Praise for
A Queen in Hiding

"This is a solid beginning to an ambitious saga of magic, intrigue, and heroism." —*Booklist*

"Kozloff sets a solid stage with glimpses into other characters and nations while keeping the book together with a clear, propulsive plot. A new series starts off with a bang." —*Kirkus Reviews*

"This series opener is literary, ambitious, and epic in scope." —*Publishers Weekly*

"A deft and exciting beginning to what I am sure will be a really gorgeous saga of a girl coming to terms with her destiny." —Melanie Rawn, author of the Exiles trilogy

"A breathtaking start to a new fantasy series that abounds in magic, backstabbing, and war. This is your new epic fantasy fix, right here." —Beth Cato, author of *Breath of Earth*

"Sweeping in scope and unabashedly epic—Kozloff has written an instant classic, here. I can't wait for the next one." —Auston Habershaw, author of *Iron and Blood*

ALSO BY SARAH KOZLOFF

A Queen in Hiding

The Queen of Raiders

A BROKEN QUEEN

Sarah Kozloff

TOR

A Tom Doherty Associates Book

New York

A BROKEN QUEEN

Copyright © 2020 by Sarah Kozloff

Excerpt from *The Cerulean Queen* copyright © 2020 by Sarah Kozloff

Edited by Jen Gunnels

A Tor Book
Published by Tom Doherty Associates
120 Broadway
New York, NY 10271

www.tor-forge.com

Tor® is a registered trademark of Macmillan Publishing Group, LLC.

Library of Congress Cataloging-in-Publication Data

Names: Kozloff, Sarah, author.
Title: A broken queen / Sarah Kozloff.
Description: First edition. | New York : Tor, a Tom Doherty Associates
 Book, 2020. | Series: [The nine realms]
Identifiers: LCCN 2019037833 (print) | LCCN 2019037834 (ebook) |
 ISBN 9781250168665 (trade paperback) | ISBN 9781250168658 (ebook)
Subjects: GSAFD: Fantasy fiction.
Classification: LCC PS3611.O85 B76 2020 (print) | LCC PS3611.O85 (ebook) |
 DDC 813/.6—dc23
LC record available at https://lccn.loc.gov/2019037833
LC ebook record available at https://lccn.loc.gov/2019037834

Our books may be purchased in bulk for promotional, educational, or
business use. Please contact your local bookseller or the Macmillan Corporate
and Premium Sales Department at 1-800-221-7945, extension 5442, or by email at
MacmillanSpecialMarkets@macmillan.com.

First Edition: March 2020

Printed in the United States of America

0 9 8 7 6 5 4 3 2 1

to Dawn,

who believed in this the most

Scattered Talents

Like dice thrown down by callous Fate

Or flotsam tossed hither and yon,

Adrift, each tumbles 'til winds abate,

And struggles yet to go on.

PRELUDE

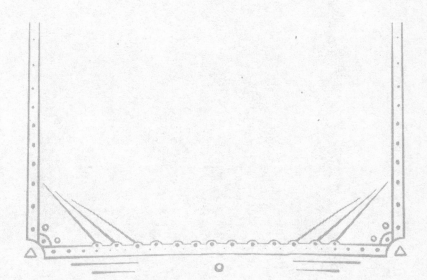

Reign of Regent Matwyck

YEAR 5

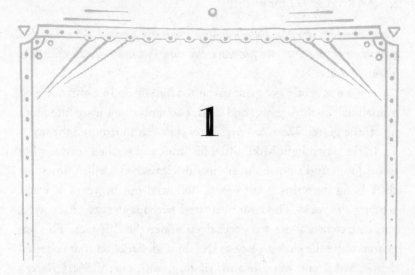

1

Off the Coast of Pexlia

Prince Mikil of Lortherrod, the worthless second son of King-that-was Nithanil; younger brother to current King Rikil; executioner of his grievously injured half sister, Queen Cressa, clung to a bit of mast from *Shark Racer* for hours, weeping and raging. He hollered until his voice grew hoarse and raw, desperate to find another survivor from the fireball attacks that had crushed his ship and *Sea Pearl*.

As the dark pressed in around him, waves and currents carried him farther and farther from the drowned, smoldering carcasses, out into immense solitude and guilt. He let go of his wooden spar and tried to sink into the cold depths.

Lautan, let me drown! Lautan, I beseech you, take me to your bosom.

He tumbled around in the waves, battered one way then another, losing all sense of direction. Seawater stung his eyes, entered his nose, burned his hoarse throat, and muffled his hearing. His energy ebbed; he couldn't swim or float but no matter how hard he tried, he also couldn't sink.

Mikil heard a rumbling laugh, neither low nor high, neither

male nor female. *No, little human. Thou art favored. Men live but a short span, but I would not have thy time cut short. Thou shalt live. Thou shalt live.*

A wave as gentle as a giant paw lifted him up and set him down on a small half circle of gravel and sand. Each incoming wave lifted him up off the gravel. *Thou shalt live. Thou shalt live,* murmured the sea.

In the dawn light Mikil lifted his head and retched seawater out of his lungs and stomach until his muscles ached. Pellish limestone cliffs hung over this small beach, hollowed out by years of water eroding the rock. The cove measured perhaps twenty paces wide, and it stretched about ten paces deep under the cliff face. This appeared to be the closest place to the ships' destruction that collected debris; Mikil saw wood beams, rigging, sails, one of *Shark Racer*'s dinghies, dishware, and bits of clothing and hand tools.

And bodies. So many charred and bloated bodies. The corpses were so disfigured he couldn't tell whether the men were Pellish, Lorther, or Weir except when he could make out hair color or an insignia.

"Lautan! Have you saved only me? Have you spared me to surround me with death? What cruel mockery is this? Why didn't you save *my sister*!"

He heard only laughter in the crash of the water.

With little hope Mikil crawled over to peer into the dinghy. He was startled to find an unconscious boy sprawled at the bottom. Pug nose and darker freckles all over his brown face—he recognized one of the cooks' lads. Mikil felt for a pulse in the boy's wrist, finding it slow but steady, and wished he had something to give him—water or wine or anything—to bring him round.

Mikil pushed against the dinghy's gunwale to hoist himself upright and looked around with more interest now that he realized he was not the only survivor. Was there a waterskin? A bottle? He grabbed the biggest piece of sail in sight and stripped a few bodies of their cloaks. If he was going to save the boy, warmth would be important. And tools. He collected daggers, swords, a mallet, and rope from the assorted flotsam.

After he finished scavenging for anything useful he strode into the cold seawater, pulling two or three corpses back into the surf each trip. He didn't want the boy to see them when he woke up. And the sailors, all of them—Pellish, Weir, or Lorther—deserved more respectful resting places.

Words needed to be said to mark the end of these sailors' lives. Mikil made up a prayer for the situation, calling out to the gray-green waves:

> Lautan, take these men, brave or craven,
> Wise or doltish, devout or heathen.
> Do not desert them, to puff and float
> In the cruel sun. Take these wretches
> Fathoms down, to your Palace under the Sea,
> Where the mermen sing and the troubles
> Of life can be set aside forever more.

As he watched, the bodies sank away. Lautan the Munificent had heard him.

Mikil checked on the boy, finding that he hadn't stirred. The prince bent his knees, stretched his arms under the boy's back and knees, and summoned his waning strength to hoist the unconscious body out of the wooden craft. He laid him on his side, wrung out a cloak as best he could, and covered him up. Then he stretched the other cloaks out on the sand, hoping there might be time before the tide came in for them to dry a little.

When he next had the time to glance toward the sea, he saw that the current had pushed a large wooden chest decorated with elaborate paintings toward the cove. Thinking it might hold something useful and afraid it might pass him by, Mikil waded out into the water to grab its edges. As he started to guide the chest to shore he was startled to hear thumping on the inner lid and—through a jaggedly formed air hole—a woman's voice crying out.

A woman. Could it be that his encounter with a fatally burned Cressa had been a dream or hallucination? He beached the chest and used the mallet to smash open the latch. An arm pushed the lid open, and a woman with green bangs stuck her head out.

"Who are you?" he barked, crestfallen.

"I am Arlettie of Pilagos, Queen Cressa's dress maid."

"But how——?"

"I was panicked. She let me hide in here. The chest slid—*boom!*—into the water. At first I was terrified it would sink, but the water only made the wood swell tighter."

Mikil was too disappointed to make any move to assist her as she stiffly climbed out of the chest onto their small, sandy haven.

"Who are you?" she asked.

"I am Mikil of Liddlecup," he answered.

"Ah. *Prince* Mikil. I recognize you. And who is that?" She pointed at the galley boy.

"I don't know his name." At the thought of his charge, Mikil stirred himself a bit. "Are there smelling salts in that chest? Anything we could use to bring him round?"

"I wonder if this would do?" said Arlettie, offering a bottle of brandy.

"Indeed," said Mikil.

He grabbed the bottle from her and took a long gulp himself. It pained his raw throat and made his eyes water, but it washed the salt and vomit tastes out of his mouth, and its warmth spread through his limbs. Then Mikil strode over to the boy, placed an arm behind his back, and tipped a little in his mouth. The liquid just dribbled out.

Arlettie came over and repeatedly tapped the boy's cheeks. His eyes began to flutter. He swallowed. Mikil poured another small amount in and was pleased to see him swallow it down right away. The boy opened his eyes.

"Hey there," said Arlettie, smiling. "Welcome back to us, darlin'."

"What is your name?" asked Mikil.

"Boy."

Mikil thought the lad's senses were addled. "No, I asked what you are called."

"Boy. My name is 'Boy,' Prince. My parents first had three sons, then five girls before they had me, and they were all out of names. Lucky, really. All the cooks knew my name right off."

"Cheeky scut. Well, are you hurt, Boy?"

Boy wiggled about, trying his limbs. "Not a bit. And you, my prince?"

"I received nary a scratch. And you?" He turned to the maid, belatedly remembering a bit of manners.

She shook her head. "Queasy, from all that bobbing around. And so cold. What happened to *Sea Pearl*?"

"She was lost. Some devilment of the Magi. *Sea Pearl* and *Shark Racer* sank with all hands. I believe we may be the only survivors."

The woman's and the boy's faces reflected shock and fear.

As much as his own grief consumed him, Mikil realized that these two were helpless. Being accustomed to assuming responsibility for others' welfare, he straightened his back and spoke firmly. "Look, it's a calamity, but we're fortunate we found each other. We haven't much time to stand around. We have to decide what to do and quickly."

"Can we stay here? Can't we rest?" said Arlettie. She stamped her feet on the sand. "I'm standing on solid ground for the first time in hours. Actually, it might be moons."

"No," said Mikil, "we can't. Look at the tidemark on the cliff wall. Soon the water will be over our heads. I judge we only have a few hours."

Arlettie shuddered, and Boy, still sitting on the small beach, grabbed handfuls of sand as if to cling to solidity.

"But we have the dinghy," said Mikil, forcing some hope into his voice. "Won't you help me load it with things that may be useful?"

The prince rigged a large piece of sailcloth on a handy spar while his new crew sorted through the contents of the chest, keeping all the clothing and a small sack of valuables, and then turned again to the washed-up debris scattered on the sand. Mikil found a plank of wood that could serve as a rough oar and makeshift tiller. Then he loaded his companions into the dinghy and pushed their craft off the spit of sand into the rising tide.

The cobbled-together craft proved seaworthy, but only just. Parts of the dinghy had been touched by fire and bashed in by a collision. In his heart, Mikil knew that Lautan guided their desperate escape from under the cliffs of Pexlia. How else to account for the favorable tide that pulled them away from the danger of the shoals and reefs, and the winds that billowed his fragile sail without tearing it? How else to explain the bobbing cask of drinking water that miraculously floated into view just as they became unbearably thirsty, or the large cod that literally leapt into their boat when hunger pangs had them doubled over?

Studying the stars, Mikil guided them northeast, away from the forbidding coasts of Pexlia and Oromondo. In the long midnight hours, holding his oar as a rudder, Mikil berated himself for the death of his Lorther crew. Why had his Anticipation not alerted him that the fleeing Oro ships were leading them into a trap? Why had he listened to Cressa's plea for an end to her suffering? Could he have saved her or healed her?

The splash against the dinghy's hull murmured, *'Twas a mercy; 'twas a mercy.*

When guilt or exhaustion consumed Mikil, he would nudge one of the others awake to take the plank and throw himself down to sleep. As days and nights melted into one another, the prince found he could lean on the unexpected stamina and determined good cheer of his companions whenever his own resiliency faltered. He suspected that these qualities explained why Lautan had chosen—out of all the people on the ships—to save Boy and Arlettie.

As far as he could judge, they were still hundreds of leagues from the shipping lanes and inhabited lands of the Green Isles. Just as their energy and spirits started to ebb away and the dinghy began to weep seawater more rapidly than they could bail it, Boy spotted a verdant island. If this island could support them, they would rest and recuperate there. Mikil beached their little craft in a small cove.

The thickly wooded volcanic isle loomed before them, the only sounds unfamiliar birdsongs. Gathering their courage, the three castaways started to search, first clustering together in trepidation, then, with more confidence, spreading out and excitedly calling out their finds, including freshwater ponds and rivulets and fruit trees. They found no inhabitants, nor any signs of human occupation. Nevertheless, grateful for the shelter it offered, they settled in, choosing a glen half bordered by rock, some twenty paces up from the beach, as their "home."

Electing himself the major provider, every morning Mikil's first task was to catch fish or collect clams, mussels, or other shellfish. Arlettie made them beds out of dried seaweed. She patched their clothes or sewed them new ones, using fish bones as needles, and then she wove them hats against the strong sun out of palm fronds. Boy gathered fruit, berries, nuts, and curiosities. The lad also discovered he could pound aloe plants to make a soothing cream for their sun-damaged skin. When weeks slipped away into spring, the youngster nimbly climbed trees to bring down birds' eggs as a change from their steady diet of seafood. And every day Boy gathered beach driftwood to provide fuel for their nighttime fires—fires that chased away the shades of their drowned companions.

The goal that drove Mikil, however, was not mere survival. He wanted to build a sturdier boat that eventually could carry them from the Gray Ocean into the Turquoise Sea, back to civilization. But how could he do this, with so few tools suited for shipbuilding?

He recalled his father's instructions to start with the best wood available. Painstakingly, he combed the island's steep and barely passable slopes, looking for cedars, firs, or oaks that grew straight and strong.

From their earliest days together, Mikil and Arlettie discovered that Boy had endured an impoverished childhood with scant parental care. The lad didn't know how old he was, but from his teeth Arlettie estimated that he had less than ten summers. Mikil found he enjoyed teaching Boy simple things, such as how to tie a real knot or read the weather. Arlettie combed his hair and made him wash. If the lad stumbled across a pretty flower, he picked it and brought it back to her and was often rewarded with a hug. Mikil doubted if the lad had ever been hugged before.

"We should give him a real name," Arlettie mentioned to Mikil one morning.

"I've been thinking that too," he agreed. "What about if we added a 'd' and made it 'Boyd'?"

"But don't most Lorther names have an 'il' sound? What about 'Boyil'?"

Mikil laughed for the first time in weeks. "No, not that! He'll think we're going to cook him!"

"Right." Arlettie giggled. "Well, I'll ask him what name he fancies. Also, would you help me teach him his letters? He should know how to read. And it would be good for all of us, to have a project for the evenings. Mayhap it would help with your bad dreams."

Mikil was not pleased that Arlettie had noticed his thrashing about at night, reliving the Magi's attack on the fleet. But dwelling so closely together, they could hardly keep secrets from each other.

In fact, Mikil often found himself studying Arlettie. With an adventurous disposition and the cachet of a wealthy, royal family, he had known scores of women, from all stations in life. Many were smarter, wittier, or more beautiful than this Green Isles dress maid. But none of them lived on this island with him. And none, Mikil soon became convinced, were as unfailingly kind as Arlettie. In a short period of time, Mikil found himself hungrily marking every time she gave Gilboy an affectionate smile or caress and often trying to read the expression in her gray eyes.

Each morning, Arlettie offered him food wrapped in large leaves, to take with him on the day's survey of the tangled, steep hillsides. Packaged in with the cold fish, boiled egg, or piece of fruit she habitually included a flower blossom.

One hot afternoon, when Mikil tried a sword against a tree trunk and in three swings the metal had snapped in two, he returned to their dwelling grove in a temper. Gilboy was off foraging, but Arlettie knelt on the cloak she used as a rug, trying to whittle a bowl out of a chunk of balsa wood.

"Why do you do this?" Mikil asked, throwing the wilted blossom in her lap. "Are you so stupid you don't know it will wither by the time I eat? Or that if I wanted a flower I need only pluck one from any branch around me? Or that the flowers leave ants walking on the food and stain it with pollen? Do you think that a *flower* will make me work harder?"

She didn't respond to his tirade, just looked up at him with hurt in her eyes, which made him angrier.

"Do you think a *flower* will protect you from me?" Mikil growled. "We're alone on a deserted island. I'm a sister-murderer after all—nothing is beneath me."

"You had no choice with Queen Cressa," Arlettie said in the tone of voice she habitually adopted whenever Mikil talked about his sister, a tone that vibrated with both regret and forgiveness. "You followed her wishes." Arlettie had said this a dozen times before, and she would patiently repeat it every day if it would help him to hear it.

She hacked at the rim of the bowl a few more times while he glared at her. "I include the flower because I want you to know that I am thinking of you and hoping your day will bring you contentment. If you don't like it, of course I'll stop.

"As for *lovemaking* between the two of us"—although she kept her eyes on her work, she stressed the word, chastising him for being too embarrassed to even speak plainly—"no matter how you tantrum, I'm confident you would never molest me."

She patted the rug, inviting him to sit down. "You're hot and tired, Mikil. Why don't you rest a moment?"

Ashamed of his words, thoughts, and temper, Mikil collapsed down on the far end of the cloak. He sat cross-legged and took out a rag to wipe the sweat from his neck and forehead. Then he propped his chin in his hand and gazed at her as she steadily (and, in truth, rather clumsily) went back to work on her carving.

"If I keep practicing," she grinned, "either I'll get better at this or I'll cut off my fingertips. We need bowls to store food away from the ants and sand." Pursuing her own train of thought, she continued, "We have a piece of net; couldn't you and Gilboy string it up high between some trees? Then our food stores would be safer from critters."

Mikil grunted his assent. He watched her slender fingers, her wide mouth, and her crooked teeth as she talked. His longing grew so intense he thought it would choke him.

As if the heat in his glance pulsed between them, she laid her handiwork aside. Arlettie stared back at him. "I know that I'm only a servant while you are a prince, and I'm sure you judge me beneath you."

"*Beneath me?* Not really. Sometimes I look up to you." Mikil said this to compliment her, but in saying it, he also knew it to be true.

Arlettie had lowered her chin, but now she raised her eyes and stared at him under her brows.

"Look, I cannot deny the gulf between us," Mikil continued. His voice sounded husky to his own ears. "But we are here, now. And we may be stuck on this isle for some time. You know I desire you. But I swear I will not touch you. I have *some* honor left." He paused, trying to read her thoughts.

"And what if I touch *you?*" she asked. "Darlin', are you so blind you cannot see . . . ?" She pushed her work away and closed the distance between them. She put her hands on both sides of his face and kissed his lips. Her breath tasted like fruit.

That night, with Arlettie lying beside him, Mikil realized that Lautan had not only rescued him from the watery depths but had also deliberately provided him with a wife, a child, sustenance, and purpose.

Though they lost track of time, years rolled by. Gilboy grew taller. The fabric that they had available wore to shreds. Once Mikil had to pull out Arlettie's tooth when it got infected. Another time, Gilboy sliced his foot on a rock and was laid up for weeks. The boy learned to read, and they used driftwood to write in the sand all around the island, *Survivors. Rescue Us.* But no ships ever came within sight.

Mikil's mood alternated between frustration and energetic contentment. He decided that a boat made out of planks was beyond his reach, but a hollowed-out log design might just be possible. He experimented with a small pine tree near the beach, felling it with their swords and sharp volcanic rocks and then getting his companions to help him drag it to the beach. After stripping the bark, he painstakingly split the log in half. Seashells and the judicious use of fire helped him hollow it out; then he cured it by storing it underwater for moons. Meanwhile, he cannibalized the dinghy to fashion crossbeams to expand the trunk and widen the center of the boat, and considered how to rig a lateen sail. Then he experimented, trying to find the best plant oils to cure the wood.

His first attempt was a disaster. He gave the misshapen boat to Gilboy to paddle around in the cove, but it wasn't ocean-worthy. However, by going through the process Mikil learned from his errors.

While he worked on the boats, Arlettie stitched the sail, braided the lines, and tried different methods of drying and smoking food to make provisions for their journey.

Years had passed by the time Mikil finally finished his second, serious attempt. His sweet craft, the *Shrimp,* turned out well-balanced. Eagerly, they sailed it in their cove, then took it out for longer trials.

However, whenever they loaded it with stores and tried to leave the island, a calamity would occur. Once they put to sea with high hopes on a beautiful day. A freak wind and a towering wave blew them back to shore before they had even left the cove.

The second time the weather stayed fair, but as soon as they reached deep water a pod of hammerhead sharks pursued them. The monsters boiled out of the water. They jostled the boat with their heads, terrifying all three travelers.

After these experiences Mikil realized that Lautan would allow them to leave only on the Spirit's timetable. Lautan had some purpose for keeping them on the island, and to attempt to escape without permission was foolhardy.

Accordingly, the prince caulked and oiled the *Shrimp* and walked the shore every morning and evening for the next years, telling his companions he combed the tidal wreckage in search of anything useful, but actually listening to the waves and looking for a sign.

Muttonshells had become one of Arlettie's favorite meals. On the brightest days, when sunbeams fingered the deep waters, Mikil dived far down, seeking the black abalone attached to the rocks. One such morning Mikil had managed to pry off a large specimen and he was almost out of air when a flicker of sunlight penetrating even deeper below made something sparkle. Straining against the overwhelming urge to surface, he forced his arms to pull him to swim two body lengths deeper. He snatched the object. With his lungs nigh to bursting, Mikil broke the surface with the abalone shell in his left hand and the golden object in his right.

The prize turned out to be a dagger—a costly, ancient dagger—with the face of a catamount carved on each side of the handle. It dazzled in the sunlight; immersion in seawater had not damaged the golden figures.

Mikil raced up to their clearing with his find. "Arlettie, do you recognize this?" he gasped, water streaming from his hair and loincloth, holding out the antique.

"That's Queen Cressa's dagger, I'm sure!" Arlettie reached for it and clutched it to her heart. "She always wore it. Where did you find it?"

"It was in the cove off the south coast." Mikil fought to breathe normally and regarded the object. "I wonder how it got this far from the wrecks.

"Finding it today . . . Could this be the signal that we should try again to rejoin the rest of the world?"

Arlettie's eyes lit up, and she gave a shiver of delight. Mikil grabbed her around the waist and twirled her a turn. "My sweet, will you be sorry to leave our private paradise?"

"It depends, my prince," she said, nestling on his chest.

"Depends on what?"

"Depends on what happens to us out there."

"Gilboy needs more opportunities than we have on this island."

"And what about me?" she asked, pulling back to look at his face.

"You? I shall take you to Lortherrod as my bride—that is, if you will have me. Though I warn you, the castle is very cold and draughty."

"What about your father and your brother the king? What will they say about a Green Isles ladies' maid?"

"They will treat you with the honor you deserve as my chosen one."

"Is it really so cold in Lortherrod?" she mused.

"Aye." He pulled her closer into his arms. "I will order the fireplaces always kept high; I will cloak you in velvets and furs and find other ways too to keep you warm. Will you have me?"

"Let's see. I have to consider my other suitors, before I give you an answer."

"Lautan won't take you," said Mikil. "The Spirit has already spit you out into my arms."

All that day they loaded into the *Shrimp* the provisions they had carefully gathered and preserved. The next morning, Mikil studied the sky and the sea. The one was cloudless and the latter softly undulating. A light but steady breeze blew from the south. Truly, Mikil had seen no better day to attempt to sail away from their small island that for so long had been both refuge and prison.

Arlettie was smiling at him from the bow, Gilboy holding the tiller in the stern.

"What do you think? Ready?" he asked them.

"Aye," his tiny crew answered. He put his back into pushing the *Shrimp* the last pace off the sandy beach. She glided neatly into the still water, and when Gilboy loosened her sail it billowed out with a satisfying snap.

PART ONE

Reign of Regent Matwyck,
Year 13

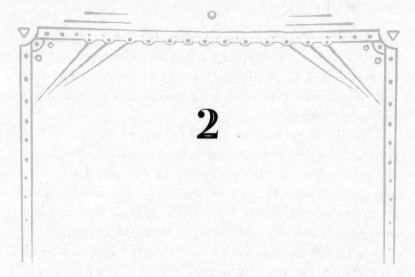

2

In the Sea

Billions of minnows lived and died without knowing anything about the Spirit of the Sea. Lautan didn't hold dominion over all sea life, just the biggest and oldest creatures in its realm, such as the few black terrapins that still lived in Femturan Estuary.

These enormous terrapins had inhabited this salt marsh for centuries, since the port of Oromondo had silted over and become worthless as a shipping harbor. Barnacles crusted their shells; their black curved claws stretched as long as human fingers. Though the mining pollution irritated their eyes and undermined their diet, they built up immunity to the metallic ores' worst effects.

The Eldest of them all, with beady eyes and a patterned shell as big and round as a carriage wheel, waited in the murky depths of the moat the morning of the Conflagration in Femturan. Of course, it was impossible that *he* could have known what was going to transpire: that Magi Two would throw a fireball at Skylark and that she would fall off her horse into the water into *this* exact spot.

A gnarled, old, ugly turtle, *he* could not foresee the future.

Nevertheless, he waited in the dirty murk.

The instant Skylark plummeted into the brackish water, he pushed off with his strong back flippers, catching her steaming, doused body on his hard shell. He swiftly bore her away underwater, hidden from sight, so that in less than a minute they swam out of the moat proper and into the salt bay.

Once he reached the edge of the open water he rose in the high grasses of the swamp to give the human a chance to breathe air. A hand weakly grabbed the ridge of his shell near his protruding, wrinkled neck. He kept his shell above the surface, making the reeds part with his four flippers. The brackish water and mud steamed with humidity, and wafting smoke made the air smell.

The human murmured one sound: "Thirsty." This meant nothing to the terrapin, and he ignored it.

After two hours the Eldest entered the ocean proper, where the sand bottom fell away and gradually cleared of plant life. This was not his territory: the cold currents and waves moved with a force that made him uncomfortable. The weight on his shell had long become burdensome. He yearned for his warm habitat. But he was old. He knew patience.

A small group of sea lions approached with their typical, noisy commotion, sending ripples through the water.

"Urt! Urt! Urt! Urt! Urt! Urt!" they hailed the Eldest. These vocalizations meant nothing to the terrapin, but he was relieved they had finally arrived.

When the terrapin submerged, the human let go. She floated loosely on the surface while a fat sea lion dove underneath and took over as the human's flotation support. His own part played, the Eldest headed back to his mud.

Sea lions prefer to swim in arches, diving and rising. To them, skimming the sea's surface—keeping their backs in the air, the Thin—feels unnatural and awkward. And their black, slippery bodies provided no purchase for the human, nothing whatsoever for her to hold on to.

She be slipping right off, blubber-puss, one juvenile female said to another. *Look out! There she goes!*

Thou gripest, thou taketh her!

Okay! One wilt take her next. See, blubber-butt? Thou gotta keep thy back flat and thou gotta kink thy head a bit, make a wrinkle round thy neck, a handhold for her strange flipper. See? She grabbed on.

Bet she wilt nay stay long.

What wilt thou wager?

Bet thee a whiting.

Agreed.

Although sea lions prefer to hover near their feeding grounds along coastlines, this group, following orders, swam deeper into the ocean, heading away from the lowering sun. The human lost strength in her fingers and slid off to the side again. This time she didn't float, but rather plunged into the colder depths. She didn't struggle, and only a tiny trickle of bubbles surfaced. The eldest female barked an alarm.

Swim beneath the creature, she ordered one of the adult females. *Lift her up to the Thin.*

The human made strange choking noises when the sea lion got her back up into the Thin.

Don't drown me, the human sent.

Not our fault, human. 'Tis bad enough to have to stay on the surface of the Thick for such a queer, misshapen thing as thee. Hey! Do nay grab at one's whiskers!

Something had scorched the human's skin, the sun had burned it further, and instead of providing relief, the night seawater scalded her again with its harsh salt and icy cold.

Burning. She sent to the sea lion.

Tell no one thy troubles. One saw two yummy octopi but one could nay dive to catch them because thou needst the Thin. One's hungry. One has already raised a pup for the year. No one asked for thee.

The stars had come out by the time the group of sea lions, with

a chorus of loud exclamations of, "Urt! Urt! Urt! Urt! Urt! Urt!"
rendezvoused with the school of dolphins.

"Ee! Ee! Ee!" the dolphins chattered in response.

Where hast thou been, thou stuck-up bigmouths? Did thou get lost?
Didst thou stop to chow down? Take this burden off one's backs, ordered
the leading sea lion.

Your Majesty! We be here!

Never mind all the chatter. Got the burden? Good riddance to
human rubbish.

The sea lions swam off, barking with relief, and then dived deep,
luxuriating in their freedom.

We have thee now, cried the dolphins. *Thou art safe. Dost thou*
hear us? We will never let thee breathe water. We like air too. We suck
it in and blow bubbles with it. Sweet sea air.

The human made no reply, but she still had life.

Thou art injured, Your Majesty. We will take thee to help. No more
fear, no more worries. We be the best. Lautan loves us the most, because
we are the swiftest and the smartest.

A few times she woke enough to retch out a gob of seawater.

Well done, Majesty, said the dolphin who was carrying her.

Help me, dolphins, she sent. *I shall surely die without help.*

We know how to help thee, Little Majesty, and we are happy to do
it. We apologize for the rudeness of the whiskered flat-faced ones. They
have no brains. We call them "shark fodder"—though not when they
are about.

What a great adventure we are having! Shall we go a bit faster?
Wouldst thou like to try some leaps? Flying be the most fun.

She grabbed on to a dorsal fin for a few minutes, but then her
grip went slack.

Never mind, Little Majesty. Thou canst rest. The water lies still as
glass tonight. We will ferry thee over rocks and chasms, coral and sea-
weed, crabs and jellyfish. Some flying fish bounce beside us. We cut
through the water cleanly; one's ripples barely foam. The moons hang

*low in the sky, watching us, making their friendly shimmer-glimmer.
Perchance they smile through that little veil of clouds.*

*Hark! A pod of whales has joined us! They are always pleasant com-
pany. They do not compete with us for fish because they eat only krill and
shrimp. Be it not rich and strange, to grow so big eating only the tiniest
food? Truly, Lautan has the most magnificent creatures. We do nay often
see whales. One wonders why they have come. We be better at ferrying
thee—thou couldst fall off their backs and the whales wouldn't even
know it. (Tell them not, but they be a wee bit stupid.)*

*Oh! The whales have come to sing thee a lullaby. How nice of them.
They love to sing, though not all creatures can hear them. Listen carefully, now.*

A dozen massive shapes surrounded the school of dolphins,
swimming underwater but nigh to the surface. The females sang
their baby-calf comfort songs in tandem, with long repeats.

The moonlit water reverberated with their kind intention as it
washed over the human barely clinging to life.

Mother is here,
Sweet little calf.
Stay close to me,
Swim near to me.
In the gray-green deeps.
My tail is strong,
My milk is warm;
Your aunts will watch
So no harm befalls thee,
Beloved of Lautan,
Spirit of the Sea.
Beloved of Lautan.
Both thee and me.

3

Femturan

Thalen, dripping from three previous dives, leaned over the bank, peering into the filthy moat around Femturan for the slightest hint of movement or shadow in the opaque water. He had seen Skylark fall in; she could not just have disappeared.

For most of the morning, Oromondo soldiers had been too occupied with saving civilians from the fire, smoke, and collapsing buildings to pay any heed to three horses and strange riders perched near the city's moat. All at once, however, a squad of eight Protectors noticed their presence, pointed and shouted, and started jogging in their direction.

"They've seen us! They're coming!" Tristo warned. Eli-anna mounted Sukie, but Thalen still knelt by the water's edge, refusing to give up his hunt for Skylark.

"Commander!" Tristo pulled his shoulder. "We've got to go, now! Get up!"

Thalen heard his words without recognizing their import. But when Tristo gave his hair a tremendous yank, he lifted his head, saw the squad of enemies bearing down on them, and looked around for Dishwater. Though Dish's eyes rolled white with stress, he had remained only a few paces distant from his rider.

When Thalen tried to mount, his wet boot slipped out of the stirrup and he ended up sprawled in the dirt on his back. He lay on the ground wondering if he cared enough to rise.

Tristo yelled with more urgency, "Commander!"

Thalen almost shouted back, "Just go without me!" But he knew his duty to the comrades who had accompanied him on this failed rescue mission. With more determination, if no more strength, he succeeded in gaining his saddle.

Eli-anna had turned her horse, Sukie, around in circles searching for their best escape route. The plain around the pyre that had once been the capital city of Oromondo currently overflowed with Oro Protectors and panicked civilians.

"This way!" she shouted, heading the three horses in the least likely direction, straight into the ocean—or rather, straight into the swampy estuary that bordered the coast. What seemed a foolhardy maneuver proved instead to be a lifesaving ploy, because within moments high grasses hid them from view. And while the chest-high mud made progress difficult for the horses, a person on foot would find it impassable. The calls from the Oro Protectors faded and the Raiders knew they were safe from pursuit.

But if the danger of capture lessened, their peril from the swamp itself increased with each stride. At times the horses found solid footing for a few paces, but just as often they had to swim through a hidden eddy or yank their feet out of muck. Sukie—the strongest, biggest horse—led the way, crashing a path through reeds, then Dishwater followed in her wake, and little Cinders, carrying Tristo, kept up as best she could.

The mud sucked at the horses' and the humans' legs, letting go grudgingly. Soon the horses trembled and staggered with fatigue. Insects whined in their riders' ears, feasting on their blood and the last drops of their strength. The sun climbed higher overhead, shining through a thick layer of black smoke, making the air around them even more thick and fetid. Thalen turned his water bag upside down several times, but no matter how he shook it, only a trickle dripped down his throat.

Thalen savored his physical miseries. They kept him from confronting a greater misery.

Finally, when they were nearly a league south of the burning city, Eli-anna angled the horses back in the direction of the shoreline. With a mighty heave Sukie climbed up onto the bank. Dish needed three attempts to yank his hindquarters out of the muck and onto solid ground, where he stood blowing, his sides shaking. Fearful the horse would not bear his weight another moment, Thalen dismounted. He turned to help Eli-anna pull Cinders onto the bank. As they did so, Tristo half fell from Cinders's saddle into Thalen's outstretched arms.

Thalen took stock of his companions. Like him, Eli-anna and Tristo wore coverings of mud up to their waists, with their torsos and even their heads splashed almost as dirty. The skin on their faces both swelled with a myriad of angry bites and stretched tight with exhaustion. Their eyes were bloodshot. Sweat and grime on their faces and necks had captured strands of their hair, plastering it to their necks. If he hadn't known who they were, he might not have recognized his adjutant and scout.

Next, Thalen turned to Dishwater, rubbing his hands down the gelding's body, roughly sloughing off the thickest, heaviest mud. Dish stamped and shook himself, sending more clinging muck flying. Eli-anna and Tristo followed his example with their own mounts.

"Water," Tristo croaked. "We need water."

Surveying the featureless landscape around them revealed nothing promising. North of their position, Femturan still burned bright orange and billowed smoke.

"Drop their leads," Eli-anna said. "If there's water to be had, the horses will smell it."

Left to her own devices, Cinders just hung her head, broken and listless, but after a few more vigorous headshakes, skin twitches, and tail lashes, Sukie and Dishwater began to snuffle the air. Sukie took off at a slow trot, heading south by southwest. Dish followed.

Thalen grabbed Cinders's reins and yanked her forward as they pursued the stronger horses on foot. For a long time they were able to trace the pair's movement ahead, but eventually the horses pulled out of sight, and Eli-anna followed their hoofprints. The path showed clearly enough (and a refreshing breeze sprung up to dry their sweat), yet the Raiders found trailing their horses difficult. They had endured so much, and it had been so long since they'd slept that they could hardly walk. Every few minutes, one of them stumbled and the others had to pull their fellow up. And Cinders had to be coaxed and pulled; if they let go of her reins, she dropped her head and stood swaying.

After the third time he tripped headlong, Tristo asked, "When did we last eat?" while Eli-anna helped him onto his knees.

"Can't remember," Thalen mumbled.

Thalen patted Cinders's filthy neck. His throat was so parched he found it difficult to speak. "Come on, girl. You can do it. Don't let those knees buckle. Don't you dare die on me."

In the midafternoon they reached the crest of a small slope, and Eli-anna pointed. In the distance they saw Sukie and Dishwater drinking at a decent-sized pond that had formed in a hollow between two hillocks. Cinders sniffed and revived enough to trot off to join them. Thalen draped Tristo's good arm around his neck and pushed their bodies across the wide expanse of sere grasses.

The Raiders threw themselves down on their bellies and drank as greedily as their horses, not caring whether this pond, like so many in Oromondo, was poisoned with mining effluence or not.

Thalen had just enough strength to pull his head out of the water and rest it on the bristly grass before he passed out.

When Thalen opened his eyes it was almost nightfall—nightfall of the same cursed day that had started with the birds and their fire arrows outside Femturan.

In the dim light he made out Tristo close by, curled in a ball. Eli-anna was moving about: she had stripped off her muddy overclothes and boots and unsaddled the horses, who, freed from their burdens, rolled on the ground to scratch their maddening bug bites.

Thalen crawled to the pond and drank again, slowly now, savoring each wet, life-giving mouthful. He dunked his head into the water several times, trying to rinse the sweat and muck from his hair and face. Then he got up to help Eli-anna with the horses. Though most of the mud had flaked off, they desperately needed grooming if their coats—sweat-caked, chafed, and bug-gnawed— were to stay healthy. Thalen rummaged through all the saddlebags and felt a rush of relief when his fingers touched a brush. He swept it down the horses' matted coats in long strokes. When he got to Cinders, the filly leaned her head into his chest, and he patted her nose for several moments.

Eli-anna motioned to Thalen that he should give her his filthy clothes. The cool wind on his bare skin soothed his own bites. Eli-anna beat the caked mud off his trousers and shirt and off the horses' blankets, then doused the garments in the pond. Tristo slept on, unconscious; Thalen knew it was a wonder he had made it through the fire and escape.

The horses folded their legs and lay down in the moonlit field when Thalen finished brushing them. Eli-anna tossed herself on a damp horse blanket, staring up at the stars through the haze. Thalen thought about keeping watch, but he could not keep his eyes open, and in truth, he would almost count it a blessing if he were stabbed in his sleep. He took another wet horse blanket and copied Eli-anna in using it as a bed.

His thoughts kept incessantly reliving the last moments of their escape from Femturan, when the fireball had knocked Skylark off her horse into the moat. Whenever he closed his eyes, he saw the searing bright fire at her back; the startled look on her face below the ragged knit cap; Cinders's eyes rolled white in terror; and the black surface below.

Finding her body would have provided a modicum of solace. He could have gotten her out of that filthy moat; he could have held her in his arms—mayhap she would have even been conscious enough to know he was there in her last moments. He could have seen her actual wounds, instead of imagining the worst.

Trying to concentrate on a less painful thought, Thalen wondered what had happened to his wolfhound, Maki, who had often been a comforting presence at night. He couldn't even recall when the dog had last been by his side. Before he could figure out what had befallen the animal, he fell asleep again.

Morning came to the three survivors clustered around the pond. The pond stretched about three paces wide and ten paces in length, its edges crisscrossed with tracks of other animals that used it as a water source. To the west the land grew hillier but still unwooded; Thalen dared to hope that this pond merely collected fresh rain runoff.

"Ohhh-ohh," Tristo groaned, as he woke to pain and stiffness. "Commander, what—" but Thalen forestalled any questions or conversation with a hand gesturing, "Stop." Once he had emptied the dirt and debris out of his boots, he abruptly stood up.

"I'm going to curry the horses in the daylight, now that I can see what I'm doing," he said as he stomped away. The horses were clumped together, grazing amongst the dry winter landscape, but they turned to him eagerly when he approached.

While Thalen kept his solitude among the horses he was dimly aware that Eli-anna had set snares near the pond while Tristo alternated between digging in the dirt and collecting handfuls of burnable material.

Eventually, Tristo called, "Commander, come eat!"

Eli-anna had captured a rabbit and Tristo had roasted the creature over a tiny fire of dead grasses and twigs. The meat, along with the greens and roasted roots they'd harvested, was the first real food the three had eaten since . . . since before.

Each mouthful made Thalen hungrier. He felt the bites of undercooked meat giving his traitorous body strength.

Well, here I am: alive after she is gone. To be dragging this sorry body around while she lies at the bottom of that filthy moat feels like a betrayal.

When they had eaten every scrap, Tristo, scratching bites on his throat and chest, broke the silence. "I'm sorry about your brother, Eli-anna, I really am. And Skylark—she was something special." He cleared his throat. "Yet we burned Femturan to the ground, killed the Magi, and took out hundreds of Oros. And we survived! We should be proud. We should feel victorious."

Thalen shook his head. "I take no joy in all the death and destruction."

"But Oromondo will no longer be able to threaten its neighbors or occupy other countries," Tristo said, as if he could argue Thalen into feeling triumphant. "This is what we came for—this is what we wanted."

"Someday I may recognize the accomplishment. But today I feel only pain," Thalen replied. "Besides, we don't know what's happened to the other troop of Raiders. Wareth and Kambey and Eldie and the rest could be in danger or dead. Don't ask me to rejoice."

Eli-anna wiped her knife clean. Then, she grabbed her plait of hair, dark plum intermixed with light brown. While the men watched her, she sawed through the plait at shoulder length.

"We Mellies believe," she explained to Tristo and Thalen, "that when someone dies, her soul goes to join the stars. But it is a long journey, from the steppes to the Lattice of Stars, and the departed fly more swiftly if we give something of ourselves to aid their passage. I gave my sister Eli-dena a year of my words. I gave my uncle, Tel-bein, a cup of my blood." She yanked her tunic to the side of her neck to show the scar of a knife wound near her collarbone. "To speed Eldo's ascent, I give my hair." She threw the cut-off hank of hair into the dregs of their struggling fire and muttered a prayer in an unfamiliar language.

Tristo had watched her with wide eyes; then he grabbed his own brown hair on the top of his head and hacked off a big handful. He separated the chunk into smaller strands.

"Ooma," he quavered and threw a pinch into the fire; "Cook" accompanied the next gesture. He continued going through the names of all their lost Raiders while tears tracked down his face.

Eli-anna and Tristo looked at Thalen. He would have cut off all of his hair if it would have eased the pain in his chest, but he didn't put credence in the ritual—he cooperated for his companions' sake. He clutched a handful of his hair near his left ear with his left hand and tried to saw through it with his knife, only to discover that his blade had dulled. Eli-anna offered hers. Thalen sliced through a hank of his hair and stared at his handful numbly.

He stood up over the fire, his hand clenched. "The friends we lost were noble and brave. We must cherish their memory. We didn't treasure their companionship enough; our lonely tomorrows will teach us the depth of our folly."

He opened his hand and let the hair tumble all at once into the small flames. Then he stalked off toward the horse blankets, threw himself down on the ground, and prayed for sleep to carry him into oblivion.

The next morning, after scarfing down another meager meal, Tristo badgered him, "What's the plan, Commander? We can't just stay here!"

Thalen knew the boy was right. He looked around them in every direction. To the north, Femturan still sent up an orange glow. To the west they saw the peaks of the Obsidian Mountains, and to the east the sea pounded against a treacherous shoreline. Thalen pointed south, not only because it was the only practical route but because an outline of a plan had begun to take shape in his mind.

The three riders filled their water bags and rode their somewhat recovered horses along a desolate coastline that started to climb in elevation above the sheer rock cliffs. They stuck to the bluff, hearing the waves and the gulls' screeches, veering inland only when they had to skirt a fissure. They rode slowly and in silence, Thalen deliberately bringing up the rear. Thalen tried just to make his mind blank, and when he wasn't successful, he tried to use Dish's smooth gait to lull himself into happy memories, lingering on his aunt Norling teaching him to play the flute or on ice-skating with his brothers. Anxiety intruded on these reveries; Thalen kept imagining catastrophes befalling Eldie's squad, such as their wounds going sour or their being captured. And no matter what he tried to think about, the memory of the moat came rushing back, making him flinch.

The riders were fortunate that this coastline of Oromondo was desolate. There were no seams of metal to mine here; no volcanoes to worship; and the soil underfoot was sandy and poor. They passed no settlements and they saw no citizens. Thalen was relieved that the isolation saved him from more killing.

In the midafternoon, they dismounted to drink from their water bags and walk the horses. The chill wind blew through the rents in their clothing, making the cloth billow.

"But *where* are we *going*?" Tristo suddenly broke out as if in the middle of some argument. His awkwardly hacked hair made him look even younger and more vulnerable than before.

Thalen cleared his throat and found his "commander" voice waiting for him. "If we keep traveling down this coastline, eventually we'll reach a seacoast town in Alpetar called Tar's Basin."

"How do you know that?" asked Tristo.

"I see the map in my mind. Tar's Basin has a harbor, the first harbor south of Femturan. From there, we'll probably be able to get a ship."

"Really?" said Tristo, a brightness returning to his eyes.

"Really, Tristo," Thalen answered. "I promised I'd get you home."

They walked on a ways, Eli-anna often stopping to choose stones from the options available underfoot.

"Plenty of gulls," she commented without inflection, gesturing to the fluttering specks of white that shrieked from the edge of the drop-off.

"What about them?" asked Tristo.

"Two apiece for dinner," she promised. "One to feed our bodies, and one to feed our grief. You keep an eye out for firewood."

"Do gulls taste good?" Tristo asked.

"Everything tastes good if you're this hungry," Eli-anna answered.

As the day slowly unrolled, Thalen felt as if the three of them were the only people left alive in the world. Sometimes he cast a glance over his shoulder, half expecting to see the ghosts of the hundreds of people he'd sent to their deaths, trailing along behind them.

4

Wyndton

By late afternoon Stahlia's back, neck, and shoulders ached and the tapestry workroom grew close and confining. When she left the workshop and crossed the small stretch of yard to return inside the cottage, however, its emptiness crept into her bones. Percia regularly departed after midmeal to prepare for the dancing classes she taught in the village center. Wren wasn't puttering around or curled up with a book; Tilim wasn't playing on the floor with his tin soldiers as he had as a little boy.

Worst of all, Wilim wasn't on his way home from his circuits, soon to arrive full of praise for her cookery and brimming with stories of his day's encounters for them to chew over. It had been nearly a year since his death, and though Stahlia could struggle on when she kept busy, at times his absence smote her with renewed force.

Stahlia rubbed a palmful of liniment on her neck. Then she walked idly through the house, discontented with everything she saw. The floor wanted sweeping, the table sanding, the hearth ash clearing, and the windows washing. Baki lay in a circle near the fireplace nibbling on his thigh. That damn dog shed with every breath. And how was she supposed to make supper out of the scant foodstuffs left in the larder?

Overcome by discontent, she threw her cloak over her shoulders and went outside, Baki following by habit. The days clipped shorter, and the vegetable garden sat in a frozen, unsightly jumble of dead stalks and eddies of leaves. Idly, she checked on Syrup in the barn. His stall smelled, and he acted put out she hadn't brought him a treat. He kept lipping at her clothing. "Quit it," she told him, and then felt bad at taking out her peevishness on Wilim's faithful old friend. She really should think about selling him—the expenses for two horses were heavy—but she couldn't face the prospect. She let him out into his paddock for a change of scenery and fresh air, and his breath condensed in clouds around him. The sun fought its way through the late-afternoon clouds, piercing them in scattered places with streams of thick light.

Movement from the road caught her eye. Stahlia watched until she could make out Lemle, wearing a large rucksack. A hoof stuck out of it. Baki ran to him, wagging his stub tail.

"Afternoon, missus," he called out when close enough. "I brought down a deer, and me and my uncle thought your family might like a hindquarter."

"That's so thoughtful of you, Lemle! It's true, no one goes hunting for us these days. Come in the house for a cup of tisane to warm up and keep a grumpy old lady company."

When Lemle came in, she added logs to the fire, hung the kettle, and lit the lantern.

Of the many people who had stuck by them since the double tragedies, Lem and Rooks had been the most stalwart. It had been Lem who had encouraged Percia to start her school and who had helped her surmount every obstacle. Rooks spent a great deal of time with Tilim, teaching him the weaponry skills the boy was so keen to master.

Lemle appeared to be as eager for a good chat as she was. He told her the whole story of how he'd brought down the doe. When she topped off his cup he reported the gossip swirling around town that Thom had gotten the Daverly girl with child and was refusing to marry her.

Stahlia *tsk*ed her disapproval. Then she asked, "How is your uncle faring this week?"

Lemle lost his wicked grin. "His ankles look awful swelled up, and his breath comes short. We had the healer round four days ago—cost a drought damn fortune—but he just said something cruel about nature taking its course." Lemle's brow darkened as he muttered, "Goddard's a greedy, heartless fellow."

"I've never liked him neither," said Stahlia. "I'm sorry to hear about Rooks; I'll make a broth with the venison bones and ride up tomorrow or the day after to give it to him."

"You've no need to trouble yourself, missus," said Lemle.

"No, no. Do me good, and do Syrup some good to move about," said Stahlia. "Come look at my latest tapestry. This one's for the Millerville Church of the Waters."

Stahlia took him out to her workroom. He admired the tapestry on her loom, his finger lovingly tracing some of the outlines.

"I think, for the top of the waves, where they crest," Stahlia pointed, "I need to work in lighter colors. Lavender, maybe. Not white. Or yellow, though I don't have any on hand and I'd have to order some." She squinted at her weaving from several angles.

"It's really splendid," Lemle enthused.

"You know, just now, when I was outside, an image of a new piece came to me. 'The Lay of Queen Chilandia' describes light just like this afternoon, solid rays streaming through the clouds, when she is returning from burying her father in a crypt in Rortherrod. I've never attempted Chilandia's Trail of Mourning. She would be dressed in gray, her blue hair all falling down with grief, wearing a mourning circlet. . . . Attendants would be in the background, uncertain of how to help their queen. And it would be late fall, exactly like this."

She laughed at herself with a touch of bitterness. "But who would want to hang the Trail of Mourning in their great room?"

"Lots of people can relate to mourning, missus," said her young visitor, wise beyond his years.

"I suppose it would all depend on whether I could capture this light precisely. The light would make her grief grand, not gnawing and fretful."

"There's an engraving in your book about Chilandia," said Lemle, pulling the wrapped volume out of his waist apron. "I brought it back to you today."

He started to turn to the page, but Stahlia forestalled him. "Let's go in the cottage for some more tisane."

Inside, Lemle found the page quickly, and he pointed out the crosshatching that gave the queen's horse depth and volume. Stahlia wondered how many times he had studied each engraving. When Percia had told her that Lem's dream was to apprentice to an engraver, Stahlia had worried that the young man was now too old for any master to take on as an apprentice, but he certainly appreciated the craft.

"Well," she said, "I'll tuck Chilandia in the back of my mind. I need to finish this one about Queen Cressa's last voyage first." She slapped her knees. "I've got to get supper started, Lemle, but you'll join us tonight, won't you? It would be so nice to have company."

"I'd best get home. I hate to go because your house is so cozy, but I don't like being gone from my uncle too long. Thanks for the tisane—I always say that yours is the best brew around."

Lemle opened the door. "Ah! Here comes your family, missus," he called over his shoulder as he exited.

And in a moment Tilim and Percia tumbled inside, with cold cheeks and happy eyes, flooding the small, shabby house with cheerfulness. Stahlia was pleased to be able to promise them venison steaks—that is, after they took care of Barley, mucked out Syrup's stall, and finished all the other chores they had neglected earlier.

She secretly relished her children's grumbles as she set about fixing them a good supper.

5

Cloverfield, Alpetar

Gunnit was watching the goats in West Pasture when his young dog, Kiki, alerted him that someone approached. He held his crooked staff at the ready as he watched the trail at the far end of the pasture. Eight-summers-old Aleen, his companion from the journey on the High Road, appeared, gasping for breath after the steep climb up the hillside.

"Gunnit!" she panted. "You're wanted."

"Has anything happened?" he asked, alarmed, as his thoughts flashed back to the time he was minding the goats when Sweetmeadow was raided.

"Nothing like that—everyone is safe. It's just that Peddler is here, and he wants you. Right away, he says."

"He wants me? I wonder why," said Gunnit, grabbing his rucksack. "Are you staying with the flock?" he asked.

"No, a lad is coming. I just got here quicker."

Gunnit offered her some water, and then Aleen and he started down the trail at a good clip, Kiki bounding ahead. Aleen was doing well keeping up with him; they nodded wordlessly at the replacement shepherd on his way up to resume Gunnit's post. Thereafter, if Aleen slowed at steep spots, Gunnit grabbed her hand and helped her.

When they got back into Cloverfield, Gunnit expected to see the peddler's cheerful wagon parked in the village square. Instead, the man with round green eyes and bells tied into his light yellow hair and darker yellow beard stood beside a tall horse, dun-colored with a white face and socks. Its white silky mane and tail were fancy plaited and tied with bells, and Peddler was holding the reins of another horse that looked almost its twin, but sporting a smaller saddle.

Dame Saggeta and his mother stood near the sundial, talking to Peddler, while other villagers watched from a discreet distance. His mother had baby Addigale on her hip, while Limpett clung to her skirts, sucking his thumb.

"It's up to the boy," Gunnit overheard Saggeta telling his mother, right before they spotted him and Aleen.

"What's up to me?" Gunnit asked.

His mother turned to him, distress in her face. "This peddler says he is going on a journey and he needs you to come with him."

"Come with him where and for how long?" asked Gunnit.

"That's just it," Dame Saggeta answered. "He won't say. Nor will he say why it has to be you and no one else."

His mother chewed her lip, "And he wants you to leave right now. This instant. Gunnit, you don't have to go, just because he asks for you. We need you here; you're only ten, too young to leave home. Even if this man is Saulé's priest or some such—I'm your mother."

Aleen came over and entwined her arm around his mother's waist, which appeared to comfort her a bit.

"Peddler also says that he will protect you with his life," Saggeta put in, "which is supposed to be reassuring, but makes me suspicious where he'd be taking you that you'd need such protection."

The horses pranced a few steps, as if eager to be off. "Whoa there, Sunbeam," said Peddler, who had crouched down to pet Kiki while the others conversed. He stood, saying, "Well, Gunnit, lad, nice to see you again. These ladies summed up the situation tidily. Naturally, you don't have to join me. But I've been called on an urgent mission, a rescue mission, and I judge it wise to take you along."

The boy looked in Peddler's face, where he saw impatience but also warmth. Gunnit and his mother had only made their home in Cloverfield a few moons ago; while he didn't want to be stuck here for always, he wasn't particularly eager to leave just yet. After their trip on the High Road, maybe he'd had enough adventures and traveling . . . at least for a few years. But he remembered the last time he had spoken with Peddler, when the older man had told him he was "kissed by the Sun," presented him with the golden Sun Bracelet, and made him feel special.

Under his shirt he felt his Bracelet give his upper arm a slight squeeze. If you were "kissed by the Sun" did that mean you had a duty to go on rescue missions?

"Gunnit," his mother said, planting her foot. "I don't want you to go."

The boy looked back and forth from Peddler to the grouping of his mother, the little ones, Aleen, and Saggeta, torn and confused.

"Dame, I surely don't mean to cause you pain; I know how much you've already endured," said Peddler.

Next he turned to the young goatherd. "Before I go, lad, why not come say hello to Sunbeam? You'll never again see a horse so fine."

Gunnit walked the few paces away from his family to Peddler and the mounts. The horse's neck felt softer than silk. Its large eye blinked at him, then it nodded its head up and down.

A thought hit Gunnit. "Is this—could this be about *Finch*?" Gunnit whispered to Peddler around the horse's neck.

"Aye. Her life hangs by a thread."

"Where is she? What can we do?"

"I'm not certain, but I must try, and the Mirror told me that with you, I'd have better odds."

Gunnit drew in a deep breath and blew it out; he then strode back to his mother and leaned against her front, one arm around her neck, the other including Addigale in his hug.

"Ma, someone's in danger, and I might be of help. You wouldn't have someone die, just so's you can keep me home?"

"I don't know, Gunnit, I guess I wouldn't . . . but it's a wicked hard thing to ask me to watch my last child ride away with a man who's practically a stranger on the chance of helping another stranger."

"Ah, but you're a wicked brave ma!" Gunnit said, kissing her cheek and drinking in her scent and softness.

In their small hut Gunnit took off his rucksack and threw in his few clothes. Outside again at the square, he rubbed four-summers-old Limpett's head, kissed Addigale's fat baby cheek, and embraced his mother once again. She was trying not to sob but not succeeding very well. He then enfolded Aleen in a hug, even if practically the whole village now hung around watching these outlandish events.

Aleen hugged him back and then reached down and grabbed Kiki around the neck so she wouldn't follow the horses.

Peddler finished the ale that a Cloverfield woman had offered him and handed back the large mug. "That hit the spot. I thank you, dame," he said so gravely it sounded like a benediction.

Peddler continued, saying, "Here, lad, let me adjust the stirrups." He lifted Gunnit up to the back of the second horse and shortened the stirrup strap to his leg. Then he walked around the front of the horse to fix the other side.

"Test your foot. Did I get the length right? Are the straps even?"

"I guess so," Gunnit answered, dubious about this large horse. He was so much higher from the ground than on Butter or Taffy.

"Not to fret, Gunnit," Saggeta called out. "I will watch out for them all."

Gunnit replied, "I know that, dame, or I couldn't go."

Peddler touched his brow in leave-taking and turned his horse to the road.

"Goodbye, Ma, goodbye, everyone," called Gunnit. Without a command his horse followed its fellow. The horses moved so fast and their bells chimed so that Gunnit could hardly hear the villagers' calls of farewell.

They cantered along the road as Gunnit tried to take in the events of the last hour, events that had upended his life.

Saulė's horses flowed down from the meadows toward the High Road in a torrent of hoofbeats and dust, their silky manes and tails streaming behind and their bells jingling, while Gunnit, who had lost his left stirrup almost immediately, bounced about wildly and held on to his pommel for dear life.

6

On the Seas

The sun was not yet over the horizon, but its imminent arrival had turned the sky a luminous gray-white. Arlettie was still asleep in the bottom of the *Shrimp,* snugly covered with cloaks, but Gilboy kept Mikil company, silently passing the water bag and bringing out dried fruit and smoked fish for their fastbreak.

Taking pleasure in the perfect sailing conditions, Mikil scanned the horizon. Thus far, Lautan had kept the Spirit's side of the bargain: their four days at sea had been uneventful except for their rapid progress, and while their stored provisions tasted monotonous, they were holding up well. Mikil taught Gilboy the rudiments of star navigation (as his father had once taught the skill to him), and during dull stretches Arlettie regaled them by elaborating on her dreams of the pleasures of civilization, such as wine, hair oil, and new cotton underdrawers.

Gilboy pointed off to the starboard. Mikil saw something breaking the surface of the water, but he couldn't discern what it was. Gilboy mouthed, "Dolphins." Mikil smiled. Dolphins were fine; he just didn't want another encounter with those hammerhead sharks that had threatened the *Shrimp* the last time they had tried to flee their deserted island.

The dolphins set a course that would intersect with their little vessel, Mikil realized, but he wasn't concerned because he had seen dolphins escort many a sailing ship and enjoyed their antics. He watched them come closer and grow larger.

"There's something on the middle one's back!" Gilboy said, with surprise.

The light grew stronger, and the dolphins drew nigh, aiming straight at them; in another moment Mikil also could spy what looked like wet fabric plastered on the middle dolphin's back.

Mikil frowned, thinking he had never seen dolphins swim this far along the surface without submerging. This was just . . . not normal.

He reached down and shook Arlettie's ankle. "Best wake up," he said. "Something is going on."

"Not sharks again!" she cried, transitioning from full sleep to full panic.

"No, no," answered Gilboy. "Dolphins. With a queer object on their backs. Or . . . maybe it's a person. But how could that be?"

As they squinted at the odd blotch of color, details began to resolve—a scrap of sodden white, could be a shirt; a scrap of sodden brown, could be breeches. And clearly the dolphins were purposely ferrying whatever it was straight to the *Shrimp*.

"I see boots!" cried Gilboy. "They *are* carrying a person!"

"A castaway!" said Mikil. "Arlettie, shift over to leeward so that we can pull him up over the starboard gunwale. Gilboy, move to amidships while I tie off the tiller."

The dolphins closed to within ten paces. The escort dolphins stopped and only the carrier dolphin approached, swimming alongside the *Shrimp,* so near Mikil could have reached over to touch it. Mikil and Gilboy saw a slight, half-drowned figure lying limp, facedown, on the sleek gray back. The dolphin matched its speed to the boat's movement and rode the same swells.

"Kneel down, Gilboy, so we don't overbalance. When I count three, you grab an arm, and I'll grab a leg. We want to do this smoothly, so we don't drop him and we don't capsize. Arlettie, as counterweight, lean far out to port. Ready? One, two, three, heave!"

The castaway was not heavy. Although the boat tipped for a second, Gilboy and Mikil barely struggled in raising him over the side of the boat.

They laid the poor wretch on the keel faceup.

Arlettie whispered in shock, "Vertia save us! 'Tis a woman! Let me take care of her." She crawled over, putting a cloak under the rescue's head to pillow her and pulling the sodden hair off her face. She felt at the neck for a pulse and then put her head down on the chest to listen.

"She's barely alive."

Mikil spoke to the dolphins. "We've got her," he said. "We will do all we can for her." The dolphins jumped into the air making dramatic splashes as if to show they understood. Then they sped off in another direction.

The water-soaked girl's hold on life ebbed. Her brown face had a gray-blue tinge, and her skin was crusted with sea salt. Her eyes were puffed closed. Even in the bright morning sunlight, Mikil found it difficult to get any impression of her features.

"She's too cold," said Arlettie. "Help me get her wet clothes off and wrap her up."

Mikil pulled off the ruined boots and stripped away the wet stockings, rubbing her icy feet and toes vigorously for a moment. Meanwhile Arlettie and Gilboy peeled off her ragged shirt, in the process discovering that she had burn blisters down her back, across one shoulder, and licking up one side of her neck under her chin.

"Oh, for Vertia's sake!" cursed Arlettie, shaking her head. "Poor thing."

They laid the girl on her uninjured side and covered her up with all their spare clothing. Gilboy chafed her hands and forearms; Mikil returned to work on her feet and lower legs, trying to get the cold blood moving.

Arlettie wet a cloth from their freshwater store and washed the salt from her face and from her burns. She smoothed the aloe paste they had brought along on her sunburn and burn blisters.

"She's still too cold to the touch," said Mikil.

"Could be my heat will help warm her up." Arlettie got in under the cloaks and pulled the drowned girl close.

"Her best hope is a skilled healer," said Mikil, untying the tiller and raising their sail.

By midmorning their passenger's eyelids fluttered now and again, and once in a while she made indistinct sounds. Her color improved enough that Arlettie could crawl out from under the blankets. She offered the girl sips of water, which she swallowed. But her breathing was shallow and she remained semiconscious.

Mikil caught every breeze, heading the *Shrimp* northeast as fast as it could go.

They speculated endlessly about the castaway: who was she? Her dull brown hair gave them no clue as to her nationality. How had she been injured, and how had she survived for them to find her in the middle of the ocean? How had she come to be floating on the back of a dolphin? How had the dolphins known to bring this person to their little craft?

The next day their patient grew restless and feverish; she moaned more often. The burn blisters changed from red to white, puffing up high with fluid, oozing and bloody, while her breathing sounded as bad as ever.

Late in the afternoon, Gilboy woke Mikil, who had fallen into a doze, slumped across the tiller.

"Sail in the distance. I can't tell what country it's from."

Mikil rubbed his eyes and looked where Gilboy pointed. "It's from the Green Isles. See the green flag and Vertia on the figure-head? A trader, not a fishing boat. Has she spotted our distress ban-ner yet?"

"No, don't look like it."

Arlettie anxiously moved to the bow. She held her woven toppie in one hand and a jeweled cutlass they had found in the cove in the other. She waved her arms wildly crosswise—making the *Shrimp* jostle—and shouted, "Over here! We're over here! Islanders, coun-trymen, help us!"

"Hey! Hey! Lookouts, are you sleeping?" Gilboy joined in, an-grily.

"Lookouts get a kind of sun-blindness," Mikil explained, but he took cold comfort from his expertise.

The trader kept to her course.

Soon it would be out of range.

Arlettie screamed, "Help us!" Mikil joined her and took the jew-eled sword to wave in wide arcs. After several agonizing moments the trader broke course, and after a long pause it tacked to head in their direction. The voyaging family cheered.

As the ship drew nigh Mikil could see the sailors pointing at the *Shrimp*. He also read the ship's name: *Island Dreamer*.

"Now this will be the trickiest part of being rescued," said Mikil, licking his lips. "Get ready, Gilboy. The sailors will throw down heavy lines. We must catch them and tie them off on the cleats. One line still leaves us unstable, free to crash against her side or slide under her bow—either of which could easily crush us; two lines make us secure."

Island Dreamer came about neatly and drifted slowly toward the *Shrimp*. The first rope was the light one; Gilboy caught it himself and tied it to the cleat. The second rope was thick and heavy. It fell aft from the *Shrimp,* but the swell brought it within reach; it took both of them to grab it and wrestle it into a knot. Now they were affixed to the bigger ship, knocking against it in a medium swell.

Several sun-darkened male faces peered over the side at them. A rope ladder was hooked to the side and then dropped down into the little craft.

"Let me go aboard and make sure of things," Mikil said. "Hand me that sword." Mikil tucked the jeweled cutlass into his belt and climbed the rope ladder. He was met by a group of gaping Green Isles seamen on a tidy vessel.

"Well, this don't happen every day! Rescue at sea!" said a man with a green mustache, wearing a seamaster's hat. "And who might you be?"

Mikil's clothes were threadbare, his hair and beard overgrown, his skin tanned deep walnut brown, but his bearing was as regal and assured as ever, and the cutlass provided just the right touch of status, threat, and money.

He sketched a slight bow. "I am Prince Mikil of Lortherrod. My companions and I have been shipwrecked on a small island since the sea battle between Queen Cressa of Weirandale and the Pellish many years ago. Whom do I have the honor of thanking as our deliverer?"

The captain's eyes went round with surprise, and his mouth fell open.

"Well, I'll be a rat-fucker—ahem. I am Captain Bajets of *Island Dreamer* out of Pilagos, homeward bound. And these are my crew. We're glad we can be of service to a prince."

Mikil shook the captain's offered hand. "Not half as glad as we are that you saw us. I have two companions waiting below: my betrothed and our adopted son. Also, there's a mistriss whom we rescued from the sea yestermorn, who is gravely ill. Do you have a way besides the ladder of fetching her on board?"

Arlettie and Gilboy waited for the sailors to lower down a sling. They loaded the unconscious woman on it as tenderly as possible, and the sailors hauled her up, knocking her against the ship's side only a few times and not hard enough to do her any more damage. Arlettie climbed aboard once the patient was safe. Then the sailors threw down the sling again so Gilboy could load into it a cloak that they had bundled around their swords and the few precious items they'd scavenged from Cressa's trunk. Finally, Gilboy cut the ropes that tied the *Shrimp* (who had served her purpose, and now could be unceremoniously jettisoned), and climbed up the ladder himself.

Mikil watched his little boat, which he had spent years perfecting, bob away on the breast of the waves. The loss cut him to the quick; he wished he'd asked the seamaster to tow it along *Island Dreamer,* though he knew if he were captain he would have to refuse to be encumbered by such an extraneous burden. Now that his long-sought goal had at last been accomplished, a wave of depression and weariness washed over him.

Gilboy, by contrast, was exhilarated, eager to talk with the crew, who were the first new people he had met since he was a small boy. He introduced himself to everyone in turn, savoring the new names and faces, shaking hands, chattering like a magpie.

Arlettie worried about their castaway; she asked the captain who served as his shipboard healer. The first mate had a little skill in this area. When he saw the state the young woman was in, the mate had her moved into his own small cabin, where he coated her burns and gave her watered rum to drink. But when he listened with his ear pressed against her chest, his brows fell, and he told Arlettie he thought something had gone wrong with her left lung—something beyond his abilities to heal. They set a galley boy to watch over her and alert them should she come to consciousness.

While Gilboy followed the sailors around like an eager puppy, Mikil and Arlettie shared a quick repast with the captain, explaining their story of being marooned and relishing the extraordinary tastes of cheese, soda biscuits, and citrus jelly. Mikil wanted to know everything that had happened since he dropped out of world events, but exhaustion caught up with him. Seamaster Bajets graciously offered his stateroom, and the prince readily accepted. Arlettie climbed into linen sheets for the first time in many seasons with a sigh of deep appreciation. Mikil first knelt at the foot of the wooden bed.

"Lautan the Munificent," he prayed. "You promised to rescue us and you have done so. We are forever your grateful servants. Please show your mercy too on that injured woman. If your dolphins were carrying her, might her life be precious to you?"

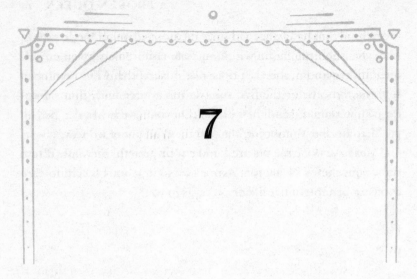

7

Femturan

General Sumroth and the five hundred troops under his command arrived at Ingot, a hamlet that had formerly been a suburb of Femturan, two days after the start of the Conflagration.

The ten thousand survivors of the fire had swamped the small village. Thousands of people milled about, some injured and all distraught, while exhausted Protectors sat leaning their backs against walls and cushioning their heads in their sooty hands.

Riding up the road through this chaos, Sumroth turned to his high flamers: "First, establish a chain of command over these troops and get them off their butts. Get the men to triage the wounded and put them in whatever shelter you can find, separate the dead, and—especially—round up the orphans. My tent goes there. Picket the aurochs out of town near the river; requisition that barn over there for supplies."

"Yes, sir. Will you be in your tent?"

"No," said Sumroth, sliding off his beast. It had taken all his discipline to waste time dispensing these commonsense orders. "No. I have to find my wife."

His only thought was to find Zea. He ran through the crowds of survivors shouting her name. Desperate children and women saw his uniform and grabbed at him—he pushed them off. Femturan soldiers and officers saluted and tried to confer with him: "General! How should we—?" "General! Do you have healers?" "Sir, all praise to Pozhar—" Sumroth bulled them all out of his way.

"Zea! Zee-aa!" He put his hands to his mouth and dashed into the deepest press of people. "Zee-aa!" No answer. He ran toward a cluster of more citizens in a small square; he banged his sword against his breastplate for silence, and he screamed again, "Zee-aa!" He climbed onto a wagon and shouted. "Zee-aa! Zea, where are you!"

Faces swarmed around him, but he recognized none of them. If he saw a woman her height, he would grab her shoulders to turn her around, but she was never the one person he wanted to find.

He began searching the major buildings of Ingot, the tavern, the school, the livery stable. He dashed into Ingot's modest Worship Citadel, where people too injured to stand lay stretched out on the benches. Women walked among them, trying to nurse them without any medical supplies. General Sumroth stood in the doorway and bellowed, "Zee-aa!"

A woman halfway down an aisle turned, ran at him, and threw herself at his chest. He clasped her against himself with both arms. "Are you hurt?"

"No. I escaped unharmed," Zea answered.

"All praise to Pozhar," he whispered. Sumroth held her away from him so he could see for himself. Her sleeping shift showed singe marks, her white hair had turned gray with soot, but arms, shoulders, face, hands, feet, ankles—unmarred. Again he folded her against his body. She shook with emotion; he gathered she'd been through a terrifying ordeal. But she was alive, and that was all that really mattered.

Once he had seen Zea fed, decently clothed, and resting in his own tent attended by adjutants who understood that their careers (perchance their lives) depended upon their making this woman comfortable, General Sumroth agreed to see the sixth-flamer who had been the highest-ranking officer at the Forge during the Conflagration.

The brigadier standing at attention outside his tent swayed on his feet. He had burns up and down his arms and a large gash in his scalp. "Sir, I regret to report that we have good reason to believe the Magi all died in the fire," he said to Sumroth. "The Octagon burned and no one escaped."

"Really?" Sumroth was astonished. "Then I'm assuming command here now—over both civilians and military. I'm sure you did the best you could in these circumstances. Get yourself tended and get some sleep. Report when you are fit to stand."

Ignoring the people trying to importune them, Sumroth and two fifth-flamers walked a short distance on the Broad Way east of Ingot to survey Femturan itself from a slight hill. The capital city had burnt to its foundations; the obsidian-paved streets wandered past piles of charred ruin. Small orange embers still smoldered in scattered corners. Not a building stood to represent the great metropolis that once stood there. The Octagon, the Bejeweled Gates, the Library of Reverence, the central Citadel of Flames—all gone. The stone city wall had collapsed in several places. The fire had completely destroyed the Forge Army Headquarters outside the wall as well as spread partway into the western valley. Pine trees stood as blackened fingers. Ash covered the ground, and smoke lingered in the air.

Returning to Ingot, Sumroth soon learned that civilians had died by the hundreds from being trampled, caught in burning structures, or inhaling smoke. Sacrificing themselves, the Femturan Protectors had done their best to save the populace until they too had been overwhelmed by the billowing, black clouds.

His first orders concentrated on establishing an organized camp and starting the funeral pyres for the dead. Protectors set up tents to shelter the weakest citizens, including the children and the elderly, and medical stations where healers could tend to hurts. They fed the civilians the soldiers' rations they carried and sent for more supplies from the patrols in the Iron Valley and from Drintoolia. The chaos that had reigned right after the catastrophe began to give way to orderly—if lengthy—lines for information, food, or medical care.

The next morning Sumroth convened a court of inquiry into the cause of the tragedy. This court was held in a tavern room big enough for the three judges and two dozen of the most important surviving officers and civilians as witnesses. The chairs his soldiers had scrounged together formed a motley assortment, and the table he sat behind wobbled, but in such a situation these rough surroundings hardly registered.

When Sumroth questioned city dwellers they could recount only their own trauma trying to escape the raging flames. However, one officer offered a credible story that three strangers on horseback, followed by birds, had penetrated the city through the Bejeweled Gates. Other seemingly sober figures spoke of birds spreading fire.

"Birds carrying fiery brands!" Sumroth shook his head. "I hear you, but I can hardly credit such a notion."

"Smithy will vouch for what we say," said a man who had identified himself as the head of the Obsidian Bank. "He stayed in the thick of the city longer than anyone else. Shall we send for him?"

Sumroth assented. Smithy, so large and so marked by his deafness, had long been a famous figure in Femturan, a figure Sumroth had known vaguely ever since he and Zea had first arrived. Although he worked as a lowly blacksmith at a forge near the central Citadel, he didn't carry himself meekly. Sumroth believed he had some ambiguous religious function but he had no title and no other name.

Watching the burly man now as he strode into the tavern, Sumroth's first impression was favorable: clearly, here stood neither a sick, loon-headed Magi nor a pewling, fanatical priest. And his bravery spoke in his favor; during the inquiry Sumroth heard again and again that Smithy had dashed back into the fire to single-handedly save many children. Yet Smithy did not carry himself with the arrogance of the late (and to Sumroth, unmourned) Champion Tulsham. Perchance in this strange character, garbed in a leather apron dotted with scorch marks, Sumroth might find a much-needed, and much-longed-for, ally.

"Smithy, I would like to commend you for your rescues," Sumroth began. "I hear they were quite remarkable."

The dour man had stared closely at his lips. He responded flatly, "I didn't do them for you. I save children for Pozhar."

"No, I'm sure you didn't, but just the same they showed valor," Sumroth replied, determined not to take offense at the man's brusque manner. "Our purpose here is to discover how the fire started. Do you know anything about how all this happened?"

"A Weir witch penetrated the heart of our capital. With the help of enchanted birds, she brought down a rain of fire."

"What!? A Weir witch?" Sumroth was incredulous, and the room broke out in surprised exclamations.

"How did she invade a guarded city?" Sumroth pressed.

"She didn't invade. She was brought into the city as a captive," Smithy stated.

Sumroth started. He remembered sending the girl he had captured on the Iron Valley battlefield to Femturan. Surely, *that* unassuming bitch wasn't— Could *he* actually be responsible for this catastrophe? He rubbed the open cut on his chin and shifted in his seat uneasily. Did this strange man know of his role? Might he be about to expose his blunder publicly?

"What do you know about the birds?" Sumroth asked, changing the subject.

"They helped the witch. She could command them." Smithy shrugged.

"How do you know such things?"

"I just do."

Abruptly, Sumroth stood up. "Gentlemen, thank you for your time," he said to the assembly. "We can proceed no more today. The air in here is smoky, and I tire of sitting.

"Will you walk with me to discuss this further?" he asked Smithy.

Smithy shrugged again as if being invited to converse with an eighth-flamer was the equivalent of being offered ale instead of water.

Leaving the other attendees of the court of inquiry to discuss the information and reach whatever conclusion they wished, Sumroth walked out. He shooed his orderlies behind, and together he and Smithy strode the perimeter of the survivors' camp alone. Smithy walked to the side of the general so that he could read his lips when he spoke.

Soon Sumroth relaxed. If his companion knew that he was the one who had sent the girl into Femturan, he appeared to have no intention of speaking of it. The general couldn't figure out what Smithy's role had been in Femturan or how he came by the knowledge he possessed. But he quickly discerned that the man's priorities did not lie in self-advancement—all his concerns were for their countrymen.

As they discussed immediate survival, the general asked, "What do you see as the biggest issue?"

"Food," said Smithy.

"Aye," said Sumroth, rubbing his chin. "That's been the problem for years. The granaries and storehouses are the most dire of our losses, worse than the historic buildings. All that work to send food here from the Free States, only to have it all burn to cinders!"

He kicked a rock on the ground in front of him to vent his frustration. Smithy said nothing.

"I have been thinking," Sumroth continued, "since we have no food stores for the people, we must take these people to food."

"Where?" asked Smithy.

"Alpetar. I marched through it years ago. The Alpies are cowards, and unlike Melladrin, their land is rich and fertile. I would lead these Femturans through the Trade Corridor and settle them in the flatlands of Alpetar."

"Occupy Alpetar? Farm there?" Smithy sounded reluctant, as much as his limited vocal range could express.

"Aye. If we had tried this in earlier decades, perchance there would have been an international outcry, but I think we can count on our enemy's quiescence now. We may not wish to settle in an alien country, but we must stay until we can lift the plagues that poison our land. Do you know how we can get out from under this curse, Smithy?"

"Kill the witch's spawn."

"How do you know that will do it?"

"It will avenge the Initial Crime."

"The Initial Crime?"

"Aye. When Weirs killed Oro immigrants for worshipping Pozhar."

"When was this?" asked Sumroth.

"Four centuries ago," said Smithy.

As they tramped with their equally long strides, Sumroth smiled at the thought that this man, who probably was unlettered, would be a student of ancient history.

"Well now, this 'witch's spawn.' Where is she? Are you sure she survived the fire?"

"Don't know where she is," said Smithy, biting off his answers. "But one day she will return to Cascada."

"Ah, there's the rub. We have never had any method of marching to Cascada in force."

"Don't need to," said Smithy. "Assassinate her."

This suggestion surprised Sumroth. "Well, that's as may be. If we knew where she was. Though there's honor only in battle, not in assassination."

"Honor," said Smithy, in such an uninflected tone that Sumroth couldn't tell whether he agreed with the sentiment or mocked it.

Overall, Sumroth found the craftsman impenetrable. He appeared to know things that no one else did, but Sumroth found his emotions even more inscrutable than his officers'. And to his deep disappointment, the man made no friendly overtures, offered no respect or comradeship.

They walked awhile in silence. Sumroth snapped orders to Protectors who were loafing on duty.

"Pellish ships," Smithy said out of nowhere.

"Have the Pellish rebuilt their fleet?" Sumroth asked in surprise. "And if they have, why would they loan them to us? Their ships are their national treasures."

"There are other treasures."

"Hear me, General," interrupted a bedraggled but bold woman who had seen them approaching and moved to intersect them. "When will we have something to feed our children? My youngest one cries that his belly is empty."

"More supplies will be arriving soon, sistern. You must be patient. Protector," he shouted to a red uniform in the distance. "Deal with this woman." He turned and shouted to the fourth-flamers following the pair. "See that we are not interrupted again."

Sumroth picked up his conversation with Smithy. "Yes, well, if I had an eighth of the riches the Magi hoarded, even just one of their fuckin' chairs—don't imagine you ever saw one of those—I would have more options. But they took their riches with them into the Eternal Flames. . . ."

Sumroth stopped short as a thought struck him. "Ahhh! No. Jewels don't burn."

"They lie in the rubble." Smithy nodded his head in the direction of the destroyed Octagon.

Sumroth's face brightened. "Excellent! All we need is to sort through the ashes. . . ." Sumroth called to the nearest soldier, "Find a fifth-flamer. Tell him I want him to collect all the rakes, pickaxes, and hand tools he can. I don't care where or how he gets them; he must find us dozens."

Sumroth rubbed his hands. "I'd wager the ashes are still too hot to work in. As soon as they cool I'll send in teams of eight. I'll have the teams work naked; that way no one can pocket the stones.

"Meanwhile, I have issued orders to pull in all my troops that are spread throughout the Iron Valley. In a week or more we will escort these evacuees into Alpetar. We will set them up there with food and protection. I will march on to Ixtulpus with all the riches of Femturan in my purse."

Smithy nodded approval. "I will stay with our people in Alpetar."

Heedless of the comment (for he really didn't care where this strange, deaf blacksmith settled), Sumroth carried on outlining his plan. "If we have to wait moons, years, we will set sail for Cascada, burn *that* city to the ground, and I will personally cut out the liver of the witch and roast it over a fire!"

"We will have the vengeance we've been owed for centuries," said Smithy in his longest sentence in a while. "And then we will have salvation." He offered Sumroth his hand, and the two men sealed the pact.

8

Sutterdam, The Free States

The jellyfish venom and its antidote left Gustie dizzy, headachy, and fatigued for over a week. Norling baked her berry cobblers and fussed over her. Gustie bore this clucking with ill grace, because she would rather have had information as to how the insurrection progressed after she had poisoned so many high-ranking Oro officers.

Norling went out twice a day and returned with news she conveyed in terse reports: a battle at Artisans Bridge had ended with the stronger, trained Oros crushing the motley Defiance fighters, and the attempt to liberate the infirmaries and healers from Oro control had been abandoned because the Oros threatened to kill Free States hostages.

Gustie wanted to know much more, not just how local skirmishes fared, but the overall condition of the conflict. How many captives had escaped Oro imprisonment? Were they in any shape to fight? How were the low-level Protectors reacting to the death of most of the high flamers? Were citizens who had been frightened now emboldened to flock to the Defiance? What was the situation in the other major cities?

Norling's answers to these questions did little to sate Gustie's hunger. And she kept making comments on the order of, "You must not fret so, my dear, or you will slow your recuperation."

The old woman meant well, and by hiding Gustie she risked her life. But Gustie could not countenance Norling's desire to keep her safe in Sutterdam Pottery while the battle raged between the erstwhile slaves and the Oromondo occupiers. She burned for more revenge against the men who had enslaved her and other Free States women.

Finally, as she grew in strength, Gustie realized that she didn't need her host's permission; she was a free woman who could do as she pleased.

"Norling, I am leaving to join the Defiance. With your forbearance I will take this worker's shirt to hide my red ball gown and cover my brigadier chain. I thank you for all you've done for me."

"Do you know *where* to go, my dear?" said Norling, surprising Gustie by her lack of protest. "Isn't it true that you've only lived in Sutterdam a few moons? Do you have contacts here among the Defiance? Wait half a tick while I get my market basket; I'll escort you. Look out the window for me, dear. Is it windy?" She wrapped herself in a shawl.

Gustie tapped her foot while the older woman made herself ready. The two women left the safety of Sutterdam Pottery's living quarters for cold and empty streets. Citizens and occupiers appeared to be hiding from one another and laying their plans for nighttime attacks. Norling led her over Potters Bridge toward the middle of town. Gustie noticed a dozen broken shop windows and torn-up cobblestones. Dark, wet splotches on the ground must be blood, but the combatants had dragged away their wounded and dead.

They passed statues of people made of stone. Someone had painted "Freedom!" on the base of a pedestal.

"I approve of the sentiment," said Norling, *tsk*ing, "but not of defacing the Statue of the Martyrs!"

After several blocks, they came to a business with a carriage wheel hung above the door. Norling knocked a complicated signal, and a large man with an almost black beard, holding an axe over his head ready to strike, opened the door a crack.

"Ah, Norling!" he cried. "You shouldn't be out right now."

"I know that, Ikas, but the young are ever restless," she answered.

"The young? Who are you?" asked Ikas, addressing Gustie as he ushered them inside.

"Gustie of Weaverton, formerly a student at the Scoláiríum of Latham. Until recently the comfort woman of Brigadier Umrat."

"Brigadier Umrat, eh? So was you there during the Poison Banquet?"

"The 'Poison Banquet'?" Gustie tasted the label and smiled. "News of that has spread, has it?" She held her head even higher with pride.

"I'm Ikas, the leader of this unit. This is my concern we're hiding in."

Looking past him, Gustie saw a large workshop full of many odd-looking tools and conveyances of all sorts—several sitting cock-eyed because they missed a wheel or a shaft—that stretched into the shadowed recesses. Other men sat scattered about in the vehicles, resting or waiting.

"How many are you?" asked Gustie.

"We number nearly fifty. Some of us aren't in great shape, though."

"And what's your next target?"

Ikas looked over her head at Norling. "Our assignment this evening is to wrest the guardhouse near the wharf from a squad of Oro soldiers. At least three dozen Oros have barricaded themselves in there."

"I see," said Gustie. "And what's the strategy and how many weapons do you have?"

"We don't have nearly enough swords, daggers, or bows. Mostly we're working with crude pikes and hand tools. As for a plan, we're awaiting our ringleader's advice."

"Who is your ringleader? May I meet him?"

"I believe you've already met our ringleader," Ikas replied with a grin. "In fact, you know her quite well."

Norling patted Gustie's shoulder. "And she knows *you* quite well. Smart and brave, you are, my dear, but headstrong and proud. I have enough to worry about, thank you, without fretting over keeping you alive. If you're going to join with us, sit yourself down there on that carriage seat and don't speak until spoken to."

Gustie's mouth fell open in shock. In a daze, she moved over to the seat indicated.

Norling took off her shawl and bonnet and emptied the wicker basket she had insisted on toting along.

"Ikas, I have brought quicklime and small jars. If we fill the jars—very carefully, mind you—to lob them at the enemy so they break, the quicklime will burn their eyes. You need to construct some sort of slingshot. You can do that, I trust?"

More men had gathered closer around them, materializing out of the dark corners of the wheelwright's shop. Norling greeted several and asked how they were faring.

Then she walked over to a wheelless carriage sitting in the middle of the room. Two men lay on cushioned benches, covered with blankets. Ikas gave Norling a hand to step into the vehicle. She moved the bandages off one man's middle to inspect a wound. The other man didn't move when she touched his cheek and stroked his hair. Norling sat with him a spell, and during this time no one interrupted her.

Meanwhile, the men in the shop had sprung into action. A few painstakingly filled the jars with the white powder; others dismantled a small wagon yoke and tested different materials to serve as the sling band. Although Gustie could tell at a glance that some of the materials didn't have enough elasticity, she held her tongue and kicked her feet as she sat.

Eventually, two men brought out a brew pot and a half dozen mismatched mugs.

Norling sighed and called to Ikas, "Dear, will you help me down now?"

A man poured tisane; Ikas pulled up a chair for Norling; several men gathered around her, squatting on their heels. Norling looked over at Gustie. "Join us, dear. I could use your quick mind." A man handed her a full cup. Gustie was thirsty, and the bitter tisane was bracing.

"All right, my dears," Norling began. "The Oros will be expecting us to attack over Sailmakers Bridge. We want to keep their attention focused on the bridge, but we'll send the bulk of our squad around to the south, over the Shipwrights Bridge, and come up on the Oros from quayside. Those men will have the quicklime grenades. The question is: how do we keep the Oros' attention focused north, and how do we get them to leave their shelter and stand around outside so we can lob our missiles at them?"

"A diversion?" suggested Ikas.

"What do we have to make a diversion *with*?" a man asked.

"Carriages?" said Ikas. He swept his arm around the shop. "We have plenty of carriages."

"That's what I'm thinking, but we have no horses to pull them," answered Norling.

"Sailmakers sits at the bottom of a bit of slope," said the man who had brought out the brew pot.

"So a carriage would roll?" asked Norling. "And who would steer it?"

Gustie raised her hand like a child in under school asking for permission to speak. "Let me do it."

"Why you?" said one of the group.

Gustie took off the work shirt she was wearing, showing off her low-cut red gown and striking a pose.

"Because the Oros are much more likely to watch me than any of you lot."

The men chuckled, but at that moment, their discussion was interrupted by the signal knock on the door. Ikas grabbed his axe and opened it a handsbreadth. A young boy entered the wheelwright's business.

"Got a note," he said.

"Give it here, dollface," said Norling, stretching out her hand.

She read it. "Mother Rellia says that the attacks start tonight when Ghibli's Wind Mill chimes at midnight," she told the men gathered around her. "We'd best make haste. You've got a long tramp all the way to the customhouse and back. Sansam, you'll lead the Shipwrights squad? Choose the men who can walk the farthest and the quickest, and who will be bold in the hand-to-hand that ensues."

Norling looked at the boy. "Now, dollface, I know that bows are in short supply, but we need one bow and at least one quarrel of arrows from headquarters."

Frowning, Ikas said, "Norling, we're mostly townsfolk and tradesmen. None of us hunt; none have practiced archery."

"Ah, but I know someone who boasts of her archery skill," said Norling. "Now, let's think more about those carriages."

Ikas, Gustie, and several other men halted the heavy lorries behind a corner of a brick building, just hidden from sight of Sailmakers Bridge. Gustie tugged at the brigadier chain, which chafed around her neck.

"If we survive tonight I'll cut that off for you," Ikas whispered.

"If I die, will you still do so?"

"Aye, I vow. I'll even cut it off if *I* die. I have two daughters. I'd hate—"

"Thank you," said Gustie.

Norling had volunteered to stay behind to tend the wounded. One of the most severely wounded, Gustie learned from Ikas, was Norling's brother, Hartling. He had been the first to charge the Oro guards when the keys were smuggled to their cells; thus he had sustained serious injuries.

A bell rung.

"That's not from the Wind Mill," said Ikas. "But our chimes should ring out any moment. Best get ready."

One of the smaller, more nimble men scurried, bent over through the darkness to take the position they'd agreed upon. He carried the bow and quiver tightly, as if they were treasures.

Gustie climbed into the driver's seat of the first, horseless lorry. Ikas had jerry-rigged a makeshift harness to the shaft that would give her some ability to steer the vehicle as it rolled down the cobbled incline to the bridge. Ikas lit the lamps posted on both sides of her carriage to throw light on the driver. If all worked as planned, the Oros would stare in wonderment at this pretty woman in a red dress on an "out-of-control" carriage.

The men positioned themselves, one each behind the wheels of the lorries, and prepared to push. *Chime.* The men heaved the carts, but the inertia of the vehicles made them difficult to budge. *Chime.* They put their backs into it, and Gustie's front carriage started to roll down the slope. *Chime.* The second lorry, lashed behind, began to clatter against the cobblestones as well; the first now gained momentum. *Chime.* Gustie looked behind her; the third carriage had joined its fellows. *Chime.* Ikas sprinted to catch up with the second wagon and threw a shoulder into the rear corner, forcing it onto a truer course. The heavy vehicles made a terrible racket, drowning out any further sounds of the church bell (or of the seaside squad's approach).

Gustie started to scream, which was part of the plan, though the terror in her voice was genuine. She heard male shouts as the lorries trundled toward Sailmakers Bridge, gathering speed. She pulled her makeshift harness, aiming the carriage in between the bridge parapets.

Her lorry had just enough momentum to climb the shallow incline of the bridge, but as it reached the crest it slowed and almost stopped. Then the second, heavier lorry slammed into it from behind, giving it a jolt forward.

Just after the collision, Gustie, who had been poised, managed to struggle to her feet. Nimbly, she jumped from the carriage seat to the thin railing of the bridge. She didn't want to perch on the edge, but rather just surmount the barrier. Her right foot made contact, and she pushed off with it, letting her weight carry her forward. She landed in an icy tributary of the Sutter, which, as she'd been promised, turned out to be only knee-deep.

Three thoughts flashed through her mind: she'd managed the leap without injury; there was no way to drown in a knee-deep stream; and the water was *freezing*. She glanced up and across the river to see her lorry roll smack into the guardhouse with the sound of wood splintering. The second lorry again struck the back of the first, sending it shuddering deeper into the damaged structure; the third had lost its path, broken its rope, and careened off course, ending up lodged slantwise, blocking the bridge. The flames from her lanterns began to spread into the oil-soaked straw the Defiance had packed in the back of her carriage.

The confederate who had assumed his position waited for her at the safe side of the stream bank. He pulled her out of the water before she even had time to fully register how cold her feet were or how heavy with water her skirt dragged. As planned, he thrust the bow and arrows into her hands.

Oros spilled out of the guardhouse, shouting, flourishing their weapons in the wavering flames. A quicklime grenade exploded in their midst. They screamed like scalded cats and scrubbed at their eyes. Another grenade. The Protectors were trapped by the heavy lorries blocking the bridge and surrounded by the attackers who had come up behind them. Some tried to escape in the half-frozen branch of the Sutter River, but Ikas and other Free Staters waited there with axes and clubs in hand.

A few thought to flee along the shore to their right. These ran straight into the arrows Gustie rained down on them from her position across the stream. At twelve paces, and with the light from the now-burning guardhouse illuminating their silhouettes, she couldn't miss. Her arrows sunk deep into Oro flesh. Each satisfying strike felt like killing Umrat all over again.

But she did not have the opportunity to kill as many as she wanted to. The quicklime grenades incapacitated most because the powder reacted with the moisture in their eyes and lungs to cause severe burning. The Oro soldiers screamed in agony until they could push no more air through their damaged throats.

If it had been windy, the quicklime would have killed the Free Staters involved in the mission too. Gustie shuddered at the chances Norling had taken.

The customhouse squad took a dozen prisoners and marched them over the ice patches developing on the river's shore and through the cold water.

The Free Staters rendezvoused in the dim wheelwright shop.

The captured weapons and prisoners pleased Norling. Then the young messenger reappeared, and they learned that one of the other coordinated attacks that night had also been successful, though with many more Free States casualties. Muted congratulations and back-slapping ensued.

"Ikas, 'tis very late. I need to take my houseguest to her bed; this is her first day fully up, and now her feet are sopping wet," said Norling. "Keep these prisoners securely tied. And take a count of the swords and pikes."

"As you wish, mam," said Ikas. He shook off the man who was trying to bandage the slash he had sustained on his upper arm.

"Wait one moment—there's something I promised to do." He squished through the shop in his own wet boots to a set of tools. He rummaged through the mess, finally hoisting a metal cutter.

The brigadier chain was so tight against Gustie's skin Ikas had to snake the lower blade under it while she held her chin stretched up. With a mighty snap, he freed Gustie of the accursed necklace. It fell to the floor with a clatter. Ikas bent to retrieve it and handed it to Gustie with a bow.

"Thank you," she whispered, holding the chain in her hand and feeling its weight.

"Much more becoming, my dear," agreed Norling, with a satisfied sigh. "Though we must do something about that red gown. For one thing, it makes you a target, even in the depths of night. And for another—'tis so immodest! I really don't know how you can go around in it. Really, the fashions young women wear nowadays!"

"I didn't choose it for fighting!" said Gustie. Norling's condescension grated on her. "I selected it for distraction at the banquet. It helped me poison one hundred Oro officers—which is more than we killed tonight!—so I'll thank you to keep your criticisms to yourself."

9

Aboard Island Dreamer

Skylark woke from her unconscious state intermittently. She became aware of a woman feeding her spoonfuls of broth. Another time someone tried to move her left arm, and the agonizing pain briefly brought her round. "The bone's broken right below her shoulder," a male voice said, and then he bandaged her left arm and shoulder tightly against her body, even though she tried to tell him that the bandages' pressure on the burn blisters was excruciating. Someone sponged her forehead. Later, they gave her milk of the poppy.

The next evening, Skylark surfaced from the drug to greater awareness of her surroundings. She was in a bunk bed, on a ship. A woman with bangs of leaf green flecked with brown sat sitting by a lantern in the tiny cabin. The color of her hair brought back memories of her Slagos friend Zillie.

"Water," Skylark croaked.

"Ah, darlin', you're awake again. I'll get you a cup of water. Oh, rot, this pitcher's empty. I'll be back in a tick."

When she left the cabin, the ship's orange cat pushed the door open and jumped on the bed.

Your Majesty, he purred. *Your Majesty.* He kneaded the bed-clothes next to her, then walked in a tight circle in front of her face.

Hullo, cat. What's your name?

The sailors call me Lazy, because they do nay see me catching rats.

Hullo, Lazy.

Your Majesty, your hair grows in blue at the roots.

Has anyone noticed it?

Not yet.

Skylark tried to think. She had returned to brown before the Battle of Iron Valley because she'd run out of chamomile.

Coal tar, acorn water, and bergamot oil. That's what I need to cover it up.

One does nay know these things, sent Lazy.

Probably not on the ship, anyway, she told the cat.

What else couldst thou use?

Skylark closed her eyes and drifted off a moment, hovering on the verge of consciousness; with milk of poppy fogging her mind, she found it hard to care about anything. The cat batted her nose to rouse her; when Skylark didn't open her eyes, he batted again with a touch of claw.

Ouch. Don't do that. Does the captain write in his log with black ink?

Yes.

Can you bring me the ink bottle?

One does nay know how, but one will try.

Thank you, Lazy.

Exhausted from the conversation, Skylark fell back to sleep before the water arrived, with her good arm holding the cat close to her heart.

The next time she woke (perhaps the next morning), a young man dozed in the chair.

"Please, could I have some water?"

"Ah, you're awake!" said the young man, starting up with a grin.

He filled a glass of water, propped her up a little, and held it to her lips. She gulped long swallows, grateful that it was not seawater, even if it did taste slightly brackish.

"Good! How did you come to be riding on a dolphin in the middle of the ocean?"

"I don't remember," answered Skylark truthfully.

"How did you get burned?"

That, she did remember, but she didn't want to say, so she just shook her head.

"I'm Gilboy. Me and my mother and sire pulled you from the ocean. We rescued you at sea. It was the most exciting thing, ever. This ship is headed toward Pilagos in the Green Isles."

"Thank you for rescuing me," said Skylark. "And for the water."

"What's your name?"

"I'm called Phénix," she said, her caution kicking in sufficiently to choose a new name.

"Odd name," said Gilboy. "Never heard it before. Pleased to meet you, Mistriss Phénix."

"Aye," she agreed. "I had unusual parents."

"Oh, I know all about that," he answered. "Will you eat something? I could fetch you a bowl of porridge?"

"Please," said Phénix, and this time she was hungry enough to stay awake during a caretaker's absence.

Yet even those few words had left her panting. When she pushed herself up higher in the bed each breath brought sharp pain. Her burns felt on fire, and her shoulder and side ached terribly. The sun-exposed skin on her face itched. When she scratched, she noticed large strips of dead skin peeling off. The uncovered burns that she could touch along her neck must look ghastly (they felt disgusting to her exploring fingers)—blistered, bleeding, and oozing.

Gilboy reentered with an older man on his heels. This second man had the bearing of a nobleman, but she couldn't tell what country he might be from because she couldn't see his hair color in the dim room. He took the bowl to feed her himself. She found it hard to eat; she needed to pause for air after each spoonful.

The nobleman waited patiently and unconsciously mimed her mouth and smiled approval at each swallow she got down. "Mistriss, we should arrive in Pilagos in another week or two," he told her encouragingly. "There we will be able to get you seen by a real healer. You just need to hold on a little longer."

Phénix found his steady gaze disconcerting. She began to worry about her blue roots.

"The light hurts my eyes," she managed to gasp out, between mouthfuls.

"Oh. Of course," the man said, "I'm sorry. I should've realized you'd have eyestrain." He nodded to the lad, who rushed to cover the porthole.

"I will send Arlettie to care for you this evening," the man continued. "And the mate who comes, he serves as the ship's healer. I appreciate that he doesn't pretend to more knowledge than he has. He's doing his best for you."

Phénix nodded and lay back on the bed.

Lazy crept in when the crew and passengers were eating their evening meal. He held a small, stoppered bottle in his mouth as if it were a mouse he'd killed. He dropped it in her hand triumphantly.

Phénix poured small amounts in several places around her scalp. Then, with great difficulty, she single-handedly tore an edge off the bandage that was wound around her torso and shoulder. She covered two fingers with the bandage to try to keep her hand clean, and rubbed the ink all around her head, stopping frequently to catch her breath. She recapped the bottle for Lazy to return, and hid the ink-stained rag under her mattress, all the while leaning on her elbow, holding her inky hair off the mattress until it dried.

But the ink had soaked through the rag and stained her fingers. Looking about the cabin she spied a pitcher, basin, and soap just a pace across the narrow room, but to Phénix they might as well have been on Mother Moon.

Lazy started licking her stained fingers with his sandpaper tongue.

Don't, said Phénix. *It can't possibly be good for you.*

One will eat some roughage and throw up later. One throws up all the time. One has favorite places.

The cat licked and licked, and gradually the worst of the stain wore off.

When Arlettie joined her after their meal, Phénix was exhausted from her efforts and holding Lazy's purring form tightly. She was grateful for the watered rum that Arlettie gave her to drink and the small bites of cheese she gave her to eat. She was even more grateful for the cooling poultices placed on her burns, and the sponge wash that took the sweat and grime (and ink) from many parts of her body.

"Darlin', I really should wash your hair," Arlettie commented.

"Not now. I'm so worn out," Phénix pleaded, and the kindly woman accepted the excuse.

Fire. In the night her body caught on fire with fever. Her breath came in shallow pants, and she coughed too much to sleep. Arlettie changed her sweat-soaked shift when she grew unbearably hot and piled on more blankets when she shivered. Phénix became too nauseated to eat any longer.

Consciousness slipped away, but in her fevered doze her dreams turned evil. A Magi branded her shoulder with a hot iron again and again, though she begged him to stop. In the distance she saw the Nargis headwaters; she was crawling over rocks trying to get to the pool of cold, clean water while wolves laughed at her mockingly. The flaming brand burnt through her skin and into her heart.

In her dream a low rumble spoke to her. *Thou hast been touched by my Power. If thou useth thy Talent thou wilt burn!*

She woke screaming with terror, "No! No! Never!!" The frightened galley boy ran to fetch the nobleman.

"I hear you're having nightmares. There is no fire here. You're safe on the *Island Dreamer*. We are doing all we can for you. Lie back, now. Relax, mistriss. Lie back. Good. That's good.

"Shall I sit here to watch over you a bit? Will you mind a pipe? Some people say that tobacco is good for the lungs. This is the first smoke I've had in eight years." The man went on, more to himself than to Phénix, "I too know about frightening dreams of Fire."

The tobacco smell reminded her of home. Wren slipped into a dream about the Wyndton cottage on hot summer evenings, just as the dark brought in the cooler air and night swallows cavorted through the sky. Stahlia sat with her darning on the step while Wren and Percia played "chase the fireflies" with Tilim out in the yard, the little boy shrieking, "Ire lies! Ire lies!" all the while. Wilim watched over them all from the chair he had brought outside and propped slantwise against the house, a contented smile spread across his face, smoking his pipe.

She woke and dozed again. This time Skylark dreamed of Thalen. She dreamed that Thalen was covering her face with kisses.

Lie still, Lazy ordered, *one needs to lick you clean. Stop this coughing.* The sandpaper tongue worked on the sweat and the tears that pooled under her eyes.

Someone held a lukewarm tisane to her lips. She drank as much as she could, slurping greedily, spilling all over the bedclothes.

"I'm sorry," she half shouted over the fever ringing in her ears. "I'm so sorry I couldn't do it."

"You're raving, Phénix," said Zillie, the owner of the Blue Parrot in Slagos. "You've naught to apologize for."

"Oh, but I do! I failed. I tried! I tried so hard," she cried, sure that she was dying with her task unfulfilled, her people condemned to suffering, and the line of Nargis Queens judging her harshly.

"'Tis the fever plaguing you. Hush now."

"I'm sorry," she said before another spasm of coughing, each cough like a knife wound of pain.

"Hush now. Go back to sleep."

"Oh, Zillie, I'm so glad you're here. Perchance Gardener can help. I can't use my Talent anymore. It's tainted. I'm Powerless."

"You're making no sense at all, darlin'. Try to relax. Here, I'm going to give you more milk of the poppy."

Kestrel lay back down, but her eyes stared at the small cabin's low wooden ceiling.

"Vertia the Bountiful," Zillie prayed aloud, "let this woman, thy child, walk among thy green fields, growing in strength and peace, under your protection."

"Please, Vertia, let me grow strong," Kestrel intoned.

She dreamt again, but this time of sitting with Gardener in his courtyard. Fire licked against the stone walls—desperate to get in and burn all the lush and precious plants—but Gardener ignored it, instead droning on in his pedantic way about separating bulbs.

"Bulblets must be separated off from one another or they will never reach their full size," he said. "They will cling to one another and grow misshapen."

10

Tar's Basin, Alpetar

Thalen, Eli-anna, and Tristo had been waiting in Tar's Basin for about a week, long enough both to recover from the rigors of their journey down the coast and to worry over whether a vessel would ever pull into this tiny excuse for a harbor. They ate in the general store cum tavern, which called itself "Everything You Desire," and received permission from the guard of the one warehouse to bunk down on the piles of goat hair stored near the dock. The people of Tar's Basin assured them that a ship would stop, sooner or later. Tristo whiled away the time by playing games with the village children, though Thalen preferred to keep to himself.

On a chill and windy day, while the sun played hide-and-seek amongst gray clouds, Eli-anna spotted the shape on the horizon first. Thalen watched as the speck grew bigger and more substantial, turning into a midsized trading ship that unshipped its oars and tied up at the wharf.

"*Island Song*," called Thalen. "A word with your seamaster, if you please."

The seamaster came down the gangplank to join them on the wharf. He was a stout and grumpy man. "Well, what's your pleasure?" he asked.

"I'd like to book passage for my two companions and myself."

"Book passage to where?"

"Where are you headed?"

"Back to Slagos, our home port."

"Perfect. That's where we want to go."

"We ain't a passenger ship. We have no staterooms."

"We'll bunk with the crew."

"What about the woman? She with you?"

"Not in the way you mean, but we'll look after her." Thalen knew that any sailor who dared molest Eli-anna would get the surprise of his life—that is, if he managed to escape with his life.

"We ain't a passenger ship," said the seamaster. "I keep saying this, but no one ever listens. Put us out something awful to take you aboard."

Thalen had sold Dishwater, Sulky Sukie, and Cinders to the liveryman in town, after receiving many assurances that Culpepper would see to it that their horses found good homes. Thalen's money pouch was heavy with coin. He threw the pouch at the seamaster. The man hefted it, opened it, and opened his mouth to whine that the funds it contained weren't sufficient.

Thalen's temper flared. He hadn't gone through all this fighting, lost so many friends, starved and thirsted and saved the Free States, only to bandy words with a greedy lackwit. His face grew taut, and his hand moved toward the hilt of his rapier.

"I have given you enough to make this worth your while, twice over. I will brook no further discussion."

"You look like rough characters," said the captain, stepping backward. "I'll have no trouble on my ship, I'm warning you. On *Island Song,* I'm in command."

"Right now we stand in Tar's Basin, not aboard your territory. But even here there will be no trouble," said Thalen, pinning him in a fierce stare, "as long as you agree to take us to Slagos."

"Hmmpf." The seamaster hefted the pouch again, and avarice won out. "We'll shove off after we off-load commissioned cargo and upload the fleece. Cool your heels here awhile on the dock, Master Impatience."

While the sailors took care of those chores and refilled their water casks, the seamaster drank the morning away at Everything You Desire. Two of the mates grabbed the chance for a hot bath in the bathhouse while the crew, in rotation, was given leave to come ashore for a few hours.

Thalen slipped back to the stable, to bid one more—now final—goodbye to the horses, even though he knew the visit would just make him sad. Dish huffed into his hand, and Cinders leaned her heavy head on his shoulder. Sulky Sukie showed her teeth and pulled away when he tried to stroke her.

Afterward, the Raiders had no choice but to wait idly on the weathered dock. Thalen threw a handful of little pebbles at a piling, testing if his aim was true. Eli-anna, who had never before been to sea, drew in on herself with trepidation.

Once the *Song*'s cargo was stowed securely, the first mate bought all the crew fresh rolls from the tavern and invited the would-be travelers to come aboard. "We need to shove off with this high tide," he explained. "I'll fetch the captain." He ordered the sailors to ready their oars and prepare to depart.

Just as the three Raiders stepped from the top of the gangplank onto the deck, they heard the noise of horses, galloping fast. Two stunning mounts came into view on the High Road, bells in their tails jingling. Their riders were an older man and a stripling lad.

"Wait! Wait!" yelled the man. "I mean, 'ahoy'! Ahoy, *Island Song*!"

The seamaster and mate, and most of the townspeople, came into the street to see what caused such a commotion.

"What in tarnation are you?" asked the seamaster, fairly drunk.

The townspeople, however, recognized the strange figure. When he dismounted, twenty-odd villagers all gathered round him as if he were a celebrity, all talking on top of one another.

"Peddler, haven't seen you in a long time!"

"What news?"

"Where's your cart?"

"Where'd you get that beauty of a horse?"

"Who's the boy?"

"Did you see my brother on your way east?"

"Hey, did you hear if my girl had her baby?"

Peddler smiled at the villagers and patted a few shoulders, but he didn't answer their questions. He approached the swaying captain with a genial smile.

"Caught you just in time. And I remembered the word 'ahoy'! Sir, we need to sail on your boat."

"Sure," said the seamaster, wrinkling his nose and throwing his arms open in a wide gesture. "Come aboard. Join the floating circus. Come one, come all. Already got me a one-armed freak, a Mellie whore, and a ruffian; why not a jingling peddler and his suckin' bumpkin?"

Like a cloud blocking the sun, Peddler's cordiality vanished. He struck the man a backhanded blow across his face, a blow of such force that the seamaster, unsteady to begin with, lost his footing and fell down in the dirt.

"We rode so hard to catch you," said Peddler to the drunk on the ground. "You *will* keep a civil tongue in your mouth.

"Culpepper." He turned to the stableman, who was out in the street along with everyone else. "Will you rest and feed Sunbeam and Sundrop for a few days, then turn them loose? They know how to take themselves home to their stable. Hold on to their tack for me?"

He stroked the larger horse's nose a moment before grabbing

a saddlebag. He flipped a gold coin to Culpepper. "Oh. Saw your youngest sister two nights ago. She and her family are thriving. She sends her love."

"That's swell news, Peddler," said Culpepper. "Don't worry about your horses."

Peddler smiled and addressed the boy, "Come along, Gunnit. We made it, just in time."

The yellow-haired man and yellow-haired boy walked up the gangplank a bit warily. Peddler stopped halfway, turned around, and shouted to someone in the crowd near the horses, "Darrott! The babe was a boy. Healthy as can be. Mother and father are busting with pride." A cheer went up from several throats.

Thalen had watched these events with great interest. When the new passengers reached the safety of the deck, he offered his hand. "I suppose I am the 'ruffian.' Actually, I'm Thalen of Sutterdam, and these are my companions, Eli-anna of Melladrin and Tristo of Yosta. We are the ones the seamaster was complaining about.

"*That*"—Thalen inclined his head toward the captain, who was being helped to rise by his mate—"was very well done."

"Ah, fellow voyagers!" said Peddler, his tone switching in an instant to effusive friendliness. "Well met! Well met indeed! I go by 'Peddler,' and I'm pleased to present my young assistant. This is Gunnit of Cloverfield. We are both completely at your service."

In a lower voice he said, "Could you be the folk responsible for that fire in Femturan a short while ago, hmm? I am so *very* pleased to meet up with you."

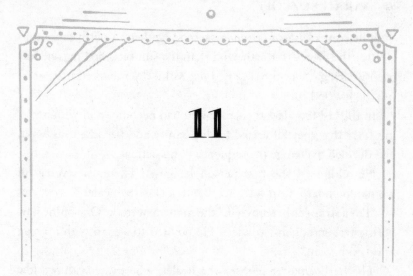

11

Pilagos, The Green Isles

As the leagues of turquoise water slipped by *Island Dreamer,* Mikil diverted himself by devising an elaborate plan for what he would do as soon as they docked in Pilagos. First, he would declare himself to the local authority—from his earlier life he recalled a very competent magistrar. Then, he would sell a portion of the valuables they had found in the queen's chest or the swords from their scavenging that night under the Pellish cliffs. This, in turn, would allow him to properly reward the captain and crew of *Island Dreamer,* purchase wardrobes for himself, Arlettie, and Gilboy, and hire the best healer on the island for Mistriss Phénix. Finally, when these tasks were completed, Mikil would inquire when the next Lorther ship was due in harbor.

If needs dictated he sail on another vessel, he would, but the prince preferred to return home from the dead on a ship of his own. If they had to wait a few weeks, Arlettie would enjoy showing him her former lodgings and looking up old friends, and Gilboy could sample the diversions of city life. They had waited years; a few more weeks meant nothing.

The crew of *Island Dreamer* pieced together an outfit more suitable for the prince of Lortherrod than the sun-bleached rags he had been wearing. Once the ship tied up, Mikil disembarked first, bearing the jeweled cutlass.

In the last few days their castaway had become so ill with a raging fever that they all feared for her sanity and her life; thus Mikil had decided to change the sequence of his actions.

He addressed the first person he saw. "There's a severely ill woman on board. Can you fetch the best close-by healer?"

"I'm a stranger here myself," the man answered. "One of the harbormasters stands just yonder." He pointed to a man with a green braid on his cap.

The harbormaster sent for the healer, who came within a few minutes, carrying her bag.

Mikil led her aboard and waited on deck while Arlettie helped her examine Phénix.

While Mikil watched the crew start to unload their trade goods, the healer rejoined him.

"What happened to cause such nasty injuries?" she asked.

"Mistriss Phénix either doesn't recall or won't tell us."

"Well," the healer sighed. "The burns on her back have gone sour; that's why she's burning up. We can try to treat the miasmas with various unguents and draughts. But the worse problem is her left lung is impaired. There's a condition called 'lung abscess,' but it is beyond my skill—or that of anyone else on this isle—to treat. So even if I could clear the burns of corruption, the infection in her chest will eventually kill her. Actually, I'm amazed she has survived this long."

Concern drawing down his brows, Mikil asked, "What can we do? What would you do if she were your responsibility?"

"If she was mine own, I would have placed her on that ship you see under full sail, nearly out of the harbor. It's from Wyeland; the

Wyes specialize in the arts of healing. If you could get her to Salu-briton, the Wyes might have the means to save her."

"When will there be another ship heading to Wyeland?"

"No one can say; that one was the first Slagos has seen in over six moons. Could be tomorrow; could be a year."

"What!? Her best chance of survival is sailing away before our eyes?"

"I'm afraid so." The healer raised her hands helplessly. "If only your boat had docked a few hours earlier . . ."

Mikil grabbed *Island Dreamer*'s first mate and Captain Bajets by their shoulders. "I must have your help in finding a boat that can chase down that Wye ship!"

The three men ran about the harbor shouting questions. Their quest led them to a catamaran and its Green Isles owner, a man willing to try his craft's swiftness against the larger ship's head start.

"Get the patient on here," he yelled, "as I ready the boat."

Mikil pointed to the jeweled cutlass tucked in his waistband. "Get her to the Wyes safely, and this is yours as reward."

Four crew members from *Island Dreamer,* each holding a corner, brought Mistriss Phénix slung in her sheets, Arlettie clasping her hand at her side as they ran, and they loaded her onto the catama-ran. There was no room for additional passengers and no time for goodbyes. Unceremoniously, the catamaran cast off, immediately cutting through the waves at high speed.

Arlettie turned to Mikil with tears in her eyes. "I worried about her all alone and friendless amongst strangers. I grabbed a dagger for her and a piece of the queen's jewelry she can change into coin and tucked them in her bedclothes. Was that all right with you, my prince?"

"Of course, my sweet. Clever and kind of you."

By now, the Wye vessel was out of sight, around the curve on the island. Mikil sighed. "We have done what we could for her. Let's find that magistrar and get ourselves settled."

Magistrar Destra, looking essentially unchanged through all these years, came running to the door when a secretary brought her the names of the petitioners in her entryway. She recognized Mikil from all the times she had met him as part of the Allied Fleet fighting the Pellish pirates.

"Prince Mikil!" The magistrar moved forward as if she wanted to pinch him to ensure he was not a phantom. "You're—alive!" Her eyes went wide, and she took a couple of steps to regain her balance. "We all assumed that everyone perished when the Magi sunk the fleet."

"Go ahead; you can touch me to make sure I'm real. Aye, we thank Lautan for our lives and Green Isles saviors for our return to civilization. I'd like to introduce my fellow survivors: an Islander, Mistriss Arlettie of Pilagos, and this young man, Master Gilboy of Liddlecup, who once served on *Shark Racer*."

Destra took Arlettie's hand and held it for a long moment. "Welcome home."

Mikil continued, "As far as we know, we three are the only ones who lived through the wrecks of *Sea Pearl* and *Shark Racer*. Do you know any differently? I've nursed a slight hope. . . ."

"Alas," said Magistrar Destra. "The Fountains of Weirandale confirmed the death of Queen Cressa. Though I am pleased to report that they flow on for your niece, who is still undiscovered.

"There are many other events of the world—in the Free States and elsewhere—to relay to a prince of a Great Power, but those can wait until you have a chance to refresh yourselves from your long ordeal. Do you recall the guesthouse where you lodged during the war? Let me put that accommodation and its staff at your disposal. Perchance you and your companions would do me the honor of dining with me tomorrow night?"

One of the guesthouse footmen retrieved their belongings from *Island Dreamer*, and the house chamberlain transmuted two of the lesser swords into ready cash. Finally, the prince was able to show his gratitude to the sailors who had saved them and been so considerate to poor Mistriss Phénix.

Once upstairs in their rooms, Mikil, Arlettie, and Gilboy bathed in big copper tubs and found Green Isles craftans hanging in the wardrobes to replace their worn or borrowed clothes. Mikil sent for a barber and felt much more comfortable after the man shaved off his beard and cut his hair into Lorther style.

Rather than requesting a formal meal, they asked the guest-house servants to set out a buffet of longed-for foods, such as meats, dairy foods, baked goods, and sweets.

Mikil had slathered a thick layer of butter on bread and topped it with a piece of ham when they heard a knock on the front door. A servant escorted the catamaran owner into the dining room.

"Please, sit with us," said Arlettie.

"Let me pour you some wine," offered Mikil. "Then you can tell us your story."

The sailor downed a cup of wine as if it were water. "Ahh! Well, the Wye ship spotted me about two hours after I set out. Islanders don't like to boast, but my sweet craft—she just flew above the waves! The Wyes pulled in all them queer-colored sails and waited. I climbed up and told them about the patient. They took her aboard readily enough. I saw them give her healing draughts right there on the deck. Their healer said something about draining an abscess from her "pleural cavity" but waiting until they got her to Salubriton for surgery." He helped himself to another glass of wine while the family exchanged relieved smiles. "I've heard tell those folk are marvels at healing."

"How was Mistriss Phénix?" Arlettie asked.

"She'd been coughing pretty awful the whole time."

Arlettie cocked an eyebrow at the sailor. "Did she have anything with her?"

He laughed. "You mean that dagger? Or that hair band of jewels? Or the bottle of black stuff? All those things you hid under the sheets, as if I would steal them?"

"What bottle?" Mikil asked, puzzled.

Gilboy chimed in, "Weeks ago she'd told me that she longed for a hair tonic, so I borrowed coin from the third mate and ran and got it for her while you were hiring the catamaran. It was the one little thing I could do for her. . . . It didn't seem important to mention."

The catamaran owner grinned at the family as he poured himself more wine. "Not to worry. She had all three things when I left her."

"Was she strong enough to speak to you?" asked Arlettie.

"Actually, when I was leaving she made a big effort. When I bid her, 'Farewell, go with Vertia's Grace,' she got up on one elbow-like and said, 'May the Waters bless you, kind sir.'"

"That's so nice," said Arlettie, her shoulders falling with relief. She picked up a piece of creamy cheese and nibbled at it.

Mikil, however, became agitated at the sailor's words. "May the Waters bless you," he repeated.

With a stab of premonition, he turned to Arlettie. "My sweet, which dagger did you give her?"

"I grabbed the first one on top. I think it was the catamount dagger. I'm sorry—did I err? Was it too valuable a gift? It was all such a mad rush. Surely, you're not mad at me?"

"Of course not; you did exactly right." Mikil tugged his Lorther braid. "I just was . . . curious."

The Waters. She deemed a hair tonic important enough to send Gilboy for it. Of all the possibilities Arlettie just happened to grab the catamount dagger and Cressa's headband. She blessed us by the Waters.

Mikil tugged his braid again and drained his wine, staring blankly at the table of food that had lost all its savor.

No. I would have recognized Cerúlia. Of course I would have recognized her. I couldn't fail to know her; she would have looked like Cressa

at her age. I couldn't have lived by her for weeks and not known her!
I couldn't have touched her and not known her! And what would the
princella be doing floating on a dolphin!

Arlettie was speaking still to the catamaran owner. "We are
so grateful to you for your daring race and overwhelmed that you
managed to get our friend to safety. Prince Mikil will get you that
jeweled cutlass now."

"No, I thank you, milady. I didn't do it for the reward. Sometimes a good deed is a reward itself."

"A few coins, then, man," urged Mikil, rousing himself from his
reverie. "Just to pay you for your time."

"Nah, thanks. I feel paid aplenty."

Mikil rose to thank the man profusely, show him to the door,
and shake both his hands. He stood a moment in the evening air of
the cobble-patterned courtyard; then he called back to Arlettie, "My
sweet, I am going to walk a bit. Stretch my legs after all those weeks
on board. I'll return very soon."

He headed back to the waterfront. After so many years on a
quiet island, he should have been overwhelmed by the passersby and
the horse carts on the busy streets, the taverns filling with evening
revelers, the odors of roasts and beer, the shouts and the whistles,
the music and the clatter. But Mikil's thoughts engulfed him so that
he walked through the tumult unheeding, drawn by he knew not
what, back to the ocean's edge.

But whom else, besides Cerúlia, would dolphins have saved? In-
deed, why would dolphins have rescued anyone except by the will of
the Spirits?

What an idiot I've been! Sitting beside her, unknowing. Sending her
off, alone and so very ill.

Tomorrow I must hire a ship to sail to Salubriton. I must find her,
see her healed, and help her regain her throne.

Mikil reached the harbor side. Unlike the breezes of their former refuge, which smelled of fresh flowers and fruit, the air here

smelled of brine and rotting fish. On his way to a view of the water, Mikil walked under fishing nets stretched out overhead on poles to dry. A gust of wind shook down a patter of drops on his head.

Suddenly, Mikil felt quite strange—as if he had been somehow changed, anointed. He felt his restless heart quiet, and he knew his purpose.

Lautan spoke to him from the surf hitting the seawall, in the voice that he had heard before under the Pellish cliffs. A voice that was unearthly and neither discernably male nor female.

Prince Mikil of Lortherrod, henceforth thou wilt serve as mine Agent in the world of men. Thou art my Sailor.

I am honored among men, Lautan the Munificent. What is Your will?

Thou must return to Lortherrod now. Our people need thee.

What of Cerúlia? That was *Cerúlia, wasn't it?*

We have passed her on to Restaurà and Healer across the Gray Ocean. We have done all that is in our Power.

But—I kilt her mother. I have a duty to save the daughter!

The roar of the waves carried something like a chuckle. *Thou didst save the daughter, fool. Well, with some assistance. Sailor, have faith. Thy duty now lies elsewhere.*

Mikil's heart and head swirled with self-blame, guilt, amazement, and hope.

He stood a few moments gazing out west, in the direction the Wye ship had sailed. The horizon was shrouded with dark clouds; actually, though he struggled against the blackness, he could see nothing at all. With a sigh, Mikil turned back to the guesthouse.

Exhausted from all the changes and emotional strain, now he trod slowly, unseeing, stumbling over the uneven cobblestones, and his thoughts turned to his long-gone sister.

Cressa, remember that dolphin I carved for her when she was small? Lautan brought it to life and used it to rescue her. I rubbed her frozen feet and fed her porridge. I fed your daughter warm porridge, and I passed her on to those who can keep her alive.

Could it be that at the last moment she recognized your dagger? Could that be why she sent a Water blessing?

Oh, Shrimpella! My sick, suffering, orphaned girl.

May all the Spirits love and keep you. May your hurts be mended and your soul made whole. Lautan, Lortherrod, and I will be waiting for you.

And we will stand beside you, against all enemies, with all our might.

PART
TWO

Reign of Regent Matwyck,
Year 14

WINTER

12

Wyndton

Percia was so excited she couldn't stop twirling. The letters from Lordling Marcot and Duchess Naven had arrived a week ago. After spending time in the other two Eastern Duchies, Marcot had chosen to return to the duke's manor house for Winterfest. The duke and duchess had invited her, her mother, and Tilim to spend a week with them and their special houseguest from Cascada. They would be sending a coach for their visitors on the morrow.

"I'm so pleased," said Stahlia. "Holidays are the hardest time; we miss Wilim and Wren keenly then. Being somewhere new will be a welcome change. How very thoughtful of the duchess."

Percia privately wondered if the invitation came at the duchess's instigation, or whether the duke and Lordling Marcot had pressured her into the invitation, but it really didn't matter because she was overjoyed to see Lordling Marcot again.

Marcot had visited their cottage once more in the fall. He had invited Percia to show him Wyndton and her dancing school, and they had had several hours alone together (if one didn't count the Cascada guards, who followed him discreetly). They had talked and talked; they could have gone on for hours. When he left that day, he had bowed to her and kissed her hand.

Percia had hardly been able to think of anything else since meeting Marcot. Thoughtful gifts had arrived from Barston—a lovely bowl for her mother, a practice sword for Tilim, and a wrap of the finest silk for her. Just as precious was the note that accompanied the gifts.

Mistress Stahlia of Wyndton,
Greetings.
 My visits with your family have been the high point of my journeys. I hope you will accept these small tokens of my esteem. In addition, I entreat you to permit me to visit with you again before too long.

Your servant,
Marcot of Cascada

When the letter had come, Stahlia had said to Percia, "We should not encourage this young man if you do not fancy him. Do you know your own heart?"

"Aye, Mother, I do."

"You'd like to get to know him better?" Stahlia had asked with a teasing smile.

"Oh, yes!"

So her mother had written back, thanking Marcot for the gifts. And she'd allowed Percia to add a line.

And Percia would see him tomorrow! She ran about in a joyous flurry, unearthing skirts from trunks, trying to get Tilim to sit for a haircut, and arranging for Lem and Rooks to tend the horses and chickens while they were away.

Stahlia took care of gifts to give their hosts. With her backstrap loom she had stayed up late into the nights, creating sashes for the duke, duchess, and all their daughters, each colorful and one of a kind.

For Lordling Marcot she wove a blue river running through a green embankment, with a fringe of green and blue.

Percia hugged her mother with gratitude. "Oh, Mama, such a special gift!"

When they arrived at the manor house, the duchess greeted them with formal politeness. But Percia didn't mind; she only had eyes for Marcot, and he only for her. When they could escape on a walk together, they didn't notice the frosty temperatures.

Their hosts planned for dancing in the manor's great room, so Percia organized everybody into lessons to refresh their knowledge of the Winterfest Reel. Tilim and the children of the now-wedded duchettes who were also visiting for the holiday went wild with delight. The house servants joined in, as did the lordling's Cascada guards and even the duke and duchess. The practice sessions sent them all into gales of laughter, especially when Marcot collided with a footman.

"Oh, I beg your pardon," Lordling Marcot said. "Let me help you up."

"My fault entirely, my lord," said the footman, whom Percia recognized as one of Nettie's cousins. He added, with a wry smile, "I should have known better than to take my eyes off a man in his cups." Although no one had been drinking any spirits, Marcot was obviously drunk on *something,* so the room rang with laughter.

The night before the feast it snowed heavily, and white blankets decorated every tree and shrub. The manor house overflowed with candles, and the fireplaces glowed; candied nuts and hot mulled cider were set out in every room. Two other families—one a wealthy sawmill owner, and the other distant relations—came for the feast, which was served at midday. The table grew so cluttered with cuts of venison and roast goose, potatoes and glazed carrots, spinach in walnut paste and stewed apples, that passing the dishes around became an exercise in finding space to set them down.

During the meal, much talk ensued about conditions in Weirandale. All the older guests wanted to ask Lordling Marcot about his father's plans to quell the flurries of unrest they had read about in the broadsheets. While most of the Weir gentry stood behind Regent Matwyck (Percia saw Duke Naven raise his eyebrows at his cousin's protestations), everyone worried whether the common folk would rise up. Percia found the political situation confusing and slightly frightening, and she was eager to spare Marcot any discomfort or embarrassment. The children inadvertently aided her, because they grew bored by political talk, started wiggling, and interrupted. Another day, they would have been disciplined and sent to the nursery, but Winterfest was a time of indulgence.

After the meal, the furniture was pushed back, the musicians invited in, and the floor belonged to the dancers. The older generation paraded through the reel with dignity. Duke Naven escorted his female relation, and Marcot accompanied Duchess Naven. Then the young adults and children took over—twirling, capering, and shouting with laughter. Every time Marcot and Percia touched hands, she felt a tingle; when his hand held her waist, she grew warm.

The dancers got so overheated they had to throw wide the room's windows for a spell. Light snow fell steadily—and with curtains drawn and windows agape, it looked as if it were snowing inside. Then servants opened the house to everyone from the hamlet surrounding the manor for dessert: throngs came to enjoy hot apple custard cake and snowballs with pumpkin-honey syrup, while Duke Naven passed out coins and toys and Duchess Naven bestowed bars of her lilac soap. The adults were servile and quiet but their children ran wild with excitement.

The hour grew late. As the servants cleared the dishes and restored the great room, the houseguests gathered in the manor library to exchange presents. When her mother passed out the sashes, the duchettes exclaimed over them and Percia beamed with pride. Marcot thought his was "magnificent," but he pretended he didn't know the best way to wear it, so Percia had to go help him tie it on, standing so close she could smell the honey on his breath and a whiff of pomade in his hair.

Marcot gave her mother a set of small porcelain bowls that matched the large one he'd sent previously and handed Tilim a small archery bow. He passed Percia a box; she held on to her gift as long as she could, watching other people open their packages, savoring the expectation. When she finally opened the box she found two bracelet cuffs of hammered gold nestled in silk, perfect accents for a dancer's arms.

Percia looked at the glittering bracelets. The library, so full of chatter a moment ago, fell awkwardly silent. Such jewelry was too costly a gift for a friend or an acquaintance. (He had given each of the duchettes a fox fur hand warmer—a nice gift, but impersonal.) By giving her golden jewelry, in the duke's house, no less, Marcot had publicly announced his intention to court her.

"Mother," Percia asked quietly, "may I accept these?"

All eyes turned to Stahlia. She kept her face neutral when she answered, "That's for you to say, my daughter."

"If the choice is mine," said Percia, carefully looking down, "then I am grateful for such a lovely gift." She slipped her hands through each cuff and held her arms out.

One of the young duchettes squealed and clapped.

"The bracelets are not half as fair as she who wears them," said Marcot.

The day guests had their coaches brought out to ferry them home, and much fuss ensued about blankets and foot warmers, and many cautions about snow-covered roads. In the bustle, Marcot grabbed Percia's hand and pulled her into a servants' stairwell and up half a dozen steps.

"Do you like your present?" he asked.

"You know I do," Percia answered, cheeks growing hot.

"Percia, may I speak to your mother about courting you?" He kept his court poise, but his eyes danced.

"Oh, is that what you've been doing?"

"Vixen!" He bent to kiss her.

In a moment she pulled back. She looked at him seriously a moment and brushed his amber top curls back from his forehead. "Scoundrel!" she chided, and kissed him back.

"Well, may I?" he asked, shaking her arms just a little.

"You'd better," Percia answered, "because by now I'm sure everybody has noticed our absence."

A quiet rap sounded on the door to the staircase and the lovers sprang apart, anxiously looking down. After a beat the door was pulled open and Tilim poked his head in. "I've been watching the door," he said, "but you'd better come out now. Mama is looking for both of you."

Percia patted her hair and tried to smooth her cheeks.

"Not to worry, Percie, you look fine—or you would if you'd stop grinning like a lackwit," said her little brother with a judicious air. "You come first, Lordling. I'll come back for you in a tick, Percie."

Mother shot her a stern glance when their paths crossed, but she wasn't actually angry. When they went up to bed, Percia twirled around the room with her skirt flaring and her golden bracelets twinkling high above her head and then threw herself on the feather mattress to make it bounce. Her mother, seated on a chair rubbing her stiff neck, smiled wistfully and did not chide.

13

Aboard Island Song

Thalen kept his distance from Peddler for two weeks, sensing that the man had some strange connection to Magic. How else could he know about their involvement in the Femturan Conflagration? He had seen in Oromondo how Magic could be used to turn wolves into demons. Thalen would not let down his guard just because this stranger had a twinkle in his eye and treated the boy who accompanied him kindly.

The boy—Gunnit. Thalen remembered every detail about Skylark and recognized the name of her younger brother. But this lad said he was from a town called Cloverfield and that his older sister (who had died) had been named Linnie. He had never heard of anyone named Skylark. Besides, he looked nothing at all like her, because his hair was a different shade of yellow, his nose wide, and his chin square. Talking the coincidence over with Tristo, Thalen concluded that Gunnit must be a common name in Alpetar.

Peddler assumed a polite and detached demeanor with the Raiders. He did not press an intimacy with Thalen, though on such a small ship—the surly seamaster had been honest in saying it wasn't designed to accommodate passengers—they ran into one another all day long. Though Thalen often sensed the older man apprising him in return, they maintained a discreet reserve.

In fair weather, the passengers spent most of the daytime hours on the stern deck. The cook allowed only Eli-anna to pass the time sitting at the tiny mess table in the galley. Eli-anna's terror at being on the water subsided somewhat, but whenever the sea turned rougher either Tristo or Thalen would seek her out. She never got sick, but her face would show strain and her hands would clench the table edge. Then they would try to distract her, Tristo by telling wild tales about his orphan life in Yosta and Thalen by reciting Rortherrod poetry.

Today the ocean swells lifted the ship in a soothing four-four time while the wind held steady. Gunnit slid down from the mast with the third mate, rejoining the group of passengers standing or seated on casks around a low makeshift table.

"Play Oblongs and Squares with me, Tristo," he cajoled.

"Sure. But what do you say—let's make the game more interesting. Whoever loses has to pay a forfeit."

"What kind of forfeit?"

"Oh, you have to make a fool of yourself, like stand on your head and sing 'Bang the Mug and Pour the Ale'!"

"I don't know that song," Gunnit said, face falling.

Peddler, leaning his elbows on the ship's handrail, smiled with his twinkle. "We'll find you an appropriate song. But by all means, let's make the game interesting. Whoever wins has to play *me* next!"

Gunnit laid out the first mate's board, and he and Tristo played. Tristo let the boy make some good moves, then finished him off without braggadocio.

Tristo forced Gunnit to stand on his head and sing "Nine Ducks Went a-Courting." The boy only managed a bar or two before falling over in a fit of giggles to the applause of everyone nearby.

When Peddler settled in against Tristo, Thalen noted that other people gathered round to watch. Tristo was a crafty player, having gambled on many a game for his only meal of the day in Yosta bars. Peddler enhanced everyone's enjoyment by offering an exaggerated running commentary: "Oh no! Don't move there—you'll kill me if you move there!" or "Got out of that trap just by a hair, didn't I?"

Yet Thalen discerned that Peddler held back, allowing Tristo the same dignity that Tristo had granted Gunnit. When Peddler won, he exclaimed magnanimously, "I really don't know how I did that! What a lucky move!" Tristo's forfeit involved singing the aforementioned "Bang the Mug," which he did, with all the nearby sailors joining in the chorus by pounding on wooden surfaces.

"The winner plays me," Thalen remarked, smoothly sliding into Tristo's place across from Peddler. "But I propose a different kind of forfeit."

"What do you have in mind?" asked Peddler. "Do you want me to climb the mast and strip to my skin?" This raised a laugh out of all the onlookers.

"No," said Thalen. "When I win I want truthful answers to a few questions."

Peddler regarded him with narrowed eyes. "*Three* questions," he agreed. "When *I* win I get truthful answers to *three* questions."

"But Commander," protested Tristo, "I've never seen you play!"

"You're right, Tristo, I've never played before, but I've watched a few games," Thalen replied, not mentioning that in his youth he had read and memorized three books on the strategy of Oblongs and Squares by grand masters. Addressing Peddler, he asked, "You won't mind if I'm slow in choosing my moves?"

"Of course not. Take all the time you need. Gunnit, my lad, would you fetch my hat and a sip of water?" When the boy returned, Peddler proclaimed, "Well, well, the game's afoot!" He moved first, and Thalen followed his lead into a maze he recognized as "The Fool's Gambit." Thalen slipped out of this gambit ("Oh, what a slippery devil you are!"), and then Peddler pressed his attack with a series of moves the masters termed "Fox and Hounds." Thalen's fox pieces eluded the hounds. *("Tsk, tsk, tsk, tsk.")* Peddler attacked with the usually deadly "Oblongs to Crush"; but Thalen blocked the attack with his Squares. ("Well now, well now, quite a clever move for a novice!")

Their game continued. Even Eli-anna came to join the crowd, resting her hand on Thalen's shoulder. Peddler's face grew lined as afternoon shadows fell on the board. His amusing comments fell away, replaced by intense concentration.

Thalen decided he had let the older man keep his pride long enough. He set his pieces into the "Broken Wing Snare," a strategy detailed in only the most recent of the books he had read. Peddler walked his Oblongs right into the trap, and Thalen won the game.

"Well now! Well now! Skillfully played, young man," said Peddler, his bells jingling as he stroked his beard. "Haven't had such a fine game in many a year."

Thalen shrugged. "Beginner's luck. A cup of watered rum on the bow to celebrate?"

"My pleasure, my pleasure. Oh! I'm so stiff!" Peddler got to his feet, stretching with dramatic exaggeration.

The opponents strolled to the bow with their drinks, studiously ignoring the scowls sent in their direction by the captain standing near the wheel. Behind them, Thalen heard excited chatter as the onlookers dissected the match.

"I know I don't get to ask the questions," said Peddler. "But if you've honestly never played before, how did you do *that*?"

Thalen had no reason to lie, so he told his opponent about his ability to memorize anything he read and the three books by expert tacticians. This put Peddler back in a good humor; he chuckled to himself. "O-ho! Then I wasn't actually playing a rank amateur, but three grand masters at once! I did quite well for a humble peddler."

At the bow, the slight breeze—no longer blocked by the forecastle—felt refreshing. All they could see was turquoise water cut with white ribbons, stretching in all directions. Below, they heard the ship's wake splashing *ka-thump, ka-thump, ka-thump.*

Thalen turned to address the older man face-to-face, holding up one finger. "Who are you *really*?"

Peddler's face grew serious. "I really am a peddler—I've been one all my life—but 'Peddler' is also the title of the Agent of Saulė, Spirit of the Glorious Sun above, patron of Alpetar. 'Peddler' is the honorific because, like the sun, one is constantly on the move, bringing joy."

Thalen sputtered a bit. "This is not my question but I just have to remark, so Agents do exist?"

Peddler nodded. "You've heard of us before, I take it. We are pledged to keep our positions secret, but over the centuries, with so many people filling these roles, I'd imagine some rumors have leaked out."

"I don't think Agents are general knowledge," Thalen reassured the older man. "I had a friend at Scoláiríum who studied magic. Actually, at the time, I didn't really believe her."

"Hard even for me to believe, most days. I can't tell you anything more, and of course I trust that you will keep this confidence?" Peddler took a long swallow of his rum.

Thalen nodded his agreement. He held up a second finger. "Why are you on this ship?"

"I am going to Slagos to confer with a confederate of mine about business of the Spirits."

Thalen asked, "What business?"

Peddler shook his head. "I can't tell you that. I've already told you more than any unanointed person should know. Choose another question."

Holding up a third finger, Thalen was going to ask about how to lift the Occupation of the Free States, but this was his only chance to talk to an Agent, someone who knew secrets he would never know. Despite himself, Thalen broke out, "When she fell into the moat, where did she go? I couldn't find her body!"

Peddler did not insult him by pretending he didn't understand who "she" was. "I don't know," he answered, in a mournful tone. "Really, I don't know."

"What is your relationship with Skylark?" Thalen pressed, though he knew this was one question too many.

"That is the fourth, but since my last answer was so unsatisfactory I will tell you this much: I've never met her, but I tried to help her."

"Why could she talk to animals? Was she an Agent or Saulė's priestess?"

Peddler just shook his head. Thalen drew in his breath and tried to compose himself. Together they drank their rum in silence. *Ka-thump, ka-thump, ka-thump* went the waves against the hull.

"Saulė is starting to set in the clouds in the stern. Come listen to me say my evening prayers," offered Peddler. "Saulė will help you bear your grief. Sunshine helps us push up the beam."

They started to walk down the ship, the peddler with his hand on Thalen's shoulder.

"By the by, young man, the book you got that final strategy from—who wrote it?"

"Catreena of Weirandale, mother of Queen Cressa. Her sobriquet was 'Catreena the Strategist.'"

"Sometimes," Peddler said, with a smile like winter sunshine, "I think the Spirits have a sense of humor."

Thalen, who again was visited by a vision of Skylark falling into the moat, didn't respond.

14

Pilagos

Mikil discovered that a Lorther vessel, *Moon Racer,* was expected to dock in Pilagos in ten days, which was just enough time for the island tailors to finish his family's wardrobes.

While they waited for the clothes and the ship, Arlettie took Mikil to meet cousins and former friends from her life before Queen Cressa hired her. Although he was only mildly interested in meeting these chatty commoners who exclaimed over him and looked at him under lowered lids as if he were an oddity, he had vowed to please Arlettie, so Mikil compelled himself to behave graciously. Seeing her this happy amongst her own people, in her native land, he began to worry about dragging her off to Lortherrod, where again she would be a castaway.

Gilboy, a restless youth on the verge of adulthood, caused Mikil more acute anxiety. Every night after dark he set off exploring this big, new city on his own, and every time he left his parents feared that, being so unworldly, he would be set upon by robbers, cozened by tricksters, captured by a press-gang, served bad liquor, or seduced by whores. Invariably, Mikil would retire for the night uneasily, with one ear cocked for Gilboy's return—and he would not find sleep until he heard the guesthouse door quietly open and then click closed.

Tonight Mikil attended another dinner hosted by Magistrar Destra. Arlettie had begged off, shy to meet grand people, but the prince saw no one particularly impressive in the room. Destra presented a man named Shetdrake—apparently a banker from the slightly smaller isle, Slagos, and a young woman he claimed was his daughter. Mikil doubted very much that the lithe, black-haired woman actually shared his bloodlines, but if Shetdrake was stepping out on his wife, that was not Mikil's business. The woman was quite comely, but she kept twitching her pert, upturned nose. Mikil wondered if she was *smelling* everyone she met and found the surmise unappealing.

Other guests standing in the reception hall included the mayor of a nearby island, some seamasters, a rotund spice merchant named "Olet," and two men who hailed from the Free States, one of whom sat in a wheeled chair. Mikil realized that Destra had assembled for him people who had their fingers on the pulse of the latest tidings.

After all the introductions had been made and pleasantries exchanged, Magistrar Destra ushered them into a dining hall. The low table glittered with goblets, porcelain, and candles and was strewn with vines twisted in elaborate patterns, and Mikil remembered that by Green Isles custom one reclined on pillows rather than sit in straight chairs. Mikil tried to tactfully look away as the man without the use of his legs was helped down to the floor by his friends.

After the fish soup had been cleared, Olet addressed the table. "Islanders don't like to boast, but nothing happens harborside that we don't all hear about. Won't you tell us, Prince Mikil, the story about the shipwrecked woman you rescued?"

Reluctant to talk about Mistriss Phénix in public, Mikil told them only the bare bones of the tale, hoping he merely repeated what people had undoubtedly already learned from the crew of *Island Dreamer*.

Just as all the guests were speculating as to who Phénix could be and how she came to be riding on the back of a dolphin, the next course—giant clams stuffed with lobster meat—was served. The other guests exclaimed over the offering, but Mikil sourly thought that he had eaten enough shellfish to last a lifetime. He wished that the magistrar had served another dish. He washed the food down with more wine.

One of the Free States visitors helped him shift the conversation by bringing up a new topic. "What have you heard about the fire in Oromondo?" the man named Quinith inquired of the seamasters in the room.

"A Zellish ship that passed the coastline says she saw the whole city of Femturan ablaze. Her crew seems certain that the fire burned along the coast and not in the mountains, and that it couldn't have been volcanic eruption," answered a Green Isles captain.

"A fire." Magistrar Destra shuddered. "Those of us with responsibilities for cities, you know, worry about fires as much as outbreaks of plagues."

"A disastrous fire in Femturan," commented the man with crippled legs, "might be very good news for the Free States. It might help us free ourselves from the Oro Occupation."

"Indeed," Magistrar Destra agreed thoughtfully. "I wonder if this could spell the end of Oro expansionism." She turned to the servers, ordering, "Please serve the sweet now."

The party lasted late, and Mikil had difficulty disentangling himself without being abrupt or rude. He strode back the short distance to the guesthouse with weary steps; he had discovered he had less of a head for spirits than in his previous life. When he got home he crawled into bed beside Arlettie, who slept on peacefully.

He had only been sleeping a short while when a commotion coming from the nearby sitting room woke Mikil. He sprang out of bed to investigate.

As he ran, he smelled smoke and his eyes started to smart. In the room, curtains and a couch blazed with flames. Small tables and decorations lay scattered about the floor, hurled there by Gilboy, who—dressed only in his own nightshirt—had preceded him in rushing to combat the fire.

Mikil grabbed a pair of cushions and began swatting at the couch.

"Should we rouse the house?" Gilboy asked, coughing. "Get the servants?"

"We've nearly got it," Mikil answered, coming over to help him with a smoldering chair. They smothered the larger flames until finally only some scattered embers still burned. Gilboy raced to the kitchen and brought back a bucket of water, which he poured out everyplace Mikil spotted a winking light.

Gilboy inspected the room, looking for any cinder they could possibly have missed. "We got it."

"Let's open the windows now to get some air," said Mikil, and he waved the fresher air inside with the hem of his nightshirt. Gilboy copied him on the other side of the room.

"What happened?" Mikil asked. "How did this start?"

"I was about to ask you the same thing," said Gilboy. "I was asleep, but I smelled smoke and came down to find this just about to flame over. Why did you light a fire in here? Why didn't you screen it?"

"Light a fire in here?" repeated Mikil, confused. "We didn't—I'm certain. I dined late with the magistrar and didn't use the sitting room tonight. I went straight to bed."

"Could a servant have lit it to warm the house when you returned?" offered Gilboy, pushing the windows wider to air out the smoky room. "Though it is a particularly warm night."

"Or perchance Arlettie used the room?" Mikil coughed some more. "Could be, but who would have been so careless as to leave a fire ungrated? Besides, I think I would have noticed it as I passed through." He paused by the open window to get a lungful of fresh air. "What luck, Gilboy, that you woke up in time. We could all have burned up in our beds." Mikil gave a shiver of distaste. "I don't like fire."

"Scary," Gilboy agreed, batting the lingering smoky air toward the open windows with a charred pillow.

"Your Lorther Anticipation, Gilboy—that sense of where danger lurks, those seconds of forewarning that led you to hide in the dinghy—is still strong."

Gilboy grinned at the compliment. In his freckled face Mikil saw the vestiges of a little cook's lad from years ago.

But the grown young man snorted, "Then you shouldn't get in a dither when I go roaming around the city!" Gilboy took one more scan of the ruined room. "Are you all right? I'm off to bed again, now. We'll sort this out tomorrow."

"Goodnight, Son."

In the morning, Mikil questioned Arlettie and the servants. The last time anyone had lit a fire in the sitting room—with due care—was days ago. No one could figure out how the late-night blaze had started, and all exclaimed how lucky they were that Gilboy had noticed it.

While Magistrar Destra tried to pull him into Great Power politics, Arlettie roped him into circles of her family and friends, and Gilboy stirred the disquiet of a father, much of Mikil's mind pursued a wholly different track. Whenever he could get free he walked by the seashore to speak with Lautan. He didn't tell the Spirit about his petty human entanglements in Pilagos; mostly they discussed what his duties would be in Lortherrod.

Sailor, instructed his Master. *As soon as thou reachest the land of the Lorthers, my favored realm, thou must visit each of my Dwellings. The tallow has been used up; the wine has been pilfered. My waves crash still into the open naves, but few of the faithful celebrate their force and magnificence. I saved thee; by coming back when all believe thou hast perished thou wilt be a symbol of my Might and my Munificence.*

So it shall be, Mikil said, bowing. *I was not particularly reverent in my life beforetimes. I have much to make up for—so many years of negligence.*

Mikil's encounter with *Moon Racer* exemplified the impression that the Spirit of the Sea expected its new Agent to make on its people.

Garbed in gray silk, with a short purple cape blowing behind him in the wind and his hair restored to Lorther style—that is, cropped everywhere except for the short, neat tail at the nape of his neck—Prince Mikil stood astride the dock when the Lorther ship pulled in. The officers and most of the sailors of *Moon Racer* had served under Mikil in the fight against the Pellish pirates, but had been spared on that fateful day because their vessels had been too slow to keep up.

This unexpected vision of their long-lost admiral suddenly materializing in Pilagos overwhelmed the crew. They gaped and pointed; they thought they were seeing a ghost. One seaman even fainted.

"Well, lads," Mikil shouted at the trembling sailors and officers gathered at the starboard bulwark. "Sorry I've been gone so many years.

"Did you get into any trouble without me, you lazy lubbers? We're going to have to work on your seamanship—you were slow as a waddling duck the day of the Magi attack! Were you at the back of the pack or second to last?"

"Prince Mikil!" shouted the seamaster, finding his voice. "Seas Below! What an unlooked-for miracle!"

"As you gather, I'm not dead after all," said Mikil. "Lautan the Munificent decided I have more chores to do on land before I am worthy of entry to the Kingdom under the Seas."

"We are indebted to Lautan!" exclaimed the captain.

"Well, lubbers," drawled Mikil, "are you planning to lower the gangplank this morning or just stand there gawking and wait for Midsummer's Fest?"

The men rushed to lower the plank. Mikil strode aboard. When he told the story of Lautan's rescue, the sailors' mouths gaped in astonishment. He led them to the bow and poured a libation to the Spirit, giving thanks for his deliverance and mourning his lost crewmates. He was pleased to see how many sailors knelt and reverently chanted the proper responses.

"Seamaster, I am assuming command. Provision the ship well but with dispatch.

"We sail on the morning tide for Liddlecup and Tidewater Keep. I have been absent from my homeland too long."

15

Slagos

Having never traveled anywhere except the one trip on the High Road of Alpetar after the raid on his village, Sweetmeadow, Gunnit found sailing on *Island Song* a fabulous adventure. He loved the experience of the wide ocean and was fascinated by the ship, its oars, and its riggings. After many moons living almost exclusively with women, he especially enjoyed the company of so many men. The sailors treated him as a pet and showed him all the workings of the sails and lashings. The youngest Free Stater, Tristo, especially, let Gunnit follow him around like a little brother and taught him songs and card tricks.

As the ship neared Slagos, Gunnit glumly realized that he would be parting from Tristo. Indeed, as soon as the ship tied up at the dock, Commander Thalen, Eli-anna, and Tristo bid the Alpies farewell, explaining again that they intended to sail immediately to another island to join Commander Thalen's brother. The two sets of passengers embraced warmly as they made their farewells.

Gunnit didn't have a chance to absorb or grieve over this parting, because in a trice Peddler hustled him to shore. "We have an urgent meeting to attend," said Peddler. "Afterward, I'll buy you a fine dinner at a tavern. We owe ourselves good grub after the wretched shipboard fare."

Peddler took no notice of the stares that the island people directed at his yellowish hair and his bells. He stopped a few strollers to ask directions, then headed for a wide street that led uphill from the harbor.

Trailing after the old man, the boy was surprised by how hard he had to struggle to walk on solid land. He barely had time to gape at his new surroundings: all the people (some with green in their hair), the many stone buildings, the cobblestones covering the street, or the unfamiliar-looking trees. After many weeks captive on the ship, Peddler strode in such a terrible hurry that Gunnit fairly had to run to keep up with him.

Presently, they arrived at a courtyard on the top of a hill. In the center stood something Gunnit had never seen before: an extraordinary large statue of marble, half woman, half man, and covered all over with plants.

An elderly man in a green robe and a battered straw hat had walked toward them. He bowed low to Peddler. Peddler quickly assisted him to rise and clasped forearms with him.

"The honor is mine, Gardener," he said. "I am overjoyed to meet you in the flesh. And I'd like you to meet my, my—"

"Apprentice?" supplied the old man.

"Exactly so. My *apprentice,* Gunnit of Cloverfield. Someday, he will fill my role. Gunnit, lad, Gardener doesn't see the way other people see. Will you come close and let him touch your face?"

Gunnit complied. The old man's milky gray eyes appeared to be sightless. "But I'm not sure I want to be a peddler," he said, belatedly reacting to the term "apprentice" as the soft hand skimmed the surface of his face, learning his features.

The two old men just laughed at him.

Squawk, said a multicolored bird. "I want to be a peddler," it repeated, in Gunnit's exact voice. The boy jumped in surprise.

"Gunnit, would you mind letting me touch Saulé's Bracelet?" Gardener asked.

"How did you know I am wearing it?" Gunnit wondered.

"I told you, lad," said Peddler, "that Gardener sees things his own way. Go on, roll up your sleeve."

Gunnit did as he was bid. Gardener touched the gold Bracelet with reverence. Then he turned back to Peddler. "How fortunate you are, to have a Chosen Apprentice! I do not know who will care for Vertia's Garden when I'm gone."

"Yes," said Peddler, tousling Gunnit's hair. "I recognize my blessing. I don't have to tell *you* that being an Agent can be a lonely life."

"Gunnit, would you like to tour my garden?" Gardener led Gunnit through a stone portico and down a set of stone steps. "I'm certain that my garden would like to see you."

The garden looked like nothing Gunnit had ever seen or imagined. In Alpetar everyone enjoyed meadows of wildflowers, but no one deliberately grew one flower next to another in such patterns. Gunnit was in awe of the garden's luxurious textures, colors, and scents—the tropical flowers, shrubs, and trees arranged in bright masses, with each bed uniquely designed.

After his tour, Gardener brought Peddler and Gunnit to sit on the stone steps. He served them a tisane that tasted like peppermint, along with slices of an exotic fruit, green and filled with tiny red seeds, which Gunnit found delicious. He worried he was making a pig of himself, but neither Peddler nor Gardener chastised him when he reached for more pieces.

"Shall we begin, my friend?" Peddler asked Gardener.

"Let us tarry a few moments longer. I am expecting another."

"Another? Another *Agent*? Really? Who can it be?"

Gardener smiled, as if enjoying his secret.

Peddler frowned, "It can't be Water Bearer. She doesn't have the money to travel."

"Ah," Gardener exclaimed. "This is a newcomer. The Ninth is

stirring." He grinned mischievously. "Coming out of Its sulk, or so it would seem."

Squawk! "The Ninth is stirring. The Ninth is stirring." Gunnit peered around, trying to figure out which bird had imitated Gardener.

"No!" Peddler slapped his knee. "After all these centuries? I never dreamt this would happen!"

"What is 'the Ninth'?" asked Gunnit. Peddler was generally close-mouthed about exactly the things Gunnit felt he should know, but Gardener's manner encouraged questions.

"The Ninth *Spirit,* my lad. Mìngyùn, the Spirit of Fate."

"Has the Spirit been sulking? *Why?*"

"In the beginning of time, each Spirit chose a land to adopt as its own. Saulė—"

"Chose Alpetar," Gunnit cut in.

"Exactly so," replied Gardener. "And Vertia"—here he waved at the marble statue—"decided to bless the Green Isles. Mìngyùn selected a small country then called Iga, but centuries ago Mìngyùn grew wrathful at the folly of the king and the equal brutality of Iga's people. We call this Spirit 'Fate,' but that term doesn't really convey . . ." Gardener trailed off, as if at a loss for words.

"Let me see if I can explain," Peddler jumped in. "When we say that Saulė is the Spirit of the Sun, we mean the sun in the sky, but we also mean something within each of us." Peddler pointed to his own chest. "Something like the yearning for happiness. The desire to be happy."

Gardener nodded agreement. "Like Vertia is the Spirit of growing plants"—he gestured toward the lush garden—"but also, for people, the desire to grow. To grow strong. To reproduce. To have children."

Gunnit had knit his brow and stuck his tongue a little way out in his effort to understand. "So is Mìngyùn the desire to be lucky?"

"No. 'Fate' is not tied to luck," said Gardener. "Haven't you heard the saying 'He deserved his fate'? It is linked to our hunger for righteousness. Just as everyone wants to be happy or grow, everyone wants to see justice prevail. We have an instinct for it, a craving.

"So when the citizens of Iga behaved so very badly during a war we call the Bloody Rebellion, Mìngyùn decided to withdraw. Decided not to favor Its land. For centuries Mìngyùn has chosen no Agent and has not become involved in human affairs. In my terms, the Spirit went into hibernation."

"Now, is the Spirit coming here?" asked Gunnit, shifting his eyes around, terrified of being judged and found wanting.

"Oh, no! Spirits don't *come anywhere;* they don't appear. They don't have bodies. They are neither men nor women." He looked in Peddler's direction with raised eyebrows. "Don't you teach him what he needs to know?"

"But," Gunnit interrupted, "there's a statue of a man-woman right over there. Maybe you can't see it, but you must know that it is right there in the front courtyard."

"Leave this topic," Peddler said to Gardener. "We can explain 'incorporeality' and 'ambisexuality' to him another time. *Who* is coming here?"

Gardener smiled. "Mìngyùn is sending an Agent. Or rather, the person who is about to become Fate's first Agent in many centuries. I can see her climbing up the hill this very minute."

Gunnit waved his hands in front of Gardener's eyes, and the man didn't blink. "But if you can't see, how can you see her?"

"I'm not certain—'tis one of the gifts that my Spirit, Vertia, gave to me, like the gifts Saulė gives to you and Peddler."

"Saulė doesn't let me see things that are far away," said Gunnit.

"No," said Peddler, "but Saulė does tell you who to trust, right?"

"Does that come from Saulė and not from my own head?" asked Gunnit.

"Hard to tell the difference, eh?" answered Peddler. "Saulė's light helps us see people clearly."

"People like Finch or the Pellish kidnappers?"

"Exactly so, and our Free States friends on *Island Dreamer,*" answered Peddler. "And Saulė's strength gives us courage. Didn't you notice that you were not afraid to leave Cloverfield and come with me? That wouldn't be true of a boy who hadn't been kissed by the Sun."

Gunnit pondered these statements. Gardener pushed the plate of fruit in his direction, so he grabbed two more pieces, nodding his thanks. One of the talking birds fluttered on the step near him; Gunnit broke off a bite of fruit and tossed it at the bird, but the parrot disdained his gift. They all sat silent with their thoughts, enjoying the peaceful beauty of the Garden. The parrot repeated "kissed by the Sun" in Peddler's voice several times, but nobody paid any attention.

In a few moments a woman in her middle years walked into the Courtyard of Vertia. She was dressed all in white, with a long side plait of hair.

"Gardener, are you about?" she called.

"Here I am, Magistrar Destra," answered Gardener, stiffly getting to his feet. "And I have other special visitors this day, from Alpetar." Gardener introduced his guests.

"All the way from Alpetar! What brings you to Slagos this day?"

"Something similar to what brings you here, Magistrar," replied Peddler. "Like you, we were *summoned.*"

"That's right." The lady's eyes went wide with surprise. "That's exactly how it felt. Seven days ago—it was the queerest sensation—I suddenly knew that I must board the *Island Hopper,* come to Slagos, and confer with Gardener. Gardener, did Vertia summon us?"

"In your case, Magistrar, I believe it was Another."

"Really? What *can* you mean?"

"I think you might find out if you took off Vertia's bracelet and walked through my garden. I assure you Vertia will not judge you disloyal."

"You think the answers to all mysteries lie in your garden," she smiled. "Nevertheless, I will hazard a stroll." She unwound the vine around her wrist, handed it to Gardener, and closed his fingers around the symbol of her fealty to Vertia.

"Dame, come see this flowering tree," said Gunnit, eager to share his favorite discovery. "'Tis the most beautiful thing I've ever seen!"

As she walked under an arbor, however, a slight sprinkle of raindrops left over from the showers the night before blew down on her head. Magistrar Destra stood stock-still, and Gunnit saw her body glow for a moment.

"*Oh!*" she cried.

"Are you hurt?" Gunnit asked. "Is she all right?" he called to the old men when she didn't answer.

"Just be patient, Gunnit," called Peddler.

Magistrar Destra returned to Gunnit as if she saw him clearly for the first time. "I'd like to enjoy that tree you fancy, young servant of Saulė, and then I must consult with the other Agents."

Gunnit showed her the tree, covered in blossoms of pink, orange, and scarlet. He plucked a small sprig for her, and she entwined it in her braid. Then they returned to the steps.

"Hail to thee, Gardener and Peddler. I find I—I—have the honor of carrying a new name. I am now Mìngyùn's 'Spinner.'"

Peddler bowed. "Hail to thee, Spinner. We are overjoyed to have you among us."

"Aye," chimed in Gardener, "though it is a sign of changed and desperate times."

Spinner sat on the top step in between the men, while Gunnit perched himself several steps below. He couldn't follow much of what was discussed, but he gleaned several important facts. This was the first time Agents had ever met outside "Moot Table," and they might get in trouble for doing so. But all three were concerned about the well-being of a particular woman. They had gathered together here in Slagos because someone else (or maybe several people?) had behaved "abominably," a word Gunnit didn't understand. Mìngyùn—the Ninth—was so disturbed that the Spirit had decided to intervene.

"We"—Spinner indicated Gardener, Peddler, and herself—"feel personally involved in her survival."

"Very much so," said Gardener. "I love her like a daughter."

"I am in her debt. She saved my charges at risk to herself," said Peddler. "Including that special one." He pointed to Gunnit.

"And I was close friends with her mother and father," said Spinner. "Her parents did the Green Isles a great service, and for Cressa's and Ambrice's sakes, if for no other reason, I would do my utmost to save their heir."

Spinner continued, "But we must set our personal feelings against this edict: Mìngyùn believes that discord amongst the Spirits over one human life constitutes the height of folly. Apparently, Pozhar and Nargis have already been trading blows, and the Others are prepared to follow."

"We saw as much at the last conclave at Moot Table," said Gardener. "Peddler had to break off the dream. Smithy almost killed Sailor—for all we know the man has died by now—and open warfare commenced."

"'Chamen has produced small earthquakes in Oromondo," said Spinner, "Lautan has sent tidal waves against Alpetar's coast, and Ghibli has whipped up tornadoes in various places. Not devastation yet—just small provocations, as if the Spirits test how far they dare to go."

Gardener covered his face in his hands, making soft noises of distress.

"Dangerous folly!" said Peddler; then he too listened to an unseen voice. "Saulė agrees: *this must cease.*"

Squawk! "This must cease," intoned a parrot.

"But does that mean we must sit still and do nothing while Pozhar destroys her?" asked Gardener. "I just can't accept that!"

"Wait! Wait one moment. *Who* are you talking about?" Gunnit interrupted, with a sudden stab of fear.

"Dame Saggeta spoke to me about a woman named 'Finch,'" said Peddler, addressing the boy, "though she wears other names too. Her truest name is 'Cerúlia,' and she is heir to the throne of Weirandale."

"Air to a throne?" Gunnit shook his head, bewildered. "What does that mean? But I don't care what her name is or what country she's from! Sit on my hands while someone kills Finch?" Gunnit protested. "Not never. Tell me who would hurt her, and I'll protect her!"

The Agents smiled at each other and at him. Gunnit was offended.

"You think I'm just a goatherd. But isn't that why I'm here—to help Finch? Isn't that why Peddler brung me this far from my ma and the tykes? He said someone's life was in danger, and he thought that maybe I could help."

"In truth, I don't know why I brought you," said Peddler, a cloud passing over his face as he worried his beard bells. "I saw you in Saulė's Mirror and, well, it struck me as a good idea at the time. I've been glad of your company, lad, but I don't have an answer as to why you are here."

"What is this Mirror?" asked Gunnit. "You promised to tell me before, but you never did."

Reluctantly, Peddler pulled out a pouch attached to his belt. Inside was a looking glass. It was about as big as Gunnit's hand, rimmed with gold. The back bore the image of a golden sun; the front looked like a normal mirror. When Peddler showed it to them it just flashed the colors of the garden and the blue of the sky.

"I know it looks normal now," said Peddler. "But every morning and night, if I catch the first or last rays of sunlight in the Mirror, it changes. And then I see whatever image Saulė wishes to show me."

Pointing to the silver face he continued, "Gunnit, I saw the Oro raid on Sweetmeadow. I saw Finch with you when you fought with

Pellish drovers. Some weeks ago I saw myself and Commander Thalen drinking rum on *Island Song*. And I have seen you, boy, sitting right on this step here in Gardener's Courtyard."

"Aha! Then via the Mirror, Saulė also provides its Agent a kind of Magic sight," commented Gardener. "I wonder, Spinner, if eventually you too will discover a new way of seeing."

The lady looked discomforted by the idea. "Gracious. There's an immensity I don't understand."

Peddler commented, "To get back to Gunnit's offer, this discord between the Spirits is too big a problem for a young boy. I vowed to protect him against all dangers. I can't send him into earthquakes or tidal waves!"

"Wait a minute," said Spinner. "Mìngyùn forbids Spirits from destroying the natural order over one woman's life. But Mìngyùn says nothing about us *as humans* doing what we can to help her, as we would help any person we cared for."

"But I can do naught as a normal human, except some weeding and digging in the dirt," said Gardener plaintively. "I am *rooted* here. I live in that lean-to behind the magnolias. Were I to leave this Garden I would wither and die."

Peddler sighed. "I can travel, but yesterday morning Saulė warned me to return to Tar's Basin as fast as I can find passage. The Mirror showed me that Oros have marched into Alpetar. My highest duty is to the people of my home."

"I still feel more human than Agent, and I have some skills in negotiation," said Spinner. "I could—" She broke off, listening to inaudible orders. "Ah. No. Mìngyùn instructs me that I must return to the Alliance of Free States. Iga is torn by war, and I am much needed there."

Silence fell. Peddler swore "Darkness abounds!" a few times—a curse that Gunnit's father would have whipped him for uttering. Gardener distractedly picked at his already-broken straw hat. Spinner stared at the sprig of flowers Gunnit had given her.

"All right then—none of you can travel and stand beside her. What about me?" said Gunnit. "Can't I help Finch? I'm awful fond of her. And I have fought by her side once before, you know."

"Bravery," said Gardener, almost mournfully. "Didn't I tell you?"

Spinner commented, "It almost seems, Gunnit, as if you are offering to be *our* Agent, to act in our stead to protect the Nargis Queen."

"That's it!" said Gunnit. "I want to be the Agents' Agent, if this means I can help Finch."

The three adults exchanged glances.

"Right now she lies in Healer's care," said Spinner slowly. "I think we can trust Healer to do her best for Cerúlia—though no place is completely safe."

Gardener put his head in his hands and rocked back and forth.

"Maybe you would all think of a better plan over food," Gunnit hinted.

"You're hungry," said Peddler. "I'm hungry too, and a break might refresh our minds. I promised Gunnit a tavern meal." He stood up and offered Spinner his hand. "Won't you join us? It is so special to spend time with fellow Agents in the flesh."

"I cannot leave the Courtyard of Vertia," Gardener reminded them. "But I suggest you sample the fare at the Blue Parrot. Tell Zillie, the innkeep, I sent you, and you will be treated to her specialties."

"How will you eat?" Gunnit asked, concerned about his new friend.

"Vertia provides everything I need," the elderly man said, gesturing around the Garden. "Take your time; I often take a short nap after midday. The bees get drowsy too. And even those chattering parrots put their heads under their wings."

As they left the Courtyard with a promise to return soon, Gunnit was struck by a fresh worry. "I've never eaten in a tavern before. Will people see I'm just a goatherd? Will they laugh at me? Are there customs I don't know?"

"Gunnit, Green Islanders are friendly, and they are accustomed to all sorts of travelers," said Spinner. "Besides, you'll be with me, and I have some influence here."

Gunnit sat between Spinner and Peddler at a wooden table. A cheerful woman recognized the magistrar and piled before them savory dishes that delighted the boy, especially the fried crabs and the vanilla and chocolate sweetcakes. Peddler and he concentrated on eating, and no one took note of the way they used their table-ware.

Spinner, who dined more sparingly, wiped her mouth with a napkin. "Now that I've been favored with Mìngyùn's touch, I have a terrible fear that a few nights ago I met another Agent. Tell me about your fellows."

Peddler spoke of someone named "Sailor" who, the last time he'd seen him, had a cracked skull; of a stout, middle-aged woman named "Water Bearer"; of a young woman called "Hunter"—

"Hunter!" said Spinner. "What does she look like?"

"Thin and strong, with black hair and kind of an upturned nose," said Peddler.

"Aye," she sighed. "She sat at my dinner table a week ago!"

"Why?" asked Peddler. "You weren't even involved then."

Spinner squinted her eyes closed, thinking hard. "'Hunter,' you said? Ah! She hunts Cerúlia."

"What can we do?" Gunnit dropped his knife with a clatter, his mouth full of chocolate cream.

"Let's look in the Mirror at sunset," suggested Peddler. "The Mirror led me here; it may provide guidance."

After eating their fill, paying their tab, and washing up, the three climbed back up to Vertia's Courtyard. Gunnit stole two sweetcakes to bring to Gardener. Two friendly dogs followed them from the tavern, inviting Gunnit to play with them.

In the early evening the sun began sinking. Fortunately, all the clouds had decided to cluster to the south, so the western sky, holding the setting sun, stayed clear. The Agents and apprentice gathered with trepidation around the small hand mirror.

Just as the sun started to dip, the image in the mirror transmuted; instead of seeing their own reflections as they stood in the Courtyard, Gunnit saw a tiny version of himself standing next to an enormous, elaborate fountain. Gunnit gasped.

"What? What to do you see? Tell me," Gardener prodded anxiously.

Spinner replied, "The Mirror showed us Gunnit in the Courtyard of the Star in Weirandale."

"*Really?* When? Did he look older? What season clothing did he wear?" asked the blind man.

"Gunnit looked about like now; I couldn't tell the season," Peddler answered.

More discussion ensued, now that the grown-ups were finally convinced that Gunnit had an important role to play. Finally, the three Agents decided he should stay in Slagos with Gardener for some moons; Gardener would know—"in the ripeness of time"—when was the right moment for Gunnit to travel to a city called Cascada. As an important official, Magistrar Destra could arrange for one of the Green Isles ships that traded with a country called Weirandale to take him on as a cabin boy and transport him there.

"Are you brave enough to part from me, Gunnit, and throw yourself into the unknown?" asked Peddler. In a lower voice, he added, "You know, Dame Saggeta will skin me if she finds out about this. Skin me alive. I very much doubt that even the Spirits could save me from her wrath."

"I think so," said the boy. "But when I get there, what am I to do? How will I find Finch? How will I, just a goatherd, help her?" A wave of uncertainty passed over him, and he thought with a pang of his mother waiting for him to come home.

Peddler worried his own beard. "We have to trust that Saulè—consulting the other Spirits—will guide you."

"Vertia," Gardener intoned, "let us grow in wisdom and bravery."

"Aye," said Spinner, "as Fate disposes."

Gunnit, who missed his dog, Kiki, stroked the big terrier that had fallen asleep on the ground next to him, but said nothing. He felt quite worn out, slightly daunted, but very determined.

The sun had sunk below the western horizon, though the sky remained bright.

PART
THREE

Reign of Regent Matwyck,
Year 14

SPRING

16

Cascada

Matwyck experienced a certain sentimental regret when Tirinella passed away: food lost some of its piquancy, and he found himself musing over the shortness of life and the preciousness of each moment. Occasionally he paused over memories of their years together. He attended all the tragedies at the Aqueduct or Peacock to sound the depths of his sorrow.

His grief did not last long, however, which was fortunate, because in the past weeks the realm had been beset by troubles. Mysterious fires repeatedly broke out in scattered places around Weirandale. The Lord Regent received reports of an inferno in the heart of Barston that destroyed whole sections of the city, a large blaze in Prairyvale that scorched league upon league of grazing land, and even a fire inside the Abbey of the Waters on Nargis Mountain. Was it lightning? Carelessness? Arson? No sooner had the populace and his soldiers succeeded in extinguishing one blaze than another would begin to flare up far away.

Curiously, rains materialized each time before the destruction grew to catastrophic proportions. But the unexplained fires and the out-of-season rains unsettled his already-restive citizens, forcing him to make trips out of the capital to survey the damage, comfort the afflicted, and spend his dwindling treasure on relief.

On his return trip from such a tiring visit in Vittorine, listening to the depressing rain patter on his coach while it lurched its way down the muddy Royal Highway, sitting alone and bored, Matwyck came to a decision—he would marry again. His pride recoiled at the thought of mistresses, bed warmers, and the like; besides, he wanted a life partner.

Tirinella's status was as high as I could reach as a young man. Now, however, I am in a completely different position. I will have my pick of the most highborn women in Weirandale, and I will choose more wisely a second time.

This woman must be ambitious, with none of that tedious scrupulousness that had forced him to hide his projects from Tirinella. A true helpmate who could accompany him and assist him in his work. Beautiful, of course. Every strand on her head must gleam amber; no half-brown wife could be suitable for the Lord Regent. Fertile too, because Matwyck realized that he would like to have more children. However, because he was loyal to a fault, he would insist that his second wife respect Marcot's claims as firstborn.

But who was worthy of being his bride? Not a foreign claimant. No, he found foreigners repellent. A duchess or duchette, then. Duchess Pattengale had been widowed these many years, but she was much too ancient either for his lust or for children. No one else immediately came to mind. He would have to review the contenders: the realm's most eligible women must be put on display without realizing he was choosing amongst them.

A party? I'll host a celebration of Marcot's homecoming. That's the perfect occasion. Marcot's ship is due back from the Eastern Duchies; two weeks should give my chamberlain time to prepare a banquet and all the women time to choose their gowns.

A gust of wind drove rain against the side of the carriage. Matwyck leaned against the upholstery, pulling his fur blanket closer, pleased with his own clever decisiveness.

Now he could look forward both to seeing his son and to this party. Marcot had dallied long in the Eastern Duchies, which perplexed his father, as those backwater provinces held so little of interest. Actually, Matwyck had expected the boy home moons ago, especially after he'd sent the tidings of Tirinella's death.

A truly dutiful son would have rushed home to his father's side to assuage his grief and help carry his burdens.

When Matwyck met the *Sea Wave,* the young man who disembarked looked more mature than when he'd left Cascada nearly a year previously. He walked more firmly and held himself straight. His father felt a flush of pride at the man his son had become, but also a momentary nostalgia for the child left behind.

Shaking hands, he noted his son's eyes still resembled Tirinella's, which gave Matwyck a minor pang.

"Welcome home, my son," he said with quiet dignity, determined not to show that his prolonged absence had rankled.

In the carriage to the palace, they deliberately did not discuss their recent bereavement.

"Well, Father, how are conditions in Cascada?" asked his son.

"The city has so far been spared," said Matwyck, "though there has been a rash of fires in the countryside."

"Fires? Really. Do you know the forest called Anders Wood, near Duke Naven's manor?" Marcot asked. "There was a terrible forest fire a few weeks before I left. No one could guess how it could have started, and the place is too remote for fire brigades to combat it. I've ridden through that forest—such magnificent timber!—what a terrible loss."

"Did Naven lose it all?" Matwyck found these strange fires distressing, but he wouldn't mind if one of his least-favorite dukes suffered.

"No. It was the strangest thing. The fire had consumed about a third of the wood and looked hungry enough to finish the job—we sat our horses watching in despair—when a sudden storm appeared and poured rain down in buckets. Saved the rest of the forest and the surrounding villages."

That evening, over a private dinner served in their quarters, Matwyck reassured Marcot that the occasional flares of unrest among the people—the mobbing of a tax bureau, a painting on a city building shouting "Where is Cerúlia?"—were nothing to worry about. Matwyck had formed a special cadre of soldiers, loyal to him, to keep the palace safe. If Marcot left the palace, his father wished him to be accompanied by a squad of guards in red sashes.

At the end of the meal, Marcot pushed away his plate and said, "Father, there is something important I'd like to discuss with you."

Matwyck hid an indulgent smile at his son's serious tone by taking another sip of wine.

"If the matter is important to you, it is important to me. Pray continue."

Marcot took a deep breath. "In Androvale I met a young woman. A wonderful woman. I should tell you straightaway that she is not of noble birth, and her family—while more than respectable—is neither wealthy nor influential." The last words of his obviously rehearsed speech came out in a rush: "Nevertheless, I intend to marry her."

Matwyck felt his temper rising as these sentences continued, but he mastered himself. "Tell me more about her," he replied with studied neutrality.

So Marcot told his father about this Percia—her grace and laughter, her dancing skills and her dancing school, her mother and brother, and their humble cottage in Wyndton. Matwyck kept a benign smile on his face, but inside he fumed.

When Marcot ran out of words to describe his infatuation with this village wench, Matwyck chose his response with care. He had seen the depth of Marcot's feelings play over his features, and he knew how stubborn the young man could be if he encountered opposition.

"Marcot, you think of me as an old man. But I remember feeling just as you do now when I first met your mother. The first flush of infatuation! Oh, how warming, how intoxicating!" Matwyck jerked his left hand; he'd been about to clasp it on his heart but decided midgesture that this would look too theatrical.

"You know I would be lying if I said I was overjoyed about this match. And it is not, my son (despite what you may believe) because I covet riches or position. No, all I want is for you to be happy—really, truly happy—in your marriage."

Matwyck took another sip of wine to give him a chance to negotiate this thicket. Marcot's face had frozen into immobility.

"I will speak to you man to man," Matwyck continued. "Choosing a wife is one of the most important decisions you will make. You can't make it hastily, or while you grieve from the loss of your mother."

"I know my own feelings," said Marcot, staring at the table linens. "And I met Percia before Mother died."

Matwyck pressed a bit harder. "Marcot, it is because I want you to be content that I am going to speak frankly to you. I fell in love with your mother; I knew just the passion and urgency that you describe. But you know that as it turned out, she and I were poorly suited to one another. I will not speak ill of your mother; no doubt the problems in our union were all my fault. But I would not have you make the same mistake I made."

Marcot's jaw tightened during Matwyck's last speech.

"Father, since you yourself made a match of commoner with no-bility, you have no standing to criticize my choice!" His voice grew louder. "I will marry her with or without your permission. I will marry her even if you disown me, even if you disinherit me. We will go live with Duke Favian and Duchess Gahoa of Maritima. I'm certain they will welcome us."

"Son, have I said anything that preposterous? Have I made any threats?" Matwyck rubbed his eyebrow and was distressed to dis-cover that the boy's outburst had made him perspire. "During your voyage you worked yourself up to imagine such threats, did you not? And practiced the role of stalwart suitor, resisting the pressure of a dictatorial father, just as in a play."

Matwyck steepled his hands and lightly tapped them together. "No. All I ask—and it is a little thing—is that you wait. That you wait until more time has passed since your beloved mother's death. You wait until you can be sure how well suited you two may be to one another. You test yourself, and you test your intended. If, while you are waiting, she runs off with the village dandy, you will have saved yourself and the realm a deal of grief."

As the last sentence escaped his lips, Matwyck knew these words were a mistake.

"Percia is not running off with anyone!" Marcot banged the table with his fist, making the cutlery bounce.

Improvising quickly, Matwyck said, "There! You passed the first test! Such fervent faith in your beloved. Speaks so well of you."

But he already had in his possession the key lever to influence the headstrong idiot; he just had to use it adroitly. Matwyck let a pause grow. Then he said, softly, "But Marcot, if your mother were here, what would *she* say? Might she not also counsel you to wait?"

Marcot appeared to consult his heart and then reluctantly nod-ded. "How long would you put Percia and me to this 'test'?"

Matwyck smiled inwardly; he recognized he had the boy on the hook. He poured them both more wine.

"What do you think would be reasonable?"

"Until midsummer?" Marcot proposed.

"How about a year? If in a year you are still set on this match, I will welcome Percia of Wyndton with open arms. Wouldn't you like to see her in a gown of silk made by the palace dressmakers? Wouldn't your girl and her family be happier knowing that you had your only parent's openhearted blessing? A glorious early spring wedding."

"If I agree to this year, you promise to bless the wedding?"

Matwyck held out his hand for a handshake. "My oath on the Waters."

17

Moot Table

Flaring with indignation, Smithy stood in the center of the flat stone surface on the barren dream island they called Moot Table. He knew that in this matter he had justice and custom on his side.

"I called you all to a Judgment because they are meeting *in the flesh* to plot against Pozhar!"

Smithy turned in a circle, challenging the eight other Agents. Peddler and Gardener did not deny this charge; they continued standing beside one another calmly, content to observe how the rest of the Agents would react to this unprecedented news.

Two of the people this morning were new to Moot Table; Smithy stared at them, wondering whose side they would take, though he recalled from his own experience that one's first trip to the dream island might be so disorienting that these newcomers probably would understand very little of the proceedings. Pozhar was mightily displeased that Mìngyùn had chosen *this* as the moment to take renewed interest in the world of humankind.

"And you know about these meetings—how?" Healer looked troubled.

"Pozhar has friends in Slagos who saw them," answered Smithy. "Peddler doesn't wear that gold cloak in his natural life, but his yellow hair and bells"—he gestured toward his own hair—"are unmistakable."

"I met them in Vertia's Garden too," broke in Spinner, the Agent newly anointed by Mìngyùn. Since her arrival a few moments ago she had been distracted by the costume her Spirit granted her, which was a gown of gossamer threads so fragile they looked as if they would tear if you touched them. She had paced this way and that, watching the gown shiver, and her hands still grabbed the golden pendant around her neck. Apparently, she had just broken through her fascination with these fripperies to concentrate on business.

"Well, to be strictly accurate," continued Spinner, "I went to the meeting merely as *myself*, and it was while I was there that I became Mìngyùn's Agent."

Smithy eyed her balefully, though if his gaze intimidated her she did not show it. He could tell this one came from the upper class, which he resented.

"Plots and more plots!" growled Smithy. "We are supposed to meet here, all open and aboveboard, to discuss our differences together, not sneak around behind shrubs in the Green Isles. Secret meetings lead to secret maneuvers and factions.

"Of course, *you* don't care." Smithy pointed at Water Bearer, whom he considered the prime conspirator. "*You're* willing to break all the time-honored customs of the Spirits to help your precious, murderous princella. But I hope that the rest of you now realize how underhanded Peddler and Gardener are."

Smithy turned to the two Agents just mentioned. "Will you tell us why you met? Or what you discussed?"

Peddler and Gardener remained quiet, though Peddler shook his head and the damn bells braided into his hair tinkled. In another circumstance Smithy might have allowed himself to enjoy hearing these delicate chimes. Gardener, as always, peered around like a mad owl, mesmerized by having his vision restored during their meetings on this enchanted isle. (Smithy would never admit it, but he also found hearing sounds again disorienting and disquieting.)

"No? See, they connive against us still," Smithy grumbled.

Water Bearer, an elderly woman with frizzy hair, tried to fend off Smithy's insinuation. "I had nothing to do with this," she said with her hands in the air. "This is the first me and Nargis heard tell of it."

"Actually," said Spinner calmly, "now that I learn that conversing in the flesh is a violation of protocol, I feel duty bound to tell all of you about *another* meeting of Agents in the Green Isles, though this earlier occasion was purely accidental and stayed on human concerns."

"Aye," said Sailor, who was the other novice to Moot Table, with a graceful bow. This man was much younger and more fit than the last Sailor, though he too wore a gray Lorther braid.

Sailor continued, "I am very pleased to make your acquaintance, *Spinner*, in your new role."

"And you, Sailor," she answered, with a smile that Smithy suspected contained secrets.

Spinner addressed Hunter. "And unless I am sorely mistaken, you too sat at my table a few weeks ago, did you not? At that time, I was insensible of your true vocation, but perchance you knew Sailor and me?"

"I did," admitted Hunter. "I can smell Agency. I don't expect the rest of you to have noticed, but you all emit a distinct aroma, not unpleasant, rather similar to pineapple sage." The dark-haired young woman in hunting garb sniffed several times.

"I can vouch," continued Hunter, "that this second meeting did not involve matters related to our Spirits. It was . . . a dinner party. The wine was excellent, but I don't particularly care for fish. No amount of preparation can cover up the fishy scent."

"A dinner party?" Smithy said, confused. "Then leave it aside; it has no bearing on the matter at hand." He wanted to return to the issue of secret plots.

"What say you, Mason?" Smithy asked.

"About what?" asked 'Chamen's Agent in his cloak of stone dust.

"About Peddler and Gardener and Spinner meeting outside of Moot Table!"

"I'm curious," Mason responded. "What's it like to talk to an Agent in the daytime? How did you recognize one another? Were your Spirits listening then as they are now? 'Chamen is not always with me; sometimes my Spirit attends to business far away from Rortherrod."

Oh, he's a hopeless fool, thought Smithy, not attending to the responses as he turned his body around to gaze at everyone surrounding him. *Healer avoids my gaze. She's in league with them too, even if she didn't travel to the Green Isles.*

Mason walked over to prod Peddler and Gardener with his questions. Detecting a break in the formal proceedings, the new Sailor crossed to bow to the new Spinner; then they whispered together like old friends. Only Healer and Water Bearer kept their positions at the edge of the circle, though both assumed uneasy frowns, and Water Bearer chewed her finger.

Hunter took advantage of the pause to beckon Smithy, who gave up his central speaker's position to cross to her side.

"I confess I am troubled by this news," Hunter said in a low voice. "The Wind treasures freedom. My Spirit is *not* pleased by factions and hidden meetings."

Although he was not skilled with words, Smithy tried to find the right note. "Ghibli grasps the heart of the matter. The issue lies not just with this or that pet human, however favored or disfavored. It is the principle of Spirits being in league against each other in conspiracies. In this case they team up against Pozhar, but what if at some later time, factions teamed up against Ghibli and tried to hem in the Wind?"

Hunter stood still, consulting with her patron through the interior connection they all shared with their individual Spirit. "We agree, Smithy, that factions violate the fundamental trust of Moot Table. How would you have us help you?"

He whispered, "Where do you abide in waking life?"

"I was born in Agfador, but I ran away from home when I was quite young. When need arises I make my living as a street performer—juggling, acrobatics, that kind of thing. I move from one nation to the next."

"If you tracked down the pet woman who is the root cause of the quarrel . . ."

Hunter laughed. "I've already picked up her trail. She leaves a distinctive scent behind her: a mixture of many animals with bergamot and chamomile. Ghibli, as usual, moves faster than all of the other Spirits."

Spinner interrupted the separate conversations with a raised voice. "Mìngyùn prompts me to speak," she said. "Am I correct that to take the floor I should enter the center of the circle?"

Healer, who presided over proceedings at Moot Table, answered, "Yes, Spinner. That is our way."

The new woman walked into the middle and addressed them all in ringing tones. "Mìngyùn bids me speak of something much more important than Green Isles meetings or dinner parties.

"Your Spirits may believe that their destructive actions have passed unnoticed—a small fire here, an earthquake there—these things often happen without ill will, from human causes or from our Spirits' casual stretches, releasing natural tension. However, Mìngyùn has noticed. Mìngyùn is displeased. More than displeased.

"Mìngyùn bids me convey that your Spirits will cease these attacks upon each other's realms. Immediately."

"Your Spirit has no right to order us about!" Smithy shouted. "Why is Mìngyùn even meddling? What's this sudden interest in humankind?" His loud outburst was followed by stunned silence.

Smithy tapped his fire tongs against his chain mail, making (to him) a pleasing clank. "Our Spirits will be at peace when the Nargis heir is dead." As ever, when he became very angry at Moot Table, a crown of flames appeared upon his brow.

"All of this destruction over *one woman*?" said Spinner, still calm, indeed maddeningly so. "This is more than irrational. It is folly. You are using her as a proxy for long-term grievances, is that not the case?"

"'Chamen only started the quakes because Weirandale has not returned its Truth Stone," Mason put in defensively. "'Chamen has a right to insist that its treasures be returned."

Spinner held up her hands for silence.

"In Pilagos, where I have lived for many years, we cherish a funny anecdote. It goes like this: Two brothers set sail for Orchid Isle, but soon they lose their way. The younger brother says to the older, 'We're lost.' The elder brother says, 'Aye, you're right. We're completely lost.'

"Then the older brother says to the younger, 'The most important thing to do now is figure out who's to blame.'"

Several of the Agents chuckled at this story. Smithy realized that Spinner had succeeded in turning the meeting away from his goal.

"Who started this conflict and who is to blame are not material facts when Spirits toy with disaster," she continued with quiet authority. "Mìngyùn insists that this destruction cease forthwith."

"Oh, yes, please, it must stop," put in Gardener, who to Smithy's mind had always been a weakling. "The trees, the fruits, the grains—drowned, burned, or swept away. Such a waste."

"And so many innocents have died and suffered," added Healer.

"If Pozhar stops starting fires, Lautan will create no more tidal waves," said Sailor as if *he*—a first-timer at Moot Table and wearing that ridiculous sea-foam hat—had the right to bargain. Smithy couldn't quite place this new Sailor; his hands and skin showed the marks of hard labor, but his bearing was proud, almost regal.

Smithy had called for this Judgment to expose other Agents' sneaking around, conspiring against his country and his Spirit. He certainly had not called this Moot Table for Mìngyùn to give Pozhar orders. Instead of shaming his fellows and calling a halt to their deceitful behavior, Spinner had put him in the wrong, stealing the floor away from him.

Smithy strode back into the center of the flat stone, tapping his tongs against the ground while his crown of flames stretched higher.

Frightened, Gardener covered his eyes while Water Bearer took a couple steps backward, spilling more rainbows. Though he towered over her, Spinner did not yield the speaker's position.

Healer broke in, "Can we come to some resolution? What say you, Peddler? Will you promise not to break our protocols in the future?"

Peddler hesitated, and that Spinner—who seemed too smart for her own good—answered instead. "Protocols are important," she conceded. "We all work better when we can trust one another to abide by the same rules. But one might inquire if procedures per se are the highest aim of this gathering. Pray, forgive me; I am new to your company—what is our foremost goal?"

"We meet whenever one of our Spirits believes another has encroached on its realm, powers, or people," Healer answered Spinner. "We gather to reason together and come to a Judgment. Smithy called this meeting." Healer cleared her throat. "By our traditions, if you and Mìngyùn wish to raise different matters, our procedures would have you convene a separate meeting."

Spinner inclined her head toward Healer and ceded the middle of the stone, though she did not step all the way back to the circle's perimeter.

"I demand a Judgment censuring the plotters and forbidding future meetings or putting into action any plans that were discussed outside Moot Table!" shouted Smithy. "All in favor?" He held his fire tongs high in the air. None of the other Agents voted with him, though Hunter turned sideways and whistled into the sea breeze, detaching herself from the proceedings.

The moment grew intolerably tense. Healer shifted her weight on her feet and said, "I think we can make no more progress at the present time. Let us return to our lives and consult with our patrons. Perchance, at a later time, we can find the harmony and agreement that prove elusive at this moment."

With a clap, Healer dissolved Moot Table. Smithy woke up in his tent in Alpetar, grinding his teeth.

But his first thought was not anger at the other Spirits, but a flash of self-consciousness. In his waking life he had long ago adjusted to his deafness and knew himself complete, even superior to those who didn't use their other senses as well as he did. Every time he left Moot Table, Smithy had to reexperience an unsettling transition. After the noise of voices, wind, and surf, a welcome silence pressed in upon him, familiar and warm.

This reminded him of his proud separation from others, as Pozhar stood alone against all the other Spirits.

18

Salubriton, Wyeland

When Phénix came out of her weeks of fevers and drugs, she discovered herself lying in a large bed, with lusciously cool, clean linens. When she opened her eyes, she noticed that the room—much more expansive than any of the cabins she had occupied during the sea voyages—remained quite still. An open window let in a view of sky and trees and the scent of an herb garden.

The whitewashed chamber was sparsely furnished. Her dagger, her headband, and her hair tonic sat on a table just to the side of the bed.

She wore only underdrawers; her upper body, which was everywhere damp with a light sweat, boasted various bandages. Her movements made her aware of areas of soreness. She lay down in the bed, taking inventory of the various dressings around her arm and her chest. What was this knifelike pain under her left breast?

Her memories of the last weeks came only in snatches—painful coughing, gasping for breath; terrifying dreams that haunted her days and nights; cooling poultices laid on her burns; a cup of fish chowder spooned to her one night; and a tonic from a tin cup that left gritty residue in her mouth.

She heard footsteps and tried to compose herself; she could not say why, but she felt guilty for examining her own wounds and embarrassed by her state of undress.

A woman of about forty years old with a quick step entered the room. She wore her hair pulled back into a snood, yet Phénix could tell that her hairline was mostly lavender. Her face was disfigured by a jagged cleft through her upper lip area, pulling the lip up and showing teeth careening in the wrong directions. Trying to be polite, Phénix looked away from the visitor's face to the tray of food she carried in her hands.

"Good morn to you, Damselle Phénix. I knew it was time to taper off the milk of the poppy. I'm pleased to see you awake."

"Good morn to you. Have you been the one caring for me?" Phénix struggled to her elbows. "What is your name?"

"My name is 'Myrnah,' but you can just call me 'Healer'; that's the name I prefer."

Phénix couldn't repress a chuckle. "I have a friend who once said something similar to me. In his case, I was to call him 'Gardener.'"

"Indeed?" said Healer, carefully setting the tray down on the bedside table.

"Yes," said Phénix. "I miss him terribly."

Healer changed the subject. "Well, you've been through quite an ordeal. Most of your burns became infected, and then your left lung did too. Those who tended you on *Misty Caravan* worked day and night to keep you alive."

She helped Phénix into a straighter sitting position, laid a soft shawl around her shoulders for warmth and modesty, and put a large cloth over the younger woman's lap. "They told me they often despaired. But you just would not slip into the final sleep, the ultimate refuge. Some force or Spirit wants you to live."

"I barely recall the journey, but I must thank those healers. What are these bandages here and here?" Phénix pointed to the various dressings.

"Scar tissue had grown between your arm and your left side because someone taped your burned arm to your burned side to set the broken bones. Undoubtedly, whoever did this meant well, but he should have wrapped the injured skin to keep it separate."

Healer gestured from her armpit down her side on her own body. "We had to slice through the scar tissue to free the arm—you have these long gashes that must heal, though they are not very deep. At least the broken bones set well enough, though it will take much work to build back mobility and strength.

"That," she said, pointing to a spot to the left of her own sternum, "is the incision we made into your chest. We drained out the corruption that had formed an abscess in your lung and pleural cavity. Such a tricky procedure, and we are quite proud we pulled it off! We just closed that hole three days ago, so yes, it is still tender."

"How long have I been here?"

"Five days since your ship docked and your surgeries."

"How long . . . ?" Phénix had lost all sense of time.

"Did you sail on *Misty Caravan*? It takes close to three moons to travel from the Green Isles to here. Today is the fifth day of the moon we call Spring Renewal." Healer moved the tray onto her patient's lap.

Phénix eyed the food with appetite, but she also hungered for information.

"The fevers? My coughing?"

"Your fevers are gone. You probably will still cough as the lung dries out more, but less than before."

"And the burns?"

"You've been seriously burned, Damselle," said Healer. "If I'd had you the first day after your injury I could have mitigated the scarring, but by the time you arrived in Salubriton, 'twas much too late. The burns, which must have been bad enough to begin with, festered and broke repeatedly. Scar tissue has grown to close the wounds, but it is fragile and we will have to watch that it doesn't break and tear more."

Phénix closed her hand around the warm cup and averted her face from the older woman. "I hope you don't think me very vain, but how do I look?"

"Whatever burned you didn't touch your face. You look gaunt: your cheekbones are pronounced, and your complexion has a gray-ish tinge. I'd very much like to see more healthy color and rounded-ness there. As for your hair, we kept up applying your tonic once a week, because even in your fevered state you insisted on it."

Phénix half expected a scolding or some curiosity about her pre-occupation with her hair while she was so ill, but Healer passed over the subject without comment.

"Your eyes . . ." Healer paused. "Your eyes hold a shadow that distresses me."

Phénix touched the lizardlike skin on her neck with her fingers. Her arm was wrapped, and she couldn't reach her back to judge the texture. "My neck? My arm? My back?"

"You will always wear the scars of your accident. Some of the scars are ridged; some discolored."

"I'd rather know the worst," said Phénix. "Can you bring me a looking glass?"

"As you wish," said Healer. "But aren't you hungry? I really want to get some flesh on your frame; I imagine that, being so undernour-ished, you've lost your courses?"

Phénix nodded. In fact, she couldn't recall the last time she had had her moon blood—it might have been in Alpetar, before she crossed into Oromondo.

Once she started eating she discovered that, indeed, she was famished. She ate everything on the tray and asked for more, but

Healer refused; she wanted to ease her into eating solid food. After the meal, she brought Phénix a night-robe and clogs and bid her rise. Phénix found she could hardly make it the six steps to the window and back. From the window seat she noticed that her bed was oddly constructed—it had curved runners along the bottom, like a rocking chair. She fingered the scars on her neck several times, trying to learn their new texture and ridges and incorporate this change into her self-awareness.

For the next several days, Healer fed her, checked her bandages, and encouraged her to move about as she regained her strength. The older woman reminded her of Nana in her firm but gentle ministrations. Soon she could look the woman in the eyes, no longer even registering her facial disfigurement. Phénix felt safe under her care, as if the touch of her hand or the sound of her voice provided an extra medicine.

When she voiced this thought to Healer, the older woman smiled. "In this Healing Center you are under the protection of Restaurà, Spirit of Rest, Sleep, and Recovery. 'Tis the Spirit that comforts you, not I." Then she gave the foot of the bed a strong push, and the bed rocked. As Phénix relaxed she began to piece together the similarities between Restaurà's Healing Center and Vertia's Garden, and between Healer and Gardener, but these were subjects best not spoken of out loud.

Within two days Phénix had grown strong enough to venture into the corridor. She almost didn't want to leave her room, which connoted safety to her, but Healer had mentioned a washing room. And there it was, decorated in hand-painted tiles: a small room that, to her amazement, offered water spigots and indoor plumbing like the palace of her long-ago childhood. She wanted to luxuriate in the running stream of water, but a large sign on the door warned "Remember the Drought!"

On the fifth day, Healer brought her two large looking glasses and held one behind her; by moving the front one carefully, she could see that the side of her neck was red, leathery, and creased, but not too unsightly, while the worst-affected area—the left half of her back and the back of her left arm down to the elbow—was puckered with lumpy, angry scar tissue. Phénix let out a long sigh of regret but refused to weep.

A few hours later, she sat by the window. A flock of swallows dipped in wild circles through the gathering evening gloom and then began to gather in a stand of birches that rose outside the herb garden. Their nighttime calls echoed. Phénix yearned to speak to them, and for a long moment she considered reaching out with her Talent. But she feared her Talent had been corrupted, either by direct contact with the Magi's fireball or by the fevered dreams she suffered on board the ship. The last animal she could recall speaking to had been the ship's cat.

The sixth day, instead of Healer, a short young woman with brown hair pinned up entered Phénix's safe cocoon.

"Damselle, I am Betlyna, an apprentice healer. It's the custom here, when patients are on the mend, to move them to a recovery house where they can profit from being around other patients," she said. "At present Healer is busy with other, more critical cases; but she sent you her good wishes. The Bread and Balm Recovery House has reported a vacancy. I have been instructed to take you there this morn and get you settled."

Phénix did not want to leave her sanctuary (and she experienced a twinge of unreasonable jealousy at the thought of anyone else receiving Healer's attention), but she recognized she had no choice. She reached for the folded clothing that Betlyna proffered. The top was an odd rectangle of cloth with a hole for the neck and then long pieces like sashes sewn on the bottom corners. As these sashes tied around, closing up the sides, Phénix discovered that the shirt would fit people of many sizes and be soft against any injury. Then she pulled on a floor-length, loose skirt that also tied at the waist. Both were of a soft material dyed in different swirls of lilac.

Betlyna held out another garment for Phénix to wear. It was an overcoat constructed of stiff white canvas, loosely falling to knee length. Seeing the puzzled look on her face, the assistant healer explained, "This is a 'dust-coat,' damselle. We wear them to keep street dust off our clothing. And here, I've got a snood for you." Phénix tucked her hair into the crocheted netting, but she couldn't tie the band herself with one arm; Betlyna had to help her.

Betlyna packed up her dagger, jeweled headband, bottle of tonic, nightgown, and night-robe in a satchel. The clogs Phénix had used earlier served as shoes.

An open carriage with a large umbrella affixed on a pole to the rear in order to shade the passenger seats waited outside the door to the infirmary. Phénix was surprised that in the traces stood an animal the likes of which she had never seen before. It had long, spindly legs, a long neck, and a small round face. Its coat—a mustard brown with white spots—looked smooth and silky. Its black tail stretched long enough to switch its face, but it had no mane.

"What's that?" Phénix asked, agog.

"Oh, never seen a gamel before?" said Betlyna. "We use them for all our carting. Horses, we keep only for leisure riding; gamels' backs are too high, and though they don't mind pulling, they won't tolerate a person sitting on top of them."

The gamel bent its long neck around and peered closely at Phénix, its odd face assuming a curious expression, almost as if inviting her to talk to it. She reached for it with her mind, and immediately felt a flash of fiery heat throb through her forehead, so fierce she staggered.

The coachman and Betlyna must have ascribed her swaying to her general weakness. The man lifted Phénix by the right elbow and Betlyna by the left waist, careful not to touch her injuries, and aided her up the three steps into the conveyance.

The ride through the streets offered Phénix her first look at Salubriton. She discovered that the infirmary had been situated in a quiet park; as soon as they left the grounds for city streets, bustle and noise rose around her. This city sat on a flat, featureless plain, and few trees provided shade from the sun. Most houses were built of concrete, painted in a variety of gay colors, and all the buildings featured rounded archways rather than rectangular doors. Small scrubby plants and rocks set in intricate patterns provided decoration in islands in the middle of the boulevards and along their sides.

The streets, thronged with gamel vehicles, stretched wider than any Phénix had seen before. Smooth walkways on either side afforded foot travelers a path that kept them safe from the carriages or carts and away from the large piles of gamel droppings. Everywhere Phénix looked, the people, wearing dust-coats, carried extravagantly decorated parasols, some fringed with tassels, some stitched with embroidery; all were a riot of color and pattern.

Such movement and color overwhelmed Phénix. She searched for something familiar and soon realized that she had not spotted a single dog.

"Betlyna, where are the dogs?"

"Dogs? Salubriton does not allow dogs. You needn't worry about those dirty animals that spread disease and foul the streets. We take precautions to keep our city free of such pests."

After a lengthy drive they arrived at the Bread and Balm Recovery House, a beige, two-story building with a red tile roof, boasting an ornate and heavy wooden door. The landlady, wearing a little white apron over her loose long skirt, came out to greet the carriage.

"Betlyna, good health to you! I'm real glad you brought me a woman this time, because I need one to sleep with the Ward. I trust she's an easier guest than the last. Weren't sorry to see the back of *her*, you know."

"And good health to you, Dame Tockymora!" said Betlyna, who

exited the carriage and then turned to help Phénix descend. "Now, dame, no gossiping about the guests. Salubriton treats all graciously."

"Oh, it's healthy to blow off a little steam. Restaurà don't mind just a little grumble now and then. What's your name, damselle?" Tockymora, like all the other Wyes Phénix had met, spoke with an accent that sounded alien to her ears, with more liquid consonants, noticeable particularly in the "r" of "Restaurà."

Phénix introduced herself and explained how she was a stranger in their land, a refugee from a ship that had burned and sunk.

Dame Tockymora said, "Well, I knew you wasn't a local, damselle, 'cause if you was, your family would have taken you home. The main folks as come to a recovery house are those from faraway places, or those who don't have any relations, or those whose relations are hard-hearted. Restaurà will see *they* suffer from pink eye or piles or pinworm. Well, don't stand out here in the blazing sun all day. Come in, come in, see the place and meet my other current guests."

Taking the arm Betlyna offered for support, Phénix entered the house. The interior was laid out like an inn, with large rooms as common spaces and small rooms for sleeping. Dame Tockymora introduced her to half a dozen men (brown hair everywhere, cropped close to the head), but worn out by the stimulation of the carriage ride, other than noticing that one of the men had a wooden leg, Phénix could barely attend. Betlyna assisted Phénix up a steep staircase, taking her to an attic room with two rocking beds and open shutters trying to catch a whiff of breeze.

"There's a washroom across the hallway," said Betlyna. "Rest a tick; I am going to check on the progress of the other patients. I'll stop up to see you before I go."

Phénix collapsed on the bed; the stairs had made her pant.

Once I climbed a rock cliff into Oromondo. Now I can't climb a set of stairs. Once my Talent flowed easily. Now I'm afraid to use it. Once Adair found me attractive. Now he would find me hideous. I used to live amongst people who cared for me. Now I'm left alone with people who don't know me at all.

A few tears wandered down her cheeks, but she was too tired to cry. The bed was lumpy, but the room smelled of the fresh lavender that filled a vase near the window. Although she would have preferred to lie on her uninjured side, she didn't even have the energy to shift about, so she fell into a half doze in an uncomfortable position.

Noise on the stairs roused her and heralded the arrival of Betlyna with one of the men from downstairs, the one with the wooden leg.

"Damselle Phénix, may I present Syr Damyroth. Syr Damyroth, I'm going to show you how to change her bandages and what to watch for. Sit up, damselle."

Phénix instinctively grabbed the bow of her sash tie tightly. She did not want to undress in front of a strange man.

Betlyna chuckled. "Oh, I *am* sorry. No one has explained to you the principle behind the recovery houses. I suppose I am the one who should have done so.

"The point is, you see, that over the centuries we have found that patients recover more quickly if they take over each other's care. Dame Tockymora isn't a healer; she's merely your landlady.

"Each of you must contribute to each other's recovery; we believe that 'We are all fingers on one hand.'

"An apprentice healer, like me, will drop by every other day to check on a house's progress and update routines, but in your case, your bandages still need to be changed frequently, and we'll give you a salve that needs to be rubbed into your scars so the tissue doesn't split or crack. So damselle, sit up here"—she patted the side of the bed—"and let me show Syr Damyroth the routine."

Damyroth's right trouser leg hung loosely, and a wooden stump hit the floor. He stood tall but so rail thin that his swallow apple protruded from his neck. His eyes were mild, and his short brown hair did nothing to hide an incongruously tiny pair of ears.

"I assure you, damselle," he said in a deep voice, "that I have no interest in your body, except to the extent I can assuage your injuries. In a recovery house one soon becomes accustomed to human bodies and all their agonies."

Ashamed of her truculence, Phénix moved forward so that her legs dangled off the bed. Now she saw the efficacy of the way the blouse was constructed: untying the one knot allowed access to a patient's entire upper body without further disrobing.

Damyroth sat next to Phénix and followed Betlyna's instructions, unwinding the bandages and inspecting the recent incisions for signs of redness or oozing. His hands were warm and dexterous. He made no comment and refrained from gasping when he saw her burn scars, and for this Phénix felt deeply, absurdly grateful.

Betlyna took a jelly jar of salve from her satchel. "You can start rubbing this on your neck now, damselle. It will moisturize and protect your skin. When the bandages come off in a few days, you'll want to ask another patient to rub it on your back as well.

"Tomorrow is soon enough for you to participate in caring for your housemates. They will tell you what needs to be done. For the remainder of today, you should just rest and get settled. Dame Tockymora will fetch you your meals. Either I, or another apprentice, will return soon.

"Good health to you, damselle." She inclined her head over her hands pressed together, the fingers interlaced. And then she and the tall man exited the doorway, leaving Phénix alone in an alien house, in a land far across the seas from Weirandale.

Phénix had been passed about like a parcel ever since the fire. From creature to creature, from boat to boat, and from healer to healer. For moons she had been too sick to take much notice; all her concentration had focused on taking the next breath or swallowing the next medicine offered to her.

Now, on the path to recovery, she fully realized that she had lost everything. The Raiders, her friends, her kin, her looks, her half of the world—even her contact with animals. Oh, how she longed for the closeness and companionship of a dog!

And yet Healer expected her to live and even take on the responsibility of care for others.

As wretched as I was when I was at my sickest, my sense of duty didn't prod me. If I get better, I have to pick up my burdens again. How can I rebuild my life, much less defeat the usurpers and regain the Nargis Throne?

Casting her gaze morosely around the new room, Phénix spied a ceramic water pitcher and cup near the bed. A drink of water would make her feel better. She reached for the pitcher with her good arm, her right arm, but the vessel turned out to be heavy. She didn't have the strength to hold it, and she couldn't swing her left hand to help. In her unsteady grasp, water sloshed all over the tabletop, her own legs, and the floor. And then as she gave up and tried to replace the pitcher on the surface, her fingers slipped on the wet handle and she dropped it to the floor, breaking it and splattering water everywhere.

She stared at the mess, guilty and defeated, wondering if she now had angered Dame Tockymora and if she would be set out on the street.

Phénix lay down and closed her eyes, letting her fatigue wash over her, inventorying all her losses, aches, and miseries, longing for the milk of the poppy or other drugs that had kept her numb during the voyage. She would even have welcomed the fevers that had plagued her for so long, because they made her woozy. Desperately, she reached for the haze of exhaustion that she had fallen into when she first entered the room.

But she had no drugs or any other means of summoning oblivion. She remained beastly conscious, thirsty, with wet knees, lying in an attic room now covered with crockery shards and a wasted puddle of precious water.

Outside she heard the sounds of people, gamels, and carriages on the street. From downstairs she smelled cooking. Life—so pitiless in its demands—went on for her, just as it had for Gentain after he lost his daughters, for Tristo after he lost his arm, or for Thalen after he lost his mother and brother.

And Thalen had risen up from those twin blows to lead the Raiders into Oromondo to free his countrymen.

But I've lost more! I've lost the most! she wailed in her mind, but even she could hear in those wails the echo of the spoiled princella she had once been. Her lips quirked into a self-mocking smile.

Well, it looks like I am going to live. So the sooner I make some effort, the better.

She heard the clink of dishes and the murmur of voices from downstairs. She was hungry, and she didn't know when anyone would bring her food. Besides, she didn't want to be waited on like an invalid.

Sliding to the edge of the bed, she placed her feet on a dry patch of floor and stood. At first her head swam, but after a moment's pause she recovered sufficient steadiness to proceed. Placing each foot deliberately one after the other, she trod down the stairs, holding on to the wall for balance. Gaining the ground floor without falling had been difficult, but she felt a tiny surge of pride that she managed on her own.

A group of people was gathered around a table covered by an enormous green-and-black-striped parasol in an interior courtyard, passing dishes from one to the other; Damyroth, three other men, and one woman. They paused their conversation when they saw her in the doorway.

"My dear damselle, we would have brought you a tray, but we are delighted you feel strong enough to join us!" said a portly gentleman whose brown coloring was decidedly yellowish. He sprang to his feet, bowed slightly, and came to hold her elbow. "The paving stones of this courtyard are quite uneven; you don't mind if I escort you to your seat?" He steered her gently but firmly to the open chair;

the others had already laid her plate and started to heap it with food by the time she sank down, drained from her exertion.

"Betlyna made brief introductions before, but let me present myself formally. I am Syr Lymbock, a businessman from Arri. I ate some bad shellfish and have presumed upon the kind hospitality of Salubriton for my jaundice for moons." He nodded to the man beside him. "I believe you've met Syr Damyroth?"

"Not socially," said Syr Damyroth. He too stood and bowed. "I am Damyroth, one-leg amputee from a work accident. Born and bred in Haven, a town far from here, north and east. I was a builder; my boss saved my life by removing me from the stones of a fallen wall and carting me to Salubriton."

"So pleased to meet you," answered Phénix, then turned to the next person.

The listless woman sitting next to Damyroth had her hair untidily pushed into another snood; she neither looked up nor spoke.

Lymbock cleared his throat. "Ah, may I present Restaurà's Ward. We don't know what her real name is. She suffers from melancholia and will not speak to us. One of us always keeps an eye on her; she's attempted suicide twice—once before she came to Bread and Balm and once while here. She is your roommate, so you will need to keep watch on her in the nighttime."

On the other side of the Ward an elderly little man got up and made a small bow. "Damselle, I am Syr Jitneye; I live here in Salubriton. I am recovering from my third heart attack. My wife died last year, and there's no one at home to watch out for me."

The last person at the table had bright magenta streaks in his intricately braided hair; he wasn't sitting in a regular chair, but rather half reclining in a sloped rocker. His own accent was slightly nasal, to her ears, but his syntax sounded stranger. "My name is Sezirō. I be a sailor from Zellia. I was stabbed in a fight. I started it, so my own is the fault. In my belly. Forgive me, I cannot stand. And I cannot eat; I join the table for company. And for favor, damselle, no need to term me 'Syr.'"

They all looked at Phénix expectantly. She felt bad about lying to such open, gracious people. "My name is Phénix of Sutterdam," she said. "Sutterdam is a major city in the Alliance of Free States. I was on a ship to the Green Isles, and the galley caught on fire. The captain put me on *Misty Caravan* to bring me to your Healing Center. Oh yes, my injuries are burns, infections, broken bones, and a lung abscess."

She looked down at her still-damp knees, which the other guests had failed to notice. She confessed, "I just broke the pitcher in my room, and I couldn't even clean it up."

"Oh, don't bother about that. I will see to it after our meal," said Syr Jitneye.

The sympathy around the table undid her. Phénix added, very softly, staring at her plate, "And, on top of these physical hurts, I am so very homesick!"

"Of course you are," said Syr Damyroth. "Low spirits accompany all our ailments. They take just as much time to heal."

Syr Jitneye beamed at her. "You are very welcome to share our table and our house, damselle." He removed the cover from a dish. "May I serve you a bite of this? Dame Tockymora is a wonderful cook. If any of us recover, it shall be because of her fricassee."

19

Salubriton

Before she went to sleep that night, Phénix labored to pull her bed slantwise in the room so that the Ward couldn't reach the door without climbing over her. She also tucked the catamount dagger under the sheets beside her, cuddling it almost as if it were a doll. She knew it had been her mother's, but she took it to bed not for her own comfort but to make sure that the Ward did not have access to a deadly weapon.

In the morning, first thing, Syr Damyroth clumped up the narrow staircase. He carried a canvas bag with bandages and salve in it, but also a cup of coffee, winning Phénix's heart immediately with this thoughtful gesture. While he changed her bandages, which had become rumpled in the night, he told her the instructions that Betlyna had given the recovery house for her care. She was to move about as much as possible, but always with a housemate at her side in case in her weakness she became dizzy. She was to eat and get fresh air. And she was to join in the care of others.

"We are rather short of people who could walk with you these days," Syr Damyroth said. "Possibly the Ward would be the strongest one to support you—or maybe Jitneye. Healer ordered him to lose a little weight to help his heart. My stump isn't tough enough to take street walking yet. Lymbock must rest to recover from his infection of the liver, and Sezirō, the Zellishman stabbed in the belly, can barely get from rocker to bed."

"What can I do to help anyone else?" Phénix asked.

"Well, if you could get through to the Ward, that would be a miracle. We've all tried, of course, but none of us has had any success. And then Sezirō's bandages need to be changed often. I sometimes get cramps in my stump, and massaging eases the pain. Lymbock should stay still, but he gets restless and breaks the healers' orders. And he has to be cajoled to drink his elixirs. I think he may be losing hope that they will cure him."

When Damyroth left her, Phénix walked over to the other bed to look at the Ward. Her eyes were open but unfocused. She was a woman of perhaps twenty-five summers, with pale gray eyes, brown hair, and thin, colorless lips. The scars where she had tried to cut her wrists had knit closed, but they were still angry and red against her caramel skin. Though her eyes were open, she gave no sign of rising.

"Let's get up and see what Dame Tockymora has cooked up for fastbreak," Phénix said with fake cheer. She looked around for clothes for her roommate; a long skirt and matching top that once might have been fetching hung in the wardrobe. Phénix helped her get dressed, noticing that the dress hung loosely because she had lost weight. Spying a nearby hairbrush, she tidied the Ward's hair, making a note that it could use a good wash.

As she approached the fastbreak table, half leaning upon, half pulling the Ward, she was greeted by Dame Tockymora, who was setting out dishes.

"Good health to you, damselle. Did you sleep well?"

"Yes, thank you."

As she straightened up, the landlady's glance fell more fully upon the two women. "Damselle, being a foreigner—where they have such strange customs!—probably you don't know. Here in Wyeland, women never walk around with their hair loose. That is why they gave you the snood. Our hair must always be pinned up"—she gave her tight bun a satisfied pat—"or otherwise confined. Loose hair is so unsanitary!"

"I'll keep that in mind from here on," said Phénix.

Ten minutes later, Phénix addressed the group enjoying the egg pie, cold meats, and pickled vegetables. "We can't keep calling her 'Restaurà's Ward.' Does anybody have a name they like?"

Syr Jitneye offered, "My sister was called—"

"No," Syr Lymbock interrupted. "That's a ridiculous notion. Nobody dead. A lively name, a name full of life and hope."

Sezirō chimed in, "Hope. 'Hope' as a name, I am meaning. Damselle Hope."

They all agreed that this was perfect.

Phénix asked Hope to walk with her around the recovery house to help her learn the layout of the rooms. Hope said nothing, but she allowed Phénix to take her arm to steady herself.

The downstairs washing room had a bigger sink than the upstairs facility. Phénix gently pushed Hope into a bent-over position and washed her hair. And then fingering her own locks, which had grown during her illness and currently stretched down her back, she leaned over the sink and washed her own.

When she emerged, Dame Tockymora was lying in wait in the hallway. "Gracious! How much water did you use?"

Nonplussed, Phénix truthfully replied, "As little as possible."

Her landlady sniffed disapproval and stalked away.

After this effort and chastisement, Phénix felt drained. She took Hope's arm and walked back to the indoor patio.

Syr Lymbock lay on a reclining rocker in the spring sun, as did Sezirō. Sezirō called the women over to him.

"I love hair to fix," he said. He threw some pillows down on the ground. "Damselles, kindly you will sit where I can reach you?"

He combed Hope's wet hair through and skillfully twisted it

into little ringlets, then gathered the ringlets up on the top of her head with a ribbon that Jitneye fetched for him. Then he asked for scissors and meticulously trimmed the ragged ends of Phénix's hair, catching all the cut pieces into a bag. He began braiding it, starting with one lock and then, incorporating more and more, ending up by pulling all of her hair into a complicated chignon situated precisely to cover the burn on her neck.

While Sezirō worked and she sat there on a cushion in the sunshine, Phénix asked, "Syr Lymbock, why all the parasols?"

"The parasols! Yes, they would be new to you. Well, the sun here will burn your skin. Wyes take great pride in their perfect complexions. Unblemished skin is the premier mark of beauty for a Wye lady." He seemed unconscious of the irony of raising the subject of smooth skin with Phénix.

"The Wyes also mark their social status by the parasol they carry," he continued. "Certain patterns and colors are set aside for certain social classes, trades, and gentry, and every tassel has a meaning to the initiated. If I went strolling, I have the right to carry a parasol with an ebony handle and a geometric pattern."

"Everyone has a predetermined parasol pattern? What happens if you start as a tailor and become a merchant—does your parasol change?"

"Oh goodness, damselle! That never happens," said Lymbock. "The tailor is a tailor because his parents were tailors, and the merchant is a merchant because he inherited his business."

"So no one ever changes his—or her—social standing?"

"No. In Wyeland we know that everyone is content where they are. That striving for advancement creates stress."

"Who does a tailor marry?"

Syr Lymbock stared at her as if she'd lost her mind. "Either a tailoress or the daughter of a tailor, of course."

"What happens if the tailor falls in love with the daughter of a dairy farmer?"

He looked scandalized. "That would be a very unfortunate situation. Unhealthy. Perverse."

Phénix pondered awhile. Sezirō had finished his labors, and she smiled her thanks at him. "What do Wyeland's rulers say about this staying exactly where one is born?"

"Ha!" said Syr Lymbock. "We have no royalty—we do not believe in such elitist folderol. We are governed by a Council of Ministers. Every five years the council chooses a new first minister."

"And how does one get to be a minister?"

"Obviously, as a foreigner, you don't understand the way things work here and why Wyeland is such a peaceful land," said Syr Lymbock, trying to be patient and succeeding only in sounding patronizing. "You become a minister by being born into a ministerial family."

Phénix considered this information for a while and then turned to ask Sezirō about the relation between Pexlia and Zellia.

"Ah! We come from the same forebears, but now archenemies be we! Zellia is an island large, separate from the mainland. My people moved there centuries ago, when the stinkin' Pellish took to piracy and made our people among men pariahs! With the Pellish we are in a constant state of war."

"So that is why your hair is a darker shade?"

"Ah, Phoenix-bird-from-the-fire, you have met my cousin rascals? Did you like them?"

"I did not!" she replied, recalling the caravan drivers who had tried to steal the Sweetmeadow children.

"See? They are heathens."

"Heathens? Do the Zellish worship a Spirit?"

"Of course. We bow to Ghibli, the Spirit of the Wind, who fills our ships' sails. Our Spirit stands for freedom, for novelty, adventure! Although Ghibli lives nowhere, we like to believe we be the Spirit's favorite."

Sezirō started rhapsodizing about his Spirit, but Phénix grew more and more sleepy in the warm sunshine until—resting her head on her right arm, which lay propped upon his chair—she dozed off.

Her new Zellish friend woke her for a tasty midmeal—a bread with mincemeat baked in the center. Afterward, properly robed in her dust-coat, and with Syr Jitneye clutching on to her elbow, she went outside and walked to the street corner. On their return five minutes later, the others greeted her with such cheers Phénix felt she had won a race.

She devoted a good part of the late afternoon to playing Oblongs and Squares with Syr Lymbock to amuse him, discovering that she had to lose because he grew peevish if she bested him. Then she took a long nap in her attic bed before supper while Syr Damyroth kept watch on Hope.

At the dinner table everyone remarked on Hope's hair, which had dried into perfect ringlets. She looked quite pretty, but showed no sign that she heard any of the compliments her fellow guests paid to her. From conversation, Phénix learned more about Wyeland, including that Salubriton—enormous though it appeared to her—was not the capital city. The capital, Somniton, was located some hundreds of leagues inland.

After supper, Phénix assisted as Syr Lymbock tended to Seziro's wound. It was a horrifying sight: a ten-inch gash, half-open and suppurating. But recalling how important Damyroth's impassivity had been to her, Phénix steadied herself to show no reaction whatsoever as they washed it with a rag, smeared on unguents, and rebandaged it.

The next day passed much the same way; she made small forays outside and cared for her fellow patients.

On the day after, Betlyna visited. She said that Phénix no longer needed to wear the bandage on her left arm and that it was time for her to start rebuilding strength in that arm and shoulder. Since Damyroth also needed to strengthen his arms, she showed them exercises to do together. These motions caused Phénix considerable discomfort, but the apprentice healer offered her scant sympathy. All of her attention focused on Sezirō, whose wound worried her.

However, Betlyna did pass on a note from Healer. It read:

My dear, I trust you are regaining strength and mobility. It is best if you confine any social interactions to your housemates and nurses. Not everyone in Salubriton is to be trusted.

With loving prayers for your recovery,

Healer

Phénix's heart beat fast. To realize that even here—at the edges of Ennea Món—people might be searching for the Nargis heir sent a chill through her body. She disposed of the missive in Tockymora's stove.

On her fifth day, properly attired in her dust-coat, Phénix went walking on the sidewalk with Hope. She had come to enjoy the sight of the gamels on parade; at first glance their gait appeared ungainly, but they covered ground efficiently. A white cat sunned itself in the middle of a decorative rock-and-scrub pattern in front of a wealthy-looking house. Phénix almost extended her mind, but instead, she reached out her hand and called, "Here kitty, kitty, kitty," as an untalented person might. The cat stood up, stretched nonchalantly, and sauntered over so that the arch of his back just barely brushed against the offered caress. This inferior contact provided Phénix little comfort. She longed for the recognition that animals had always provided.

Hope and Phénix pushed on another block. A woman with a costly parasol jostled her, and Phénix lost her footing. She broke her fall with her hand, and she didn't feel any scars tear open, but the incident made her frighteningly aware of how weak she still was. She pulled herself up, brushing off her knees, and turned on Hope in a fury. "You're supposed to watch out for me! You're supposed to balance me! I'm still so weak. Why weren't you paying attention? Don't you even care if someone gets hurt?"

Hope blinked rapidly a few times at Phénix's tirade, but as usual she didn't speak. Phénix returned to the recovery house ashamed of her outburst. And she turned her mind to the impenetrability of Hope's catatonia.

When they were out-of-doors Hope walked straight beside Phénix, eyes unfocused. Inside the house she ate without tasting and used the indoor privy when so ordered with the same mechanical obedience. No one knew how well she slept, but she would rise from bed only when forced to. The breaks in her routine were distressing: occasionally, she would have a fit where she whipped her arms around in strange movements while repeatedly bending her neck so her ear touched her shoulder. Phénix questioned the other guests, but they knew almost nothing about Hope's history; she had been brought there by healers. The only time she was known to act with true volition was the midnight her previous roommate had discovered her coiling ripped bedsheets into a noose.

Phénix brooded on the possible causes of Hope's melancholia. Syr Lymbock told her that Hope's gown indicated she came from a lower middle-class background, but that was all they had concluded about her past.

20

Pilagos

When the *Island Breeze* pulled into Pilagos harbor and Wareth and the other Raiders spotted the Commander, Tristo, and Eli-anna waiting at the dock a kind of joyful madness had seized them all. The shipboard Raiders and the dockside group whooped with excitement and relief to discover that both squads had made it out of Oromondo alive—in fact with no additional human casualties. Dalogun had thrown his hat overboard, and Jothile had burst into tears.

Recounting the events that led Thalen's band to Tar's Basin, then to Slagos, and finally here—while Eldie's group rode to Needle Pass, through the vastness of Melladrin to Metos, and then boarded the *Island Breeze*—led to a jabber of excited talk and back thumps. Wareth twirled Tristo around in the air, while many of the Raiders embraced Eli-anna. Then they all repaired to the Fruitful Vine to celebrate their reunion and toast one another. Of course they proceeded to toast their faithful suppliers—the mysterious demigods Olet, Quinith, and Hake, now present in the flesh—from whom all bounties had flowed and who had sent the ship to Metos as soon as they confirmed tales of a fire in Femturan.

As the night wore on, however, everyone's high spirits evaporated; the Raiders turned morose, mourning the comrades who had fallen before the retreat. Wareth wrote Codek's name in the moisture on the table and then wiped it out. Several fell asleep with their heads on the liquor-stained tables, and in the end Olet and Quinith were forced to carry them to their beds.

Yet despite the rum he had consumed, instead of sleeping all day in the Fruitful Vine's featherbed, Wareth awoke at daybreak in the room he shared with three others (which had painted grapevines running up the walls), beset by anxiety about a duty unfulfilled. Lying on the soft mattress, listening to his friends' snoring, nursing the pain from both his shoulder and his hangover, he realized they'd all totally forgotten about their horses. He assumed that the crew of *Island Breeze* would have off-loaded and stabled them, but the Raiders should tend to their own mounts. Custard had saved his life more than once.

In the inn's kitchen, Wareth found Cerf and Dalogun making free with the proprietor's brew pot while the kitchen help clustered together on the other side of the room, wanting to rid themselves of these intruders but not knowing exactly how to get them to leave.

"Come with me, fellas. We need to find our horses," Wareth urged, and the two agreed to join him. The three Raiders stomped the streets of Pilagos, taking in the sights of an island city, but not breaking their long strides. Wareth noticed that the townsfolk, garbed in some loose garment tied at the waist and wearing straw hats, moved away from them and grabbed on to their children as if the three of them posed a threat. He found this odd and insulting until he glanced at his companions in their travel-stained leathers. Cerf wore a sword and a dagger, and his crushed beaver hat tied under his chin resembled a dead and mangled animal. His expression warned all and sundry against casual conversation. The same could be said of the surviving twin, whose face had lost all its youthfulness and who now boasted a scruff of a beard. As for himself, Wareth shivered to think of how disreputable he must look.

Or how hardened he had become, compared to his prewar cheerful self.

A short tramp brought them to the wharf. Cerf approached a couple of men shifting cargo to ask about the nearest livery stable. They suggested two. The first one didn't have the Raiders' horses. But at the second they found their reduced string: Brandy, Cinnamon, Cloves, Custard, Gander, and Sandy. Two horses had died of water poisoning on their trip through Oromondo, and because the Raiders had been able to transport only six horses on *Island Breeze,* they had given the other survivors to the Mellies as gifts. (As was only fair, given the aid the Mellies had provided in helping the troop, so injured and dispirited, safely return to the coast.)

The horses nickered with excitement at their approach. Dalogun immediately entered the stalls, checking on his sea-stressed charges, stroking and cooing. Custard, Wareth's own mare, nodded and blew at him when he whistled to her. He leaned his pounding head against the mare's neck a moment, but after a while she pulled away to nibble at her hay.

Cerf and Wareth went outside to talk to the stable owners, who were currying a stallion in a front yard in choreographed partnership.

"So you brought 'em back safely after all," said the woman.

"I don't take your meaning," said Wareth.

"Our horses—the ones Olet bought from us, the ones he named after spices—you brought some of them home. We miss the gelding with the reddish patchwork. We called him Chichi: I disremember what Olet named him."

"Chili," said Wareth, recalling the horse that had died. "And there was Pepper too, a black."

"Aye!" said the male owner. "Anyways, we was right joyful to see them. We had a time last night, didn't we, Wife, moving all the others around so your string could clump together, but we did manage it."

"Thank you," said Cerf. "Yes, they are accustomed to being together, as their riders are."

"How long are you planning on boarding them with us?" said the wife. "We need a deposit, for so many. Though if you're friends of Olet, mayhap that's not really necessary."

Wareth said, "We're not the owners, just a few of the riders. I don't know the plans for the horses, whether we are going to take 'em with us or sell 'em, but I'll convey their whereabouts to the money folk. Either way, we leave Pilagos in less than a week."

They took their leave of the stable owners, and the three Raiders strode onward.

"Less than a week? How'd you know that?" asked Dalogun.

"I sat next to Hake part of the time last night. 'Mander says we must hurry back to the Free States where there's still Oros and fighting going on. After all, we can't lounge around, kicking up our heels in the Isles while our people are fighting an occupation."

"Makes sense," Cerf grunted. He continued, "You know Hake from before, right?"

"Right," said Wareth. "I spent a few days with him after the Rout. When he was first crippled and all."

"Is the commander very close to him?"

"I dunno. Why?"

Cerf looked abashed. "I'm shamed to admit it, but I find it hard to share the commander. A blood brother might mean more to him than brothers-in-arms."

Since Wareth felt something similar, he smiled through his headache.

The three Raiders then wandered into the heart of the old town. They pooled their coins and discovered they had enough to buy fastbreak at an outdoor stall. The vendor sold them what he described as a local specialty: a flapjack rolled over and filled with strange fruit with lots of cinnamon. They took their flapjacks and tisane mugs and sat on a stone balustrade with an overview of the large and busy harbor, which sported all manner of vessels, warships and traders, heavily oared or bearing multiple sails. Overhead, flocks of swifts swirled and twirled in dizzying patterns.

"He looks grim," said Cerf to Wareth, and Wareth understood immediately that "he" was Thalen.

"Aye," Wareth answered. "They must have had a time in Femturan. Compared to their trials, our sneaking through Needle Pass was easy times. Especially since all the Oro soldiers immediately scooted out of our way, heading toward the Femturan Conflagration."

"Easy times!" scoffed Cerf. "Well, maybe you thought it so, being full of poppy milk, but I worked my sweat dry to keep you and Kambey breathing, and the others had to keep their eyes on Jothile every moment. Ask Dalogun here how easy he had it with all those horses."

Dalogun didn't complain about his labors. Instead, he interjected, "I feel awful about Skylark."

"Hm-mm," said Wareth. He had liked the Alpie girl too. But she no longer seemed real or substantial, more a dream connected to another place. Nor could he see how Thalen and she could have built a life together. Or maybe he just felt grim about women in general since Eldie had chosen to stay in Melladrin with her own people, rather than accompany him. He couldn't *make* her board *Island Breeze*—and he understood the attachment to one's homeland and kin—but his heart ached as much as his shoulder and head.

Cerf looked sideways at Wareth. "Your shoulder throbs? You're lost in thought."

"Huh?" said Wareth, returning to the balustrade. "I was thinking how glad I am to be on land, not tossed about on a cramped, stinking ship. I'm not looking forward to another long voyage."

"But to go home!" said Dalogun, kicking his heels against the stone wall. "Mind you, my folks, they'll probably whip me for running off to fight. And what will they say when it's just me that returns? They'll look behind me for Balogun and it'll break their hearts that he's not there."

"Your mention of folks reminds me: I have Nollo's letter to post. When we finish, let's look for a postal business."

"Why would we post it from here? Why not when we get back to the Free States? Better yet, shouldn't we *take* the letter to his mother and say nice things about Nollo to her?" asked Dalogun. "Isn't that how things should be done? Deliver the news personal-like."

Wareth answered, "Nollo didn't hail from the Free States. The letter is addressed to a woman in Cascada."

"So *that's* how he knew all those Weir ballads," said Cerf. "Remember them singing together? The three of them?"

"Aye," Wareth agreed. "Hard to forget." He finished his last swig of tisane and gathered the mugs to return to the vendor.

"Let's keep a lookout for a bathhouse too," said Cerf with a side glance. "A warm soak will ease that shoulder. From now until we embark, I prescribe hot baths every day for you, Kran, and Kambey."

"And what about Jothile?" added Dalogun. "Mayhap the water would help him relax a bit."

"Good thought, boy," said Cerf. "And you too."

"Why?" asked Dalogun.

Cerf probably had been thinking about the loss of his twin, but Wareth was sick of dwelling on losses. "You smell," Wareth said, and he cuffed the boy, gratified to see his grin.

21

Wyndton

Although her mother had warned a storm looked imminent, Percia waited outside the Wyndton Arms for the post wagon, as she did every delivery day, rain or shine. The rest of her life had lost its color; her heart revolved around these treasured letters. Marcot was a faithful correspondent, and she rarely walked away empty-handed. This morning, with a friendly wink, the driver handed her an envelope, which she ripped open.

She read through his news about continuing to hunt for a home for her family in West Park and his father's keeping company with a woman named Duchette Lolethia, but lingered over and reread his avowals of affection, then tucked the letter into her purse.

As she walked through the familiar streets toward her dance barn, tugging Barley's reins, she wondered if it was selfish of her to expect her mother and Tilim to move to Cascada just because she happened to have fallen for Marcot's dimples. But Marcot was doing everything he could to make them happy. And her mother kept reassuring her that a change would be good for all of them: that the house reminded her too much of Papa, and that in the capital Tilim would have broader opportunities.

And Marcot had promised that if they weren't happy in Cascada or at the palace, he would approach his friends, the duke and duchess of Maritima. He said he was eager to earn his keep with honest work and would welcome the opportunity to supervise their estate and holdings. Percia could open a dance school in Queen's Landing. But then Mama and Tilim would have to move a second time.

Percia dawdled, staring through a window at a dressy hat, but not really seeing it. The windowpane reflected the dark sky behind her. She would take cover in her dance barn in a minute. She pulled her cloak closer around her as the wind picked up.

Goody Gintie, on her way to the market, hailed her. Talkative as ever, Gintie regaled her with the latest bits of local news, raising her voice as the gusts made more noise.

They were just chuckling over the tale of a new father's faint upon discovering that his wife had borne twins—"We all shoulda guessed; that gal was as big as a house, but Ribat, he just falls like a tree!"—when Percia suddenly realized that the horizon looked strange. Ackerty, driving by in a cart, reined in his horse; he too stared in consternation. Goody Gintie's story about reviving the father died on her lips. The old lady who owned the sweetshop came to her doorway, and Kittie, her hands still covered with flour, dashed out of her house into the street. Before long, all the shopkeepers and their customers had come pouring out-of-doors to point and gawk.

A light patter of leaves and twigs began falling on them, but that wasn't what was disturbing. The sky had turned decidedly greenish.

"What is it? What's happening?" villagers called to one another in alarm.

"Look there!" someone called, pointing to a black, funnel-shaped cloud, wider at the top and narrow at the bottom, that whirled around in a most unnatural manner.

Percia stared at the cloud openmouthed. She had never seen its like nor imagined that such a thing could exist.

Sister Nellsapeta appeared in the doorway of the Church of the Waters. "Take cover! Take cover!" she screamed, motioning that they should join her inside. Percia grabbed Goody Gintie's arm; together they fell in with the crowd hustling down the street. No one objected when Percia pulled Barley inside after her. Barley wasn't the only animal; one boy had brought his dog, and one lady carried in the calf she'd been bottle-nursing.

By the time they were all inside, the wind had grown so it took four people to push the door closed. Everyone ran about trying to latch the wooden shutters on the side windows; they rattled ferociously, and three immediately tore out their hinges, pulling away from the wall and letting gales of wind inside. The glass window behind the little fountain broke with a hail of fragments and these shards, mixed with Nargis Water, flew around the room.

Just at that instant a ferocious slap of rainwater hit the roof, drumming down hammer strokes. Rain came pouring in through the open windows, making deep puddles that quivered on the floor. Even above the sound of the rain, however, they heard a horrible, unearthly noise—a noise that Percia could only compare to carts hurtling headlong down the cobbled streets of Gulltown. Percia, like everyone else, dived for the floor. She took cover with Gintie, Dewva, and Dewva's toddler under a wooden bench. They held on to the bench tightly, though the wind sucked at it, trying to pull it away. The roof creaked ominously. The loose shutters slammed against the wall with a tremendous clatter. Barley screamed and reared.

And then the strange, loud cloud had passed over them, heading southwest, and the horrible noise abated, though the rain still fell in torrents.

Percia sat up and looked around. Everyone was wet because of the rain, and a few people had sustained cuts from pieces of airborne glass. Gintie brushed a piece of glass out of her own hair and reached over to pull a shard out of the back of Percia's hand where it had impaled itself.

"Is everyone all right?" Sister Nellsapeta called out.

Dewva, Percie's friend since childhood, sat up, the child in her arms too frightened to fuss. Dewva's eyes tracked the direction the funnel cloud had moved, and she screamed, "The school! It's headed straight toward the school!"

Disregarding the heavy storm, the villagers poured out of the church, taking in that a few of the stores and cottages had collapsed. Ackerty's cart had been blown into the door of the dry goods shop, and his horse—sounding vigorously aggrieved—was all tangled up in the traces. Chimney bricks littered the street. The old oak tree in front of the church was uprooted and leaned precariously against the roof. Watering troughs overflowed.

The blacksmith's helpers stopped to rescue Ackerty's horse, but everyone else took off in the direction of the school. The wind and rain slowed the townsfolk's progress, and the street had turned to mud, snatching at their shoes. People from outlying farms joined the crowd, everyone racing toward the school.

Downed trees snapped in two blocked the road to the schoolhouse. The men vaulted them and ran ahead; the women, dragging their wet skirts, helped each other over the obstacles, crying out the names of their children or kin.

By the time they neared the building, set half a league outside of town, the sky behind them had started to brighten to a light gray and even the rain had slackened. Percia saw some black-and-greenish clouds scudding away in front of them, but nothing as ominous as Wyndton had just faced.

Finally, Percia and Dewva turned a corner in the road and the building came into sight. It had lost its roof, and one wall looked as if it had been smashed in by a giant fist. The men who got there first were busily untangling the heap of sixty-some children huddled on top of one another in a corner.

"Tilim!" Percia shouted as she ran the last paces. "Tilim!" He turned at the sound of her voice. He looked uninjured; at least he was walking. The light rain washed just a trickle of blood off his temple.

"Percie!" he said, grabbing her around the waist. "Are you all right? Is Mama safe?"

"I'm sure Mama's fine. The cloud didn't go that way. What happened?"

"This thing, this wind hit the school out of nowhere. Help me with Daverly, would you? I think he broke his elbow and he looks near to puking."

It took a while to sort out the students and masters and take stock of the casualties. This task was made harder by the children's fear: several had hysterics so badly no one could calm them down. By the Grace of the Waters, no one had perished. One master had a concussion from being struck on the head by a wooden strut. The healer, Goddard, who had had the presence of mind to bring his bag, set a few broken bones, the disaster making him less gruff-tempered than usual. Carneigh, the blacksmith, fetched a carriage to take the injured and distraught to town; and Hecht, the peacekeeper, formed men into a crew to clear the roadway for the horses.

The master who wasn't concussed informed everyone that this kind of storm was called a "tornado," and to his knowledge this was the first such event in the Eastern Duchies.

"Will it happen again?" Dewva, clutching both her toddler and her five-summers boy, asked him repeatedly, but she could get no answer.

The rain stopped altogether and the sun came out, making all the broken glass sparkle amidst strewn-around slates, chalk, hats, and books. Percia and Tilim, feeling weak in their knees, sat morosely on the edge of the school grounds on a downed tree trunk, watching some neighbors examine the damage to the building and conclude that it would need to be totally rebuilt.

Finally, Percia stood up and gave herself a little shake. "Can you walk to town, Tilim?" Percia asked. "I'm really anxious about Barley—I left him inside the Church of the Waters. I hope he's not drinking from the fountain or pissing on the floor, but I suppose, given everything, that if he did, no one would be wroth today. Then we must get home; Mother must be frantic. No one will be dancing today. And I'm dying to take off my sopping hose."

"I can walk," said Tilim, and he stood up to prove his hardiness.

"Are you sure? I could fetch the horse and ride back for you."

But Tilim had already taken a few strides. Then he bent down to pick up something that had glittered in the sun and caught his eye. He held it out to Percia. It was a tiny bird, just a common nuthatch, with its characteristic white throat and the black stripe on its head.

The innocent little thing's neck was broken. Percia bit her lip at the waste and cruelty of the sudden calamity.

PART
FOUR

Reign of Regent Matwyck,
Year 14

SUMMER

22

Sutterdam, The Free States

In the commercial city on the Sutter River, where nightly battles raged between the Free States Defiance fighters and Oro occupiers, Gustie of Weaverton did *not* catch a grippe from her wet feet after the skirmish at Sailmakers Bridge. This was fortunate, because she would never have heard the end of Norling's chiding if she had. Besides, she needed to be healthy for the tasks ahead. A few days after that battle Norling's brother had grown strong enough for Ikas's crew to move him to his house on Lantern Lane, where the women also relocated, leaving behind their temporary quarters upstairs at Sutterdam Pottery.

Hartling was in a sorry state. One of his hands had been crushed, and the bones had reknit distorted and useless. Also, blows had knocked out many of his teeth. But his most grievous injury was his splintered mind. Norling hoped that familiar surroundings would comfort him; yet mostly he lay wherever they put him, still and impassive. He had to be spoon-fed. They had to remind and assist him in using the chamber pot. Intermittently he would surface from his fog, recognize his sister, and speak to them lucidly; it always broke Norling's heart when his personality slipped away again into a dull apathy.

Gustie wandered through the dusty house, unoccupied for more than a year, opening windows and airing out the musty smell. The room that Thalen had once shared with his brothers sat untouched, its very neatness a sign that no one lived there now.

In the days that followed, when she wasn't occupied Gustie would leaf through Thalen's books, bemused by his eclectic collection. She wondered whether he was still alive, and she wondered how her life would have turned out if she had had a love affair with him rather than Quinith. She had heard nothing of Quinith's whereabouts, and every day his image in her mind grew fainter, though she found that if she closed her eyes and concentrated she could still hear his voice in her head—not any specific words, but the music of his mellow inflections.

Nursing and homemaking hardly lay within Gustie's ambit; still, she did what she could to help, whether this meant heating broth or sponging Hartling clean. Now, suitably attired in a more modest though slightly moth-chewed dress that had come from an upstairs chest, she was also the person who went out daily, both to scan the sparsely stocked markets for food and to gather news of the latest skirmishes.

She knew that when General Sumroth had left the Free States he had taken with him most of his best troops. At the Poison Banquet, Gustie had killed a large proportion of the officers stationed in Sutterdam, and the fighting with the freed Sutterdam slaves had further reduced the strength of the Oro garrison. Still, the leaderless Oro soldiers fought back against the Defiance with skill, discipline, and weapons the civilians did not possess. The Sutters lost as many engagements as they won and took more casualties.

Finally, the Oros—deciding they could no longer defend themselves against raids in Sutterdam—decided to pull out.

The news spread that the occupiers, more than two thousand strong, had retreated en masse behind the ancient walls of Jutterdam, the largest city in the Free States. Through torture they uncovered the names of the most highly placed figures of the Defiance there; the Oros burned the bodies of the Crones and children in the town square and left them hanging as an object lesson to Free Staters not to plot against them.

Ikas told Gustie that Mother Rellia had relocated her headquarters to the outskirts of Jutterdam and that fighters from all over the Free States flocked to her banner, the Free States four-quadrant flag. Two days later, Ikas and his troop gathered their sparse weapons and departed Sutterdam to lend their might.

Gustie wanted to leave immediately, but her conscience pricked her at the idea of Norling alone, caring for such a sick man. Besides, she admitted to herself, the Defiance needed Norling's strategic mind more than one semi-skilled archer, no matter how eager she might be. Gustie tried to swallow her pride and impatience.

Finally, one afternoon when Norling and she sat at a table in the kitchen of Lantern Lane over cups of tisane gone stone-cold, Gustie could keep quiet no longer.

"Norling, they need you in Jutterdam. You should go. I will stay here and care for Hartling, the very best I know how."

Norling smiled wanly. "Goodness, child, you are growing up quickly."

Gustie refused to rise to the condescending "child."

"Norling, think clearly. This is the only sensible solution."

Norling stirred her tisane.

To demonstrate her willingness to serve as nurse, Gustie got up to check on Hartling. He was sleeping, his broken hand cradled on his chest. She cracked the shutter so the room would get fresh air.

When she returned, Norling had her arms folded on the table and her forehead resting on her hands.

"Are you all right?" Gustie asked.

Norling ignored the question about herself and picked up her head. "You know, Gustie, you've never really told me your story."

"My story? How can that be relevant? There's not much to tell."

"Every person has a story. And every story is important. Start at the beginning," said Norling.

"If you wish," said Gustie, humoring her. "I was born in Weaverton, which you may know is a smallish city in Wígat. It's famous for its large textile workshops, but actually my father is a silversmith. He is a man of some standing and repute, consulted about the city's important issues. I never knew my mother, she died birthing me. My older brother went to live with her family, but my father insisted on keeping me close."

"The apple of his eye," murmured Norling.

"Yes, well, when I was ten I found myself supplanted by a stepmother, who was kind enough, I suppose, though I found her gauche." Gustie really didn't know why she was telling Norling these personal details. "My stepmother produced a litter of children—she popped one out right after another—and they wailed and peed and puked. And the house, which had always been so quiet and tasteful when it was just the two of us . . . Anyway, I asked my father if I could lodge at Weaverton's Upper Academy. It was there that I became interested in languages."

Gustie brushed some strands of hair off her face. "Ancient Languages are fascinating. They present whole new ways of thinking; they bear the traces of lost cultures and customs. Do you understand?"

"Not really," said Norling, "but go on."

"So after Upper Academy, my father agreed to pay so that I could enroll at the Scoláiríum, where I studied with Tutor Andreata, who knew twice as much as my master in Weaverton. I was happy at the Scoláiríum; I had a lover there, named Quinith, but I hadn't really decided whether to marry him when—"

"All this happened and upset your life, just as you were beginning it on your own terms," said Norling. "No wonder you feel such anger. Aye, this is all so unfair."

Gustie took a steadying sip of her cold tisane. She was not going to let an old lady's sympathy inside her armor.

"Let me tell you my story, child. Perchance that will help you understand why I cannot leave Sutterdam.

"When I was some years younger than you are now, really just a green girl, I married a man I fancied, a man who knew how to make me laugh. His kisses tasted like butter . . . Well. We used my inheritance from my parents to buy an inn on the Post Road. Awful hard work to run an inn, upstairs and downstairs all day and all night long, cleaning and fetching and cooking and smiling. My husband did little of the labor, arguing that chatting up the guests and pouring the drinks was his part of the enterprise.

"Anyways. It became an unhappy marriage—like so many. And when my husband saw a way out to another life, he grabbed it. Ran off with the barmaid and all our valuables.

"This was twelve years ago. I thought my life was over. I had no children, no husband, no coin, and not even any neighbors on that lonely road.

"And then my younger brother—aye, the man who lies suffering in the room yonder—said, 'Norling, come live with us.' More than being willing to take me in, he made it as if I was doing them a service. Then, of a sudden, I had a second chance, a true family. For many years I knew deep contentment. I've worked hard, but my labors helped those I loved.

"But then the Oros invaded." Norling listed for Gustie all the tragedies that had befallen her family. "So now you ask me to choose between my brother and more bloodshed? There is no choice. I will stay with Hartling. When he is hungry, 'twill be my food he eats. When he wants to talk, it must be to *me*, someone who knows the ghosts flitting in each room, yet can remember when this house overflowed with laughter. The best healer in the world can't give him what I can offer him."

"I understand," Gustie said, twisting her hair around her fingers. She had dismissed Norling as a boring old biddy, but she realized now that Norling's life had its own color and drama.

"But just because I'm going to stay here, doesn't mean I haven't been pondering on how best to help," said Norling. "I'm going to send *you* in my place. I've hatched a plan to lift the Occupation of Jutterdam, but these instructions are not for the faint of heart. You'll have trouble getting the citizens to follow them. Even Mother Rellia . . .

"Let me put it this way." Norling sat up very straight. "You will need every drop of that haughty, stubborn arrogance to see this through."

Gustie sat silent, refusing to rise to Norling's bait. Privately, she knew that her stubbornness and arrogance were what had kept her alive in Umrat's quarters.

Norling spoke again. "I've visited Jutterdam, but you lived there for some moons?"

"Yes," said Gustie. "My brigadier was originally stationed there."

"Good. Tell me everything you recall about the layout of the city. Oh, and fetch a piece of paper—tear a sheaf out of a book if need be—and a quill. Together we may be able to fashion a sketch that will serve."

The next morning Gustie set off on a mule with a limping gait. At the end of a week of tedious riding she came upon a Defiance roadblock four leagues south of Jutterdam. After a great deal of arguing with guards, Gustie succeeded in gaining a meeting with Mother Rellia.

Mother Rellia had made her headquarters in a farmhouse not far from the main road. It was merely a one-story building with a thatched roof, but over the years, with their growing prosperity, the owners had appended extra bedrooms in a rambling fashion. Around the central structure, hundreds of Free Staters camped haphazardly in the barn and the fields. Their clotheslines of drying garments festooned the yard like holiday decorations.

When Gustie finally gained entrance to the farmhouse's sitting room she realized that the light wheeze she had heard in Mother Rellia's breathing during their walk away from the Poison Banquet had worsened into a constant hack. Rellia, seated in a chair, could hardly speak for coughing, though the farmer's wife and grown daughters bustled around her with hot drinks.

For all her ill health, Rellia's eyes still shone brightly and she recognized Gustie. She looked avid when Gustie explained that Norling had sent her with a proposal.

"Is it a strategy to dislodge the Oros holding the Jutters captive?" she asked.

"Aye," said Gustie. "And having lived here for a year and seen the strength of the walled fortifications, I believe Norling is right. This is the only way."

"And what is it?"

Gustie unrolled their sketch on a table. The farm women moved Rellia's chair close and gathered round.

"The walls around Jutterdam stretch in three directions for over a league," said Gustie, pointing at the sketch. "They are high and thick. The Defiance cannot breach them. We do not have siege towers, ladders, trebuchets, or sufficient fighters. So a direct assault is out of the question."

Rellia coughed into a kerchief but nodded as if she'd already concluded as much.

"Jutterdam has a deep and large port, around here"—Gustie touched the place on the map—"which is why it has grown into such a great city and why it has been valuable to the Oros for shipping food to Oromondo. We need to send boats in on a dark night to see how many ships are still anchored in harbor. Can we do that?"

Rellia cleared her throat. "I would think so."

"Good. Well, Norling suggests that our people sink these ships."

A general cry of surprise arose from the other people in the room.

"Go on," said Mother Rellia.

"With the ships sunk, the Oros could not escape by sea. The only ways to leave Jutterdam would be through these two gates, Electors Gate and Kings Gate, both of which lead first to the Jutter Plain." Gustie indicated the place on her map. "The plain is this area here we've marked with the hatch marks—it's a flat and pretty meadow by the Jutter River. Before the occupation, the city folk used it for carnivals, fests, special markets, and such. My father brought me there once for a Solstice Fest.

"But *here,* we have the two bridges over the Jutter River: Electors Bridge, the newer, and Kings Bridge, the older one. Norling suggests, and I concur, that the best solution is to block the two bridges. I think we can do that; we—that is, the Defiance—should be strong enough to take and hold the bridges. Then we just keep ahold of these blockades."

"Why?" asked the farmer's wife with a frown.

"We'd box the Oros *into* the city. It's like a siege only from a little farther away. We don't let any farm carts pass. No foodstuffs."

The farm women looked confused, though Mother Rellia nodded.

Gustie clarified, "We starve them."

At these words, a woman carrying Mother Rellia another hot drink dropped it on the floor with a crash. The room grew still except for the sound of Mother Rellia's hacking.

When Mother Rellia regained her voice, she remarked, "You realize—Norling realizes—that while starving the Oros we would *also* be starving their ten thousand captives."

"Obviously. Though if any managed to flee the city we would let them through."

"Kind of us," said Mother Rellia, ironically. "What about those too old or injured or jailed by the Oros?"

"They will die," said Gustie, lifting her chin. She continued in a rush, "But however we proceed there will be deaths. If we tried to attack the city, how many hostages would the Oros kill? How many of our fighters would fall on the walls or gates? And if we attack we'd have no assurance of winning out in the end. We could all be wiped out—after all, their soldiers are much stronger and much better trained than ours. In laying implacable siege to the city, we could be sure of eventually killing or capturing *every single Oro* encamped there."

"Why couldn't they simply swim the Jutter and flank our bridge blockades?" pressed Mother Rellia, pointing to the river on the map.

"I lived with Oros for moons. Ask anybody: *Oros don't swim.* And the Jutter runs wide and deep here at its outlet. Even the bravest, most experienced swimmers would have a hard time getting across."

"That's true, Mother," echoed one of the farm women. "Why, in my day, the farm boys used to dare each other to swim the Jutter and the Nimuel boy drowned. Drowned dead. And those lads, they were good swimmers."

Rellia tapped her fingers against the empty mug she held in her hand. "Could we hold the bridges against determined strikes? As you say, the Oros are stronger, more numerous, and they have better weapons."

"But they don't have archers and we do. If we can lay our hands on enough bows and arrows, we'd have more than a chance," said Gustie.

"I have arrows, and we've been fletching hundreds more each day," said Mother Rellia with a tiny nod of satisfaction. "How long are we talking about? Jutterdam boasts many granaries and warehouses; wouldn't these keep them supplied?"

"Yes, mam," agreed one of the hangers-on. "There's blocks and blocks of 'em down by the harbor."

"I believe that most of the granaries are empty these days," Gustie argued. "The Oros have already sent those stores across the sea. It took them moons to drain our caches, but that was their first priority." She raised her chin even higher. "I concede, however, that an undercover expedition to confirm the state of their supplies might be wise."

"Suppose you're right—suppose that the Oros have precious little supplies left inside of Jutterdam. When they get hungry enough, what's to keep them from eating . . . ?" Mother Rellia couldn't finish the thought aloud.

"Our countrymen?" Gustie spoke without a quaver. "Nothing. They *will* butcher Free States women and children."

A woman in the room wailed, "My sister! My sister is trapped inside Jutterdam!"

"But what's the choice, Mother Rellia?" Gustie pressed on. "Allow the Oro army food, allow them to sail reinforcements into their harbor, allow them to spread out and assert control over more of the countryside again? Allow them to imprison, enslave, or burn us all? We've harried them until they've bottled themselves up in Jutterdam. If we can trap them there, *eventually* they will all die. Or surrender."

Mother Rellia closed her eyes, coughed into her kerchief a few times, and then opened them again.

"I will go down in history as a monster," she said.

"Not at all," said Gustie. "You will be remembered as the only person strong enough, clear-sighted enough, to save the Free States."

At that, Mother Rellia muttered something Gustie couldn't hear. "Excuse me, what did you say?"

Mother Rellia repeated, "My people come from the steppes of Melladrin. We are not faint of heart. The Stars will guide us." But all brightness had died in her eyes. She looked ancient and ill.

23

Salubriton

Time, food, and rest aided Phénix; she regained mobility.

She would have recovered more quickly if she slept more peacefully at night. Now that she was away from Healer's (or Restaurà's) protective aura, her nightmares, or rather a single, recurrent nightmare, plagued her again. In her sleep a red-eyed face—whether of man, bat, or wolf she couldn't say—laughed at her and taunted her. Once Hope shook her shoulders to wake her up, and Phénix gathered that she'd been thrashing and crying out.

As she became better acquainted with her housemates, she learned that the qualities that mattered most in a recovery house differed from those prized amongst the Raiders. The Raiders had focused on fighting skills, and then on bravery and self-sacrifice. In this circumstance, by contrast, the most appreciated trait was empathy. Phénix prized Damyroth above all her fellow lodgers because he could always read the pain in her face and invariably sought to ameliorate it or distract her. Everyone grew impatient with Lymbock, the jaundice patient, because he rarely pitched in with anyone else's care. And though they understood that the injury to Hope's psyche must have been severe, the fact that she walked by Sezirō without even noticing that he shivered with fever infuriated them all.

Tonight Phénix put off retiring to her bed and evil dreams. In the common room, Lymbock had rubbed her sore shoulder until he got bored; Phénix smoothed salve onto the raw tissue on the bottom of Damyroth's stump and offered Sezirō sips of lemon water. Hope sat unmoving where they'd placed her in a chair. Jitneye brought out a strange stringed instrument that was something smaller and more rounded than Phénix had ever seen before and strummed it. Phénix softly began to sing a common children's song that counted up to nine ducks and back. Although Jitneye often fumbled, Damyroth and Lymbock joined in.

Halfway through the song, tears started flooding down Hope's mute face. They all noticed but pretended not to. Phénix and Jitneye exchanged meaningful looks; purposely he kept playing and she kept singing children's songs until they had made it through all such songs they had in common.

When Hope and Phénix retired to their attic bedroom, Phénix lay on her back, listening to nighttime street noises of a busy city.

Phénix whispered to the gable, "Not so long ago, I spent time with a group of children. Their worlds had been turned upside down because most had lost their mothers. I haven't yet met a mother who's lost her children. Did something happen to your children, Hope?" She did not actually expect an answer.

"He killed them," said the woman in the bed next to hers, startling her with a voice rusty from disuse.

"Who killed them?" asked Phénix softly.

"My husband." She was silent for a long moment, and Phénix held her breath. "He killed my boy and my baby right in front of me."

Phénix gasped at the thought. "How? Why?"

A sniffling sound in the dark attic room indicated that Hope was crying again. "With his butcher's knife. Because he thought I was making eyes at a neighbor."

"Oh, Sweet Waters," whispered Phénix, as tears flooded her own eyes. "Did the guards arrest him? Hang him?"

She heard a muffled "No," as if Hope had her hands over her mouth.

"Why ever not?"

"Because after he cut the baby's throat, he smiled at me and cut his own."

"Oh, the Waters!" Phénix breathed. She could too readily imagine the gush of blood, the lifeless little bodies. Her heart ached for her roommate, who was now wailing full-out into her pillow. She thought of crossing the room to her, but speech itself was such a breakthrough that she didn't dare jeopardize this progress by adding touch.

When the sobbing abated a notch, Phénix asked the darkness, "What is your name? Would you prefer we call you by your real name?"

"'Hope' will do."

"May the Waters bless you, Hope," said Phénix, and she lay in her bed staring at the ceiling for a long time even after her roommate fell asleep, thinking about different varieties of pain.

All of Phénix's burns and incisions closed up. She had recovered sufficiently that she could walk the streets of Salubriton alone, though she found the experience unpleasant because, since she didn't carry a parasol, people looked through her, assuming she must be a low-class servant or a whore. In her strolls she found a bookseller not far from the Bread and Balm that offered old broadsheets from the other continents, but she had no ready money. She also hankered for different clothes, hair tonic, and other small items.

So she took the amethyst headband Arlettie had given her and carefully dislodged several of the smaller stones. Dame Tockymora accompanied her to sell the gems to make sure she got a fair price (though she asked for a 10 percent commission for her time). Phénix then bought herself two sets of rugged trousers and linen shirts similar to those she had worn as a stable manager in Slagos. She spent several sessions roaming cobblers' shops, finding a cobbler who would craft boots to her specifications. Finally, she purchased a belt and sheath for her dagger. When she strapped it about her waist, she sighed with relief.

Buoyed by her success, she walked to faraway shopping streets, looking to buy presents for her housemates with some of the money she had left over. She purchased a book to help Lymbock pass the time, a new frock for Hope, and a cheerful hand fan for Seziro. For Damyroth and Jitneye she bought bottles of local fruit juice. With water rationed, the juice was quite expensive, but she knew that after their exercises they grew thirsty, so this was a special treat.

She realized that the principle behind the recovery houses was the same one behind the Brothers and Sisters of Sorrow in Weirandale. In caring for others, you heal yourself.

She held her breath when she presented Hope with the new gown and was pleased to see her roommate eagerly change into it. These days Hope would talk to Phénix, their landlady, or the female healers if she had to, though she still shied away from any conversation with men. She fetched and carried as needed, but now that she could recall her own history she would not touch or allow male patients to touch her. The house rejoiced that she had made this much progress; her improvement lifted a weight off of all of them. Betlyna predicted that with time Hope's psychic injury would heal even more, though they were still supposed to watch her constantly.

By contrast, Lymbock never cracked the cover of his book. His yellow color worsened rather than subsided; his legs began to swell; he lost his appetite and often complained of pain in his belly. Meanwhile, Jitneye had grown strong enough to return to his home but he wheedled the apprentice healers to be allowed to stay in the recovery house because he would be so lonely in his own lodgings. "Heart Attack Number Four is waiting for me," he told Betlyna. "I'd rather not meet that wicked fellow all alone."

Next to Damyroth, Phénix became most fond of Sezirō. As she changed his bandages, washed, or fed him, he told her colorful stories about his adventures. He had sailed across all the seas, marveling at floating islands of ice and flocks of seabirds so dense they shut out the sunlight. He told her there were lands beyond Ennea Món, a concept that thrilled and frightened her.

"How did you wind up here?" Phénix asked him one day.

"Several of us signed on to a trade ship *Agfadorian*. When we stopped here the seamaster gave us shore leave and then put to sea in the night to avoid paying us what was due."

"How low!" Phénix exclaimed.

"Aye, but he got what was coming to him," Sezirō commented with a note of pride.

When he wasn't talking of his travels, he would boast of past duels with relish.

"Why did you fight?" she asked him one day.

"I fought to prove I was the best. Or I fought for honor."

"What does 'honor' mean to you?"

Sezirō was shocked by the question. "Honor means everything— do you not have honor in the Free States?"

"Well, yes. To act honorably would be not to cheat your customers. To keep your promises and such. But where I come from, most people are not eager to die for their honor."

"Ach, Fire Bird. Let me see if I can explain. In Zellia, few people own much land or big estates. Some rich people, it is true, own ships or shipyards . . . but that's another matter. What every man is born with is his own and his family's honor. You must prove your devotion to Ghibli. You must prove you are a man of your word. You must care for your family. And you must not allow someone else to show you disrespect or show you the coward. If you do so, you will lose face. And your face, your honor, is all you possess truly."

"Do women in Zellia fight for honor too?"

"Sometimes, yes. Though Zellish women are not as competitive as the men, they too train with swords and daggers and they will challenge anyone who tries to them dishonor. In Pexlia, our cousins with pink hair have a view idiotic of women's honor. They do not teach their women to fight. They think their women's honor lies in chastity, and they stone women who know pleasure." He made a spitting noise.

"What do the Zellish believe?"

"We believe that a woman's honor, like a man's, doesn't lie between her legs, but here." He laid his hand on his heart.

"How do you love with honor?"

Sezirō opened his eyes wide in surprise at her utter ignorance. "One is honest with one's bed partners. Once one has found the mate, one loves with the whole heart. One loves forever. In Zellia, a woman does not taunt men. She does not neglect the children or her family." He lowered his voice. "Lymbock's daughter, the daughter who has never come to fetch him, she is a woman with no honor."

"Are men expected to love so faithfully too? If Lymbock had a son, instead of a daughter, would you say *he* had no honor?"

"Indeed," said Sezirō. "The difference is if that son came to this door, I would run him through with my sword immediately. I swear, up from this couch I rise."

Phénix thought through these concepts as she poured Sezirō some cold willow bark tea and sat on a pillow next to his rocking chair.

"What if Lymbock's daughter doesn't come to fetch him home because Lymbock was cruel to her? I can imagine he was not a patient or loving father."

"Then, I should run Lymbock through with my sword to avenge her. To be the unloving parent is most dishonorable. But, alas, one cannot attack the ill. To do so would be to act without honor."

She laughed. "Sounds like the rules about honor are very complicated."

"Indeed. The purpose of life is to learn to live honorably in all situations."

He grabbed her hand and changed the subject. "It is very honorable, Fire Bird, to comfort a dying foreigner, just as honorable as taking a stranger into one's house."

Phénix smiled at him. "But I do not do it to build my reputation. I do it because it pleases me when you feel more comfortable."

"Even better." He pressed her hand. "Damselle, someday you will want to travel back to your homeland, no? This you must not do as a woman alone and young. You have jewels, money. You must hire the Zellish bodyguard. They are the fiercest fighters and the most loyal defenders. Promise me that this you will do. I die easier if I know you will be safe."

"What?" She recoiled a little at the prospect. "Sezirō, how can I find a Zellish bodyguard? How can I be sure that I am hiring someone skilled and loyal?"

"This is what you do, damselle. You go to the tavern called 'Shipmates' near the river. You ask for a man called Ciellō. You will remember—'Ciellō.'"

Scratching the burn scars on her neck, she asked, "How do you know that this 'Ciellō' would be the best bodyguard?"

Sezirō smiled a shark's grin. "Because he is the man who has killed me. He is very skilled."

"He may be a great swordsman, but I am your friend. Why would he be loyal to me?"

"You understand so little," Sezirō replied. "A Zellishman would not accept a commission unless he would be loyal. Also, he owes me a life. He will take this obligation with most seriousness. Promise me you will go to Shipmates and meet him? Promise me that, Bird of Fire."

Phénix could hardly refuse, especially when Seziro's condition worsened. Healer herself visited the Bread and Balm, trying to persuade him to return to the Healing Center so that she could cut out as much as possible of the black-and-green infected tissue that slowly spread poison through his body.

Seziro kissed Healer's hand but shook his head. He knew he was dying; he wanted to stay in the recovery house among his companions. Healer warned them that while an apprentice would visit every day, much of the care would fall on the other patients. "No easy slipping away here, I wager. He's young and strong: his body will fight for life."

The five others nevertheless agreed that Seziro should stay "at home." Even Hope nodded (though Tockymora looked none too pleased). The patients all decided to short themselves on their water rations so that they had more for Seziro's needs.

Although everyone helped, Phénix ended up becoming the dying man's primary attendant. His suffering grew terrible to behold; sometimes he writhed in agony. Yet he almost never complained.

Tired and anxious, she would sit by his side, marveling at his stoicism.

In a recovery house one learns about pain.

Seziro still had hours when he rallied and his housemates were able to give him sips of sweet lemon water while chatting quietly with him.

During one respite, Phénix asked, "How do you feel? I mean, are you frightened, do you have regrets, are you angry?"

"Frightened?" He made a scornful face as if he would reject such a dishonorable suggestion, but then he gave a crooked smile. "Frightened? A bit. Like a small boy who is to swim in the sea for first time. It looks so immense and I feel so tiny.

"I would be more frightened if I were deserted. To have friends by is everything."

Phénix commented, "They say that in the end, all persons die alone."

"That's as may be. But to suffer or to slide toward death all alone, *that* would be hard."

She stroked his hand.

"Not angry. I have lived many summers. I do not miss the growing old, the losing my teeth.

"What else. . . . Regrets? Ah, shall I tell you, Fire Bird, why I travel so?"

"Please."

"In my town there was a girl—Zorah her name. We go to school together, you understand? When we grow up, Zorah, she falls in love with me, but I, I—look elsewhere for the dance. Zorah decides to leave Zellia; she signs on to an oceangoing trader."

Sezirō's voice had grown husky so Phénix propped him up and offered him more sips of lemon water. He waved his hand when he was done.

"One day—that day I sail home from fishing to the harbor and I see Zorah—she leans over the side of *Winds of Trade.* I see her face—I really see it—for the first time." He looked off in the distance, as if again visualizing her face before him. "I know I make a mistake terrible. A mistake that dishonors both of us. Now, I search for her," he made an openhanded gesture, "everywhere."

Phénix's eyes had filled with tears during this story; it seemed immeasurably tragic that this Zorah would never know of his change of heart and his efforts to find her.

As the days progressed Sezirō could no longer talk and no longer fiddle with Phénix's hair. What pleased him most was for her to sing to him. He didn't care what she sang, so she pleased herself by choosing hymns of the Waters. The familiar melodies reawakened all her memories of Sister Nellsapeta, Stahlia, Wilim, and the small white church in Wyndton. The hymns appeared to comfort Sezirō; certainly, they comforted Phénix through these long, grim days.

In the afternoon about ten days after the prognosis, Seziro's eyes fluttered and his breath became even more labored.

"Hope! Fetch the others. Seziro worsens."

The housemates kept a vigil by his bedside in the quietest room the Bread and Balm had to offer. But the end did not come quickly: his strong heart refused to stop beating for another day.

Phénix was still holding his cooling hand and wiping tears off her face when Betlyna arrived.

"Do not grieve so," said Betlyna.

"Would you have me caper about?" Phénix snapped.

"No, damselle," Betlyna murmured to her, "but death is a release. When Restaurà can do no more, the Spirit grants the Ultimate Sleep. We must not fear death, because ofttimes it comes as a blessing."

The apprentice made arrangements for Seziro's body to be taken away for burial.

That night while laying out the dinner dishes, Dame Tockymora said, "I've reported the vacancy. We'll be getting a new guest soon. I do hope it's not another Zellishman. I'll never get the smell out of the bedding."

Dumbstruck, no one voiced a rebuke.

The next morning, Healer herself paid them a visit. After she checked on all the other patients' progress, she turned to Phénix.

"Might I have a word with you, damselle?"

"Certainly." Phénix led her into the inner courtyard, which, for the moment, they had to themselves.

"I wanted to warn you again about people who might be looking for you," said Healer. "I've heard renewed gossip."

"Thank you."

The older woman peered into her face. "You've not been sleeping well. Seziro's decline?"

Healer's concern undid Phénix's resolve to keep her negligible problems to herself, "That, and I have these terrible dreams that have clung to me ever since I was burned."

"What kind of dreams?"

"Dreams that my mind has been tainted. That if I were"—here she paused, but her intuition told her to trust Healer as she had trusted Gardener—"to use my full abilities, I'd find these abilities corrupted."

"I see. Come close to me, would you?" She held the younger woman's hands and peered closely into her face. "Always before, I saw something of a shadow in your eyes. I don't know how to describe it; it looked rather like a dark flame. But it's gone now."

"You could *see* it?" Phénix asked. Knowing that the taint was discernible to someone else meant so much to her.

"Aye. I mentioned this in the Healing Center. You might have been too weak to attend."

"But it's gone now? Are you sure? Are you totally sure?"

Healer took Phénix's chin and slanted her face in and out of the sunlight, staring at her intently. "Completely gone, I am certain. Have you done something different in the last weeks?"

"Nothing." Phénix shrugged. "I've done my exercises as well as I could while caring for our friend. I've walked less than I should, but I sang a great deal."

"Sang? Sang what?"

"Hymns of the Waters. They seemed to soothe Sezirō."

Healer tapped Phénix's cheek with gentle "how-can-you-be-so-stupid?" taps. "Water washes away any lingering taint or corruption, does it not? I would wager you will have more restorative sleep in the nights to come."

The next day, after a deep sleep, restlessness beset Phénix. She was eager to escape from this lodging, full of illness and suffering.

Healer had told her to stay close to the Bread and Balm, but she had gone shopping without incident.

Dame Tockymora gave her directions to the closest stable, which was named Vigor Hostelry. Phénix bypassed the office door and walked down the rows of stalls, overcome by the smell of horse and the animals' blows, stamps, and nickers.

The liveryman entered the stable with a bale of hay on his shoulders. Either her trespass made him surly or he was naturally so, because he made no effort to be pleasant. The hostelry generally rented horses for riding parties; someone who wanted to ride alone, he implied, was just an unprofitable nuisance.

"You're not from Salubriton, that's for sure," he said. "Where do you hail from, damselle?"

Though he'd used the polite term "damselle," Phénix didn't like the way he squinted at her. "I was born in the Free States," she said. "In Sutterdam. Does that change the weight of my coin?"

"You don't sound like any Free Stater I've met," he muttered. The man took her silver coin and hefted it in his palm.

"Oh, you're an expert on all the Free States accents, is that right?" Now this man irritated her, but she would not allow him to deprive her of a ride.

The only horse that the liveryman was willing to rent her for an afternoon was a stocky white mare he called Pillow. Phénix needed to use a mounting block to get to the horse's broad back because her arms were no longer strong enough to lift herself so high.

"Which way should I head to get to the countryside?" she asked the stableman.

"There's nothing there," he said. "Best to ride in one of our beautiful parks. We keep them green."

"Just point me the way."

Though annoyed at her insistence, the liveryman complied.

Phénix felt clumsy on the mare. The saddle was a foreign design without a cantle, and the leather was slippery. Also, this horse didn't come close to fitting her hips—her legs were spread too widely for comfort or to grip the mare's flanks. After only ten minutes her left shoulder and back started to ache fiercely. She started to regret this adventure.

My discomforts are real, but the true problem is that Pillow is not Cinders. She's indifferent to me. She's just a horse, plodding along with a rolling gait. And I am just like any other stranger she has had on her back. There's no sense of connection and rightness.

The horse stopped in her tracks and neighed loudly.

Hesitantly, Phénix fumbled to find the latch to the door to her Talent.

One be not indifferent to Your Majesty! cried the horse plaintively. *Thou art nay answering one!*

Ah! Forgive me, Pillow. I am out of practice; I had my mind closed. Do you really recognize me?

One may be overfed, but one be not stupid.

I am delighted to speak to you. Do you hear me without taint?

"Taint"? One does nay understand.

Like a mash that has sat too long, and when you eat it, it makes you sick.

Thy thoughts have no odor.

Ahhhh. I'd like to see the countryside beyond Salubriton. Do you know the best way to go?

Naturally. One may be heavy, but one be not stupid.

Phénix began a long conversation with the mare, asking her whole life history (which was not very unusual or action-packed), just for the delicious sensation of using her Talent. Her ability to converse flowed as easily as ever. And that the mare identified her filled an empty corner of her heart.

The buildings thinned out, and the city's hectic bustle fell away. Eventually Pillow swayed alone on a flat dirt road. The landscape was barren and mostly level, with a few small foothills in the distance and red rock formations scattered randomly. Ditches that might have been streams in wetter times were bone-dry. She passed a small pond that held only a cupful of dirty water at the bottom. Phénix saw no other travelers. She recalled what Damyroth had told her: Salubriton was situated on the edge of a thinly populated desert. The Wyes traveled by sea or river barge to other cities in the more fertile north of the country. Even though the inhabitants were accustomed to drought, this current dry spell was the worst in anyone's memory.

The greater distance she rode, the hotter and drier the air became. She wished she'd thought to bring a hat and some water. Rooks or Codek would have chastised her (with good reason) for riding out so unprepared.

She was almost dozing in the heat and the monotony of the landscape. All of a sudden, Pillow reared in panic and dumped Phénix *bang* on her rear on the dirt road. The horse galloped a ways back toward the city before stopping her headlong flight. The young woman was too astonished by this event to even think of conversing with the horse about what had frightened her so.

If anyone had been around to see, Phénix would have been mortified by her lack of skill. She couldn't recall ever being unhorsed before. She stood up, noticing that she was uninjured except for bruises on her seat, but feeling uneasy. She pulled her dagger from its sheath and looked in all directions.

In a few heartbeats, a tawny-colored catamount, which had been camouflaged by the dry grass until she moved, leapt onto the road in front of her.

Phénix regarded the mountain lion levelly. Perchance she should have been frightened, but the catamount gazed back at her with its yellow eyes, eyes a princella remembered from long, long ago.

You should not have frightened my horse, Phénix sent. *That was very rude.*

One wanted to meet thee, sent the catamount.

I didn't know that catamounts live wild in Wyeland.

Indeed. This be where we live.

Some live in Weirandale.

One knows nothing of that.

Why did you want to meet me?

One has a new litter of kits. Wilt thou bless them?

Certainly. Bring them out of hiding.

Phénix sat in the middle of the dirt road. Three young kits crawled out of a dry rivulet, scampered over to her, and crawled around her lap. Phénix rubbed their fat bellies, caressed their soft fur, and let them lick her fingers with their rough tongues. They tried to climb up her clothing with their claws to reach her face, but she disentangled them.

The female catamount stood nearby, casting proud glances. Then she addressed Phénix.

Why art thou here, Your Majesty?

Here in the road? Because you frightened my horse.

Here in this realm.

I've been recovering from serious injuries.

Thou dost not bleed; thou dost not limp; thou rides a horse.

Aye, I am somewhat better now.

Then why art thou here, Your Majesty?

Are you saying it is time to leave? Truly, female catamount, you are most insolent.

One believes thou hast duties elsewhere.

Phénix firmly moved the kits off her lap and stood up.

This audience is at an end, she told the animal. *Leave the area so that I can call back my horse.*

The catamount blinked at her challengingly. *Thou hast duties elsewhere,* she repeated. *The Waters ebb.*

I TOLD YOU TO GO! commanded Phénix. The cat rounded up her kits and slunk off toward the foothills. Phénix sat back in the dirt of the road.

That the catamount had been instructed by a Spirit to accost her, she had no doubt. Phénix saw no streams or greenery, but it didn't really matter if the Spirit had been Nargis, Vertia, Saulė, or one of the others. The point was that the cat had asked her to consider that question: "Why am I still here?"

Defensively she answered: *I'm here because this is the first day I've even ridden a horse. I'm here because this is the first day I've even known whether my Talent survived uncorrupted. I still need rest.*

True enough. But I'm also here because I'm afraid to leave. I don't want to abandon this new fellowship at the recovery house. I don't want to pull myself out by my roots once again.

She picked up a handful of road dust and let it sift through her fingers.

Yet this is not where I belong. This is not my soil.

I have played at being a wren, a kestrel, a finch, a skylark, and a phoenix. I can't keep putting off what I know I have to do. If I am not ready now, I will never be.

She brushed the dust off her hands, rubbed them clean on her dustcoat, then used her fingertips to wipe the sweat that had pooled under her eyes and on the sides of her nose. She then stood up and slapped the dirt off her seat.

I must journey to Cascada and claim the Nargis Throne alone. It's just taken this long for me to face it. Or, perchance, to be truly ready for it.

Pillow came to her whistle, full of apologies. Remounting posed a problem, but Cerúlia found a rock that she could scramble onto and then reach the horse's stirrups.

Take us back to your stable, Pillow, she ordered. *No, I am not angry with you.*

On the long ride back, Cerúlia shifted in the uncomfortable saddle, trying to relieve her aching back. Eventually Pillow brought her back to the outskirts of Salubriton. Twilight fell, and a cooling breeze rolled in from the direction of the riverfront. The streets quieted, and lantern light glowed from interiors.

Cerúlia decided that tomorrow she would visit Shipmates tavern. A bodyguard would not really help her with her major task, but he might make the journey home less anxious. She should not scruple to use the gifts the Spirits had given her, such as her Talent, or the dagger and jewels that came from her uncle, Prince Mikil.

Besides, she had promised a dying man she would consider a bodyguard, and she wanted to prove that she was a woman of honor.

24

Cascada

Nana knew that the princella was still alive. First, because the two Fountains, the one in the courtyard and the one in the Throne Room, kept flowing (even if less vigorously). Second, because at the confrontation at Moot Table Lautan's Agent had said that the Spirit of the Sea had saved her from Pozhar's Magi.

So Nana bided her time, obeying Nargis's orders and trying to keep tabs on conditions in the palace and around the realm.

The chamberlain who had taken over after Martza was fired (because the soup was not hot enough at an after-theater dinner), was a man named Vilkit. Regent Matwyck had wooed him away from the duchy manor of Woodsdale: he had no previous experience with the palace. Vilkit struck her as smart and ambitious, smart enough to know that Nana, as one of the longest-serving staff members, had crucial information that would be helpful to him. So he treated her with a certain oily respect, which she found both flattering and off-putting.

This week Vilkit had ordered a massive inventory of the palace linens and had asked Nana to supervise this task for the most precious chambers, the royal rooms and the second-floor guest rooms. And she'd told him she'd be happy to do so, once she returned from visiting a sick friend in Cascada.

Brother Whitsury, Nana's ally among the Brothers of Sorrow, had met her at the Courtyard of the Star, and together they'd hired a carriage to take them to the feedlots on the far west outskirts of Cascada. As they disembarked at the third business, Nana shuddered at the too-familiar smells of cattle. But she also brightened at the sight of the silhouette she sought: Pontole, one of Queen Cressa's Shields.

Fortunately, at the moment he worked in a paddock of some thirty cattle alone.

"Nana!" he cried, putting down his bucket. "What are you doing *here*? If you wanted to see me, why didn't you send for me?"

"Ah, Shield Pontole! 'Tis so grand to see you! Obviously, I wanted to speak away from the palace."

"So you found me out, clever mittens. This is my brother's lot." His arm gestured over their surroundings. "I've been working here since I returned. But my plan has always been to put in for a position as a guard for a trader's caravan. Pay's better, and that would get me away from crowding my brother's family, now that they've got even more mouths to feed. I guess I've been a lazy cuss; somehow I've never taken the step."

"But if you went off with caravans, wouldn't you be sent long distances?"

"Of course. Their wagons crisscross the duchies. But I don't mind the traveling life. Might help me forget everything I want to forget."

Whitsury spoke at this point. "I find that I can't ever leave my troubles behind me. Pesky things; they tag after me wherever I go."

Pontole put down his bucket and slapped some cattle on their haunches to get them to move out of the way. He crossed to the split-rail fence.

"Shield Pontole, let me introduce you to Brother Whitsury; he's the head of the Abbey of Sorrow here in Cascada."

"My honor," said Pontole, looking at his dirty hands and deciding not to offer them to shake. "Do you mean, Brother, that I can't ever escape the picture of Kinley dying on the deck? Kinley, she was a mate and a swell fighter. Or my guilt at not being with the rest of the fellows in the last sea battle? I know it's crazy, but I keep imagining that I could've helped, that I could've saved someone."

"Time will help. Time and drinking Nargis Water," said Whitsury.

"It's been a lot of years already, Brother. If time would help, you'd think it woulda done so by now. But I haven't tried the Waters—I haven't really felt worthy. . . ."

Nana spoke. "But you've no cause to feel guilt, because Queen Cressa sent you home with the horses."

Pontole spread his hands and then made a fist and tapped his chest. "I understand that in my mind, but I still feel that I should've been with my mates and my queen."

"What if," Nana dropped her voice and spoke with great care, "I was to tell you about ways to serve Queen Cressa still?"

Pontole ducked through the fence crossbeams so that he now stood on their side. Forgetting his soiled hands, he reached for both of Nana's hands.

"Nana! The princella!" he said in an excited whisper. "Do you remember the day Seena and I went riding with her? I think of it all the time. All the time! Have you found her? I would give my life to help the princella!"

Nana smiled at his enthusiasm. "Nay, Pontole, I don't have the princella hidden away. But I know she'll be coming back, and when she does she is going to need our assistance."

"That's for sure," he said. "My brother's wife, some nights she reads me the broadsheets—they are full of stories about what a wonderful regent Lord Matwyck has been. Methinks he's got the writers by the shorthairs. And those statues of his ugly face that have been showing up more places . . . It's a wonder he hasn't put his likeness atop the Fountain! And the rumors floating about, saying that anyone who even talks about the princella had better shut his trap or else. Has something changed, this last year?"

"Yer a shrewd customer, Pontole. I've noticed this too. My guess is the death of his lady-wife has allowed the coxcomb to strut more.

"Pontole, do you know the whereabouts of the other two shields who came back with you?" Nana asked.

"Sergeant Yanath and Branwise?" Pontole shooed away a horsefly. In the distance two other workers came out of a barn and Pontole waved at them.

"Aye."

"Branwise has fallen into his cups. He does odd jobs and drinks away the money. I see him quayside, outside whatever tavern that day offers the strongest drink for the least coin."

"And Yanath?"

"Yanath got married. Imagine that! A widow woman with two sons and fifteen acres. He spends most of his days hitched to a plow and his nights chasing varmints away. I see him now and again. He invited me to the farm for Harvest Fest. Actually, it's not very far from the city. 'Twas so grand to spend the holiday with him. I wondered if I'd be in the way, but his missus was right cordial to an old pal and made me feel ever so welcome."

"Are they still loyal to the throne?" Nana asked as she lifted a boot to inspect the bottom.

"Nana! How can you ask that? Of a surety."

Whitsury had a practical streak. "How are their fighting skills, Pontole? For that matter, how are *your* skills?"

"We all hung up our swords when we returned. That was somethin' like nine summers ago. We'll be rusty for sure. And if Branwise has the shakes . . ."

Nana turned to Whitsury. "Can we even trust a drunkard? Wouldn't he sell us out for a pitcher of brew?"

"In his day Branwise was a great swordsman," Pontole put in eagerly. "Water's sake—what a fighter! Better than me, for sure. Couldn't we give him a chance? Something to sober up for, something to live for?"

"I'd like to see 'em both before I decide," Nana said slowly. "Pontole, forget the caravan jobs; stay in the capital, even if you change positions or move lodgings. You can always reach Brother Whitsury at the abbey near the Fountain. Keep in touch with him and always tell him where to find you. If you get Branwise sobered up and get Yanath to come to town, Whitsury will arrange for us five to meet. In the meantime, polish the rust off yer sword, restring yer bow, and lose that roll of lard on yer belly."

"Nana! Hey, you call to mind my old captain. He wanted us all to stay trim. Are nursemaids now soldiers?"

Nana chuckled. "Takes a lot of backbone to handle princellas. And everything has turned topsy-turvy these days."

"What would you have me tell Yanath and Branwise?" asked Pontole. Despite his soiled work clothes, the man already held his back straighter.

"Keep me and Brother Whitsury out of it for the nonce," said Nana. "The Lord Regent is always sniffing around to find out what I am up to, and General Yurgn tries to root out every Royalist. But I'm hoping they may just have forgotten about you three. So tell yer fellows this: while you was praying at the Nargis Fountain for the souls of the departed shields, Nargis spoke to you."

Pontole's mouth fell open in awe. "What did the Spirit tell me?"

"What else? Nargis said, ''Tis time to prepare for the return of the queen.'"

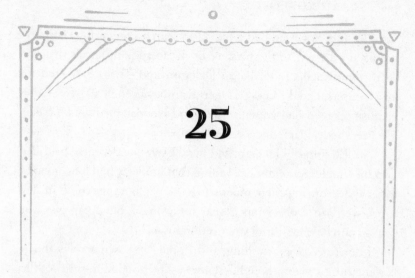

25

Sutterdam

On top of his happiness at finding Hake as hale as could be expected at Olet's Olive Oil and Spicery in Pilagos, Thalen felt great relief in shrugging off some of the burden of decision-making onto his brother's muscular shoulders. True to his word, Hake was able to arrange passage for the surviving Raiders and their two Free States quartermasters, Quinith and himself, home to Sutterdam on a ship that was slated to depart in five days.

Thalen left the decision about the horses to Hake, who decided to sell them to the livery stable to spare them another long, cramped voyage. Thalen felt no regret, because Brandy reminded him of Adair, who reminded him of Skylark; Cloves reminded him of Eldo, who reminded him of Skylark. . . . Every damn horse reminded him of Skylark, or of someone else who had gotten killed following his lead.

Two days before they were to embark, Eli-anna knocked on the door of the quartermasters' office. Most of the Raiders had assembled there to pick through the stores of supplies Hake and Quinith had gathered for clothing or weaponry they needed to replace. (Cerf and Quinith, however, had gone off to search Pilagos for Pemphis's kin or any answer to the mystery of the fortune in jewels that had been found in his saddlebags.) Dalogun and Tristo hankered for new trousers; Fedak, a new dagger; Kambey needed all new clothes because his own had gotten so torn and bloodstained; and Thalen, like everybody, wanted a new neck drape.

"Ah, Eli-anna," Hake greeted her. "Everyone decent?" he called over his shoulder, not understanding that modesty had long gone by the wayside during their moons together. "Come in, come in. I'm sorry, we didn't collect much gear for women, but I can give you coin to purchase anything you need in town."

"I don't need new clothing, and I prefer my own arrows. There is something I want, though," she said. She nodded toward Jothile, who wore a new hat that Kran had insisted he try on. "You should take that, Jothile. It suits you." Jothile came close to smiling at the compliment.

"Name it," said Thalen, who was sitting on a chair trying on new boots. "I'd lay the riches of the Green Isles at your feet."

Eli-anna paused until everyone looked at her expectantly. Thalen felt a premonition the split second before the words came out of her mouth.

"I want to go home."

"Eli-anna, no!" exclaimed Fedak. "What would we do without you?"

"You're our best archer," said Wareth, dropping the shirts he'd been sorting through onto the floor.

"Eli?" said Tristo. "Have we done something wrong? Something to offend you?"

Thalen felt her gaze rest on him. If *he* asked her to stay, he thought she might relent. But he felt she might want something from him that he couldn't give, certainly not now, and maybe not ever.

Kran went down on one knee. "Marry me, my marvelous Mellie maiden, and always protect my back."

Everyone was stunned, because no one knew how serious Kran was. After a moment of silence, Eli-anna took this as a joke and started laughing. "Someone else will have to protect your back. I'd as lief marry an aurochs.

"Besides," she turned from Kran to the whole room, "you'll all be fighting to protect your homeland. The Free States is not *my* home." Very softly she repeated, "I want to go home. Eldie is there and my mother."

"Even though you'd have to sail on a ship again?" asked Tristo. "And this time, without us?" He pointed at Thalen and himself.

"Even so," she said.

Thalen cleared his throat and stood up. "I understand, Eli-anna. We will grieve to lose both your bow and yourself, but we will rejoice at the thought of your reunion with Eldie. We will think of you often, riding under the Lattice of Stars . . . with gratitude, pride, and comradeship."

"Fuck, Commander," said Fedak, "you put it that way, you're going to make me cry." And he walked over to wrap Eli-anna in a hug, a hug that Jothile joined from the other side. Dalogun and Tristo piled on so that Eli-anna was enfolded in Raider arms. When they finally let go, Kran insisted on a hug of his own and he kissed the top of her head with great tenderness. Thalen wondered if the proposal had been serious after all.

"If this is what you want, I'll get to work immediately on finding you passage," said Hake.

Dalogun broke in, "We gave Eldie a bunch of our horses—can you claim one and make it your own? I'd like to think of you on one of our gang. And if I get some sugar lumps, could you give them all treats from me?"

Bidding farewell to Olet caused Thalen no pain, because Olet was so effusively happy that their mission had succeeded and so (deservedly) proud of his role in the expedition. He turned the goodbye supper into a joyous fest. "Islanders don't like to boast," Olet remarked, "but we do give the best parties."

Eli-anna's ship back to Metos wouldn't leave for another week. So the next morning Eli-anna, weighed down with a bag of sugar and two bridles decorated with silver and jade jewelry that the Raiders' treasury had bought as gifts for the Mellie sisters, stood with Olet on the dock to see the Raiders off when they departed Pilagos on *Island Voyager*. The Raiders waved their hats goodbye as the *Voyager*'s sailors rowed the ship out of harbor. Soon the slim figure standing next to the heavyset man vanished from view.

"We'll never see her again," Tristo said to Thalen, his voice filled with misery.

"That seems likely," Thalen admitted. "Life is full of sorrowful partings. At least we got to say farewell and we know that she is hale and following her own stars. Take comfort in that."

It was lucky that *Island Voyager* turned out to be a more spacious ship than *Song*; the winds turned against them, and the ship sat becalmed for days at a time. Since all the Raiders had fallen slack, Kambey made use of the time by instituting sparring drills on deck, especially for those who had been injured. Their activity provided great entertainment for the Green Isles sailors, who began betting on the fencing contests.

When *Island Voyager* finally slipped into the harbor at Sutterdam, Thalen rushed to the prow, eager to survey his own home. The city that stretched before him looked battle-scarred but still basically intact; the Oros had wreaked less damage on buildings and bridges than he had feared. Another positive sign was that lots of countrymen were out and about this midday.

Many of those people thronged at the wharf, shouting and cheering, when their ship docked.

"What's all this fuss about?" Thalen asked Quinith, lowering his brows.

Quinith looked at him as if he'd lost his reason. "When did you become dense? They are cheering for the Raiders who saved their country. They are cheering for *you*! You're a national hero."

Thalen pulled a face at such a preposterous notion. "But how did they even know the Raiders are on this ship?"

"I sent word on a fishing boat the minute Hake booked *Island Voyager*. And I gather that harbor lookouts can see ships a good while before they dock, and they spread the word we'd been sighted."

Thalen turned on his friend, eyes flashing with anger. "Why would you do such a fool thing?"

"But Thalen," Quinith protested, puzzled and hurt, "isn't it right, isn't it proper, to acknowledge what you've done? What your men have done? What Hake and I have done?"

"You don't understand," said Thalen. "I'm not proud of it. Any of it. You're celebrating death and murder."

Voyager tied up and lowered a gangplank. The crowd's cheering redoubled when the Raiders started to disembark. Fedak and Wareth played to the throng, doffing their hats and bowing. Jothile looked frightened by the uproar, so Kran draped his arm around his neck.

When Thalen overheard Dalogun say to Cerf in wonderment, "Are they really cheering for *us*?" he realized that even if he found the spectacle unwarranted, it might lift the hearts of his fellows.

For himself, he just wanted to slip away as soon as possible. But people in the crowd recognized him.

As he trod down the gangplank, his hat pulled low over his face, shouts rang out.

"There he is!"

"That's him!"

"I see him."

"I went to lower school with him."

A chorus of voices shouted, "Commander Thalen. Tha-len,

Tha-len, Tha-len. Hooray for Thalen and the Raiders! Thalen and his Raiders!"

When Thalen reached the wharf, men thumped him on the back, little girls pressed flowers in his hands, and old women clung to him.

"Help!" he shouted over heads to Kambey.

Kambey let the crowd lap its waves of excitement against the commander for a few more minutes, then barked an order. The Raiders pulled themselves away from the pretty women offering kisses and regrouped, forming up around Thalen and Hake in a protective box. Thalen pushed Hake's chair, and the Raiders marched him through the throngs of shouting folk toward Sutterdam Pottery.

"You're taller than me," Hake turned around in his chair and called out to his brother. "Keep your eyes out for Pallia, would you?"

Thalen watched for his brother's former girlfriend, but he didn't spot her. When they reached the factory, he ordered the gates closed behind them and sighed relief at being out of the crush.

"Those of you who have family, friends, or favorite taverns in Sutterdam, consider yourselves free to go visiting. We will meet here tomorrow at this time. Those of you who don't, just cool your heels a few minutes while I check on the old place."

Kran called out, "I'm buying the first round!"

"Hold a seat for me," said Cerf. "I've a friend I want to look for first."

Fedak, Kambey, Kran, and Cerf strode off, either genuinely in high spirits or faking excitement to buoy one another.

Thalen and Hake entered the workshop. The building echoed emptily to their calls. A quick search showed signs of occupancy, but none very recent.

Accordingly, now with fewer of the people in tow, Thalen, pushing Hake's chair, led the way over the familiar bridges—Silversmiths, Tailors, and Millers—that led from the pottery to Lantern Lane.

Norling pulled the door open before he could knock. "At last!" she cried. "Hartling, our boys have come home!" In an undertone she warned her nephews, "He's a broken man."

"So are we all, Teta, in body or mind," muttered Thalen, pulling her slight body into an embrace. "What a marvel to see you. Are *you* all right?"

"I'm much better now," said Norling into his chest.

Thalen left the other Raiders to deal with getting Hake's chair up the half flight of stairs and hurried to find his father.

Hartling lay on a bed in the room on the first floor that they had originally added on for his aunt, curled up in a fetal position. His eyes were open, but he looked completely different because of his broken nose and broken teeth. Thalen missed the calm and kindly face he'd known so well.

"Pater," Thalen whispered. "Pater, do you know me? It's Thalen." Thalen began to pat his father's left hand; the right one looked twisted unnaturally. "It's Middle. I've been away, but I've come home now. And I've brought Eldest with me."

"Eldest with me," the man on the bed repeated.

"Yes. Pater, don't you know me? It's Thalen."

"Thalen," he repeated without comprehension.

"Yes. I am going to pick you up and take you to see Hake."

Thalen had built up so much muscle, and his father had wasted so grievously, that Thalen lifted Hartling without strain. He set him down as gently as one would treat a china doll near Hake's wheel-chair in the front room.

"Hake!" cried Hartling. "Hake, my Eldest!" He recognized his son, but he didn't appear to see the wheeled chair.

"Aye, Pater?"

"Give your old man a hug, Son. It's been a long time, I think."

Hake leaned over to pat his father's ruined face.

"You're going to be fine, Pater. Wait and see."

"Where's Youngest?" asked Hartling. "Middle is around here

somewhere, but where is that young scamp? That boy is always causing me heart-pain. Throwing away his talents for excitement."

"I know," said Hake. "Harthen always causes me heartache too."

Tristo and Norling disappeared into the kitchen, jabbering excitedly about ingredients and dishes. Hake and Quinith took charge of organizing the household for so many visitors, asking Dalogun and Jothile to throw open every window to disperse the sickroom closeness, sorting out sleeping arrangements, and setting the men to fetch extra water and firewood.

"Now that I look at you (and myself), we all need serious scrubbing before we're fit to sit at a civilized table," Quinith commented; thus, a relay of washtubs became the next order of business.

Thalen left them to such labors. He took the staircase two steps at a time up to the room that had once belonged to his mother and father. He knew his mother wasn't there, but he had to see for himself. Of course the room sat empty. Thalen walked about; he picked up her pincushion from her sewing basket. He lingered over her hairbrush, recalling all the times she'd nagged him to tie his hair back. He wondered at himself, that as a lad, he'd often balked at such a simple way to please her. Now, he brushed his own hair with her brush and retied his leather tie. When Tristo came to search him out for midmeal, he was sitting on the bed fingering the silk petals of the fake flowers in her prized traveling hat.

They had set Pater at the head of the table and Norling had slipped on his businessman's wig, which restored a semblance of his former appearance. Norling's food lifted everyone's spirits. During the meal she told them all she knew about Gustie and the Poison Banquet, Sailmakers Bridge, and the Siege of Jutterdam.

"That's your Gustie!" said Thalen to Quinith.

Quinith avoided his gaze. "Well, I'm not sure she's *mine*. It's been a long time. Do the bonds from the Scoláirium last through . . . I worry we're not the same people anymore."

"I understand," said Thalen, both because he could imagine Quinith's feelings and because he wanted to make up for his harsh words on the ship. "But we can still be proud of her, right?"

"Indeed."

During this exchange Tristo got a look in his eyes that made Thalen harken back to the Mead Test. "Excuse me, Mam Teta Norling," Tristo said with his glowing, innocent smile, "but I don't understand. *How* did Gustie know about the Defiance fighters at the wheelwrights' shop?"

Then, bit by bit, Norling's own position in the Defiance began to come clear. Whenever Tristo suspected she was playing down her role or leaving out crucial parts of the story he was on her like a cat shaking the truth out of a wayward kitten.

"Norling!" exclaimed Hake. "Why you old fraud! You fake! You imposter! All those years you pretend to be just a sweet, puttering old lady, and now it comes out that *you* are the greatest tactician in the Free States! It must be from Teta, Thalen, that you inherited your skills."

Norling waved away Hake's compliments, but Thalen could tell she was pleased. He examined her face, noticing all the new lines and the way the skin on her neck and eyelids now sagged. These deep creases reminded him that as arduous as their mission into Oromondo had been, those left behind had also suffered.

"You're really the one the crowds should have hailed, Teta. Do the people know of your heroism?"

"Everyone did what she could, each in her own way," said Norling. "It's the combination that makes the difference."

"I'm so glad we got to see you before we leave," Thalen said, entwining his fingers through hers.

"*Leave?*" she said, her voice rising through the word. "You just got here. Where are you going?"

"Teta, we must ride to help the Defiance in Jutterdam. Our work isn't done until all of the Free States are liberated."

Norling didn't argue, but she blinked fast and looked down.

"*I'm* staying with you, Teta," said Hake. She threw him a quick smile.

The gaiety had fled the table. The Raiders felt the change and looked at one another, fidgeting a little in discomfort.

"I'd better get busy," Quinith announced, rising.

"Where're you off to?" asked Hake.

"If we're riding to Jutterdam tomorrow we need horses, lackwit. Dalogun, you want to come with?"

"Half a tick," said Dalogun, standing, but downing his last swallows of ale.

"Jothile?" Quinith invited.

But Jothile shook his head. This wasn't surprising; he always felt safer staying physically close to Thalen. Despite their care, Jothile hadn't fully recovered from the terror of the woro attack in Iron Valley. He twitched nervously, and a loud noise would send him scurrying for cover.

"We need battle-ready cavalry horses," Thalen said.

"I don't know how you'll find good horses left in town," put in Norling. "The city is picked clean."

"Try the neighborhood near Horse Traders Bridge," Hake suggested.

This flurry of suggestions and commentary annoyed Quinith. "Oh, shut up, all of you. Just loll at ease and prepare to be grateful when we ride back. Come on, Dalogun. Let's go scour the city and shake out all the hidden horseflesh. I've got a bag full of jewels going to waste in my belt."

When every serving plate was scraped as bare as a flock of crows left a cornfield, Hake suggested, "Let's put Pater in his chair by the hearth and get him his pipe."

Thalen thought this was a bad idea: it would only make the contrast between their father of old and the wreck the Oros had left in their wake more glaring. He held his tongue, though, knowing he had no standing to question his brother's expertise in coping with the effects of life-changing injuries.

Tristo assumed the chores of Youngest, fetching the pipe and helping Hartling pack and light it. Pater was not accustomed to grasping a pipe in his left hand. But he puffed a few times and grunted with satisfaction at the familiar aroma.

When he looked around, his glance fell on Thalen, and this time, to Thalen's great relief, recognition dawned in his eyes.

"Middle! I'm so glad you've come home for the holidays. I've lost track. Which fest is this? Are they still treating you well in that school of yours?"

"Yes, Pater," said Thalen.

"Truly? You look thin and ill dressed." Hartling looked at him suspiciously. "Or as if you've been sick." His mind wandered. "Your mother's been pining for you so, Middle," he chided. "Have you seen her yet?"

"Yes, Pater," Thalen replied. "First thing."

"Where is she?" Hartling asked, turning his head this way and that, obviously confused. "I look for her . . . I call her . . ."

"Oh, you know Mater; she moves so fast. She's around here somewhere. Everywhere," said Hake, with an airy gesture.

Thalen had been so consumed by his own grief over his shattered family that he hadn't thought about his brother's; their eyes met for a moment, and Thalen realized that in all of Ennea Món only Hake shared exactly his own enraged and bitter joy at being home in Lantern Lane again.

26

Cascada

Gunnit bid farewell to his friends amongst the crew of *Island Trader* and settled his heavy rucksack on his back. The third mate had already given him detailed directions to the Courtyard of the Star and the Nargis Fountain. Although he again experienced the funny sensation of adjusting his balance to solid land, he headed up the hill with a mixture of nervousness at being in another strange land and confidence that the Spirits would guide his path.

The Fountain pulsed into an evening sky fading into pink. Gunnit stared at the arcing sprays and rainbows of mist, marveling at the sight for a long time. The last vendors closed up their carts and started to disperse. Soon he found himself alone except for a herd of begging children and a number of mean-eyed guards.

Since Saulė's Mirror had shown him at the Fountain, Gunnit thought perchance the Fountain would tell him what to do next, but he heard only the sound of the water and the sniffles of the sickly children. As the last of the sunlight faded and the moons rose, he turned around to seek food and shelter for the night; one of the

Green Isles sailors had recommended a particular lodging house as a cheap but safe place for a boy on his own.

But as Gunnit walked in the direction of one of the avenues heading away from the Courtyard, he felt a sudden discomfort in his left arm where the Bracelet rested. He cautiously took one more step, and the Bracelet tightened so much it hurt. When he turned back toward the Fountain the stricture loosened, allowing his blood to flow normally.

Each avenue Gunnit tried, the gold circlet squeezed him, telling him to desist. Finally, he understood he was supposed to stay by the Fountain.

Gunnit took off his rucksack. He had a decent supply of ship's biscuits inside; he ate one with gulps of Fountain water to wash down its dry crumbles. As he munched, the ragged children cautiously crept close to him. He took out two more biscuits and offered one to a tangle-haired girl and the other to a hollow-cheeked boy. They snatched the offerings from his outstretched hands like feral dogs. But later, the girl returned, offering him a scrap of dirty blanket, which Gunnit accepted gratefully. He put on his extra shirt and threw the blanket around his shoulders against the cold. He leaned against the Fountain balustrade and dozed uncomfortably until morning.

He woke up to a clamor of young voices. "Did you bring us anything today?" Opening his eyes, he saw a stout older woman with a white lace collar and a blue feather on her cap.

The ragamuffins crowded round her basket as she pulled out scraps of food to feed them. She clucked over them while doing so. "Dovey, you've got to keep that cut clean, or it will fester. No, son, don't short yourself to feed your brother: I've got enough for all today. Sweetie, let me see if your eye is better? Ah, much better, right? Now don't forget to keep using them drops I got you from the Sorrowers."

When her basket was empty, the children dispersed and the

woman came to sit on the Fountain's edge. The Bracelet gave Gunnit a sharp pinch then release, painful enough to make him jump to his feet.

"Excuse me. Dame?" He moved to stand in front of her. "I'm Gunnit. I wonder if I am supposed to meet with you?"

The woman looked at him in astonishment. "Meet with me? I don't understand you, boy. I'm sorry, I've already handed out all the food I carried today."

"I'm not hungry—well I am, but that's not the point. I'm not one of those kids. I'm from Alpetar. They tell me I've been 'kissed by the Sun.'"

He rolled up his sleeve to show her Saulė's Bracelet. She traced the golden circle and stared at the dangling Sun charm, then quickly pulled his sleeve down.

"Who sent you?" she asked with narrowed eyes.

"Gardener and Peddler," Gunnit answered. "And the Bracelet itself made me stay here to wait for you."

"How did you know who I am?" she asked.

"I don't know who you are; I just know I can trust you. Who *are* you, dame?"

"I'm Water Bearer. Why did Gardener and Peddler send you to me?"

"Because I'm brave," Gunnit answered, pulling himself tall and puffing out his chest (just a little). "Because I can do things they can't. Because I'm awfully fond of Finch. She saved us after the Oros raided Sweetmeadow, and I want to protect her."

"*Sweetmeadow? Finch?* Lad, are you addled? Who're you talking about?"

"They tell me she has a lot of names. But if you know Gardener and Peddler, you should know who I mean."

The woman patted her own chest with a fluttering hand a few times and blew out a loud puff of air. "Ah, glory be to Nargis. An ally would be so useful. Especially one brave and favored by a Spirit." She smiled and held out her hand. "I'm really called 'Nana.'"

"Gunnit." They shook hands.

"Do you have parents, Gunnit?"

"I have a ma, back in Cloverfield. Dame Saggeta and Aleen promised to watch out for her. But I'm here on my own."

"Are you, now? Kind of young to be on your own, ain't you?"

"No," Gunnit contested. "Gardener said I'm grown beyond my years."

"I'm sorry you had to grow up so fast," said Nana. "Happens all the time"—she nodded toward the group of ragamuffins—"but it's always a pity to miss a childhood."

She cocked her head to one side. "I'm trying to think of a way to keep you close to me so we can work together. Are you good with horses?"

"Not really, Dame Nana. I learned how to ride, sort of. But I don't know much about caring for them or training them. I'm very good with goats."

"Unfortunately, we don't have any goats at the palace." She paused and looked him up and down. "You're a likely-looking boy, though. Or would be, dressed up. I might be able to convince Vilkit to take you on as a page." Her voice got lower, as if she was thinking aloud, and she tapped her lips with two fingers. "He owes me for ferreting out that silverware thief. Aye, a page boy actually would be even better than the stables, because then you'd be inside the palace."

"Inside the palace, Dame Nana?" said Gunnit. "Why would I want to be there?"

"Because that's where I work."

"Wouldn't everybody be able to tell I'm unlettered? That I don't know anything about fancy palace customs?"

"We train our pages; no one would expect much of a newcomer but listening hard and a smart hop when you get an order. And the palace, well—for sure—that is where 'Finch' will be coming, when she returns."

"When will she be coming?"

"I don't know," said Nana, suddenly quite cross but not—Gunnit guessed—at him. "Here I am, here you are, both of us favored by the Spirits, and neither of us knows the only damn thing worth knowing. If you ask me, 'tis a damn foolish way to run things."

She shook her fist at the Fountain. "You keep yer Agents in the dark and they're liable to bump into things! Do you hear me, Nargis?"

"I serve the Spirit of the Sun, Dame Nana." Gunnit loyally stood up for Saulė. "It makes light and sends darkness away. Gardener told me that Alpies are known for their 'Optimism.'" He pronounced the last word carefully, proud of having learned it.

"That's right," she smiled. "Don't mind me; I'm just old and kind of fretful. But the Spirits don't give us sort any Magic; they just give us knowledge. Course I guess that *knowing* is a kind of Magic, but then they dole even that out like misers. Sometimes that makes me mad."

Gunnit was trying to puzzle out her meaning when she spoke again.

"You hungry, Gunnit? Silly question, I know. What growing boy ain't hungry? And then I've got to think of how to introduce you to Vilkit. . . . Can hardly be a country cousin with that shock of yellowish hair.

"Tell you what. Let's stop by the abbey. I'll give you a close hair-cut so it's not so noticeable. And there's someone there I want you to meet. I can already foresee how having you to run messages between us might be a Spirit-send."

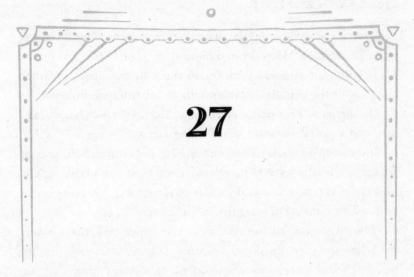

27

Salubriton

Cerúlia's body ached after her ride into the barren countryside, and she would have loved a long massage, but she didn't allow herself to rest. Early the next morning she used her dagger to pry the rest of the gems out of the amethyst headband, arriving at the jeweler's shop when it opened its shutters. Now she had enough knowledge of Wye currency and the stones' value to drive a fair bargain.

She headed toward the river district. Salubriton was a large city and her destination far off. Walkers and their parasols made navigating the sidewalks tricky and tiring.

But what impeded her progress most was that her Talent now linked her with the minds of the gamels.

Yoo-hoo, Queenie! they called to her, craning their lengthy necks to stare at her. *Yooo-hooo! Over here! Dost thou want to stroke one's soft coat? Why hast thou been so quiet? Stuck up? Yooo-hooo! Thou hear one now! Come scratch one's forehead! One wants to smell thee close.*

So many gamels called to her that Cerúlia felt under assault.

Queenie! One is right here! sent a gamel waiting by the sidewalk in front of a carriage. It nipped at her shirtsleeve for attention.

"Sorry, damselle," said the driver. He flicked his whip at the animal. "Don't know what got into him."

Cerúlia shrank away from the forward animal and forced herself to resist the blandishments coming at her from all directions.

I'm sorry I've been uncommunicative. You are all bewitching, but I can't stop to get acquainted today. I'm in a hurry.

Most people she asked had never heard of the tavern she sought. When she finally located it, around midday, she understood why. Shipmates tavern was a dark, small establishment, on a side street, with a battered sign missing the "a" in "mates."

The tavern looked so still that Cerúlia suspected it was closed, but when she tried the door, it swung open easily enough, leading her down three steps into the main room, a dingy place that was larger on the inside than it had appeared on the outside. The room smelled of unwashed wool and fried fish. A bald, middle-aged barkeep stood behind the counter. Several customers, each sitting alone, were already drinking their midmeals. A fiddler, playing tunes in a foreign scale, sawed away in a nearby room.

Cerúlia approached the barkeep. "I am looking for a man named 'Ciellō,'" she said.

"What's your business with Ciellō?" he asked without warmth, glancing at her quickly and then going back to drying bar glasses.

"My business with Ciellō is *my* business," she said.

"Hmmpf. Go away, little girl, you bother me."

"I'm not overly fond of you either, but unless you are Ciellō that hardly matters."

"*I'm* not Ciellō," he said. "You don't even know what he looks like, do you?"

"No, I don't. But I promised Sezirō of Zerplain I would speak with him, and I don't care whether that pleases you or not."

One of the customers called out in slurred speech, "How *is* old Sezirō?"

Cerúlia kept her eyes on the barkeep. "He's dead. Two days ago."

The barkeep flinched and made a gesture she had seen Sezirō make, blowing air into his hands and then setting it free.

"All right, you've told us. Now git out of here, little girl, afore I lose my temper."

"For the third time, I want to speak to Ciellō," she said, unyielding.

"I am Ciellō," said a male voice behind her. Cerúlia turned. She saw a man of mid height; his dark brown hair, with two prominent magenta streaks at his temples, was meticulously braided. She found it hard to gauge his age; he might be in his early thirties. He held a fiddle bow. "Come." He motioned with the bow toward the inner room where he'd been practicing. "We can talk in here."

She followed him into the room and closed the door behind her. They sat opposite one another at a small, scarred table holding only a burned-down candlestick. For a few moments they regarded one another without speaking.

Something he saw made Ciellō address her with more respect than the barkeep. "What must I do for you, damselle?" he asked in a low tone.

"Sezirō suggested I hire you as a bodyguard. I promised Sezirō I would consider the idea."

A sad smile played across Ciellō's lips. "Did Sezirō braid your hair, damselle? That pattern has a name—did you know that?"

Cerúlia touched the elaborate plaits, which were starting to come unraveled since Sezirō had braided them days ago. "No, I didn't."

"The pattern, it says, 'Beloved of the Zellish.'"

"Sezirō was my friend. I tried to comfort him as he lay suffering from the wound *you* inflicted on him."

"Yes, I stabbed him," said Ciellō without noticeable remorse. "Did Sezirō tell you of the fight?"

"No. Only that it was his fault, and that you were more skilled than he was."

Ciellō nodded. With restrained exactitude, he moved the candlestick on the table just a tiny bit so that it was perfectly centered.

Cerúlia noticed the grace in his movements and the ripple of muscle in his arm and his neck.

"Excuse me, damselle, but you dress like—like a boy who works with donkeys. You no look to be a woman needing protection."

"If you don't understand that looks can be deceiving you are of scant use to me," Cerúlia replied. "What good is a bodyguard who is fooled by a manner of dress?"

"I no say fooled *I* was. At your waist you wear a dagger. So sharp that it already cuts his new sheath. You keep it sharp because you are frightened, no? And it is gold because you are no a stable boy, though you hide as one. I see that too in your eyes."

Cerúlia just nodded, considering.

"And you carry a sack of gold coins above your left hip."

"How did you know that?"

"The coins make the purse sag. But you are wise to put it to the left to keep your right hand free for the dagger, no?"

"How do you know I have coins and not rocks or candies?"

"When you walk they make a very small sound."

She nodded and smoothed her hand across the empty tabletop. "I need to book passage to a destination hundreds of leagues away. I don't want to worry at night about sailors' lusts or greed. How would you ensure that I could sleep well?"

"I would hang my hammock in front of your stateroom door, damselle. No one would dare bother you."

"How much do you charge for your services, Ciellō?"

"It depends. If you want me only guard the body, I charge two hundred gold pieces. If you want me as manservant and advisor too, I charge one hundred fifty."

"You charge less for doing more jobs?"

"Aye, because on your own you make the mistakes foolish. If you take advice, it is easier to keep you alive. To keep me alive."

Cerúlia found his cool assumption of superiority irritating. "Don't you want to ask me how long the job would last?"

"Already included. We sail to Cascada, no?"

"How did you know that?"

"I hear your accent. Also, word has passed all over town of the generous reward for news of the young woman from Weirandale."

Cerúlia recalled all of Healer's warnings, and her heart sped up. "Circulated by whom and where?"

"Among the river folk and pickpockets."

"Are you going to claim this reward?" asked Cerúlia, staring straight at the man, hoping she could read the truth.

"No," he answered.

"Why?"

"Money matters to me little. And, I told you, the braid says 'Beloved of the Zellish.'"

"Take your payment now," said Cerúlia, making her decision.

"Why, damselle?"

"Sezirō would not have sent me to a man without honor. If he was mistaken, better I should know that now; better that you abscond with the money now, rather than later. Besides, as you say, the coin weighs down my purse."

She counted out the gold pieces. She noticed he laid out his palm so that the coins didn't clink on the table, and he separated the coins into three pockets with a sleek motion.

"Now, what do you advise, Advisor?"

"I want that *you,* a lone Weir woman, do not inquire about the ships; you leave such to me." He looked her up and down. "I advise also that you purchase clothes fit for the daughter of a merchant so wealthy, or peoples will question why you employ a manservant. I think—the parasol with white fringe; that is the emblem of a trading family from north Wyeland; they have the long feud with dangerous rivals. Your parents would never permit you travel without protection."

"A white fringe," she assented.

"Where are you lodging?" he asked.

"The Bread and Balm Recovery House."

He raised his eyebrows high. "Ah. Not a public house. *That* is why you haven't yet been spotted. I will send you a message when passage is arranged. You must not come back here."

"All right. Do you need money for the tickets?"

"Not now. You will pay me back and for the manservant costume when I know an exact amount."

"Agreed," she nodded.

"Now, you slap me hard—as if I to you make rudeness—and you leave the tavern angry, so angry. We will not want men in here to guess we make this deal."

"Agreed." Quickly, she concocted a story. "I came to tell you about Sezirō; you were fresh with me; and now I never want to see you again." She placed her hands on the table edge, preparing to push her chair back. "But one more thing. When you book passage, bribe the seamaster so I can bring my dog."

"You have the *dog?*" he asked, eyes opening wide. She had succeeded in surprising him.

"Not yet," she answered, "but I will."

Cerúlia stood up abruptly, making the chair screech against the wooden floorboards. "You murdering pig!" she shouted, in a carrying, furious tone. Then she slapped him as hard as she could across the face and strode out of the tavern.

Drought damn him! My hand stings so.

But that was very satisfying. I am tired of rude catamounts and ruder men telling me what I can and cannot do.

28

Jutterdam

Gustie chafed at her orders. Although Mother Rellia hadn't publicly committed to Norling's plan for the siege of Jutterdam, she had issued directives for a great gathering of materials capable of constructing barricades on the bridges. And she had sent squads to reconnoiter Kings Bridge and Electors Bridge, both of which the Oros patrolled with confident negligence. But, frustratingly, Mother Rellia had barred Gustie from involvement with either mission. Instead, she assigned Gustie to organize the blockade of Jutterdam Harbor and the covert survey of the city's food supplies. An important task, surely, but one removed from the main field of action. Besides, Gustie had no experience with boats.

Gustie found four men and two women who knew the city well and who claimed skill with watercraft and swimming. At the moment these six sat with her in the barn adjacent to the farmhouse, planning the expedition.

"The key is we need to row into the harbor without being spotted," Gustie said.

"Muffle the oars," said one grizzled fishing boat owner, as if any fool would know this.

"Low moons, tomorrow," said the youngest woman, to all-around nods. "We'll wear black clothes. Your face"—she pointed to one of the younger men with a more sallow complexion—"is rather light; use some charcoal."

"Good," said Gustie. "We'll need a small group to land on the wharf, avoid any Oro guards, and check on the warehouses. I'll be one. Who else knows that neighborhood well?"

The older woman and the eldest man raised their hands.

"All right. We three will check on the warehouses and granaries. The rest of you will count the ships and boats in the harbor. And sink as many as you can. How do you sink or disable them?"

"Stave in their bilges," said the grizzled man, as if any fool should know.

"How?"

"Hand drills, metal wedges, crowbars," he answered, with the same attitude as before.

"Won't that be noisy?" asked Gustie.

"Not much. Ports aren't ever silent—plenty of waves hitting against ships and wharves. And we'll do it from right at the waterline."

A discussion ensued about the number of holes and their exact placement. Then her squad debated the merits of rubbing goose fat on their bodies to insulate the underwater saboteurs from the cold.

"Jutterdam's a big port," said another one of the men. "There'll be too many small craft and big ships for one team. We need two more rowboats and teams of four. Two to row and two to swim. Extra tools in case some drop."

"I bow to your judgment," said Gustie. "Can you rustle up the right people and more boats?"

The Jutters tossed about some names of people they knew. Gustie felt herself the outsider; some of these people had known each other all their lives, and they all had boating expertise.

"What do you think," she asked, "of including an archer on each boat? Even if they aren't natural sailors, the Oros aren't fools. They'll be guarding the biggest ships and the harbor itself. If Oros come to investigate, it would be nice to have a way to take them down before they spread an alarm."

The grizzled man—his name was Nothafel—grunted and grudgingly admitted, "Good idea."

"We need crack shots in the dark," said Gustie, "from a swaying surface. I know I couldn't hit the target."

"My boy, Kiffen—he's only fourteen," said the oldest woman. "He's got them young eyes and steady hands."

"There's one. I'll talk to Mother Rellia about two more," said Gustie. "And we'll meet at the path to the water at dusk tomorrow."

"One question," said the older woman, Kiffen's mother, who had agreed to check on the warehouses. "How do those of us on land searching the warehouses get away?"

"We'll pull back up at the wharf at two bells," said Nothafel.

"Are you sure you'll be there?"

"We'll be there, I vow, Hulia." He reached across the circle to seal the promise with his hand. "But if *you're* not there on time, you'll have to swim."

The three rowboats—two carrying five Free Staters, and a bigger one carrying eight—rowed around the headlands toward the harbor of Jutterdam. The sky cooperated in its dull opacity, and the muffled oars dipped and fell with only the faintest swish and water dribbles. Gustie looked at the black water and regretted wearing her dress; she had detached the white collar and cuffs and decided that its deep brown color would serve. But if she had to swim, the voluminous fabric would drag her down. She decided she would rip off the skirt if she needed to.

The occupied city hulked brooding, and the harbor area sat in midnight desuetude. Gustie counted five large ships, swaying on their anchors, looming above them as blacker shadows. Smaller boats, fishing craft and such, dotted the closer waters and piers in throngs so numerous that she thanked the Spirits they had brought three teams.

Her rowboat paused a moment in the shadow of an enormous carrack to study movement on land. Oro soldiers marched in the center of the wharf area, and they probably had sentries posted where the seawalls met the land.

"Aim for the far side of the pier across from Fresnay's," Nothafel commanded their rowers in a low voice, pointing. Their craft slipped forward, threading between many anchored fishing boats, sometimes pushing off their sides rather than risking the sound of the oar. The other squads lingered in deeper water, already busy with sabotage on the big ships.

When they reached the pier, Hulia grabbed a ladder and bounded out. She reached a hand back to help Gustie and then the old man. The three crawled on their bellies from the pier in between some dark structures. Bells all over Jutterdam began to chime midnight.

By prearrangement, Gustie and the two other spies spread out to different sections of the warehouse district. Gustie took off her shoes and tucked them in her belt so they wouldn't echo on the cobblestones and ran, hugging the walls, keeping to the shadows. She and the rats had the alleyways to themselves.

Trembling with nervousness, Gustie approached one of the large granaries. She crept around to the wide front door, finding it unlocked and unguarded. She pushed the heavy door wide enough for her to slip inside—the air felt stagnant. Too cautious to risk a match, which anyways might set flour dust alight, she stumbled through the dark. Her feet felt empty floorboards covered with a light smattering of sandy grain and bits of rubbish. She put her hands out in front of her and kept going until she ran into the far wall. Which explained why a people who valued foodstuffs as much as the Oros had left the building unguarded. This warehouse was empty.

More confidently, she rushed through the large building next door, finding that it too stood vacant.

She found the large front door of the third warehouse locked. She slipped around its perimeter, looking for another entrance, and located a small back door—also locked. Whispering curses and wiping her sweaty hands on her dress, she managed to spring the catch with her dagger. Within a minute of walking around she stubbed her toe on a row of barrels and grabbed at them for fear of sending them tumbling down. But they only rocked to her touch, because they too were empty. She knocked on as many as she could, hearing a hollow echo. Then her feet encountered piles of flat sacking. Moving with care, Gustie began to back out, but she'd lost her sense of direction. Her hand hit a pile of wooden boxes. One fell to the ground with a cataclysmic crash, but no Oro soldiers came rushing to investigate. The wooden crate had been empty.

Returning to the street, her assignment concluded, Gustie realized she had forgotten to listen to the bells.

She ghosted back to the rendezvous point. She found Hulia already hiding near the pier. She held a child in her arms.

"Hey. What did you find?" Gustie whispered.

"All the buildings are empty," said Hulia. "They don't have any quantity of supplies."

"Mine too."

Gustie gestured at the child. "Who've you got there?"

"I found him hidden in the corner under some burlap. Thin as a scarecrow. I reckon he's an orphan or runaway. I want to sneak him out to safety with us."

Gustie paused to review who she actually knew in Jutterdam,

wondering if there was anyone she personally wanted to rescue. The only people she could think of were the dairywoman and her grandson who had helped her on a Defiance mission so long ago. If she could save them, even one of them, that would repay the debt.

"How long till they pick us up?" she asked Hulia.

"More than half an hour."

"I'll be back," whispered Gustie. "If I'm not, don't wait."

Lowlands Dairy lay some blocks inland from the harbor. Gustie put her shoes back on for speed and ran through the streets. She skirted a brightly lit guard station and detoured at the sound of tramping. A man leaning out a window for a smoke saw her, but didn't call out. She lost her way in the dark and had to circle around to a street that she recognized, and then finally she found the dairy barn. Deserted. No milk cows, no Creamy, no old lady or young boy. She'd risked her life to warn a pair of disused buildings that stunk of stale manure.

She worked the sticky pump handle in the yard for a handful of water—she drank a few sips and splashed the rest on her heated face. Then she headed in the direction of the pier, now worried about time and whether she'd missed the pickup boat. Surely the second boat would still be busy sinking so many ships; if she had to, she'd swim—

"Halt!" cried a male voice. "You! Woman! Halt!"

Gustie risked a glance to see if she could outrun the Oro, but he and a comrade stood only twenty paces behind her. She stopped, catching her breath, as he approached her.

"What are you doing out this time of night? You know there's a curfew."

Though she wasn't dressed the part, Gustie patted back her hair and assumed a seductive body posture and voice. "A gal's gotta make a living in these hard times. I was visiting the barracks. Got fellas there."

"Which barracks?"

Gustie's mind froze. "You know, the one by the dock."

"Which barracks?"

"The one Brigadier Umrat built when he first came here. He named it a queer Oro name." At least she could throw around Umrat's title.

"But what are you doing in *this* neighborhood? Which Protectors did you service?" his comrade asked, still suspicious.

"I don't want to get any lads in trouble, you know. Steady customers are valuable." She paused. "Breaking curfew isn't the worst crime, is it? Maybe I could do something for you and you could look the other way this one time?"

The first Oro had drawn very close to her now. In appearance he was like all the Oro officers she had ever seen: neat red uniform, black boots, white in his hair, hard face, and narrow eyes.

The officer put up his pike and closed the distance to her. He grabbed at her body, randomly, hungrily, squeezing her breasts and her bottom.

"I don't want your slit," he growled. "You're probably crawling with pox. On your knees, slut!" he pushed her down on her knees and started unbuttoning his trousers in front of her face.

The gorge rose in her throat. Gustie could not stop herself—she vomited on the Oro's shiny boots.

In fury and disgust he kicked her so hard under her chin that she flew backward into the street, banging her head on the cobblestone and facing up at the night sky stunned.

"You fuckin' slut!" snarled the Oro in anger.

His pike's blade glinted as it moved. Gustie felt something akin to a fierce punch in her chest. Then another.

She experienced no pain, only shock. In her last seconds she stared up at the black sky and rummaged through her disordered mind. She tried to translate "Time to die" into Ancient Lorther, but she couldn't find the words.

29

Jutterdam

In the early morning, when Thalen and the Raiders arrived at the foggy checkpoint on the road to Jutterdam, they found their fame had preceded them. Small crowds of Free Staters thronged around the commander of the Raiders, eager to meet him.

"How far are we from the city?" he asked.

"The road jogs up ahead and climbs a hill; then you hit the Jutter River, the bridge, the plain, and the city."

"Kings Bridge?"

"It's right there. Electors Bridge lies two leagues yonder, to the west."

Thalen asked for the Raiders to be taken to confer with Mother Rellia. A child led him to the farmhouse down a lane, which was serving as headquarters. The farm looked like a big and prosperous place, with many fields and outbuildings now crowded with wagons and tents.

Unfortunately, Thalen discovered Mother Rellia was not available: she had died two hours before dawn.

"Who's second-in-command?" he called out repeatedly. The people in the farmhouse just milled about, wringing their hands.

"There's a man from Sutterdam with a dark beard?" said one of the farmwives. "Or maybe you want that tall woman from Yosta?"

"Do you know where either of them are right now?"

"No. I don't—*I* don't know anything. I just nursed her. What'll we do? We're lost without Mother Rellia." She burst into tears.

Kambey sized up the group and murmured to Thalen, "The Defiance was never an army, just a motley group of volunteers without a solid command structure. Maybe they've got some squad leaders, but even when she lay a-dying, they didn't think to appoint a second."

Thalen grabbed the person nearest him. "Do you know a woman named Gustie? Gustie from Weaverton?"

The woman shook her head. Thalen needed Gustie's intelligence and experience to help him figure out what to do with this ragtag army. By dint of much asking around, finally, in the farmyard they found a woman named Hulia who knew her.

"We snuck into Jutterdam last night to blockade the harbor, sink the ships, and check on stores," Hulia told Thalen and his squad. "Your Gustie and I and another, we landed to scout the Oro supplies of grain. She was supposed to meet us at two bells, but she never showed. We waited as long as we dared. She could've been taken prisoner, but honestly, it's more likely Oro guards discovered her out after curfew." The woman was too weary and too hardened to be tactful. "They kill anyone on the streets."

Thalen turned away from his informant, stunned.

After all this time, to miss her by a night! One night. One miserable, stinking, fuckin' night.

Images of Gustie flooded into his mind—Gustie waiting for him and the rector that first afternoon in Scholars' House; Gustie teaching him to pull a bow; Gustie chewing on her hair while she studied antiquated verbs in the library.

After so many Raiders, Skylark, his mother .... This was one loss too many.

Thalen had taken off his hat in respect for Mother Rellia. This inoffensive object ready at hand drew his wrath. A kind of madness possessed him: he threw it on the ground, kicked it, jumped on it, and stomped on it with both feet.

"Commander. Commander! Stop! Stop, will you? Here, drink this." Tristo offered him a dipperful of water.

Thalen ignored him until Tristo threw the water in his face.

The water broke his fit of fury and he saw all the Raiders around him, staring with shocked eyes. Thalen strode over to the well and poured the remainder of the nearly full bucket over his own head. The cold water soaked his hair and face, coursed down his neck, and doused his shirt. He wiped his face with his neck drape and retied his wet hair with his hair leather.

Coming back to himself, Thalen spied Quinith sitting on an overturned bucket, his elbows on his knees and his head in his hands. Wareth was trying to offer comfort with a hand on the top of Quinith's head. While Thalen had given in to his own grief, he'd been insensitive to what this news would mean to Gustie's lover.

Thalen crouched in front of Quinith, trying to see his face. "Hang on. We'll find you some brandy or wine."

"You know, Thalen," Quinith addressed the dirt between his feet, "I never really believed I'd see her again. One night I told Hake that she was lost to me, and I was prescient, wasn't I?" Thalen saw Quinith's shoulders move. "It's awful, but I don't even know if I still love her—or loved her." He sucked in a long breath. "We'll never find out now, will we?"

Tristo approached with a bottle.

"Here, have a drink, Quinith," said Thalen. "We don't have to parse your heart. You've had a shock, that's for sure."

Grabbing the bottle, Quinith took a pull and then another. He passed the bottle to Thalen, but Thalen shook his head and handed it back to Tristo.

Quinith stood up. "Just—don't treat me like a widower or something," he said. "Keep me busy."

Thalen, recalling how Quinith had refused sympathy for his father's death at the beginning of the Occupation, stood too.

"If that's what will help. Spirits know, I need you."

Thalen glanced around at the Raiders. None of them grieved for Gustie, but their faces showed concern for their comrades and worry about the loss of Mother Rellia. Instead of joining an operational force, they had stumbled into chaos.

"All right, then," Thalen said, putting decisive force into his words. "I will assume command here. Someone's got to. I will make use of this blasted reputation. Gather all these people milling everywhere into this yard in front of the farmhouse."

As the Raiders set off to do his bidding, Thalen looked for a stand that would give him enough height to address a crowd. In the barn he found an old wagon; it was beastly heavy for one person to shift alone, but the effort required was a productive use of his wrath. He pushed it into the yard and hoisted himself up into the bed.

It took some time for all the people scattered on the holding to gather around his wagon. Most of the crowd consisted of women, children, and older men; many already boasted bandages, slings, or crutches. Thalen surveyed his "army" of some four to five hundred people. Despite their wounds, he saw in their expressions fierce determination and—when they glanced up at him—admiration and anticipation that he fiercely hoped to satisfy.

When no more people trickled into the yard, he lifted his hands, and a hush fell over the farmyard and field. Thalen pitched his voice loud.

"Free Staters! I am Thalen of Sutterdam, commander of the Raiders. Many of you have heard of our successes in Oromondo.

"Mother Rellia has passed on. This is a terrible loss for the Free States. We honor her for her bravery and service, but at this perilous crossroads, we do not have time for ceremony.

"With your permission, I will assume command of the Defiance, aided by those of you with the most battle experience. We must get organized immediately. I am going to divide you into groups and appoint lieutenants who will report to me.

"Those of you who are fit to be soldiers, report to Raider Kambey and Raider Fedak. Kambey, raise your sword.

"I want everyone with a horse or strong legs and sharp eyes to gather by the well. Raider Wareth is in charge of scouts. Wareth, raise your sword."

Thalen continued on through horse tenders under Dalogun, healers under Cerf, builders under Kran, and cooks and provisioning under Quinith. He called for those who had previously led Defiance strike teams to report directly to him.

The people sorted themselves quickly and with none of the hanging back, giggling, or jostling Thalen half expected of civilians. These folks hungered for orders and direction. Each Raider set about evaluating his volunteers' skills, experience, and courage, and apportioning them into squads.

Meanwhile, Thalen met with the two dozen men and women who had clustered around him in front of the farmhouse.

"Quickly, let's go around the circle. Tell me whatever you know about Mother Rellia's plans and your own battle experience. Oh, and tell me if you're local and familiar with the lay of the land."

"Begging your pardon, Commander, sir, but what's the report from the bridge brigades?" interrupted a man.

"Bridge brigades? I don't follow."

"Last night Mother Rellia dispatched all our archers to take down the Oro patrollers on Kings Bridge and Electors Bridge at dawn. And behind them went wagons full of logs and such to build barricades. It's near midmorn: What reports have come back?"

Thalen sputtered. "I've heard nothing—no one mentioned—do you mean *that while we're sitting here getting acquainted,* Free Staters may be dying, already taking the bridges?"

Embarrassed, worried silence greeted his question.

"Damnation!" Thalen swore. "Get me the Raiders. And my horse!"

Within ten minutes, a guide led Thalen, most of the Raiders, and some sixty mounted Defiance fighters to the Post Road. Wareth galloped ahead to reconnoiter Kings Bridge; he rejoined the main force on the road with a piercing whistle and broad gestures indicating that this bridge was secure—they should proceed west.

Some three hundred paces farther on, they swept by a horse grazing on bushes while its rider, a young girl, lay facedown in the road, the puddle of blood around her already seeping into the dirt. Thalen read in a glance that a wounded messenger racing for help hadn't completed her mission.

Another ten minutes at full gallop brought them the noise of a battle ahead. As soon as they rounded the curve, Thalen saw that Oro soldiers had control of two-thirds of the bridge, and Defiance fighters were desperately trying to hold their position on the last third. Bodies, weapons, even logs cluttered the bridge itself.

Thalen had pulled his rapier after he saw the dead messenger. As they approached the bridge, he stood up in his stirrups. Kran rode at his left, occasionally pulling a nose ahead of him; Fedak was at his right, and Wareth and Kambey pounded right behind them. His Raiders didn't need the additional goad of Gustie's death: this was their first chance to engage Oros since the night in Iron Valley, when so many of their friends had died.

"Make way!" they shouted. The Defiance fighters dodged the horses that dashed through the press, thundered onto the bridge, leapt over obstacles, and clove straight into the mass of Oro pikemen pushing forward.

The Raiders' swords flashed with fury—slicing through pike

handles, hacking off hands or arms, skewering throats, or decapitating their foes. Defiance reinforcements on their heels set upon any soldier the five Raiders missed. Loud splashes behind the horses announced men or bodies being thrown off the structure into the swift and deep Jutter River below.

Thalen couldn't find the icy control that always before had sustained him on a battlefield. He hungered to kill.

The mass of Oro soldiers staging at the city end of the bridge turned and fled before their furious onslaught.

Thalen pursued them, overjoyed to see that these pikemen weren't wearing backplates. He skewered one, pulled his blade out, and lunged for the next bare neck. This Oro, here, who had tripped and held up his hands—his bare throat was perfect. Blood spurted up Thalen's arm. He looked around for the next target.

"Thalen!" Wareth's face loomed close to his, and Wareth had grabbed Thalen's bridle. "We've cleared the bridge. Turn back."

In shock, Thalen realized that he had led his Raiders one hundred paces across a flat field straight toward Jutterdam. At the moment, scores of Oros ran from their attack, but if they stopped panicking, realized their numerical superiority, and turned around . . .

Thalen whirled his mare, glancing about. The city's walls were within sight. On top he could just make out Oro soldiers staring and pointing.

Wareth blew a piercing whistle as recall. Thalen led the way back over the bridge, keeping his lathered horse to a prancing walk.

Once on the other side, Thalen dismounted. He had to lean with his hands braced against his knees for long moments to catch his breath.

A tall, square-jawed woman with rough bandages around her head and torso and clothing spattered in blood approached.

"We'd given up hope of reinforcements. Why didn't Mother Rellia send them earlier! Did she *fuckin' forget us here?*"

"Mother didn't forget you. She died," he answered between

gasps, finally managing to straighten up. "I'm sorry—your messenger didn't get through, and I didn't know you had an action in progress."

He turned away from her for a moment.

"Fedak!" he called. "Get those wagons turned on their side and get this end of the barricade up before they regroup!"

He turned back. "I am Thalen of Sutterdam," he said, holding out his hand.

"Bellishia of Yosta," answered the woman, whose handshake was firm despite her injuries. "*The* Thalen of Sutterdam?"

He nodded. "Tell me, what happened?"

"Mother Rellia sent us to get in position in the night. We attacked the bridge guards just before dawn. They summoned reinforcements. We're closer to the city here than Kings Bridge, as you can see. We sent for help too and held them off as best we could, but we were so busy fighting that we couldn't get the barricade in place. Spirits damn those Oros, I lost so many good people."

"It was valiantly done. Let's get you and your wounded to where healers can tend you. We'll leave these fresh fighters to finish and hold the barricade."

Before he remounted, Thalen studied the bridge. Electors Bridge was built of masonry, forty paces long and rising at least twenty paces above the rushing river. Five arches supported its length; the last arch, on the Post Road side, rose to the bridge's apex.

Thalen addressed Wareth and Fedak. "Stay here; supervise the reinforcements. Make the barricade unbreakable. Send reports—every hour—to the farmhouse."

After waving the wounded from Bellishia's brigade on to headquarters, Thalen motioned for Kran to turn off with him at Kings Bridge. This older overpass, built by one of the Iga kings, crossed the Jutter at its narrowest but swiftest running point with a single-arch design. The Free Staters trying to capture and hold Kings had benefited from an essential advantage—the bridge included a tower

on the countryside, originally to help lookouts keep watch for anyone approaching the city. With the tower providing a height advantage, Defiance archers had been able to chase the Oros off the bridge
and erect a barrier.

Thalen dismounted to check the soundness of the construction.
He had knelt to examine the interlaced bracing of some logs when a
man tapped him on the shoulder.

"Those braces will hold till the end of time. Thalen, ain't it?"

Thalen stood up and whirled around. He recognized the wheelwright he had hidden with for several days after the Rout, though it
took a moment for him to find the name.

"Good to see you alive, my friend. Ikas, right?"

"That it is." The men clasped hands.

"Are you the one in charge of this bridge?" Thalen asked. "I
heard about a Sutter with a dark beard but didn't realize it was
you."

"Mother Rellia put me in charge of building the barricade, and
that fellow up in the tower with the green hat, he's in charge of the
archers."

Green Hat smiled down on them and saluted.

"Well, Ikas, I have news. Mother Rellia died in the night; I've
assumed command of the Defiance; and thus far this morning has
been a total cock-up except you've done a good job here."

Ikas chewed over this information in consternation, but Thalen
didn't have time to waste. "Here, this is Kran; he's one of my Raiders. I'm going to leave him with you to help. Send reports to the
farmhouse every hour."

Once they arrived at the farmhouse, Dalogun ran over to take
Thalen's mare.

"We need horses saddled and ready at all times," Thalen remarked as he passed over the reins.

"Did these Sutter horses do us proud?" Dalogun asked.

"Well enough," Thalen answered.

Cerf had already taken over assessing the wounded from Electors Bridge. While Thalen had been off fighting, Cerf had decided that the spacious barn would serve as the infirmary. His assistants were rigorously scouring it clean.

Thalen discovered that Tristo had seen to Mother Rellia's burial. He'd even cut off another random hank of his hair to burn to assist her journey to the stars and had begun the job of turning the building into a working command center, with maps, lanterns, paper, and other things he knew Thalen would want.

Turning about after peeking in the farmhouse door, Thalen almost bumped into Jothile, who had materialized behind him carrying a plate of food that he thrust out as an offering.

"Thank you, Jothile. Something hot to eat is exactly what I need most right now. Thank the cooks too. Maybe you could fetch me a cup of tisane? Or coffee, if they have any? I'm going to sit for a spell on that hill behind the house, out of the bustle, and try to clear my head."

Jothile returned with two mugs of coffee, one in each hand. "Give me your rapier?" he asked. Thalen passed him the rapier he had only barely wiped after the battle. Jothile sat down a few paces in front of Thalen with a rag and whetstone, his protective presence (he reminded Thalen of a dog on guard duty) serving as a deterrent against those who would interrupt the commander's chance to eat and think.

Thalen gulped the first mug of hot coffee swiftly, savoring how it fortified him and cleared his head. He slowly sipped from the second as he ate and reviewed their situation.

Norling had told him that though scattered Oro units occupied the far reaches of the Free States, they were now rudderless. Their most capable officers had all either sailed back to Oromondo, been poisoned at Gustie's banquet, or already gathered in Jutterdam. There was little chance, then, that the Oro general in Jutterdam counted upon his countrymen coming to lift the siege. The Oro's leader would accept that he had to deal with this threat from the Defiance himself.

Thalen very much doubted that Oros would sit passively behind the stone walls, waiting to starve. The Oro general would counterattack soon. He had nothing to gain in waiting while the Defiance organized itself or hunger eroded discipline and strength. Thalen blessed Gustie's mission for taking down the sea route. With that option closed, they would hurl brute force against the bridge barricades.

Tonight. Or tomorrow at dawn.

At all costs, he had to hold the bridges.

In his mind, Thalen addressed the Oro general. *When you find you can't beat down the barricades, what will be your next move? You'll try to break us with your hostages, right?*

Could this novice army hold firm? Could it sacrifice innocents? What alternatives did he have?

Thalen had no answer. He lifted his eyes to survey the farm and environs. In every direction squads buzzed with activity: many loaded more logs onto wagons, or worked on reinforcing ladders and scaffolds. Quinith, standing behind the barn in the informal armory, had set workers to taking an inventory. Women pulled down laundry, ripped the cloth, and rolled bandages. Thalen realized that for weeks Mother Rellia had been gathering the materials her forces would need to maintain this siege. Though she'd been negligent about a command structure, in other areas she had shown foresight.

Thank you, Mother R. For your wisdom and your sacrifice. Thalen saluted her memory with his coffee mug. Then he bestirred himself to enter the farmhouse and take his position at the table.

"First things first," he said to Tristo. "We must prepare the barricades for imminent attacks."

The afternoon and evening passed in a myriad of arrangements, including organizing relief shifts on the barricades, building blinds for archers at Electors Bridge, and readying weapons.

When Ikas came in to report, he said to Thalen, "I heard about Gustie of Weaverton. She was a friend of yours, I take it. I had the honor of fighting beside her in Sutterdam. Damn shame."

"If we survive tonight, I'd like to hear more about her Sutterdam escapades," answered Thalen.

"We'll survive. We have Commander Thalen leading us," Ikas answered.

"By the way," Ikas continued, "remember the healer, Dwinny, who lived with us in that first farmhouse? She's here too."

"Good. I'm delighted she survived. And we'll need her."

Around midnight Thalen personally took command of the barricade at Electors and assigned Kambey to hold Kings Bridge. Under cover of darkness, his crews braced for combat.

An hour before light, Wareth's sentries sighted Oro columns marching to attack both bridges. The defenders heard the clink of the Oros' armor long before they saw the troops. The Oros marched confidently, with no effort at silence or stealth, and approached the bridge in ranks of eight, wearing their helmets, breastplates, and armor on the front of their legs and arms. When they reached the cobblestones on the bridge's far side, orders rang out and pikes leveled with impressive precision. In the middle of their ranks they carried two large battering rams, rams large and heavy enough to do real damage to the bulwark.

The Oros crested the highest point of Electors Bridge, and their officers called out commands and pulled whips, urging their men to charge. Obediently, the soldiers broke into a run. But in the night Thalen had used ropes to lower giggling children with buckets of tar and oil and mops. They had made the downslope surface as slippery as a frozen lake.

As soon as the pikemen stepped on the cobblestones, their feet went flying out from under them. Their own battering rams fell on top of the sliding heap, crushing limbs. The whole tangled mass of men, logs, and pikes slid against the blockade with a thunderous crash that knocked part of it askew. But the shocked Oros, many with the wind knocked out of them or broken bones, were incapable of taking advantage of the damage they had wrought.

Defiance crossbows punched through the steel plating of their armor. Only a few soldiers made it past the arrows, and if they pressed against the barricade, hoping to be safe inside the archers' angle, crouching children with spears stabbed through the chinks, slashing at their enemies' feet and legs. Some Oros tried to climb the obstacle, only to be met by the clubs and axes of Defiance fighters on top.

The Oro officers called retreat, but very few men were left alive to reverse across the slippery bridge.

Free Staters whooped and laughed at the men sliding about as they tried to flee.

"I doubt it's over," Thalen warned. "Drink some water, settle yourselves, and get ready."

Twenty minutes later a larger group of about one hundred Oros came swarming over the bridge once more. These men held metal plates aloft as shields against the arrows.

"Here they come!" Thalen shouted.

Some of the tar had worn off, and the shields helped the attackers ward off arrows. This time, more upright men reached the barricade and started to batter against its wooden supports or climb up it. Just when the pressure was at its height, Thalen yelled, "Now!" Cauldrons of hot oil were turned upside down on the attackers. They yowled and ran for safety.

Without pity, Thalen watched one injured Oro try to crawl up the bridge, digging his fingers into the cracks between the cobblestones. Observing the man's unarmored backside, a Free States archer took aim and skewered him from buttock to groin.

After the noise of the skirmish, the quiet—broken only by the cries of the wounded—made the fighters' ears hum.

"Leave all the bodies and debris on the bridge," Thalen ordered. "Repair the barricade. Make it stronger still. Ferry our injured to the infirmary."

An hour later, when the Oros tried pushing burning carts over the bridge, the carts got stuck on the fallen pikes, shields, and logs that lay scattered about. They harmlessly burned themselves out without getting anywhere near the obstruction.

Thalen wondered how many times the Oro general would throw men to die against the barriers before he switched tactics. He redoubled his sentries along the riverbank, just in case the Oros tried to swim or row across. But the tumbling river looked fearsome; locals said they couldn't recall a time when the Jutter River had run so swift and deep.

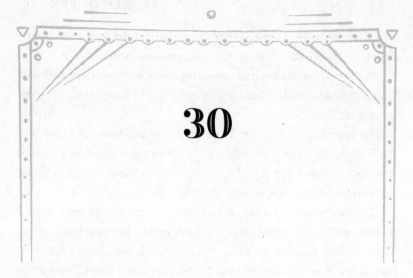

30

Cascada

Matwyck's day had been inordinately tiresome. His calculators had come to him with a discrepancy, and Matwyck had kept the books but sent them away, concluding after several hours of tracing tiny figures himself that General Yurgn was skimming off more of the budget allotted to military matters than Matwyck had agreed to.

With the populace increasingly restive, this was not the time to be shorting the funds for the garrisons! Of late, painted letters had appeared on the sides of buildings, "Matwyck the Usurper" and "Where is our Queen?" Matwyck needed all his soldiers content with their salaries and reassured by having plentiful arms at hand.

Had Yurgn's greed overwhelmed his senses?

He'd sent for his longtime coconspirator and had a confrontation that had turned ugly. Yurgn maintained that he needed the money and he refused to return it. After much wrangling, however, he agreed to stop plundering the accounts and to come to Matwyck directly with monetary requests.

Matwyck wasn't confident this promise would hold. *Old men die every day,* Matwyck thought as his valet dressed him for dinner in his bedroom. *But Yurgn's hold on the army makes him damn near irreplaceable.*

Matwyck turned his mind to a more pleasant topic: the intimate supper he had planned with Duchette Lolethia. Lolethia's pouts and stratagems, which he found so charming, would be on full display. When she casually brushed against him, or leaned over to give him a privileged view down her dress, he knew she was trying to trap him with his own lust. He approved of her clever marshaling of her assets. Besides, who wouldn't enjoy such a luscious tidbit trying to win his approval?

His valet poured hot water for him to wash his face and handed him a towel.

How will my upcoming engagement and remarriage affect the populace? Can I use the spectacle to divert the masses? Will Lolethia's beauty charm the nobles?

He snapped his fingers, and his valet handed him his glass of cognac. This servant had learned that Matwyck despised chatter.

Duchette Lolethia was a summer or two younger than Marcot, and Matwyck admitted to himself that she was neither well-educated nor mature. But her immaturity was part of her appeal. Matwyck could foresee molding her into the perfect wife to stand by his side. Besides, Matwyck appreciated her native cunning, so visible in the way she chose the tastiest morsel from each serving plate, the way she insulted old Latlie without the duchess even realizing she'd been snubbed, or the way she would cheat at games while distracting her opponents. The scrupulousness and disapproval that had tainted his marriage to Tirinella would not be a problem in this second union. He would have to keep an eye on this one, though; she was capable of trying to deceive *him.*

But Matwyck had the Truth Stone in his possession, and if he had doubts about the girl's loyalty, he could place her hand on the stone. She would quickly learn that she might trick others, but she couldn't cozen or cuckold him!

While the valet tied his burgundy cravat, Matwyck found himself dreaming up various trinkets that would make Lolethia's eyes sparkle. And also various scenarios for their wedding night. She had once made a comment about a spirited horse needing a strong master. Matwyck relished repeating this remark over and over in his head; it led him to believe that they might be compatible.

I'll give that young filly the ride of her life!

The cravat didn't lie in a neat knot; the Lord Regent tugged it loose angrily and bent for his valet to tie it again.

The one snag in his plans had arisen from her family. Naturally, her mother, Duchess Felethia of Prairyvale, was overjoyed to have her daughter the object of the Lord Regent's attentions. But the duchess had made it plain she would entertain no talk of marriage until after a full year of mourning for Lolethia's father, who had died of fever in the spring. Matwyck found this no grave impediment; he rather enjoyed the thought of moons of delay and suspense, observing how far Lolethia would go with her teasing and flirting.

Would she bed him before marriage? He would not pressure her—it must be at her initiative and desire. He might then shame her as wanton, bringing her more under his control.

But when he thought of *family* complications, his mind turned to Marcot's stubbornness.

The valet held out his weskit. Matwyck scowled both at his thoughts and because the armhole was not placed at the correct angle for his arm.

Drought damn my son! Nothing moves him from his infatuation with that village girl in Androvale.

Matwyck had made sure to introduce his son to nearly a dozen more suitable women, a few of whom had been given explicit instructions that seduction would be well rewarded. Marcot behaved like a polite gentleman with each, departing as soon as possible from the social event with a feeble excuse.

Matwyck turned his head sideways to look closely at his cheeks in the looking glass.

Should I ring for the barber? No, this bit of stubble looks rough and manly.

His people had intercepted one of the letters Marcot sent and one of the letters she returned. Matwyck had a vague plan of interrupting the correspondence or forging a note from Percia saying she had found another beau. But before he could act decisively his son found a new avenue for posting and receiving his letters that kept them out of the palace and Matwyck's grasp.

The valet stepped away to fetch the jewelry case while Matwyck stared, unseeing, at the carpet of his bedroom.

A play he'd seen a few moons ago, *Devotion and Debts,* had centered around filial piety. The young hero, who had dreams of becoming a famous artist, had not listened to his father, who knew that the boy's real talent lay in increasing agriculture yields and motivating the servants to work harder. Only after their estate had fallen into arrears—and his sister had almost been forced to marry an elderly money changer—had the son realized, almost too late, that the key to his own happiness lay in his submission to his father's wisdom and guidance. Matwyck had enjoyed the drama and had invited Marcot to attend a repeat performance, but the boy had begged off, claiming he was feeling unwell.

The scamp's constitution is about to be tested.

Matwyck realized he didn't particularly like to think of himself as the murderer of Weir girls. If Tirinella were still with him—regarding him with her disapproving eyes and daily winning out the contest for the boy's love—he might not dare to go this far, because she would have known who was behind the attack. But he could no longer hold out hope that Marcot would waver, and the girl would hardly take a bribe when she could have the husband and the country's riches too.

I have to act soon. The closer the incident to the wedding date, the more suspicious it will look.

The burgundy color of his garb was brighter than what he usually wore, and these days he was adding more jewelry than he used to wear. He had always disapproved of gaudy show, but he wished to remind Lolethia of his access to riches.

He held out his fingers splayed for his valet to place his rings and then resettled them more comfortably on his fingers. His valet sprayed him with cologne, a scent he'd been told contained "musk," which purportedly made women grow lustful.

How I'd like to make that minx as hot and hungry as she makes me! She thinks she is baiting me with a hook, but actually, I am the fisherman, reeling her in.

"I will be late," he told his valet in a brusque tone. "I'll expect you waiting for me and my nightclothes properly warmed this time."

Matwyck left his quarters for the salon, pinning a warm smile on his public face.

31

Salubriton

Buying upper-class accoutrements posed little difficulty. Cerúlia took Hope with her to the shops, guessing that the novelty might make a good outing for the melancholic and needing Hope to speak for her to female merchants to hide her Weir accent.

Hope steered Cerúlia away from silk. "We wear silk for fancy occasions, not for traveling," she murmured. Her friend helped her order split skirts, shirts with lace and billowing sleeves, and short open doublets made out of linen cambric, in light colors or with subtle contrasting stripes. For an extra payment, the seamstresses promised the outfits would be ready posthaste.

At the parasol shop, Hope assisted as Cerúlia chose two parasols with white fringe. One had a black-and-white checked pattern, and the other one she liked was white, with blue raindrops embroidered on the fabric. Cerúlia insisted that Hope choose a parasol for herself as a present and was delighted when she settled on a cheerful yellow with green leaves embossed in the fabric.

Finding a dog in Salubriton caused much more difficulty than new garb. Cerúlia admitted to herself that her need was irrational, but nonetheless, she wanted a dog. So many moons without one made her feel less like herself, as if she were missing an arm or a leg. And since Ciellō had confirmed that she was being hunted, having a dog by her side felt even more necessary.

The tabby cat at the parasol shop vouchsafed that dogs did live within the city, but she did not know where. The gamels told her to search northeast of the city center, in the area past the Park of the Dreamers.

The next day, comfortably dressed in her donkey boy outfit, she told her housemates she intended to take another ride.

"Could I accompany you, Damselle Phénix? Would you mind?" asked Damyroth. "I'd like to see if I can ride with one leg, and it would be nice to have a change of scenery. I have coin; I can pay my own way."

Cerúlia did not really want to bring him, but she hadn't the heart to say no to what would surely be a healthy outing for her housemate.

If the stableman at Vigor Hostelry recognized her, he made no extra effort at politeness. Cerúlia put Damyroth on Pillow and hired a smaller horse, Cotton, for herself. She told the stableman to place his largest double panniers behind Pillow's saddle.

They rode to the Park of the Dreamers—a large, lush, and peaceful oasis in the middle of the busy streets (irrigated, Damyroth told her, with water diverted from the River Cleansing). It had walking paths and bridle trails, a small lake, and manicured greenery. Tall Salubriton peacocks, with their lilac-colored feathers, showed off their plumage and chastised anyone who approached too closely. Damyroth relished being out, and Pillow behaved so docilely that he had no trouble controlling her, which raised his mood even further. Cerúlia's back and shoulder started to ache, but she could manage the discomfort. After a pleasant tour of the trails, they bought a meat pie from a vendor.

"What is that structure over there?" she asked Damyroth.

"That's a Restaurà Pavilion. Inside you'll find pillows and rockers."

"People nap in public?"

"That's the sweetest sleep, amongst your fellows, watched by Restaurà."

Cerúlia regarded the pavilion, which had swaying white side curtains, with more interest. "It looks appealing, but in the rain?"

"It rarely rains, but if it does, that's even better. You hear the raindrops on the roof, and a light mist blows through." Damyroth urged her to take more of the pie. Then, through his chewing, he asked, "Do you want to try it? Lie down for a bit? You look fatigued."

She shook her head. "No. I have an errand I must do."

Looking up at Damyroth, she warned, "It might possibly be a rough neighborhood. Perchance, I could even lead us into some kind of difficulty. Will you back me up?"

While his eyes regarded her thoughtfully, as if considering whether he really knew her, Damyroth's large swallow apple bobbed up and down, finishing the pie. "You know I will."

After leaving the park behind and riding a few minutes northeast, Cerúlia sensed the presence of dogs, though they were too panicked to communicate anything besides gibberish. She steered the horses first past a row of deserted buildings and then through heaps of rubbish that desperate people picked through. As they rode on, they passed men wearing kerchiefs over their noses and mouths, shoveling waste into smoldering pits. The smell was overwhelmingly foul. The horses shied in discomfort.

Damyroth opened his mouth to question her, but closed it without speaking.

The horses did not find approaching the wooden building at the end of a narrow dirt road any easier. With every pace, dogs' muffled howling grew more audible, and the horses skittered their hind hooves.

The building with a soot-stained chimney sat slightly apart from any neighbors, surrounded by packed, dry earth. Two shuttered windows and a metal door were closed up tight. The barking noise escalated to deafening levels. Cerúlia climbed off Cotton and banged on the door, but no one came to her knock.

Help! Help! Help! Out! Let us out! Out!

Cerúlia tried the door, finding it locked. Taking a step back, she searched for something to use as a tool to force the lock; but Damyroth, who had also dismounted, had already secured a rock with a sharp edge. Bashing the latch several times with his strong arms, he succeeded in busting it open.

Cerúlia's eyes didn't have much of a chance to adjust to the dark interior as she rushed inside. The building was small—even tinier than the cottage in Wyndton. In the middle of the room stood a waist-high table stained with what looked like blood, viscera, and fur, with leather gloves and several axes strewn on top. To her right was a stack of faggots and a large stone hearth capable of roasting a pig.

With the light that streamed in the doorway she made out two cages filled with half-starved, terrified dogs, penned up in their own excrement.

The noise the dogs made was unbearably distressing. Cerúlia sprinted to each cage, using her dagger to cut the twine that bound them shut and opening their sides. Jumping on top of one another in their haste, about a dozen dogs streamed out of their pens, bolting for freedom out the door. Cerúlia exited the noisome building in their wake.

Outside, Damyroth held the horses' reins; he commented, "I take it that in the Free States dogs are valued."

"Aye," she answered.

"Strange," he remarked. "Different countries, different ways."

"Hmm-mm," she agreed, turning to look in all directions.

"Now what? Is freeing the dogs what we came for?"

"Only incidentally," Cerúlia responded, glancing down at her side. "*This* is what we came for."

As she had hoped, not all the captive dogs had run away—one had stopped as if called to her side. He was a large, red-colored animal, with a white blaze on his chest, a ridge of raised, exceptionally dense fur down his back, and a cocked ear.

Cerúlia squatted down on her heels so her face was level with his warm, brown eyes.

Hullo, she sent. *How did you come to be here?*

He met her gaze for a moment, then politely looked to the side.

One came with a caravan. One had a master; after he fed the gamels he would feed one. The new smells in this big town enticed one far from familiar wagons. One could nay find the right caravan again and slept on the streets for many suns. One found naught to eat. People threw rocks, so one hid. But anon the axe man caught one and brought one here. Such a terrible place that stinks of fear.

This is a terrible place, Cerúlia agreed. *But I've come to free you.* She stroked both sides of his head. *Would you like to be my dog? My heart hurts from lonesomeness.*

The dog had had a chance to process her scent. He began to whimper and crept forward to lean his full body weight against her chest. His weight unbalanced her crouch, so she sat on the ground and wrapped both arms tightly around his back as he grew more emotional rather than less. He began to stick his black nose and muzzle into the hollow of her neck and to rub his silky cheek against hers. His tail beat wildly.

Where hast thou been! Why did it take thee so long to find one? Oh where hast thou been!

There, there. Your lonely days are over. I've got you now, and you've got me. Shh. Shh. We've got one another. Her eyes brimmed over, and the dog licked up her tears.

Looking up at Damyroth, she said, "Isn't he wonderful? Free

Staters in general do like dogs, but I—" She broke off to giggle as the dog enthusiastically licked her mouth and chin.

"Look at that funny ear. I'll call him 'Whaki.'"

"You let him lick you with his dirty mouth?" Damyroth tried to keep the shock out of his voice.

"As you see," she answered as she gave the dog a final tight hug and a kiss on his nose before she got to her feet. "I love dogs."

"What about that one?" her companion said, pointing to a small dog hiding behind Cotton's legs.

Cerúlia hadn't considered that more than one dog might be called to her side. Though dirty and matted, the white lapdog—the fluffy kind that noble ladies like to caress and teach tricks—stood up on her hind feet and walked toward them, wagging her tail.

Damyroth laughed. "Like a toy, isn't it? Kind of cute."

"She'd be adorable if we washed her. She's too small to survive running free, because the first predator that comes along will snap her up."

"Don't you think that Damselle Hope would like her?" asked Damyroth.

Cerúlia leapt at the idea. "I think that having a dog to care for might do wonders for Hope."

"Let's take her home with us then!" Damyroth enthused.

Your Majesty! sent the white dog, pawing at her knees. *Thou rescued us!*

They loaded each of the panniers with a dog—Whaki barely fit and the basket cover wouldn't latch—and retraced their route down the dirt street. By the time they reached the midden piles, a crowd had started to gather.

Shrink down, Whaki, as tight as you can.

Most of its members had the mien of rough-looking laborers, but among them stood a young, black-haired woman wearing thigh-high hunting boots and a feathered hat. This strange woman also shouldered a longbow. This was the first time Cerúlia had seen a weapon carried openly on the streets of Salubriton.

"Who might you be?" one of the men asked. "Did you see a bunch of dirty dogs running loose?"

Knowing that speaking would betray her accent, Cerúlia looked at Damyroth meaningfully.

"Dogs? Gosh no. Dogs? We're just out for a ride, friends."

Another man in the crowd pointed to Damyroth's wooden leg. "A peg leg. A recovery patient. Such don't go about causing trouble."

The suspicious woman pointed to the livery name on the saddle blankets and panniers. "Vigor Hostelry. You're a long way from that part of town," she said. "What are you folk doing hereabouts?"

"We'd heard of the beauty of the Park of the Dreamers," said Damyroth. "We brought midmeal to eat by the pond and feed the peacocks. Have you seen them?"

The woman's nose twitched. "Then why are you over here?"

"Just curious to see more of the city. Though I guess we've wandered about a bit and lost our way."

"Don't you talk?" said a second man to Cerúlia. She kept her mouth closed.

Again, Damyroth answered for her, "She's mute. Trauma patient. Melancholic. We don't even know her name; we call her 'Restaurà's Ward.'"

"Hey! There's one of them!" The crowd took off after a stray dog they glimpsed down an alley. The riders moved on at a leisurely pace that Cerúlia hoped would not raise suspicion.

She stretched her back casually and stole a glance over her shoulder. To her amazement, the smoke from the closest of the midden piles condensed as it rose in the sky instead of dispersing. As she watched, the gray wisps slowly pulled together, making a darker cloud; then the cloud took on an unnatural form. It transmuted into a giant, dark hand, standing out from the rest of the sky, with a forefinger . . . pointing straight at the princella.

They needed to hide—quickly.

Pillow, where would you go to shelter from danger?

One's stable.

No, that's too far. I mean, is there anyplace in Salubriton that is sacred to Restaurà?

Restaurà favors the parks, Cotton piped in. *A smaller park lies nearby.*

Head for the nearest park as fast as you can.

"Damyroth, hold on!" she warned.

Pillow and Cotton took off down the street at a gallop—or at least, the closest gait they could manage. In truth they ran at a speed that would have drawn even old Syrup's contempt, but at least their pace was faster than a person could run, and that was what mattered.

Cerúlia snuck another look behind. As if blown by a magic wind the smoke cloud kept pace above and behind them, pointing. In the distance Cerúlia could see the woman with the bow loping on a diagonal from a street that stretched east. She had cut them off and was almost approaching bow range.

Veer left around that building, Cerúlia sent to the horses.

She heard an arrow thunk into the wooden slat with tremendous force.

"Damyroth, duck down!"

We just have to outrace the archer. Cotton, how much farther to the park?

One smells the grass ahead, sent Cotton.

They had reached a more populated district of Salubriton, and people stared in shock at the running horses. Another arrow, shot with tremendous force, struck Pillow's pannier, the one with the white dog inside. The dog yapped so Cerúlia deduced it had missed getting skewered. Ahead she saw an archway labeled "Park of Peaceful Risings." Pillow came dangerously close to running over walkers with parasols, while Cotton jostled a mother holding a baby.

"Watch out! Make way!" Cerúlia shouted, motioning with her arms, and then finally they raced through the archway. A third arrow struck the stone on the archway's side, missing the princella by the span of a hand. Pedestrians screamed and rushed about wildly at the attack, and many cried out, "Help!" "Guards!"

Gamels! I beg you! Create a big pileup of carriages at the archway.

At last they were inside the park. The Pointing Hand hovered outside, apparently prevented by Restaurà's Power from entering. Cerúlia hoped that the chaos at the gate and the guards racing in that direction might delay the woman hunting them.

The horses, exhausted from their unaccustomed exertion, had slowed to a walk. Scanning around her, Cerúlia saw a group of well-dressed, chatting riders coming around a bridle path toward them.

"Damyroth. There's no time for any questions." She pulled her foot out of the stirrup and slid down the side of the horse, then gathered up Cotton's reins, which she passed to her friend. "Take the horses and mingle with that group of riders for as long as you can. Then just give Pillow her head and she'll take you back to Vigor Hostelry. Cotton will follow along."

Damyroth gazed at her with grave concern. "Who is after you and why? Will you be safe?"

"Yes. I'll meet you at the Bread and Balm after I've shaken off pursuit. Go, now!"

Whaki raised the basket's top by pushing his nose through, saw that she was walking away on foot, and leapt the distance to the ground.

Strollers shrieked, "Look out! There's a dog!" but Cerúlia was already running for a wooded area in the park with the offending animal streaking at her heels. With any luck the archer would follow the horses a ways, until she discovered that Cerúlia was missing; then she would double back, searching for her prey, leaving

Damyroth alone. But while the archer might have her scent, she didn't know her footprint.

Cerúlia ran as far as she could, but like the horses, she was not in any condition for such exertion. She needed to hide, but where? This park was smaller and not as manicured as the one earlier in the day; the landscapers had settled on a more rustic look. All she saw were trees and shrubs, bridle paths and footpaths, and a few small rolling hills.

She turned to head back toward the park's center. Between some trees she spied a small Pavilion, its white curtains swaying in the breeze.

I'm going to hide in there, she told the dog. *But what about you?*

This tree be empty, said Whaki, nosing a hollow log. *Raccoons once lived here, but not this day. One can hide inside.*

Trying to walk calmly, Cerúlia angled her way onto a walking path that led to the Pavilion. Inside, she saw a small table that held burning incense that smelled of lavender, and a stack of damp, folded towels that smelled of lemon water. Two of the rocking beds were occupied: a young Wyelander lay comfortably reading a book in one, and a middle-aged woman slept in the other, a lemon cloth spread over her face. Seeing that they had both removed their shoes and covered themselves with the lilac-colored blankets that lay neatly piled in the Pavilion's center, Cerúlia followed suit.

After what seemed like forever, Whaki sent to the princella, *She comes.*

Cerúlia covered her face with the lemon cloth and breathed rhythmically. Under the blanket she pulled her dagger.

If the woman even looked inside the Pavilion, she did so noiselessly.

She passed thee by.

Be sure you get her scent, Whaki.

Cerúlia must have dozed off for a little while. When she awoke the other occupants of the Pavilion had left. Whaki assured her the archer had disappeared from as far as his sharp nose could detect, so they both crawled out of their hideaways.

All right. Now we need to get off the streets. Whaki, stay in the shadows, behind bushes or trees. I suspect fewer people are out strolling this late.

Cerúlia led them back to the main walker's path. Ahead stood another archway gate, leading back into the city streets, but the princella had lost her sense of direction. She sent Whaki to hide behind a bush and approached an elderly couple.

"Excuse me. I fell asleep in the park, and now I'm disoriented. Do you know High Street? Could you point me in that direction?"

"High Street runs for leagues through the center of the city," said the old man, peering at her shortsightedly. "What part of High Street would you be wanting?"

"I'm not sure. I do know a jewel shop near where my friends are staying. It's called Many Facets. Does that help?"

"Many Facets, Many Facets," repeated the old man, and shook his head.

"I know the place," said his wife. "It's near the cobbler's where I got your clogs repaired. That's Upper Middle High Street, damselle." She pointed. "If you head that direction you can't miss it. Once you hit High Street, will you recognize your way?"

"Oh, yes. I'm certain I'll be fine. You've been most kind."

Cerúlia, with Whaki keeping to shadows, slunk back to the Bread and Balm. Anxiously, she considered that the archer had seen the livery stable name on the horses' blankets and panniers, but she didn't think she'd ever told the stableman where she lived. But the crowd had seen Damyroth's leg—how many recovery houses lay close to Vigor Hostelry?

No one accosted the woman and the dog, but the gamels' incessant cries of *Yoo-hoo, Queenie,* echoed through the dark streets, pointing her out to anyone with ears to hear.

32

Jutterdam

The sun had just sunk behind a horizon of trees when Destra arrived at the checkpoint on the Post Road outside Jutterdam. She had laid aside the flowing white robe she habitually wore as magistrar of the Green Isles, and as she had no idea what Mìngyùn's "Spinner" should wear, she'd settled on an outfit that could have come out of an ancient painting from the years of a royal court in Iga: a ruffled collar of white silk, a surcoat of beige velvet brocade with wide sleeves, and a wide, split-legged skirt of the same material. The pattern on the fabric swirled in a circular motif, flecked with gold thread. The only aspect of her appearance unchanged from her previous life was her long braid of hair, but she now wore an elaborate hat, and the gold streaks in her hair winked and shimmered next to the material.

She found these clothes stiff and confining, especially for so many days on horseback from Sutterdam. The Defiance soldiers at the checkpoint, however, were sufficiently impressed by this costume that they immediately led her to the farmhouse that they identified as "Headquarters." A bald man with an earring stood guard outside the door. He looked her over, satisfying himself that she carried no weapons. Then he knocked on the door, announcing, "A lady asking for the commander."

The door was opened by a young lad. "Won't you come in?" he invited her, rubbing eyes that looked heavy with sleep.

As he led her closer to the fire and lanterns, Destra saw that one of his white shirtsleeves hung empty. "Forgive me for waking you," she said. "I do need to consult with Commander Thalen."

The lad said, "He is sleeping now, milady. We sleep when we can. Is the matter so urgent I should wake him?"

"I regret disturbing him, but yes," Destra replied.

"Very well. Won't you take this chair by the table, milady? And may I offer you some wine or ale?"

"Wine would be most welcome," she smiled.

The lad poured her a glass.

"You are very kind," she said. "You are?"

"I am Tristo, milady, Commander Thalen's adjutant. I should tell him who wishes to speak to him."

"My name is 'Destra,' lately of Pilagos, but originally of Jígat," she answered. "But that name won't mean anything to him. Tell him— tell him, I also claim the title 'Spinner.'"

As she waited, Destra sipped her wine and gazed around the room. It was a large Free States farmhouse common room. Its ceiling pressed lower, its walls stood thicker, and its hearth stretched wider than the Green Isles spaces she had lately occupied. The furniture appeared helter-skelter; a knitting basket and children's toys had been jumbled in a corner, and assorted chairs and stools clustered around the large table. Pictures were stacked in a pile leaning against a corner, and someone had used the barren wall as a canvas for a hand-drawn map.

In a few minutes a tall man entered the room. He was young,

but his face was already careworn and hardened. Though he held his shoulders straight, his eyes showed not only fatigue, but also pain.

Destra stood, and they regarded one another across the room for a long moment.

"Tha-len of Sut-ter-dam," she said, savoring the syllables. "At last we meet. I have heard of you since before the Occupation of the Free States. Master Granilton was my tutor, my friend, and a faithful correspondent."

"Milady, then you have me at a disadvantage," said Commander Thalen. "Tell me, is a 'Spinner' analogous to a 'Peddler'?"

"Ah, so you have met Peddler and he revealed himself to you?"

"Yes, on a ship sailing to Slagos."

She nodded. "We must have missed one another by moments, then, because I convened with Peddler and Gardener in Slagos."

"Oh, there's a 'Gardener' too?" The commander raised his brows. "Won't you be seated, milady? I see we have much to discuss. But first—Tristo!"

"Aye, Commander," said the adjutant, appearing at a doorway.

"Could you fetch us some food?" Thalen pulled his hair back into a band and gestured with his chin. "And another wineglass."

He poured himself a glass and topped off Destra's. "Now, milady, you have my attention until we finish supping; afterward, I'm afraid, there are scores of things I must attend to."

Destra needed to win this commander's trust. She knew that showing trust was a method of winning it in return: she could demonstrate her faith in this stranger by putting her life in his hands.

"I know you are fatigued, and you must have many things on your mind," she said. "Pray indulge me a moment. I will sketch my tale quickly.

"I was born in Jutterdam not too far from here. My father was drawn to statecraft; he served as mayor and then as an elector; my mother, however, was the scholar in the family. She specialized in birds. I showed aptitude in both areas.

"I attended the Scoláiríum, where I read history with Tutor Granilton. In his house, I met his only son, Graville. Graville was—well, Graville became very dear to me. We made plans for a wedding. But first we undertook a trip to the Green Isles. It was part holiday and part a favor for my mother. She studied birds, as I told you, and she wanted us to pick up several specimens. When we sailed to a small isle to purchase a rare black parrot, our ship was boarded by Pellish pirates. They killed Graville.

"I did not have the heart to return to the Free States. I made my home in the Green Isles and tried to make myself useful to the people there. Not many years after I settled in Pilagos, the Islanders nominated me as magistrar. I served in that post for nearly twenty years.

"If it was not the life I planned, it was a *useful* life. Oh, often wrangling about tariffs or harbor dredging grew tiresome, but I built up relations between the isles. I played a role in the Allied Fleet's efforts to defeat the Pellish pirates. And when my friend Master Olet came to me for advice and help in setting up a supply chain for a special team of Raiders, I did everything in my power to help him and his associates, a Master Quinith and a Master Hake."

Thalen had listened intently, staring at her face, leaning forward, his hand in his chin. The last sentence moved him to speak.

"You know my brother?"

"Yes."

"Hake is in Sutterdam at present, but Quinith is here. Well, not in this farmhouse, but somewhere close by. He's supervising our provisions and arms."

"That's good news," she answered. "He's very capable. And he would vouch for me, if you need someone to confirm the public parts of my story."

Thalen made a gesture with his hand that this was not necessary.

"So," she continued, "I had made good use of my talents, such as they are. I thought I had contributed enough. Living so long in the Green Isles I had adopted their ways—their dress, their food. I gave thanks to their Spirit, Vertia, the Spirit of Growth, for the blessings bestowed on the islands."

The adjutant interrupted them at this point by bringing in two steaming plates. They waited in silence as he set one before each of them and left the room.

"Please continue your story," Thalen said, attacking his food with hunger, though his eyes didn't leave her face.

"Three moons ago, however, I was summoned to Slagos. There I met with a man I had known for decades, Gardener, who tends the Garden of Vertia. And he introduced me to a visitor, a man who termed himself 'Peddler.'"

"What does Peddler look like?" Thalen asked, and he nodded assent when she described the bells in his hair and beard and his round green eyes.

"He's very clever at Oblongs and Squares," Thalen remarked.

"I wouldn't have guessed that." Destra quirked an eyebrow. "Anyway, in Vertia's Garden, I underwent a *change*. I became Mìngyùn's Spinner. And Mìngyùn ordered me to return to the Free States." Destra drew a breath. "More specifically, the Spirit ordered me to return home, find *you,* and help you drive the Oros from our country."

There. As fantastic as the whole tale sounded once spoken aloud, she had followed Mìngyùn's order, revealed herself, and delivered her offer.

Thalen rubbed his hands over his eyes and face. The silence grew long.

"That's quite a story," he said, keeping his tone neutral.

"Yes. Do you believe me?" Destra sought to read his face.

"I believe that you are telling me what you believe to be true—I see no lie in your eyes. But I've always had some . . . difficulties with the Spirits. And I've barely even heard of this 'Mìngyùn.'"

"A skeptical mind," Destra smiled. "Granilton and Graville too. So." She held her palms up in the gesture one would use to order "halt," and then pantomimed moving something in front of her to the side. "Set the Spirits aside for now.

"I served as magistrar for twenty years—a fact that you can easily confirm with Quinith if you summon him."

"I shan't wake him," said Thalen, shaking his head. "There's no need. You carry authority on your shoulders."

"Although I am not a warrior, I counseled Queen Cressa and Prince Mikil," Destra replied, "throughout the Allied Fleet's war with the Pellish pirates. Are there any aspects of this campaign that worry you? What's the state of affairs? How stands the siege?"

Destra ate her cooling food and listened while Commander Thalen described the morning's battles and his fears of what would happen next.

"I don't know what I would do, faced with a hostage situation," he admitted. "Nor do I know if the Defiance will stand firm. But if we fold, the Oros will resupply and even retake more territory. All the sacrifice to corner them in Jutterdam will have been wasted."

"Commander," Destra said, "I have a question for you." She pushed her plate away and leaned forward on both elbows.

"Is it necessary to kill more Oros to assuage your anger, or is it sufficient that the invaders leave the Free States?"

Thalen took a few moments before he started to speak. He had to clear his throat.

"Yesterday, I learned that one of my closest friends from the Scoláiríum had been killed by the Oros. I had thought that I was done with vengeance. Yet on top of all my other losses, this death shook my sanity. I roared with bloodlust. I wanted to hack as many of them to pieces as I possibly could."

He looked at his hands and Destra followed his glance, but his hands were clean and she did not see whatever image filled Thalen's mind. "Milady Destra, this now seems monstrous. I have already killed hundreds, if not thousands of my enemies. I helped burn a city *of civilians* to the ground. That . . . is not the person I thought I was. Killing more Oros will shatter *me*.

"All I want is to save Jutterdam. Perhaps saving Jutterdam would balance burning down Femturan."

"I know well the desire for vengeance, Commander." Destra folded her hands and rested her chin upon them. "I have taken no husband, no lovers, for twenty years. Vengeance has been my nightly companion. Earlier I claimed I have lived a useful life. Useful, perhaps. But hollow and lonely, because I could not let go of my phantom. Believe me, I tried; but it always crept back."

"I tried too," said Thalen, his eyes distant, "and thought I had succeeded. And then you lose more, and fury roars again."

The room fell silent, except for the fire in the fireplace making little pops, as they each consulted with their demons.

Destra asked, "If the Jutters could be rescued, would your army agree to let the Oros escape?"

Thalen toyed with his knife. "I believe . . . I believe that I could persuade them."

"Did Granilton ever assign you a book—what was its name?" Destra felt her fatigue fogging her mind. "It was about methods of persuasion."

"Aye." A shadow of a smile tugged at his lips. "I can't wait to tell him how useful that one has been."

Destra's face fell. "I miss him so much. He used to write me every week or two. I have received no news of him since the invasion; he would have written if he lived."

Thalen hit the table with his fist. "Damnation! Somehow, I imagined if I could just return to the Scoláiríum, everything would be as it was. Granilton and I would discuss histories or cultural development; Gustie and Quinith would sit across the table from me at the refectory. . . . I would be the student who had never killed anyone and had never sent others to their deaths."

Abruptly, he stood up. "I need to check on the wounded. And if they, who have the most right to revenge, agree just to get those scum out of our country, then I will be able to manage the others."

As Thalen and Destra crossed the farmyard, she noticed that the sky was lightening. They had talked the night away.

Thalen commented to her, "Peddler really drives a peddler's wagon. Do you actually spin thread?"

"Oh, gracious no! I've never so much as touched a spinning wheel and wouldn't know how to work one."

The barn door was propped open to the summer air. The commander moved amongst the wounded who were awake, praising them, comforting them, conversing with their healers in a soft voice. He even pulled away bandages and looked at wounds himself. Both the casualties and the healers appeared to draw sustenance from his approval and attention.

Destra couldn't mix amongst the patients with as much equanimity and reassurance as he possessed; blood and gore distressed her. She leaned against the barn doorframe, her legs stiffening and aching after such a long ride.

She was not worried about Thalen's skepticism, because Mìngyùn, she now understood, differed from Lautan and even from Vertia. The Spirit of Fate asked for no sacrifices, libations, or baskets, expected no reverence, and cared not a whit whether humans "believed" or remained incredulous. Mìngyùn weighed and judged the quality of men's souls, not their spiritual devotion.

The commander rejoined Destra. "They desire their city, their country, and their lives back. Revenge doesn't rank."

"Then we are agreed?" she asked him.

"Perhaps," he said. "But you need to convince me your plan will work. You haven't told me how you are going to make this miracle happen."

"'Tis no miracle," answered the former magistrar. "The answer lies, as so many do, in a network of alliances and in finding shared interests." And she told him her plan.

Destra slept a few hours in one of the farmhouse beds. While she rested, women washed and ironed her shirt and beat the dust out of her riding habit. At midday she watched as the commander, mounted on a farm wagon, spoke to his followers, asking their permission for this new approach.

A contentious argument broke out, with people shouting out the names of kin that had been killed.

"What about my boy!"

"My daughter—they took my daughter from me!"

"They burned my family's farm!"

"We must have vengeance!"

"I came to kill the bloody Oros, not set them free!"

"I want revenge!"

Thalen allowed this airing of grief and grievances and then repeated, "More of *us* will die or be maimed. Will that bring back your family?" When some of the crowd started to listen, he shouted, "I could water the Jutter Plain with blood—but how will that ease your hearts?" When fewer holdouts remained, Thalen's tone grew steely. "I will not lead you into a battle in which you will be slaughtered."

One man from the back—a burly figure with a dark beard—then a woman in a healer's apron, and finally others in the crowd took up the chant, "Get them gone. Just get them gone."

Twelve hours later, the commander waited with her on the city side of the barricade at Kings Bridge. Thalen's troops had set up torches at regular intervals, throwing jumpy shadows. Tristo, his adjutant, had rustled up a black stallion for Thalen (with warnings that the good-looking beast was actually wind-broken and couldn't move as fast as a mule), and had tied black-and-white patterned ribbons to his harness that fluttered madly in the summer breeze. Astride the steed beside Destra and her mount, the tall commander, bareheaded but in a long black coat pinned to fit him, looked imposing. The two waited without speaking, both occupied with their own fears, while their horses shifted restlessly and the time slid toward midnight, the time they had requested for a parley.

A man called down from the bridge tower, "They're coming!"

Archers in the tower and on the barricade protected them, but when eight columns of Oros came marching into view, Destra still felt exposed. The Oros were moving stiffly and unnaturally. As they came closer into the torchlight she could see that each one of them had a child or a baby tied to his chest and a dagger in his hand.

The sight chilled Destra. She felt faint.

Mingyùn, help me. I am no soldier. I am out of my depth here.

The commander sighed, but he did not appear as rattled as she felt. He spared a glance at her. "Take a breath," he said. "Forget about the weapons. Treat this as no different than a negotiation in a council chamber. We know our lines and play our roles."

The company halted approximately twenty paces in front of them. The lines of Oro soldiers parted to let a mounted officer and his adjutants ride to the front. An officer, made even more imposing by his helmet with red plumes, rode up to within ten paces of Destra and Thalen. "Are you in command?" he barked.

"Yes," said the commander, his voice level. "And you?"

"I am Fifth-Flamer Lumrith, assistant to General Murnaut, head of the Oromondo Force."

"I am Thalen of Sutterdam. At my side is milady Destra of Jígat."

The fifth-flamer ignored Destra—not even sparing her a glance—but he reacted to Thalen's name. His nostrils flared as he glared at the commander.

"Yes," Thalen said. "I am the one who burned Femturan to the

ground. I am the one who sent all eight of your Magi to your Infernal Flames while you 'Protectors' sat here on your fat asses. Or
terrorized children."

The officer made a move to reach for his sword.

"Fifth-Flamer Lumrith," said Destra in a soft voice, "thirty archers are aiming at you. Wouldn't you rather see the dawn?"

The officer halted his movement. "If you shoot me, if you don't
follow my orders, we will cut the throat of every one of these Free
States brats."

"You could do that," agreed Destra, nodding, "but that won't
gain your soldiers any food."

Commander Thalen spoke. "You know of me. You know I am
capable of *burning down a city*; do you think I will bring down my
barricades for the sake of some kiddies?"

"You talk boldly," said the officer, "but Free Staters are soft. You
asked for a negotiation?" He barked a command, and a nearby
soldier ran up beside him. The soldier's human shield was a thin,
terrified girl of about six summers. Destra steeled herself to meet her
petrified eyes.

"We do not negotiate with rabble. You will begin dismantling
this barricade now and move aside or the Protector will kill her,"
said Lumrith, his eyes gleaming in the flickering light, certain that
the Free Staters would respond to his threat.

The vitally important element, Destra had insisted to Thalen
earlier in the day, was to show not the slightest hesitation or remorse
over the hostages. "We must remove them as a bargaining point,"
she'd warned him.

So now, Thalen raised his right arm. "I will save you the trouble," he said, snapping his fingers.

At this prearranged signal, an arrow twanged through the night.
It was fired with such force that it pierced the girl's body and hur-
tled through the chest of the Protector holding her. They fell to the

ground; the girl with a shriek, the soldier with a groan and an exhalation.

The fifth-flamer watched them both fall, stupefied. Behind him, one of his assistants' horses reared, and its rider fought to bring it under control. The Oro foot soldiers shuffled uneasily. A cold stillness followed.

The Oro officer barked another command, and a squad of eight more soldiers ran up to the light of the torches.

"Cut their throats," said Lumrith.

Thalen smiled. "Say your prayers, boys. Your Infernal Flames nip at your heels." He raised his hand in the air again, ready to snap his fingers.

"Fifth-Flamer Lumrith," interrupted Destra, knowing this was exactly the right moment. "More arrows will fly, killing your soldiers. Those would be needless deaths. And," she lowered her voice, "you might spook the rest of the platoon behind you on the bridge. I have no doubt that you are very brave, but will your general be pleased if *all* your men die tonight and you have nothing to show for the sacrifice?

"I can offer you a way out of this difficult situation. On my signal a fleet of Green Isles ships, crewed by Green Isles sailors, will sail around the headlands. I understand that it might take some hard work to clear the harbor so that they can tie up. But each ship is loaded with food, enough for your men to eat on the voyage and enough for you to return as saviors to Oromondo, bringing supplies to your hungry country. All your soldiers have to do is march onto these ships."

"What?" he said, turning his attention to her for the first time.

Destra repeated the offer.

"There's some trick here. You will sink the ships once we are out at sea."

"No. Think a moment: the sailors have no wish to drown themselves."

Lumrith stared at her, calculating; glanced at Thalen; and looked over at his junior officers.

"There's some trick here. We will take the children with us as hostages."

"You will not!" said the commander authoritatively, though he was improvising past their script. "The sea captains have orders to pull up their gangplanks and sail away if you try to load hostages."

"Fifth-Flamer Lumrith," said Destra, her voice athrob with reasonableness. "Please, consider. I'm afraid Commander Thalen will never tear down these barricades, no matter how many hostages you kill. He's a hard man, a brutal man, a man thirsty for blood. You heard about his mad dash over Electors Bridge almost to the walls of Jutterdam? You see that now. He will hold the barricades while you, your men, and every captive in Jutterdam starves.

"But I beg you to consider—*why* should you starve to hold Jutterdam? What good does it do you? The rest of your soldiers have returned to the Land you love while you are marooned and forgotten here, without reinforcements, unable to control the Free States or use this country to provision your own. Here I offer you a way to go home, *with the honor* of bringing desperately needed provisions. All you have to do is clear the harbor and board the ships. Such easy tasks."

"Where are these ships?" he asked.

Destra knew she had him.

"As I said, they anchor around the headlands. They will sail into Jutterdam on my signal."

"What is your signal?"

She reached into her saddlebag and pulled out a cylindrical object with a fuse.

"This is a powerful rocket that explodes in the air. When I set it off from the rooftop of the Jutterdam Council Hall, the ships' lookouts will see it."

The fifth-flamer regarded her closely for the first time. "Who are *you*, woman?"

"She is a minister of the government of the Free States and must be addressed with respect," snapped Commander Thalen.

Lumrith conferred with his junior officers for a few moments.

"You will come with us and set off your signal," said Lumrith.

"No," said the commander, resuming his part of the play. "I can't allow her to go with you. You would harm the only person in this country who is trying to save your worthless necks."

The Oro officer considered. "I give you my sacred pledge that this female minister will not be harmed."

Thalen shook his head.

"I swear by Pozhar."

Thalen spit to the side.

"Perchance," said Destra brightly, as if the thought had just occurred to her, "if your men would cut down the children they bear, this would be a sign of good faith Commander Thalen would accept."

Lumrith nodded and shouted orders to the men behind him. The children shrieked when the knives moved, but in each case their captors only cut their bonds. They fell in pitiful, mewling heaps on the road.

"Well, Commander Thalen," said Destra. "Isn't that enough? You don't *really* want to burn Jutterdam to the ground too, do you?" She glanced at Thalen with a look that suggested he was a dangerous madman.

"Let's ride into the city, Fifth-Flamer, before this bloodthirsty man changes his mind. The sooner I light this rocket, the sooner you set work crews to clearing the harbor, the sooner you and your men will be on your way back to your homeland."

She rode beside the officer through the ranks of Oro soldiers down the dark road. Torches on the Jutterdam wall showed the city looming ahead of her.

Mingyùn, tell me that she lives.

The Spirit answered in her head, *Spinner, I will forgive this one impudence. Thou must never doubt that I choose if the Thread of Life is snipped. The child was under my protection. The arrow missed all her vitals and pierced the heart of Pozhar's filth.*

Destra had enough presence of mind to register the Spirit's disdain toward the Oros. A little giddy with relief, she dared to tease, "Pozhar's filth?" *Mìngyùn, I understood that the noble route was to renounce vengeance?*

The voice in her head roared, *Don't bandy thy intelligence with me, Spinner. I am the One Who Judges.*

It had been Wareth who pulled the bow.

Wareth had just average skill with archery. But among the choices that night, he was Thalen's oldest companion and one of the original survivors of the Rout, which had once included Tristo (who was maimed) and Codek (who was dead). Dalogun was the stronger bowman, but Thalen couldn't ask that innocent boy to shoot a Free States child in cold blood. No, that was a burden he could only lay on Wareth.

Milady Destra had promised that the hostage would live, though how she could possibly know this was obscure. But even if this were true, when Thalen assigned him the task, both he and Wareth knew what it would cost.

Forever after, Wareth had to live with the knowledge that he had the wherewithal to shoot a Free States child in the chest.

Forever after, he would carry the secret pride that when Thalen had needed a friend to make such a sacrifice, he had chosen him.

The arrow sprang from his bow with an aim and speed Wareth realized he had not given it. He waited, hands covering his face, while the confrontation played out below; then he registered the sounds of the Oro column marching away, the bustle of the Defiance fighters opening the barricade, healers rushing to the girl, and more people running to the other freed hostages.

Cerf carried the injured girl to the other side of the barricade, calling, "She's still breathing!"

Wareth opened his eyes in amazement and peered down from his perch in the tower. Free Staters held torches as Cerf and Dwinny worked on the girl as skillfully as if they had been a team for decades. Dwinny's knife cut the arrowhead from the girl's back, where it had pinned her to her captor. Cerf pulled the arrow out from her chest. They had bandages at the ready to stanch the bleeding from both the back and the front. Cerf felt for her pulse at the neck, while Dwinny opened one of the child's eyes to look at her pupils.

"Hullo there, moppet." Wareth's straining ears heard Dwinny's familiar voice. "Everything is going to be all right now. No one will hurt you anymore."

Thalen rode his black horse through the barricade, dismounted without caring if the horse was caught or tied, and climbed the bridge tower.

"I think we've done it," he said to Wareth in a raw voice. "We've freed our country of the invaders. So much loss, so much pain, but the Free States will be free again. Your sacrifice—her wounds—should be the last injuries."

Wareth began to weep. These tears escalated into body-shaking, choked sobs. Thalen patted his back, but when Wareth glanced at Thalen he saw that the commander's own eyes burned dry and haunted.

PART
FIVE

❦

Reign of Regent Matwyck,
Year 14–15

EARLY AUTUMN AND WINTER

33

Salubriton

Cerúlia could understand why Dame Tockymora protested against Whaki's presence the next morning; he was large enough to be frightening, and he scarfed down food as if they were about to steal it away from him. But like all the other residents of the recovery house, their landlady was charmed by the lapdog that Damyroth had smuggled home, tucked inside his shirt. Hope named her "Puffy." Puffy wandered from one person to the next, showing off her tricks and winning endearments and treats from all the guests.

Whaki, by contrast, paid little attention to the other patients. With the click of nails striking the tile floor, he followed Cerúlia from room to room. When she sat on the ground in the central courtyard, he would press his head and as much of his body as possible into her lap and push at her arms with his nose until she stroked him. The princella hugged him close, absorbing the smell of dog, his silky fur, his little whimpers and noises, and the way he licked her ear.

Keeping Whaki hidden in the recovery house could not remain an option for long. The big dog needed exercise to restore his muscle tone and burn off his anxiety. But the princella couldn't walk him out-of-doors, attracting attention and disgust. Moreover, that mysterious archer might be searching for her.

But was the Bread and Balm still a safe haven? It was only a matter of time until the woman who was hunting her tracked her down.

Even more worrisome was that Dame Tockymora went missing from the recovery house for most of the afternoon. Later, Cerúlia saw her whispering with Lymbock. She grumbled no more about the big dog, but she cast dark looks at her Free States guest.

That night, Hope drew her roommate into their shared bedroom. "You can't trust Tockymora. I'm sure she's up to something. And Lymbock showed Jitneye a gold coin he's going to send to his daughter."

Cerúlia closed her eyes and struck her forehead with her fingertips, considering alternatives. She could flee, but then she'd be more exposed. And her Zellish bodyguard, Ciellō, knew this as her address.

She needed to silence Tockymora. Without taking the time to come up with a considered plan, she sprang into action. Squeezing Hope's hand in gratitude for the warning, she grabbed her dagger and headed downstairs. She found Tockymora getting herself ready for bed in her ground-floor bedroom off the kitchen. Her shoes, hose, hairpins, and apron lay on a chair.

"What ails you?" Tockymora cried in alarm when Cerúlia burst in the door.

"You're coming with me, dame," she cried, holding her dagger at the ready.

"No," said Tockymora, planting her heavy rump firmly on her bed. "No. I'm not. I'm staying right here. And where do the likes of *you* get off telling me anything different? *You,* with your hideous scars and your foreign accent! *You,* covered with dog spit!

"I don't know what this is about," Tockymora chattered on with nervous bravado. "Strange folk from strange countries. No wonder they're after you! After all I've done for you, damselle, to threaten me with a knife! I'll be glad when they come to arrest you. To think that you grew stronger on my victuals!"

"Shut up, dame," said Hope's voice behind Cerúlia at the doorway. A clumping noise through the kitchen indicated that Damyroth was hurrying to join her. From behind them, Whaki growled, sensing the tension but uncertain whom to blame.

Cerúlia sat down on the bed beside her landlady and held her knife steadily at her throat. "Yes, shut up," she echoed Hope's command. Tockymora arched her neck backward, but the anxious, defiant grin stayed plastered on her face and her hands grabbed Cerúlia's forearm.

"What now?" said Damyroth, who was dressed only in his trousers.

"We tie her up and gag her," said Cerúlia. Tockymora made an attempt to push past them and flee, but her friends entered the small chamber, each pinning an arm, and, standing guard at the doorway, Whaki gave a small lunge in the direction of her face, snarling.

The apron that the older woman had just taken off lay ready at hand. Cerúlia cut off the sashes.

"Use these to tie her arms and legs." She wadded up the apron skirt and made it serve as a gag.

"Where should we hide her?" said Hope. "The cellar?"

"I don't think we three could carry her down to the cellar without dropping her," Damyroth noted. "She weighs as much as a stack of bricks."

"We'll make her walk there, then," suggested Hope. "I'll make the leg tie more like a hobble."

Awkwardly, the three dragged and pushed her down to the cellar, sat her on a sack of lentils, and found a rope to tie her bodily to a wooden strut. Then they left the room and closed the door tightly, with Damyroth pocketing the key.

"If she thumps against the floor, there's a good chance no one will hear her," he said.

"What about Lymbock?" asked Hope. "In the morning, when she's missing, won't he cause trouble?"

"He might," said Damyroth. "But he's too ill to leave the house and fetch the city watch. Leave him to me."

The three coconspirators crossed the indoor patio, the women preparing to climb the stairs to their bedroom and Damyroth heading in the direction of the room he shared with Jitneye.

"I acted on impulse, and I would never have succeeded without you two. Why are you helping me?" Cerúlia asked. "Won't you get in trouble?"

"I don't care if I get into trouble," said Hope. "After what I've been through, what could anyone do to me?

"You made me want to live again, Phénix. Do you think I care if some city watchman scolds me? Or if Tockymora throws me out?"

"Aye," said Damyroth. "Healer'll say that we recovery patients are not really in our right minds. Or I'll argue that we had to assist you, because we are all 'fingers on the same hand.' I just couldn't help myself." Grinning at the thought of using the recovery house philosophy against authorities, Damyroth seemed to notice for the first time that he was half-dressed. He crossed his arms over his chest.

"Besides, Phénix, you've meant just as much to me. Every day, when we were exercising, you kept going, so I had to keep going too. You brought me hope."

Cerúlia had been turning over a suspicion in her mind since Damyroth had inquired about bringing Puffy home.

She looked from one of her friends to the other and squinted. "Do you mean 'hope,' or"—she pointed—"'Hope'?"

"Both—I pray," said Damyroth, with a lopsided, chagrined smile. "Now, go to bed. I'll keep watch on Tockymora through the night."

In the morning Damyroth offered up a preposterous story about their landlady being fetched in the wee hours to her daughter's house. Lymbock scowled suspiciously, but Jitneye's main concern was for their missing hotcakes. The patients fumbled about in the kitchen, fending for themselves for meals.

Fortunately, in terms of keeping both the dog and the landlady confined, that very morning a boy knocked on the Bread and Balm's front door, asking for Damselle Phénix.

She stepped out into the street for privacy.

"I's to give you a message," the boy said.

"Yes?" she asked.

"Your manservant will escort you tomorrow at daybreak. A ferry to the coast, then sea passage," said the boy.

"That's it?"

"Yeah. Now you's to give me a copper."

After fishing a coin out of her waist purse, Cerúlia went back inside. If any of her housemates had noticed anything, they gave no sign. She tried to keep up normal routines; accordingly she took a fast walk, mixed Lymbock's concoctions, and worked through her arm exercises with Damyroth one more time. Damyroth and Hope disappeared into the cellar on several occasions, and during these absences Cerúlia tried to distract Lymbock and Jitneye.

The day crept by slowly. Cerúlia feared the archer might show up any moment, but Whaki reassured her that he didn't detect her scent.

When she went up to her room in the evening, she laid out one of her new outfits and packed the case she had bought when she purchased the clothing. She also put a cushion in the bottom of the large, covered wicker basket she had found in the cellar that she had decided to use to get Whaki to the ship. She tipped the basket on its side.

I need you to try this little cave.

One doesn't want to be enclosed ever again.

Ah, but this is different, Whaki. See, it is made of straw, not metal,

*and I will not lock you in. I will be next to you the whole time. I have
made this so that you can accompany me. Come on; try it for size.*

Cerúlia was prepared to Command Whaki past his fear if she
needed to, but the dog trusted her enough to scoot into the basket.
She tipped it so that it stood straight up; curled in a ball at the bottom, Whaki fit well enough.

Are you all right? You can see out of the holes in the sides.

The straw has a strong smell, but the pillow is comfortable, Whaki
grudgingly admitted.

Hope watched her silently from her bed, with Puffy tucked up in
her arms. Then she motioned for Cerúlia to sit next to her, and she
massaged Cerúlia's aching shoulder muscles thoroughly and rubbed
salve into every one of her burn scars. Cerúlia kissed her forehead
good night, putting into the kiss her wishes for Hope's future.

In dawn's first glow, Cerúlia, dressed in an outfit fancier and
more impractical than any she had worn since her palace childhood,
waited by the front door with her luggage, her parasol, and Whaki
in his basket. She had left envelopes with parting words and gold
coins for her housemates.

Writing the letters had reminded her of the night she'd snuck
away from Wilim and Stahlia, undoubtedly breaking their hearts.
She wondered if they would ever forgive her, even when they knew
the reasons.

The unmistakable sound of Damyroth's leg hitting the floorboards alerted her to his approach.

"I wanted to say goodbye, Phénix," he said in his odd baritone.
"Farewell, and may your Spirit bless you."

"Goodbye, Damyroth. You've been wonderful to me. You've all
been wonderful. That I am able to go is due to the strength you've
given me. I hope you won't get in any trouble on account of me."

Damyroth smiled. "If we get kicked out of here, maybe that will
convince Hope to entertain my courtship. We're both maimed; if we
lean on one another we could prop one another up."

The softest knock made the front door vibrate. She opened it: Ciellō stood there, neatly dressed in black livery with white fringe epaulets, his hair tucked inside a servant's cap. Cerúlia had forgotten the glint in his eyes and the muscular menace in his bearing.

He had hired a man with a gamel cart, and together the driver and Ciellō loaded her luggage and the basket.

Yoo-hoo, Queenie! said the gamel, turning his long neck and batting his eyelashes at her. *Come scratch behind one's ears.*

Shh! sent Cerúlia. *I'm not supposed to know how to talk to you.*

Then Ciellō handed her up to the padded seat. She still clutched her parasol absently. "Let me assist you, damselle," Ciellō said, opening her parasol and handing it back to her.

Damyroth stood still in the darkened hallway, a tall and silent sentry. She met his glance one last time, and when the cart drove off, he quietly closed the door.

As the gamel cart trundled through the quiet streets, Cerúlia realized that Salubriton still slumbered. Without traffic, they reached the riverfront in no time. Ciellō assisted her down and was giving orders about her belongings when a familiar figure approached Cerúlia. This morning she wore an ordinary dress and carried a lilac-colored parasol, but Cerúlia instantly recognized Healer.

"I trust you have had a curative stay with us?" said the older woman.

"Indeed," Cerúlia answered. "Everyone has been so kind—I have no way to thank you properly. I would have died without your care."

"No, no, that would not have suited," said Healer. "You know, Restaurà is actually the Spirit of Restoration. Yet, ideally, I should be sending back a woman *more* fit for challenges than the one who arrived."

"Fitter? I'm not actually stronger than before my accident; I'm still rather weak."

"'Fitter' doesn't only mean physically."

"Ah." Cerúlia twirled the parasol handle in her hands. "I suppose

I did grow stronger in other ways." After a moment she met Healer's clear gaze. "I learned that one must turn away from oneself to see the pain of others."

"You're a quick study," said Healer. "Did you know, my dear, that when someone breaks a bone and it heals straight and true, the bone is stronger than before?"

Cerúlia laughed. "That sounds like something Gardener would say. I can just imagine him gabbing on about how resin heals a wound in a branch and makes it harder than before."

"Really? What a very strange comparison!" The older woman's lips twitched. "At any rate," Healer continued, "I came to see you get off safely. It is high time you were gone; I'm not certain you would be secure here one day more."

"Healer," Cerúlia asked, an insight striking her, "did you do something to protect me these last days? I feared that archer was just about to ferret me out."

"Who? Me?" replied Healer with laughter in her eyes. "Are you accusing *me* of putting a sleeping potion in the mead of a certain guest in the Sanctuary lodging house?"

Ciellō had been watching their interaction from a few paces away. Now, at the sound of a shrill whistle behind them, he offered his arm. "Excuse me, damselle, it is time to board the ferry."

"Be of good cheer, damselle," said Healer. "You have naught to fear on the long voyage. Surely Lautan will hold your vessel in Its hands. Go in Health."

The older woman looked off into the distant horizon, where gray clouds gathered in a darkening band. "I do believe that presently Salubriton will be blessed with a shower. We need rain so badly—such a welcome gift, Nargis!"

Cerúlia took Ciellō's arm, but she also made a half turn and offered Healer the Queen's Blessing.

Then she boarded the riverboat that would take her to the carrack *Misty Traveler,* bound for points west.

34

Aboard Misty Traveler

Cerúlia soon discovered that she needn't have worried about how Whaki would adjust to shipboard life. He trotted around to all the sailors, making friends with those who showed receptivity and learning who preferred not to bother with a dog. She instructed him to use an out-of-the-way corner as his relieving area and paid a lad to keep the area swabbed clean. The seamaster grumbled only at how much Whaki ate, so Cerúlia offered her an extra allowance for his food.

Whaki mostly stayed at his master's side, but she noticed that of his own accord he often stationed himself at the prow of the ship, the wind blowing back his ears as he gazed across the waves, looking for all the world like a second figurehead. For long hours she joined him in this perch, pondering her past and her future, and scanning the seas for dolphins or whales.

As for Ciellō, he accepted Whaki with enough grace, although she suspected a dog may have offended his sense of order. Ciellō turned out to be a methodical man. Invariably, he started his day by stripping to his skin and swiftly running through a series of brutal exercises; then he scrubbed himself roughly with a pumice stone and a mug of water. Each day he sharpened his dagger until its edge gleamed, whether it had been used enough to dull it or not.

He transferred his habit of thoroughness to the care of his charge. Invariably, before he would let Cerúlia enter her mouse-sized cabin—holding merely a built-in bed, a desk, a chair, hooks, and her chest—he checked the room for intruders or danger. At meals in the seamaster's dining mess, he stood against the wall behind her alert; when an unexpected wave hit *Misty Traveler,* Ciellō was the one whose hand flashed forward, catching the sliding decanter before it crashed.

Noticing that she still favored her left arm and shoulder, he further expanded his duties by assuming the role of assistant healer, insisting she fill her hours with Betlyna's arm-strengthening exercises. When Cerúlia protested that these tired her out, rather than relent he added fast-paced strolls of the length of the ship to build up her endurance. And if the seas were rough or the weather inclement and Cerúlia asked to forgo the walking, Ciellō would refuse, pricking her sense of responsibility: "Damselle brought a dog with her. A dog to be healthy needs exertion." To the bemusement of the sailors, Cerúlia, with Whaki trotting joyfully beside her, would repeatedly traverse from stem to stern and back again unless the seas were actually unsafe, while Ciellō beat out on a pan a tempo that increased each day.

Her bodyguard even supervised what she ate. As shipboard fare could not compare with Dame Tockymora's cookery, whenever *Misty Traveler* stopped to reprovision, he would escort her to the best tavern in town to dine, while he took the opportunity of shore leave to shop for treats such as nuts, dates, figs, cheese, and sausages to bring aboard for her to eat between ports. Cerúlia began to worry whether she would have any coin left upon arrival, but she listened to his counsel that she should use this hiatus to rebuild her strength.

Most days she could turn her mind away from her grief and losses.

It helped to forget herself in a book. Cerúlia countermanded her manservant's advice that a merchant's daughter would express little interest in the ship's small library. She read all the books she could lay her hands on, and the seamaster, noticing her avidity, offered her the volumes she kept in her cabin. When the ship stopped in Midmere, Cerúlia spent a long afternoon in a book merchant's shop.

None of the crew or fellow passengers harassed the young woman, and none acted suspicious about her true identity. (She explained her "Free States" accent as stemming from being sent there for schooling by her ambitious parents.)

One morning, after six weeks at sea, Ciellō set down the water pitcher he had brought to her cabin and motioned to the sheathed dagger she had just affixed to her belt.

"Damselle, you carry that knife golden. You know how to use it?"

"Of course I do," she answered with some pique, recalling her training with Rooks in Anders Wood.

"Show me," he commanded. "Pretend I be a robber. And your invaluable Ciellō is not nearby to protect you."

Cerúlia frowned. "Playing with daggers can't be a wise idea. I don't want to hurt you."

"Humor me, damselle," he urged, leaning lackadaisically against the wall.

So she pulled the dagger with her stronger hand and rushed in on him from a low crouch, as she'd been taught—though evidently not quickly enough, because in a second one of his hands pinioned her right wrist, and the other twisted her bad arm behind her back.

"That's not fair!" she protested. "You know that my left arm is injured."

"A person who wants to rob or hurt you will not care about being fair," he replied, with equanimity that made her angry.

Cerúlia massaged her shoulder and conquered her pride.

"Will you teach me, Ciellō?" she asked.

"So? Now you want me to play bodyguard, manservant, advisor, healer, *and* instructor?"

"Aye. And I will pay you twenty coins *less*," she smiled, "because the stronger I become, the easier it will be to 'guard the body.' You said that yourself, the first day we met in Shipmates tavern."

"No, never would I such foolishness say," he responded, laughing.

And thereafter, every morning—sometimes in her cabin, sometimes in a narrow passageway, sometimes in a more spacious hold, leaping around the sacks and bushels of cargo—he would show her exactly how to place her feet, hold her wrist, and carry through with the whole strength of her body. He taunted and teased her, goading her to improve her reflexes.

Their practices got her blood high and made sweat pour into her eyes. She often found herself grinning at Ciellō's skill or crowing with triumph when she made a good thrust. Although they discovered that her left hand would always be weaker and less coordinated than her right, under Ciellō's tutelage, drawing and striking out with her dagger became as fluid as a catamount's swipe.

In the Bread and Balm she had crawled back from being a broken invalid. On *Misty Traveler,* bit by bit she recovered the muscle, balance, and vitality she had known before she set out from Wyndton two years ago. And this recovery was as much emotional as physical, because to be delivered from hunger and pain—not to mention solitude and fear—allowed her to lay aside the tense watchfulness she had adopted. She recognized that she was safe for the duration of this voyage, protected by Lautan, a fierce bodyguard, and a loving dog.

As, after a long winter, a half-grown tree stretches in the spring warmth and puts out new shoots, so the young woman knew herself to be flourishing in the sea air and sunshine. She started to share her father's love of seafaring.

With her regained health, she began to take more pains over her dress and hair. She played with Whaki on deck, frolicking about, aware that the two of them formed a fetching picture.

The moons waxed and waned, and the waves rolled on unceasingly. In the main, *Misty Traveler* encountered fair seas and brisk winds.

Her manservant intrigued her. His idiosyncratic speech patterns came and went: eventually Cerúlia concluded that they were an affectation he put on to stress his Zellish heritage. His respectful, protective demeanor always carried a whiff of independence, if not conceit. For reasons known only to himself, at times he would be chatty and tell her stories about his past or travels; other times he would fend off her polite inquiry. She found him mysterious, and— if she was honest with herself—desirable. Or desirable because he cloaked himself in mystery.

The ship stopped in Pilagos to pick up more provisions and new passengers. When she went on shore, Ciellō insisted that she carry her parasol open and allow him to speak for her in all the shops and eateries. She bought a new book, more hair tonic, and a bottle of lilac perfume. In an herbary she wanted a packet of tisane leaves that smelled of cloves like Stahlia's had, but her shadow hissed at her that he would buy it for her later, after she had returned to the ship, when he went out to restock their provisions.

His caution brought back to mind the number of spies that frequented the Green Isles. Even after they set sail again, with no untoward encounters, Cerúlia's anxiety returned. She was halfway to her destination, and unfathomable challenges awaited her.

Nightmares beset her again—not the dreams of a red-eyed pursuer that had tormented her when she was burned, but dreams of desperately trying to get back to the Wyndton cottage and getting lost in Anders Wood. She was in the midst of tossing and mumbling during one such bad night when she dimly became aware that Whaki whimpered at her. Ciellō's opening the cabin door jerked her back into the waking world.

"Damselle?" he inquired.

"Just a bad dream," she muttered groggily. *I'm fine, Whaki; go back to your corner.*

Although she wanted to make light of the experience, the distress of the nightmare still clung to her, and her pulse beat quickly.

Ciellō sheathed his dagger, lit a candle, and poured some water on a towel. He sat on the edge of her bunk and wiped her face, neck, forearms, and hands with the compress. The touch felt cooling and comforting.

Her bodyguard, who slept in a hammock strung across her doorway, was barefoot; he wore his trousers, but his shirt was untucked and unlaced down his chest. When he made the slightest movement she became conscious of his musculature. "Better now?" he asked.

On impulse, Cerúlia leaned forward to bury her face in the warm hollow of his bare neck. Then aghast, she sprang back and put her hands over her mouth.

"I'm sorry, sorry! I shouldn't have. I didn't hire you to, to—I mean, this isn't part of your job, and I don't want you to think—"

Ciellō laughed his low and wicked laugh. In one motion he pulled off his shirt while simultaneously his belt and dagger sheath hit the floorboards with a soft thud. "You really believe, damselle, that if I had so wished, I could not have dodged away?" His voice had taken on a husky timbre.

"Of course, but—" Cerúlia felt her cheeks burning.

"Slide back, against the wall," he said. "You are too much tense, damselle. Every adult knows that the remedy for such tension is to dance"—here he whispered—"lips against lips, skin against skin."

As she had fantasized, Ciellō was a masterful lover. Abandoning herself to his lead, Cerúlia luxuriated in the sensations of this new "dance." And her tutor—as much as she could tell from his controlled inhalations or read his face in the dark—enjoyed himself immensely.

A few hours before dawn, with Ciellō's strong arm around her, she fell into a dreamless sleep.

Come morning she felt his movement and opened her eyes.
Sitting again on the edge of her bed, he had begun to dress with his
typical grace. She reached out to trace the muscles down his back.
He twitched, shying away from her touch.

"Ciellō! Have I done something wrong?"

"No, damselle." He kept his back to her. "But the Zellish have
a saying: 'Darkness may obscure, but in the light of morning, one
more clearly sees.'" She heard his belt being adjusted. He stood up,
his back still turned to her.

"To share your bed was not honorable for me. I succumbed to
the temptation, but I will be on my guard and will so not again.

"You might enjoy another partner. If you like my assistance to
choose amongst the sailors . . ."

Cerúlia felt as if she had been slapped. She bolted upright. "*Honorable? Honorable* in what way? Honorable for whom?"

Was he talking about being her employee? But she had hardly
coerced him. Could he be referring to her rank? How much did
Ciellō know or guess about her? She knew that royalty was discreet
about love affairs. But how had they been indiscreet? Besides, she
was still—publicly at least—Damselle Phénix from Wyeland, and
they were one hundred leagues from Weirandale; no scandal could
attach to the throne.

Was he pledged to another woman? He never talked about such
personal matters, and of course she could not pry.

"Ciellō! You must tell me—you must explain."

He refused to look at her or justify his rejection; only his stilted
language revealed a level of emotion. "Mine is the error. I faltered.

"Now, damselle, I will take out the dog and give you the little
time to compose yourself. With your fastbreak in a few minutes I
will return."

When he left her in privacy, she washed and dressed with jerky
motions, her shock turning to mortification and anger. She recalled
her Green Isles friend, Zillie, and the way she enjoyed bedding men;

Cerúlia couldn't understand why—having just been introduced to this new realm of experience—she should not only be deprived but so summarily dumped. Her pride burned.

Maybe he was disgusted by her burn scars and couldn't look at her in the light of day.

The rest of the day, exchanges between them remained awkward, and she could not meet his eyes. During dagger practice, Cerúlia struck at him wildly, on the cusp of actually wanting to hurt him.

Ciellō grabbed her wrist in his iron grasp. "Enough for today."

Cerúlia stomped away and went to sit with Whaki on the prow of the ship. The dog nosed her neck.

What be the matter, Your Majesty?

Human emotions are difficult to explain, Whaki.

So one has gathered. Thou mated with the male, but this has made thee unhappy.

Well, first it made me very happy, but now I am unhappy because he rejected me.

Is he the only male who can mate?

No, and he's not even the one I truly want. The one I want is far away or maybe even dead. Or maybe never wanted me.

Whaki scratched his ear with his hind leg.

Cerúlia chewed on a fingernail. *Whaki, why don't men tell you what is in their hearts? Why do they leave you so confused? Do they think that speaking openly would make them vulnerable?*

One doesn't know the term "vulnerable."

It means, "to show their bellies."

Whaki yawned so widely that his throat made a soft explosive noise. *Many alpha dogs—male or female—would rather die than show their bellies.*

Whaki twitched his nose. *Dost thou smell the seawater, Your Majesty? The sunshine on the wood? The pig fat heating in the food place? The gull dung on the sails?*

Not as well as you do.

Dost thou smell this one? His black nose nuzzled her neck again. *One smells thee. The wood be warm, and air cools one's fur. We be not locked in a cage. Soon we will eat again.*

He flopped down, rolled over, and showed his belly. Cerúlia rubbed him, unable to suppress a grin at Whaki's wiggly pleasure.

Thy hurt will heal if thou dost not gnaw at it. All be well.

Though the princella often recalled the night with flushes and long-ing, she refused to regret it or feel embarrassed.

In the days that followed, she worked hard to bring her relation-ship with Ciellō back to a more formal and controlled footing. She concluded that some distance between them really was for the best; now was not the time when she should be distracted.

Gradually, their interchanges returned, at least to any observer, to the pattern of bossy, trusted servant and sheltered mistress. And in the meantime, *Misty Traveler,* sails billowing, sliced through the waves of the Gray Ocean.

35

Wyndton

One late afternoon in the winter, as Tilim and Percia headed home from the Wyndton dance academy, two strange men lingered in front of the Wyndton Arms. Sitting in front of Percia, gazing back every now and then, Tilim saw them mount up and casually ride a ways behind Barley.

As they progressed through the village, Tilim expected the riders to turn off any moment toward a house or a throughway. But they didn't. They followed Barley, even as the gelding turned onto the less-traveled footpath through the scattered wood and meadows. The strangers both looked big and rough, but they made no effort to close the distance. Tilim didn't want to scare Percia, and the men weren't actually causing trouble, so he kept an eye on them but said nothing.

When Barley turned into their own lane and quickened his pace, eager to reach his stable and feed, the strangers continued straight on. This road didn't lead anywhere special—it just continued to two farms farther on and petered out after an abandoned orchard—so

Tilim puzzled over whether these outsiders could possibly have some business with their near neighbors.

The distraction of company for dinner drove the occurrence out of his mind.

As soon as he entered the cottage, Lemle shouted, "TIL-im!" jabbing him with fake punches, as if he hadn't seen him for years, when they'd met only last Waterday. Sometimes Lemle and Rooks embarrassed him in front of his pals, but Tilim could relax with them here at home. He snuck under Lem's longer reach to tap him a good one in the belly.

"Ouch!" Lem pretended.

"Stop that nonsense and wash up quick," said Mama. "I've got rabbit pie, and it's bubbly hot."

Percia came in from stabling Barley, and they gathered around the table.

"Mighty good eats," Rooks complimented the cook. Everybody watched to check that the old man ate with appetite tonight. His hands shook nowadays and his body had shrunken. Tilim knew that Lemle worried about his uncle's health.

"I baked a second pie—that one's just got onions and carrots—for you two to have cold tomorrow," Mama said. "After supper, Tilim, I want you to fill the woodbox."

"He doesn't need to do that, missus," said Lemle. "I can manage."

"No, he does. It's awful nice of you two to stay here to take care of the chickens and horses while we're away. Least we can do is leave the cottage in good shape."

"When's the duke's carriage coming?" asked Rooks.

"The note said midmorning," Percia answered, passing their guest more of Mama's bread. "Why do you think they invited us to stay at the manor house for a week? Lordling Marcot won't be there. And it's not as if we're actually friends."

"Oh, Percia!" scolded Lemle. "Don't act innocent. Now that

you're engaged, Duke Naven and his wife want to get in good with you. You're gonna outrank him, I wager."

"Yes," said Mama, with a bit of an impish grin. "A lady outranks a duke."

"So strange," muttered Percie, shaking her head to indicate that the changes her upcoming marriage would bring had yet to really sink in.

They had a jolly time at dinner exclaiming over the village gossip that Lemle spread. Mama liked to know everyone's business, though often she protested they shouldn't talk about their neighbors. Percia had once explained to Tilim that speaking behind their backs was Lemle's way of getting a measure of revenge for the way the townsfolk treated him.

Then Mama served a special custard that wobbled on its plate, and Lemle compared it Goody Gintie's hindquarters, which made Tilim sputter with laughter and spray his milk across the table. Mama pretended to be cross, but he knew she was having more fun than she would at the manor house.

Suddenly, Percia interrupted the merriment. "Do you hear anything? I hear horses, riding fast."

Tilim dashed out into the yard—but all was still. Maybe there was a bit of extra dust hanging in the air.

"What did you hear, Percie?" Tilim asked when he came inside. "There's nothing doing outside."

"Really? I guess my ears must have deceived me."

That set Rooks and Mama to discussing the ways they couldn't hear as well as they could when they were young, with Rooks morosely confessing that he could no longer hear the chirps of baby birds. Tilim almost told everybody about the men from Wyndton, but feared he would sound like a ninny.

After dinner Tilim laid out a pallet in the front room, because he'd given Rooks and Lemle the room under the eave, while Percie had moved into Mama's bed. But instead of lying down right off, he stared into the fire, pondering the upcoming move to Cascada. Although he knew he would miss his friends, he was excited at the prospect of living in the capital, rather than in a remote hamlet. Would he see real soldiers? A real circus? Travelers from other countries?

Baki stiffened and emitted a low growl. Tilim stared at him in shock: this was the first time he had heard the dog actually growl. For all their assumptions about Baki being a fierce guardian, the old black mutt had been lethargic all these years. He ignored fox barks and coyote howls. A caller to the cottage might merit a cursory sniff or two before the dog resettled himself. Generally, the dog didn't even bother to stand up for visiting children, and once when Dewva's toddler tripped over his own feet and fell right on top of him, Baki had just wagged his stumpy tail twice and gone back to dozing.

But now Baki leapt to his feet, fully alert, hackles raised and lips pulled back. Whatever bothered him had not passed by.

Tilim rushed to the back door and lowered its crossbeam, then did the same with the front door. His own small-sized sword hung in his bedroom. He raced up the stairs and grabbed it from its scabbard on the wall.

"What is it?" said Rooks. His voice sounded wide-awake. Either old men don't sleep well, or he had paid more attention to Percia's report of fast horses than he had appeared to.

"Baki scents danger," said Tilim.

"Lem, wake up! Wake the others," called Rooks. "Go, boy," he said to Tilim.

Tilim ran back down the stairs, sword in hand. Now he could hear the crunch of boots in the yard. He saw the front door's latch raise and the intruder discover the beam-barred entry. He heard a muttered oath in the darkness.

Smash!

Someone was trying to break into the cottage's front door!

Smash! Crash! It sounded as if an ogre were throwing his shoulder against it.

The door wobbled. Tilim had no idea how old or sturdy the beam might be; his father had been the one to see to such things. Heart pounding, Tilim placed himself just to the right of the doorframe, where he could stab the intruder when the man walked in. Baki crouched low, every nerve intent on timing his spring.

Smash! Crash!

The door broke off its hinges, and three large men rushed in, their shapes and weapons catching the gleam of the firelight. Mama and Percia, hearing the noise, had rushed out on the upstairs landing, Percia screaming, "What is this? What's happening?"

Baki took the first villain, springing into the air, latching on to his throat, and bringing him down by his own weight and the force of his attack. Tilim struck out at the second with all his strength, skewering him in his lower back with the good steel that Marcot had gifted him. The third tripped over his fellows sprawled on the ground, then regained his feet and rushed to the staircase.

On the landing, dressed in only his night shift and bare feet, Rooks had pushed in front of the two women. He held a dagger, and though his left hand trembled noticeably, that which gripped the blade remained steady. Tilim could see a small smile playing on his mouth.

Baki's man lay motionless. Tilim's target, merely injured, grabbed for and caught Tilim's ankle, seeking to pull him off his feet and down to the floor. With effort, Tilim yanked away from his attacker's grasp, pivoted around, and stuck him again in the shoulder.

"Ai-ee! Fuck!" cried the man on the floor, pushing himself up to his knees with his good arm. "Loish! I'm hurt! A fuckin' kid! Loish!"

Tilim looked up. "Loish" didn't heed the cry for help; he was intent on reaching the second floor. He took his chance on the old man and the dagger, bounding up the steps. At the last instant Rooks slipped sideways under the thrust of the intruder's sword to stab at him with his dagger, catching him in the pit of the arm that held the weapon. The big man's sword fell down to the first floor with a clatter, while the intruder staggered forward one more step, grabbing Percia's hair, pulling at her with all his strength.

Percie screamed. Mama beat at the man's wrist, and Lemle yanked Percia by the waist back from the stranger's grasp.

Then the man's hand fell nerveless, and he crashed facedown on the stairs. He slid down a few steep risers with loud thumps. Rooks sat down heavily on the step behind himself. Mama enfolded Percia in her arms.

While Tilim was watching this drama, the intruder he had injured had staggered out the front door, leaving a dark streak behind him. Baki ran after him, his claws scrambling on the wooden floor; a short scream pierced the darkness of the yard, then stillness.

Tilim's head started swimming. He sat down in a chair and put his head between his knees so he wouldn't black out.

Dimly he heard Rooks say to someone, "There don't seem to be any more comers."

"Lock her in the bedroom, Lem, and stand guard," said Mama. And in a moment his mother crouched on the floor next to Tilim, rubbing her hands up his legs and arms.

"Mama, I'm not hurt," he said. "No need. Quit it, will ya?"

"Are you sure, Tilim? Are you sure?"

"Yeah, just a little dizzy."

"Missus, I feel dizzy too," said Rooks. "A drop of brandy would not go amiss."

Mama poured them both a finger of brandy. She lit all the lanterns and stoked up the fire for more light. Tilim was able to lift his head upright, though he didn't want to try standing.

"Mama, I want to come out!" called Percie.

"No, Percie. I forbid it. Stay in my room with the chair holding the door."

Lemle helped Rooks to rise. "Are you hurt, old codger?"

"Nay," said Rooks. "Pah! Amateurs. Twice my weight and I took him down with one strike. Your uncle's still got some grit in him."

"Your name should have been 'Grit' instead of 'Rooks,'" said Lemle proudly. "And what about your pupil? A nine-summers boy fighting off a brawny man!"

"Yeah! How about that!" agreed Rooks cheerfully. "Don't guess I can take any credit for the dog, though." He swallowed down the rest of his brandy and smacked his lips.

"What was *this* all about?" Rooks said. "When has this ever happened in Wyndton? Not in all my years!"

Mama's hands worried her nightdress. "Oh, I wish Wilim was here! This can't be happening."

"Now, missus, calm down," said Rooks. "Send for Hecht. He'll know what to do. I feel a mite tuckered. How about bed, Nevvie? Help an old codger back to bed after all this excitement?"

Rooks chuckled and slapped his knee. "Feels awful good to know I'll wake up in the morning and that miserable son of a bitch *won't*."

Lemle settled Rooks back in bed, and then he rode off to fetch Hecht, the village peacekeeper. Tilim could have gone, but he really didn't want to leave his mother and Percia in case there were any more of these intruders lurking around. And truth be told, he still felt a mite shaky.

"Tilim, I'm going to wait down here for help to arrive. I'll have Baki with me," said his mother. "I need you to go up to my room and lie down next to Percie. She's miserable alone up there. Can you do that for me?"

"Don't you want me to stay with you, Mama?" said Tilim.

"I'll call you if I need you," she answered. "Keep your sword handy. But Son, would you take off your boots? And here, let me wipe you off a bit."

She washed and washed Tilim in the kitchen bucket. The water grew quite red. He cautiously tiptoed around the dead man sprawled on the stairs and went into Mama's room with Percia. Percie made a fuss over how brave he was and all, till he told her to hush up. He lay down on the bed next to her, held her hand to comfort her, and—woozy from the liquor—fell asleep.

In the morning Tilim heard the rest of what happened in the night. Hecht had come to the house, and when he'd found the tracks of four horses coming and going, he had raised a posse of locals. Hecht figured one of the scoundrels had stayed with the horses, but he had too much of a head start. The posse came back empty-handed and none the wiser about the motives of the four ruffians.

They'd moved the bodies and Mama had scrubbed the floor by the time Percia and Tilim came downstairs in the morning. The house looked a bit disordered, but not scary.

Because this was a major crime, Duke Naven and Captain Walmunt, the head of his personal guard, were sent for. No one could recall anything like this happening in Androvale—four armed strangers attacking a cottage! It was not as if they owned anything valuable. Were the intruders after the womenfolk?

Now Tilim had to tell Hecht his story about noticing the strangers following them, and the owner of the Wyndton Arms was questioned. All he knew was that one of the men asked about Percia, claiming he knew her from her years in Gulltown.

Duke Naven and Captain Walmunt arrived around midday. The captain put on a grim face about the whole business. He said he was proud of Baki, Tilim, and Rooks, but he didn't focus on their heroism quite as much as Tilim would have liked.

The duke kept repeating to the air, "A nasty business! A nasty business! In my duchy. I won't have it, I tell you; I won't have it!"

After some hours of this, when no progress was made on the investigation, Duke Naven turned to Mama. "Missus, when was your family fixing to travel to Cascada for the wedding?"

"Around Planting Time, sir," she answered.

"Pack your things," he ordered. "All of you, all your things. My men will help. You are going to stay at the manor house for the six moons until you sail, so the duchy guard can keep you safe."

"But—my school," Percia protested. "My mother's loom. Tilim's little friends and Rooks and Lemle. We can't just leave all that behind."

"No?" said Duke Naven impatiently. "Were you going to take your Wyndton life to the palace when you marry Lordling Marcot? Girl, you made your choice."

Percia crumpled in on herself. In that moment, Tilim hated Duke Naven.

"But we weren't about to abandon it all in a tick, neither," said Mama, her hands on her hips and her eyes taking on a look that Tilim knew could mean trouble for anyone who crossed her.

Duke Naven must have recognized the danger he faced from Mama, prepared to do battle. He raised his hands in exasperation. "All right. All right. I watch out for my people. I'll leave two men to keep an eye on you for two weeks. But I can't station soldiers in one cottage forever, you know.

"Finish up your business here. All your business and all your goodbyes. At the end of the time, I'll send a wagon to fetch you."

36

Cascada

This evening was the fourth time that, after bringing his winter vegetables to the Central Market in Cascada (telling Eyevie they would fetch a higher price in the big city than in their local hamlet), Yanath stayed late with his former shieldmate Pontole to search the quayside taverns for Branwise.

Tonight Pontole and he had gone around in circles, revisiting places they'd gone to before. Yanath felt frustrated and longed to collect his wagon and head home. But knowing the importance of their mission, he persevered.

Luck was in their corner, though, because after they tried Sea Wench (to no avail), they peeked into a dingy establishment called the Beached Boat. Oil lamps and pipe smoke formed a haze in the long, narrow room half full of patrons, but after a moment Pontole elbowed Yanath in the side. Halfway down the counter, visible through gaps in the sparse crowd, a disheveled man who was sitting alone, humming tunelessly, nursing a whiskey and drawing patterns in the moisture on the wood, had Branwise's physique, Branwise's ears, and Branwise's big, scarred hands. In fact—'twas Branwise himself.

Pontole moved noiselessly to sit on one side of him, and Yanath slid onto the stool on the other.

"Hey!" said Branwise, gazing at Pontole with recognition. "Hey!" he said, turning his head the other way and squinting at Yanath.

"Hey, yourself," said Yanath. "Do you still snore as loudly as you used to?"

"I don't know," said Branwise, taking the question too seriously. "When I'm asleep I cain't hear myself. Hey! Ain't seen you fellas in forever. Buy me a drink for old times' sake?"

"Nope," said Pontole. "No drinks."

"No drinks?" said Branwise. "You guys turned dry?"

"Nope," said Yanath. "We're working. You remember about staying sober when you're working?"

"Ahh!" said Branwise, nodding sagely. "What're you working *at*?"

"Actually, we was searching for you," said Pontole. "Run our feet off looking everywhere. You're a hard bloke to find."

"Searching for me? Well, you found me, so let's cele—"

With a forceful bang the door of the tavern burst open and bounced off the wall behind it. A squad of soldiers crowded in with swagger and noise. The barmaid gave a frightened squeak, and the bartender carefully laid both hands on the wooden surface in front of him.

"Don't want no trouble," the bartender said.

Yanath studied the intruders. They weren't the city watch, nor palace guards; they wore red sashes. He raised his eyebrows at Pontole.

Pontole mouthed, "Matwyck's Marauders."

The room had fallen dead quiet except for the coins the barmaid had dropped on the ground. These rang as they rolled about the floor.

These Marauders obviously hadn't stopped in for sour ale. Yanath glanced around, calculating if the three shields could escape through a back door.

"You, there!" roared the leader of the squad, a beefy, fat-faced man, directing his attention to the tables on the side. Yanath realized that the speaker wasn't paying any attention to the former Queen's Shields; he was shouting at a table of sailors on the far side of the room. "Which one of you shitwits goes by the name 'Gourdo'?"

One of the sailors stood. He wasn't in uniform, but Yanath recognized Seamaster Gourdo, part of Lord Ambrice's circle from the war against the Pellish pirates. The man had aged but still carried himself with dignity.

"I am Gourdo," he said. "Who wishes to address me?"

"I'm Captain Murgn," answered the swaggerer, "and you're wanted."

"Wanted by who and for what?" asked Gourdo.

Murgn drew his sword, and his men did likewise. The tavern was narrow for so many weapons; the other patrons pressed themselves back against the walls, overturning some chairs in their haste to get out of the way.

The bartender said again, "Don't want no trouble." No one paid any attention to him.

"Wanted by me for shooting your mouth off. You've been heard talking." Murgn's voice went up an octave and became mincing: "'When the queen returns' and 'When the queen takes power' and 'When the queen'—my arse!"

"Where's the crime in talking about the queen?" asked Gourdo. "I've been in the Queen's Navy all my life."

"Ain't no room in Cascada for mal-con-tents," said Murgn. He spit on the floor. "Come along now." He waved his free hand toward the doorway.

"Cap'n, don't go!" implored a young sailor from his table.

"Cap'n, there's six of us!" said another, grabbing his tankard of ale.

"Aye, but lads, you're not armed tonight, sitting having a pint, expecting a peaceable evening," said Gourdo. "I'd hate for any of you to take hurt."

Under the cover of the bar counter, Yanath slipped his dagger out of his scabbard.

Reaching across Branwise's belly roll, Pontole grabbed Yanath's wrist. He whispered, "Our business is too important to get tangled up with this. Let it go, Yanath."

Seamaster Gourdo walked slowly around the table toward the bullying guards. One of them gratuitously struck him in the head with a metal-studded leather glove. Gourdo's knees sagged, and the young sailors jumped to their feet, overturning their table. Instantly, Murgn had his sword tip in the youngest sailor's neck. He wasn't just touching the lad; by the amount of blood gushing down his shirt, the point had already penetrated the skin perilously close to cutting into the sailor's throat.

"My, you're a tasty morsel," said Murgn. "Do you want to keep breathing? Then sit back down and drink your pint of piss like a good little boy."

Murgn snapped his fingers at his team of guards. They grabbed Seamaster Gourdo by each arm and hustled him from the tavern. The room remained paralyzed with shock.

"Don't want no trouble," said the barkeep again, his eyes glued down on the counter.

"Then treat those sailor boys to new pints and keep your trap shut," said Murgn as he backed out of the room.

"I'm going to be sick," said Branwise. He bolted from his stool out the back door. Pontole and Yanath could hear him retching in the alleyway.

"For guts, I'd take the sailor any day," muttered Yanath to Pontole as they followed Branwise outside.

Vomiting cleared some of the liquor out of Branwise's system. Pontole and Yanath walked him around in the air, then bought him a plate of sausages at a tavern. On the second cup of tisane, Branwise's eyes cleared up enough that they knew he was listening.

"We're hoping to talk you into giving up the demon rum," said Pontole.

"Give up the demon rum?" said Branwise, holding his tisane mug protectively just at the suggestion. "Now, why would I do that? I was drinking *whiskey* tonight. And I'll give up neither rum nor whiskey. Better friends than you. *They* never desert me."

"No one deserted you, Branwise. We just had to make a living and you became a sot," Yanath said. "Let's get out of here. We'd like to talk to you about something important."

"But I haven't finished," answered Branwise, instantly truculent.

"Then swig that last swallow. We've been searching for you for hours, and it's getting late."

Branwise glanced up at them with a touch of his former shrewdness. "You guys were looking for me. Looking for *me*. You ain't just concerned about my future. Is there something you want?"

Pontole looked about the empty room; then, whispering, he told him the story about sitting at the Nargis Fountain and hearing the Water's message. Yanath studied Branwise's face as Pontole told his tale.

"Let's go there now," Branwise said, rising so abruptly his trencher and mug swayed.

"Go where?" asked Pontole.

"The Fountain, you lackwit. The ever-lovin' Fountain."

Yanath barely had time to grab some coins out of his pocket to pay the fare and follow; Branwise began running up the hill from the quayside as if his life depended upon it.

Huffing, the three men arrived at the Courtyard of the Star, which at this time of night sat deserted with the exception of a few bored city watch keeping an eye on a clump of beggar kids. The Fountain sang low in the moonlight, the Nargis Ice shining like a star close at hand.

Branwise cupped his hands and drank Nargis Water from the

Fountain again and again. Yanath cursed himself for being so out of shape that a short uphill jog winded him. Then he dipped his hand, and as water dripped off each finger he murmured each of the five prayers: Home, Health, Safety, Comradeship, and the Future of the Realm. Each of the prayers brought to mind images, painful or precious.

Yanath didn't want to just pray for the Future of the Realm; after what he'd witnessed tonight he wanted to fight for it.

"All right, Bran," he said, after he dried his hand on his shirt. "I'm tired of dicking around searching for you. I'm tired of your drinking and puking. I'm tired of thugs like that pig in the tavern. I'm tired—I'm just plain tired of a lot of things. Are you in or are you out? Right now. Tell me."

Branwise stopped lapping Nargis Water. His eyes had cleared, and he had a peaceful smile on his wet face. "Aye, I'm in."

Slightly over a week later, Pontole brought Yanath and Branwise to meet Nana and Brother Whitsury in the Abbey of Sorrow. Whitsury put a finger to his lips and led them by a circuitous route around the back of the complex, through the vegetable and herb garden, down a flight of stairs to the basement, and then through a lengthy corridor to the annex called the Queens' Rest.

This crypt held the elaborate stone tombs—each carved with representations of her Talent and accomplishments—of all the Nargis Queens of Weirandale stretching back at least three centuries. Although the crypt lay beneath the floor of the abbey reading room, glass portals had been cut into the ceiling and the coffins placed in such a way that thick shafts of natural light fell in a pattern around the room, illuminating each of the queens' resting places.

Yanath would have liked to examine the monuments, but Nana stood waiting for the three shields there. The room had two doors:

the small one Whitsury had just used and a grand double door that led to the official entryway. The Brother of Sorrow stationed himself watching and listening at the public door. The air felt dry and cool on Yanath's skin, and the shafts of light made it bright enough to see clearly. Through the ceiling Yanath could hear a choir practicing hymns in the abbey.

Nana shook Yanath's and Pontole's hands, then turned to Branwise. He'd lost weight since the night Yanath had last seen him, undoubtedly from going through a rough time getting the liquor out of his system. But for this meeting he'd washed and tied his springy hair back. The skin on his cheeks was scraped raw, and three bright red nicks showed how shaky his hand had been as he shaved.

Nana took both his trembling hands in hers and looked at him closely. Branwise hung his head for a moment, then blew out the breath he was holding and gave a slight nod.

"Shields," Nana said, "'tis grand to see you."

"Tell us, Nana, what's going on," said Yanath.

"Nothing's going on this instant," she answered. "But someday the princella will return to claim the Nargis Throne. And 'tis not bloody likely that bastard—drought damn his eyes!—will give up power easily. He'll try to stop her. The moment she steps on Weir soil she'll be in danger.

"All I can hope is that she'll make contact with me. That is where you'll come in. I want you to be the core of a new Queen's Shield, defending her through any trouble."

"Nana, we would die for her," said Yanath. "But with only three of us against the whole corps of palace guards, much less the Marauders, we *will* die before we can be of much use."

Pontole jumped in. "On our way here, Yanath and me, we was talking about allies. When we scoured the harbor dives looking for Branwise, we thought . . . what about the mariners? Those that didn't drown off the Pellish coast—*they* was loyal to Queen Cressa and Lord Ambrice. Could we recruit from their ranks to bolster our numbers? True, they don't have as much training in hand-to-hand as us shields, but during our years in the Green Isles we saw 'em fight with real guts."

Brother Whitsury and Nana looked at one another, surprised at the new idea.

"How would you go about it?" asked Whitsury.

Yanath answered, "I would first approach the seamasters like Wilamara, who distinguished herself so that time she led the raid on Jade Isle. I asked around; I hear she still lives."

Nana said thoughtfully, "Mariners was always on the steadfast side. I'd wager they'd want to protect Ambrice's daughter. . . . What would you tell them?"

"Just exactly what Pontole told me," Yanath answered.

"And what if one of the seamasters, or one of their sailors, betrays us?" asked Whitsury. "We'd all be thrown in one of Yurgn's pits."

"We have to take that chance," said Yanath. "Because three against hundreds isn't bravery—'tis idiocy. And we don't want to die *trying* to get the princella on the throne. We want to live, *succeeding*."

Nana nodded. "That we do. I've been thinking we need more allies. I'd thought of that former councilor, a man named Belcazar. Mayhap you remember him? Ach, it makes no never mind 'cause I don't know how to reach him. Besides, yer idea is more practical. Sailors are better fighters."

"We need to put ourselves in training," said Yanath, looking at Pontole and Branwise. "Hone our skills again. Once upon a time, we was pretty slick."

"And we can be again," said Pontole eagerly.

"Mebee now," Branwise interrupted, "would be a good time to pledge ourselves once again? I want to be a shield again."

"Aye," Yanath agreed. "Nana, you're our leader now—will you stand in for Captain Clemçon and the queen?"

Walking with a slower and more dignified gait than her usual trot, Nana moved next to a half-finished sarcophagus. A shaft of light revealed that it was open and vacant except for a blue silk lining and a blue pillow. Yanath grasped that it had been meant for the queen he had failed, the queen whose body floated forever alone and lost in the Gray Ocean. He grasped the bottom edge of the coffin in a tight grip.

"Queen Chinika's shields . . ." Yanath said, recalling the lore he had learned. "There was only three of them left, and they laid her body on a stretcher and carried her back from Northvale. That's about five hundred leagues. Even when they got to more populated areas, those shields wouldn't lay down their burden or accept help. She died under their watch, but they brought her home. They fulfilled their duties; we're the ones who failed."

"One never knows," said Whitsury, turning his head from his lookout, his gray eyes kindly, "when there's an opportunity for valor or what form it will take. Those shields rest in unmarked graves and we don't even know their names, but the deed lives forever. And someone like Nana, now, she's done nothing so showy, but she's stood by faithful for years. Waiting patiently can be another kind of heroism."

"I want to be a shield again," Branwise repeated. "Let's pledge."

The three men, all past their prime and with shoulders weighed down by regrets, bent a knee before Nana and piled their hands on top of one another's. Together they spoke the words that Yanath had first learned twenty years earlier, when Captain Clemçon—rest his soul—had first invited him to join the ranks.

Henceforth, I know my purpose. I join the Queen's Shield with pride, eager to uphold its trust.

My Queen is but blood and breath, yet she serves as Cupbearer of the Waters.

I dedicate my eyes, wide and watchful; my arms, strong; my nerves, steadfast in the face of fear.

I pledge these talents to my post, in life or in death, so that the Queen may reign in peace and the Waters of Life flow never ceasing.

Yanath lifted his head, feeling a flood of strength and the steadiness of duty.

It must have been the glass portals bending the light beams from the abbey above, but he saw a hint of a rainbow mist around the figure of the stout nursemaid.

PART
SIX

Reign of Regent Matwyck,
Year 15

SPRING

37

Cascada

If anyone had been watching—and no one was—all they would
have seen was a young woman, informal in trousers and a black
bodice; her manservant, wearing a uniform with white fringe epaulets and holding a case; and a large brown dog with one floppy ear
stride forward off a wooden dock and onto the soil of Cascada.

Nothing happened. No bells tolled, and no one marked her. The
people bustling about the harbor area went on about their business
and paid her no never mind. Cerúlia looked around, hoping that
something about the layout of the port would say "home" to her,
but all she saw was another harbor—less well-managed than some,
considering the chaos of noise and crowds.

Well, she thought, *at least I have returned unobtrusively.*

Today, despite Ciellō's protestations, she wore her donkey boy
garb. Really, due to his care, she had no choice, because as she had
regained weight and muscle her stylish Wyeland outfits had grown
too tight.

"Damselle, will not you let me into your confidence still?" After they passed the rocky Cormorant Isles and the coast of Weirandale had become visible, her advisor had grown avid to know her plans.

"No, Ciellō," she said. "I cannot. I hired you to escort me here, and you have done so, most assiduously. I have profited from your care, but per our contract your duties now are at an end. What I have to do in Cascada, you cannot help me with. Besides"—she tapped the purse at her waist—"as you know well, we're nearly out of money."

"I do not wish to be discharged," Ciellō insisted stiffly. "I will wait for you to finish your business so mysterious and to realize that I am invaluable."

Cerúlia regarded him. Often these moons she had thought that he would be relieved to complete his commission and regain his freedom, and sometimes she suspected that the multiple ties between them had grown too complicated to be easily severed.

"I already know you are invaluable. If you insist on staying in Cascada, I cannot stop you. Actually, for the next few days, it would be a boon if I were not burdened with my case or with Whaki. Could you keep him for me?"

A narrowing of Ciellō's eyes showed that he was offended.

"You think I am not capable of a thing so simple?"

"I should have said, 'Would you do me that service?'"

"Of course." Ciellō tapped a sailor on the shoulder. "Excuse my interruption, could you tell me of the decent inn?"

"Right in town?" asked the sailor. "Most everything is full, what with the wedding and all. But the Sea Hawk has a big hall of bunk beds. It's a safe bet."

Ciellō turned to Cerúlia. "That is where a dog and I will be. When you finish your private affairs and you want me again." He took the rope they had affixed to Whaki's neck. Whaki pulled back toward Cerúlia with pleading eyes.

One wants to stay with thee.

No. Go with Ciellō and obey him until I send for you. Go on. Don't give me that look.

She could not afford to be distracted by either Whaki or Ciellō today. She walked off the quay, past the fishmongers and the sailors' taverns, into the city itself. Above her she saw the chunk of Nargis Ice held aloft by the spray of Nargis Fountain—it mesmerized her. She thirsted for Nargis Water.

Glancing around for a horse-drawn carriage, she spotted many engaged, but none free, waiting to pick up passengers. The streets were thronged; but at least Cerúlia took slight comfort in the sight of horses rather than gamels, and in familiar fashions rather than the dust-coats, craftans, or pinafores of foreign lands. She chose a side alley, instead of the major boulevard. Within a few moments of walking, she found her path impeded by two women chatting to each other, blocking the passage between two stone buildings.

"Just the grandest occasion ever!" exclaimed one.

"Excuse me," said Cerúlia, trying to bypass their gowns stretched wide by petticoats. They stared at her and shifted their feet a fraction.

She had almost succeeded in squeezing by when she realized what they were talking about. Cerúlia halted, whirled, and addressed them.

"Ladies, pray excuse me. I just arrived by ship. Is something going on, such as a fête or a wedding?"

The older woman looked askance at her informal and salt-stained clothing. The younger was more polite. "Oh, yes, it's *so* exciting. The son of the Lord Regent is getting married tomorrow. There is going to be such an enormous celebration! All the gentry have gathered, and Lord Matwyck will be throwing such a party for them, and a feast for the townsfolk and even fireworks. Lucky for you you've arrived in time."

"Indeed," Cerúlia dryly remarked.

"And it is such a romantic love match!" continued the woman, barely pausing to catch her breath. "You're a stranger? You don't know the story? You must be the only soul in Weirandale who doesn't. You see, Lordling Marcot was traveling in Androvale, and he met this just beautiful young woman, and even though she's only a commoner and he's a lordling, he was adamant that he was going to marry her—"

"Come along," said her companion, pulling at the arm of her garrulous friend and starting to move away.

A shiver of premonition ran down Cerúlia's spine. She importuned them again: "You didn't say—who is the bride?"

"Really, Ifany, we've been inconvenienced enough by this *person*." The older woman pretended she couldn't see or hear Cerúlia.

"Tell me!" said the princella, grabbing on to the younger woman's trailing hat ribbon.

"Her name is Percia of Wyndton," said the chatty one. "Fancy that!"

The older woman pulled the ribbon out of Cerúlia's hand, which had gone slack. "Ifany! Stop encouraging the riffraff." She scowled at Cerúlia. "You! Leave us alone now, or we'll call the city watch." The two proceeded on their way.

"Fancy that!" echoed Cerúlia faintly, and she stood struck dumb in the crowded alleyway, oblivious to the people trying to pass around her.

Recovering her wits, Cerúlia ascended the hill to the Nargis Fountain.

The Courtyard of the Star buzzed with guards, tourists, and vendors, but Cerúlia's gaze focused only on the Fountain. She feasted on the Water's graceful high arcs. She cupped her hands, dipped them in the pool, and drank of the icy water—her overheatedness, fatigue, and anxiety dropped away. The cold liquid she splashed on her cheeks tingled. She sat inside the rainbows of mist; they watered her—roots, stem, and branch. She listened to the Water's splash, a song half remembered and sorely missed.

Since Femturan she had harbored a secret dream that once she got home, Nargis Water would erase her burns and heal her shoulder. Sitting on the Fountain's quartz ledge, however, she could perceive no change to her body—the Water refused to work its Magic on her. She felt refreshed, but not renewed or remade.

Cerúlia refused to indulge any sense of disappointment.

All right then. I earned these scars and the memories that go with them. If Nargis had to heal only one of us, I'm glad the Spirit chose Percie's leg.

A blue tanager preened itself in the spray. It swooped down to the Fountain edge in front of her.

He cocked his little head this way and that. *Your Majesty, high time thou returneth.*

So animals keep telling me! But you! You can't be the same tanager I knew as a child.

One has never met thee. But one has been waiting for thee just the same.

Well, here I am. At last. But I have no plan to regain the throne.

All through the moons at sea she had puzzled over the task ahead. She was no Strategist. She had no way to make people believe in her identity. She had no means to force Matwyck to give up power. All she had was a fixed destination—the Throne Room—and her Talent.

And now out of the blue she was presented with this wild complication of Percia's marriage. Didn't this mean that the Wyndton family was close by? Would this help or hinder her?

The scents emanating from the vendors' carts reminded Cerúlia that she was hungry. She had a few foreign coins in her purse. She bought apple fritters from a countrywoman, hot and greasy, redolent of home. The fritters tasted so wonderful that she went back for two more.

The worn-looking woman smiled at her. "Hit the spot, did they? This time let me slide this bit of cheese between them, summat to fill the belly."

Cerúlia accepted the food gratefully. She stood next to the woman as she ate the second helping more slowly. "I've been traveling. How is Cascada?"

"Where are you from, if you don't mind my asking?" said the vendor.

"Here," she replied. "But I left many years ago. It seems . . . different . . . now."

The woman glanced at her sideways. "The harvest came full last fall. What we get to keep. The Lord Regent's men are heavy-fingered and heavy-handed." She seemed to make up her mind to trust the traveler. She hissed, "My neighbors' son protested the tithe. . . . He's been missing four moons now."

"'Missing' kilt, or 'missing' imprisoned?"

"No one knows. You can ask at the jailhouses, but you don't get answers. Lots of folk go missing; anyone who raises his voice about the way the country is run. It's kind of safe by Nargis's Fountain. My, it runs fierce today. Don't run afoul of Matwyck's Marauders."

"I am grateful for the food and the warning," Cerúlia replied.

The vendor gave her a friendly wink and turned to another customer.

Cerúlia set out again up the hill and headed toward the palace, whose white towers she could now see at the top of the hill. But since she'd already walked up from the harbor, she wasn't eager for the tramp. If there were no carriage cabs to be hired, could she find other means of conveyance?

Alert for an opportunity, she scanned the streets for several minutes. Eventually she saw a wagon train of four carts, each heavily loaded with supplies. Roughly dressed haulers dangled their feet off the open backs. The first cart was just starting to move. The driver's seat of the third cart sat empty—the driver probably answering a call of nature. Relying on her experience from the carters' yard in Slagos, she climbed aboard the cart as if she belonged, nodded to the haulers in back, picked up the reins, and clucked the horses to pull out into the street.

She kept in line following the cart ahead. These streets and buildings offered the scenes of her childhood, but she could not gawk at the sights. (*Like that bell tower to the right, which looks so familiar—I think it is part of the abbey. Or the Church of the Headwaters—I know it lies down that street!*) Despite the need to concentrate on steering the cart away from collisions, she realized that Salubriton's streets had been cleaner, and in Slagos store owners took more pride in their decor and flowers.

She felt a stab of fear when the carts turned off the main thoroughfare to the palace. Then she grasped that the lead driver was just avoiding the most crowded byways and bringing his load in a circle around by the Kitchen Gate.

Indeed, the carts clattered up to a squad of soldiers who blocked the roadway, demanding to see the papers of the head driver. Once inside the cobbled yard, Cerúlia watched the other cart men to ascertain if they stayed with the horses or helped unload. They stayed with their teams; a couple lit pipes. One of the other drivers kept glancing at her with puzzlement written on his brow; obviously she wasn't the person he expected.

More carts jostled in noisily, bringing in more goods. A footman yelled at the haulers to work faster, get their pig-fuckin' wagons unloaded and out of the way, didn't they know this was a busy day?

Cerúlia spoke to the cart horses. *I'm getting off here. Follow your fellows out of the grounds.* She jumped down from her seat, grabbed a random cask up onto her shoulder, and carried it to the loading area, which was filling up with wooden boxes and racks of hanging geese. Kitchen workers armed with checklists marked off items as they arrived.

She tried to saunter through the porch way into the kitchen itself.

"Hey, you! Where do you think you're going?" A beefy palace guard blocked the door.

"I was just going to get a drink. Thirsty work, this," she answered in an aggrieved tone.

"Get along with you," ordered the guard, unsympathetic and suspicious. "There's a pump in the yard. Or are you blind as well as lazy?"

Cerúlia jumped on the empty cart bed of another wagon that was just leaving. The other haulers looked at her in surprise.

"Say, wench, where'd you spring from?" said one with bad teeth.

"Missed the cart I came in on," she replied shortly.

"Kind of scrawny for a hauler," said another man, eyeing her body with a leer and poking her waist with a dirty finger.

"You'll leave me alone if you know what's good for you," Cerúlia replied in a firm tone, placing her hand on her dagger's hilt.

"Temper! Temper!" retorted the man. "Don't flatter yourself. *You* ain't no prize pigeon."

A few streets outside the palace, when the cart paused in heavy traffic, Cerúlia leapt off. She scurried down a narrow and shadowed alleyway, fearful that someone would be following her. She pressed herself into a doorway, scanning both directions.

She had tried her acting skills, and this time they hadn't been sufficient.

How am I going to get into the palace? It's guarded so tightly.

Deep in her memories, Cerúlia recalled a play park and a gate that squirrels could open. It had been called . . . West Gate, so it must be on the west side of the palace. Cerúlia oriented herself and began striding in that direction.

The neighborhood of wealthy mansions near the royal grounds sat quieter than the middle of the city. Cerúlia walked purposely, pretending in her mind that she worked as a stable lad, and that her master had sent her on an important errand. The blue tanager flew over her shoulder and perched for a moment on the stone in front of her.

Where didst thou go? he asked.

I tried to get into the palace, but the way was blocked. Do you know a small gate on the west wall?

Course one does.

He led her to a small iron gate in the tall stone wall. The day had run on: light had begun to wane. Cerúlia tried the gate, only to discover that it was locked and double-barred from the inside. At her request, squirrels attempted to free the door, but they did not have the strength to lift the iron bars.

Tanager, is there any other way for me to get in the grounds?

The squirrels and the bird conferred; then the tanager led her to a stately tree that had a long bough stretching over the stone wall. Cerúlia regarded it with a scowl. This tree would be difficult for Ciellō; how could she, with her compromised shoulder, manage it? She studied the handholds and footholds carefully in the gathering gloom. After looking around to make sure she was unobserved, she took a running start to jump up a pace high, grabbing a lower branch and wedging her feet into rough spaces in the bark. She clung for a moment, then reached for another handhold. The bark under her left foot gave way, and she slid, scraping against the trunk, all the way down.

Thinner trousers would have ripped. Even with her thick material her legs felt chafed inside the fabric and her hands and forearms sustained deep scratches. Cerúlia rubbed her hurts a moment while studying the tree more carefully, trying to recall the way she had climbed the cliffside into Oromondo. She tried again. This time her foothold broke only after she had grabbed the treasured upper bough with her right hand. She hung there perilously. With great effort she got her left arm around the branch too, but even both arms lacked the muscle to pull her up and astride. She swung her legs a little, then a little more, making her feet hit flat against the stone wall; then she walked her feet horizontally up the wall so she could cross them over the branch, leaving her hanging upside down like an opossum. She wiggled her body forward along the branch and over the wall until the palace grounds appeared below her, then dropped her feet and hung by her weary arms. She let go and tried to absorb the fall in her knees. The twinge in her ankle was insignificant; she could walk off the sprain.

The tanager had flown over the wall easily and now perched a pace in front of her. *All right. I'm inside the palace grounds. Now what?* she asked the bird.

The palace lieth a long way in this direction.

Her legs were tired, but the princella set out at a steady pace, grateful for all her training aboard *Misty Traveler*. Soon the tanager, a daytime bird, took his leave. The moons came out, both just slivers in the inky sky. She passed amongst trees and shrubs that might remember her from her childhood, but which loomed about her as unfamiliar shadows. Had she ridden this path on Smoke? She tripped on a root in the darkness and just barely caught herself before she tumbled.

Finally, after more than an hour, when she could see lights from the palace, she paused to consider her next step. Could she climb a roof? Find an open window? Sneak inside the palace?

Then her eyes fell upon the base of the building, and she noted the ring of guards stationed at intervals of fifty paces around the circumference. The palace walls stretched low around the entire grounds, and as she had just proven, they were hardly impregnable. Matwyck's Marauders—their sashes bloodred instead of the white of the ordinary guard—encircled the palace itself, providing another layer of protection. Cerúlia watched these men for a while. They had been marshaled out in force, and from their posture and stance she judged that they were vigilant. She had little chance of sneaking by.

So. With guards everywhere she turned, she couldn't steal into the palace. She would need to be *invited*.

38

Lemle couldn't sleep, but that was not unusual. The jail cells were so crowded with men caught up in the Marauders' dragnets that no one could find a place to stretch out, and the air hung fetid with waste and body odors.

Noises reverberated against the stone walls. The prisoners would cough, mutter, or moan, while the guards would laugh amongst themselves or purposefully make a clatter to destroy desperate dreams of open air and freedom. Lemle found that he missed the quiet woodland sounds of crickets and birdsong that had surrounded Rooks's shack as much as he missed the sunlight that he used to take for granted.

As near as Lemle could count, he had been held in captivity for two moons. When Rooks had died last winter and Stahlia and Percie had returned from their safe—if stilted—refuge in Naven Manor for the funeral, Lemle had told Percia he wanted to move to Cascada and pursue his dream of becoming an engraver. Stahlia had loaned him the money for his voyage, and Lordling Marcot had kindly arranged a position for him at the Type and Ink Press in a commercial neighborhood of Cascada.

Lem recalled how excited he had been by his job and the sights and crowds of the capital city. He'd felt as if a new world had opened to him and he was finally about to live on his own terms. He'd gazed at the men on the streets and wondered if an unrecognized future love was right that moment passing by.

He'd been such a naive fool.

Lemle had only been working at the press for a fortnight when the shop was raided by guards in red sashes. They had grabbed the owner and thrust a handful of leaflets in his face.

"Did you print this? Did your shop print this?" their leader demanded.

Lemle's new master had denied it ever more vehemently during the repeated questioning, but the soldiers didn't believe him. Picking up one of the leaflets from the ground, which was a cartoon of Lord Matwyck as a bloated pig, Lemle didn't believe him either, because he recognized the paper stock the Type and Ink used, and the page had a small tear at the corner characteristic of one of their hand presses.

The men started beating the owner. They held back Lemle and the three other apprentices either with rough handholds or pointed weapons. Then the brutes stuffed his master's mouth with leaflets and held his nose while he choked, thrashing on the floor, clawing on their hands, and his face took on a purplish color.

After this display of sadism the guards gathered up the four stunned workers and carted them off to jail.

"I've only been here a fortnight!" Lemle protested. "I had nothing to do with this leaflet!"

"Shut up," said a guard, and he punched Lem in the stomach for emphasis.

When they reached the holding cells on the edge of Cascada, Lemle tried again, shouting to the jailers, "Just let me send a message. I'm sure my patron will want you to release me."

A uniformed man delivered a volley of blows to his belly and finished him off with a kick to his privates. Lemle shuddered, remembering the agony.

When Lemle came out of his shattering pain on the cell floor, a group of wiser prisoners set him straight.

"Look, boy, it don't matter if you are guilty or innocent. Most of us are innocent, or at least innocent of what they say we done."

"Look, boy, no friend nor family nor patron can help you here. No one can get word to wives or fathers. Once Matwyck's Marauders have you, your only choices are imprisonment or death. If you wise up, you might yet live awhile."

Death might come any number of ways, Lemle learned, as he wised up over the next weeks. Guards randomly selected men for the public executions that were held to frighten the populace. Or if you caused him too much aggravation a jailer might just bash in your head. Or a desperate fellow prisoner might strangle you for your rations. You could also die of the flux or any one of a score of other illnesses.

Anonymity and mistrust added to the prisoners' miseries. Lemle didn't know whether the fellow printers he'd been arrested with were already dead or whether they, like him, had just been shifted to another holding place. The population of the cells shuffled almost daily with new prisoners coming in and others being taken away. Lem shrank from trying to form a bond with another prisoner, because the pal you made today might be gone tomorrow, or might sell you out to the guards for extra rations.

Tonight Lemle gave up trying to sleep and sat up. The old man sitting on the bench in the corner nodded at him. Lemle had noticed the elderly prisoner when he'd been brought to this cell a couple of weeks ago. The man's lank hair floated all the way down his back, indicating he'd been in captivity a long time. He looked frail, but the jailers didn't mistreat him; in fact, Lemle observed that when passing out food they often gave him a large portion and served him first.

Smiling encouragement, the old man patted the bench next to him and beckoned Lemle. Lemle was so disconsolate that he snatched at any offer of companionship, so he threaded his way over his other dozing cellmates, trying very hard not to step on anyone, getting cursed at when he didn't succeed.

The ancient prisoner slid over to make room for Lemle on the bench.

"You're not from Cascada, are you?" he whispered.

"No, I just came here recently, from Androvale," answered Lemle.

"Androvale. Major city, Gulltown. Principle crops: apples and hardwoods," muttered the old man.

"That's right," said Lemle. "Have you ever been there?"

"Been there? No. But I could tell you were country-bred by how much you tossed about. Rural folks have a hard time adjusting."

"Where are you from?"

"I believe this is my nineteenth jail," his seatmate answered, ignoring his life beforehand.

"*Nineteenth!* How do you stand it? How long have you been captive? How do you keep from going mad?" Lemle kept his voice low and cast his eye on men lying nearby; he really didn't want to disturb anyone from their escape in sleep.

"How do I stand it? The trick is to find little boons. For instance, this place is better than the one that had mold and much better than solitary confinement. I get to talk to people here, such as a smart young man like you."

"Focusing on tiny benefits has kept you going?"

"I refuse to go mad, and I refuse to die. I just won't give them the satisfaction."

"How long have you been imprisoned?" Lemle repeated.

"What year is it?"

"Year Fifteen of the Regency."

"Really, is it now?" The old man grinned. "Then I've been held for fifteen years. How are things in the outside world?"

"Not great," said Lemle glumly, seeing in his mind an image of the owner of the Type and Ink choking to death. "You've been held since the beginning? That's forever."

"You are a young man; you should hold on to hope of outliving this regime. I am an old man, and *I* refuse to give up. What's your name?"

"I'm Lemle of Wyndton. What'll bring about this miraculous turn for the better? What'll save you and me and all the other wretches?" Lemle gestured out at the sea of misery that surrounded them.

His cellmate patted Lemle's knee and whispered in his ear, "The queen's return."

"Pah! What makes you think she's coming? She might be living a life of ease in Lortherrod, she may have abandoned us, or she could be dead by now. Or she might try to return and not be able to overthrow *them*."

"No. She's too strong for that."

Lemle snorted at this rosy vision. "You're living in a fantasy, sir. Or, no offense, but you *have* lost your senses." He closed his eyes, feeling weary and wondering if he could nod off sitting up on the bench. But he didn't want to desert the first person who had treated him kindly in days. "You didn't give me *your* name."

"No, I have faith," said the stranger, picking up lost threads of the conversation. "You see, I knew her when she was a child. A strong and smart child. I had the privilege of serving as her tutor. I am Master Ryton."

"So what?" Lemle wasn't usually rude to his elders, but the man's persistent optimism grated on him. "I'm sure that hundreds of people knew her. That doesn't mean you can see the future."

Stubbornly, the elderly man batted away Lemle's doubts with frail hands.

Lemle insisted, whispering, "And even if she comes, is she bringing an army with her? Do you think this lot"—he nodded his head toward the coarse jailers down the hallway, drinking and playing cards—"is going to roll over for one queen?"

"'One day the drought shall be broken,'" muttered the old man, reciting a line from the famous poem about the queen's eventual return.

"Yeah, yeah, I've heard that too. 'And the wondrous Waters will course clean' and all."

"*Really?*" The old prisoner was astonished. "*You* know those lines?"

"You've been in jail too long. Everybody knows the whole 'Dusty Throne'; that's gone around for ages."

"Truly?" asked the old prisoner.

"Of course." Lemle scratched his neck, wondering if there were fleas here. "You'll hear it in every tavern in the land and ofttimes in a Church of the Waters. Or at least you used to, until reciting it became a crime."

"Has it now?" Master Ryton broke into a self-satisfied smile. "I didn't know. You see, I wrote it in jail five. Jail five had rats—I had to stay up nights to fight them off—but there I was blessed with paper and ink."

He marveled, "How did my composition travel? Mayhap a jailer picked it up. . . . But you are from Androvale, you say. My verse traveled that far!"

Despite his depression, Lemle was impressed to meet the poet of the now-famous rhyme. He was about to say so when a jowly passing guard called out, "Hey fellas, come look at this. The loon's found himself a young beau."

Only one of the jailers was interested enough to stir himself. He came to the bars of the cell and leered at Ryton and Lemle, then made a rude joke to his fellow that had the two guffawing.

"Isn't that pretty boy on our list for the gibbet?" one jailer said to his chum.

"Yep, but all executions have been halted this week. Orders from above 'cause of the wedding. The old loon can enjoy his pet for a short while."

And the jailers puckered up their lips and made kissing noises.

39

Cerúlia slept fitfully under a thick lilac bush that was threatening to bloom, until a skunk that kept watch over her through the dark hours woke her in the morning.

One must seek one's den. It's getting too bright for one.

Did anything happen while I was asleep?

No human saw you. A male came this direction, but one chased him away. The skunk chortled. *Just a determined little rush and they always flee!*

Thank you for your help. Cerúlia stroked the small animal from the top of its dapper head to the end of its long tail. The skunk flicked his long tail in a goodbye salute and scampered out of sight.

As the light grew bolder, Cerúlia tried to make herself more presentable, rubbing the dirt and dried blood off her hands and patting her braid (she had allowed Ciellō to fix it in a chignon to hide her burn) back into shape as best she could.

She spied on the red-sashed guards, noticing with relief that their rounds ended in the daytime hours. Servants, administrators, gentry, and white-sashed guards began carrying on their business around the palace; everyone looked busy and excited rather than wary. The princella carefully chose a place to join a traveled footpath and strolled out of the bushes with a pretense of normalcy. No one on the grounds paid any attention to a lone woman in working garb.

She asked the tanager to lead her to an inconspicuous doorway. It looked promising; only one footman, holding another clipboard, stood outside the unprepossessing entrance.

Cerúlia smiled at him. "Is this the way into the palace?" she asked in her most innocent voice.

"For servants of the wedding guests," he frowned.

"Ah. What if I am Mistress Percia's maid?"

"The wedding party came with no servants. And you're not in livery." The footman started frowning. "Guards!" he called, grabbing her arm. Immediately, two burly soldiers appeared from an interior vestibule.

Not a good choice, tanager, she sent to the bird, who looked away and pecked at nothing, avoiding responsibility.

"This woman tried to walk in," said the footman to the soldiers. "Yet she can't be a visiting servant. Look how dirty she is!"

"What's your business here then, eh?" asked the taller of the guards.

"I'm a friend of the bride's family," Cerúlia answered, falling back on the truth.

"Ah! That would explain why you come to the palace dressed like this! Bumpkins! I told you!" said the footman to the guards with undisguised contempt.

The guards still harbored suspicions. "The bridal party didn't invite any guests from Androvale, except for the duke and duchess, and they're already in residence. Besides, how'd the likes of you get into the grounds? Show us your pass."

Cerúlia ignored the question about entrance, again relying on the truth. "They didn't know how to reach me. I have been traveling. Nevertheless, they will want me at Percia's wedding, I am certain. Send for them and see."

A bit of doubt crept into the guards' eyes.

"Keep the minx here and keep a close eye on her," said the shorter one, "while I check with the sergeant." He disappeared inside.

The footman told her to "rest her arse" on a stone bench in the small patio outside the entrance. Cerúlia sat, trying to ignore such insolence and calm herself by looking around at the garden plantings, some of which were just coming into spring bloom. An azalea bush was studded with buds, each offering a tiny slash of pink.

A short walk to the left, down a stone pathway, she recognized the palace's Church of the Waters. The building called to her; she longed to visit its Fountain to wash her face and drink cool water. She must have attended Waterday services there as a girl; some buried memory stirred.

She wiped her hands on her trousers and tried to think of how Percie's Wyndton friend, Dewva, would handle this situation. How would she convince the guards that she really was part of the wedding party?

The guardsman returned after an absence of only a few minutes.

"Sarge says that the gentry are busy and he thinks it would be his head—or rather, *our heads*—if they were disturbed. He says to bring the dirty wench to him."

"I don't want to see any more of you fathead guards." Cerúlia flared up with what she hoped would sound like a country woman in a huff. "Actually"—she stamped her foot—"I *refuse*. You've treated me so rudely! The Wyndton visitors are going to be angry. Where does your sort get the nerve!" She thought of Dewva and put her hands on her hips.

"Look, fatheads, why don't you give me a piece of paper and a quill and I'll write a note you can pass to the bridal family? Then they can decide. The longer you lot ill-treat me, the more trouble you're gonna be in."

The footman shuffled uneasily, exchanging glances with the

guards. "I don't see too much harm in that. . . ." He disappeared inside and came back with a sheet of paper, a quill, and a pot of ink, which he thrust at her.

Cerúlia stared at the writing implements a moment; her mind tumbled, empty of stratagems regarding how—all of a sudden—to address a note to her Wyndton family.

"I can't write on this rough stone bench; I need a wooden surface," she mumbled to the men watching her, before leaping up and speeding off into the Church of the Waters.

The taller of two guards and the footman followed after her, muttering "What's this nonsense, wench!" But she didn't care; she just wanted to be inside Nargis's house. There she would be able to quiet her nerves, and she'd find the words to write to the family she had deserted.

The palace Church of the Waters was modest-sized, intended only for the private prayers of the palace community; but even so it possessed its own unique elegance and aura of peacefulness. Light flooded in through stained glass windows, making the polished walnut paneled walls and benches shine. The Fountain situated in the center stood as tall as Cerúlia herself; it had waterfowl images carved into rose quartz and water lilies blooming in its lowest basin; the water flowing down nine levels made a tinkling sound. At this midmorning hour on a hectic day at the palace, the room stood empty, its air soft and refreshing.

Cerúlia walked up to the Fountain, letting its movement and murmur soothe her.

The guard growled, "Hey! Wench! We've more pressing duties. If you're going to write this letter do it now; otherwise we'll tumble you off the grounds posthaste!"

Cerúlia found a smooth wooden bench to use as a desk and knelt on the floor beside it. She still didn't know how to phrase this note, but the church had comforted her enough to start.

Teto Wilim and Teta Stahlia,

   Fate has washed me up in Cascada. I've learned that you are here too,
for Percia's wedding. If you could find it in your hearts

At this moment they all heard a commotion outside the church
of laughter, voices, and bustle. Cerúlia's first instinct was to hide herself, but that was impossible in this open nave and, besides, her wary
escorts stood watch over her. She just stiffened in her kneeling position like a terrified doe who hopes if she keeps completely still no
one will see her half-hidden behind a shrub.

The double front doors opened from an energetic yank, letting
in a flood of bright sunlight that edged a group of ten people in
fancy dress, led by a Brother of Sorrow. Duke Naven's bulk made
him easy to recognize. And gliding in behind him . . . *Stahlia, Percia,
and Tilim.*

Cerúlia's breath caught in her throat. The guard and the footman
bowed to the entering party, but busy with their own matters, the
newcomers ignored the bunch of palace workers.

Quietly, Cerúlia stood up from the floor.

The Brother of Sorrow spoke to the assembly in a mild but au-
thoritative tone. "Now, Duke Naven, you will escort the bride down
this center aisle, while Lordling, you and your father and Master
Tilim will be waiting at the end of the north aisle." He was pointing
out the locations to everyone. "We need to practice the pace of the
walk so that everyone reaches the Fountain, where I will be standing with the nuptial cup, at the same moment. All right? Why don't
we take our places? Duchess Naven, would you oblige us by standing in for Lord Matwyck this morn?"

"I'd be honored," said the duchess.

Chattering and laughing amongst themselves, the wedding
party dispersed as he had directed them. Stahlia and a few others
seated themselves on wooden benches to watch, while Duke Naven

and Percia retraced their steps to the front entrance. Duchess Naven and a handsome young man walked toward the opposite lane without passing near the three onlookers, but Tilim chose the aisle that led him closest to the Fountain and thus closest to where Cerúlia, clutching the writing implements against her chest, stood, her heart thudding.

The guard gripped her upper arm to protect the gentry from this stranger under his supervision. As Tilim neared the grouping, his forward pace faltered.

Wonder at seeing the boy she had helped raise overcame Cerúlia. In three years he had grown much taller and his face had matured, losing the baby roundedness that had been so dear to her.

Almost without meaning to speak, she burst out, "You're going to be as tall as your father or taller."

Tilim's shock rendered him mute.

"Don't you recognize me, Tilim?"

His face came alight. "I knew you'd come back. I knew it! I told everyone. I knew it! I knew it!" Tilim launched himself at her, gathering her in a hug so forceful it almost knocked her over, while the inkpot spilled all down her leg.

"This is my *sister*," Tilim shouted at the man holding her. "Let go of her! This is my *sister*! Mama! Wren has returned to us!"

40

When the tempest of shouting and embracing started to slacken, Stahlia realized they were no longer in the Church of the Waters.

Someone—had it been Marcot? it must have been Marcot—had ushered her family out of public scrutiny and into a nearby antechamber of the palace. Oil cloaks and umbrellas lined the wall; rows of boots sat in labeled cupboards. She found the vestibule's order and privacy a comfort at a moment when her world had gone askew.

Stahlia pulled her wayward daughter back from the embrace to look at her again. Here she was, live as day, not a phantom or a dream. Yet so changed.

"Where have you *been*? How could you leave us?" Stahlia gave her a little shake.

Wren just mutely shook her head.

"Why didn't you write to us? Don't you know how much we fretted? Three years!" Stahlia demanded, shaking her again. "You like to broke our hearts! And the worry!"

Wren looked stricken, but resolute. "I couldn't. I couldn't write to you or have any contact with you."

"Why? What possible reason could there be for being so heartless?"

"Mama! Mama, leave off! She's here now," said Percia, pulling her sister from her mother's grasp, hugging her and rocking side to side almost in a dance step. "What a miracle! I always pictured you returning to us in Wyndton, and when we moved I left a message for you at the Wyndton Arms. But you've appeared out of smoke, here in Cascada, just in time for my wedding!"

"Are you really getting married tomorrow, Percie? Are you happy? Do you love him?" Wren asked, speaking into her tall sister's neck.

"Oh, Wren, if you'd been home I would have had someone to talk to about how wonderful Marcot is."

Tilim broke in, "She's told us often enough. Do you mean you wanted to talk about him *more*? Percie's been a lovesick cow."

"But Wren, he *is* a swell chap. I wouldn't let Percie go to just anyone."

Perhaps Wren caught something in Tilim's inference that he would grant his sister permission to wed. She looked at them all with her forehead scrunched.

"But why is *Duke Naven* walking you down the church pathway? Where is Wilim?" she asked. She pulled back, stood still, and glanced around the room. She asked again, *"Where is Wilim?"*

"She doesn't know," Percia told her mother quietly.

Stahlia sighed, took Wren's hands, and sat her down on a rough, low bench made for pulling on boots. "Birdie, Wilim is not with us here in Cascada. He joined the Waters shortly after you left us."

"No! No, that can't be true." Shaking her head, she looked around at Tilim and Percia for confirmation. "What? Why?" She must have read the truth on Percia's face. "How did he die? Did he sicken?"

"He killed himself," Stahlia said, biting the words. "We don't know why."

Wren's face began to crumple like a broadsheet being wadded up. She hid it in her hands.

"This happened—when?" she spoke into her fingers.

"About a moon after you disappeared," Stahlia answered. Her voice hardened. "He couldn't recover from your disappearance. Do you know anything about it? I need answers. I've gone nigh crazy not understanding how he could leave us."

"But it's not your fault, Birdie, of course it's not your fault." Percia jumped in to protect her sister from Stahlia's probing. "You couldn't know what he would do after you left."

"All this time . . . while . . . I've been gone I've pictured him at Wyndton. I thought he was riding Syrup, keeping the duke's peace, caring for the ward. You mean, all this time he was already gone?" She started rocking herself back and forth on the bench.

"Hush now, hush now," said Percie, sitting next to her and patting her shoulder.

"You mean I'll never get to thank him for . . . everything. I never dreamed—" Wren choked out.

Tilim broke in, his voice strained. "Stop crying! *Everyone stop crying!* I mean it. I can't take any more tears! This is a happy day! I order you all to stop this crying this instant!"

Her son had inherited some of Wilim's sense about people, and Stahlia knew he was right. The remnants of this family would shatter under the strains of joy, guilt, and recrimination. It was hard enough to be here in Cascada, hard enough to deal with these gentry and their strange customs, hard enough to think of Percie getting married and leaving them. And now to have Wren suddenly rejoin them and to dig up all the past heartache!

It's up to me to pull us together. Wilim would want me to weave us back whole.

Stahlia found her linen kerchief tucked in her belt. She wiped her own tear tracks, then turned Percie's face up to the light from a narrow transom and wiped hers.

Kneeling by the bench, she said, "There now, Wren. I'm sorry. Get aholt of yourself. I know you feel the pain now, but this happened long ago. Wilim has been safe in the embrace of the Eternal Waters for years now. We four are here. Tilim's right. Let's be thankful for being reunited at last."

Wren took a few ragged breaths.

"Come on, Birdie. Wipe your eyes and blow your nose," said Stahlia. "I know this came as a shock. We're all having a few shocks today." She let out her breath in a noise that became a ragged laugh. "We'll hang on tight to one another and see each other through."

"Good girl," said Tilim, encouraging, patting Wren's knee. "You don't want Percie to look a mess when all these strange people are staring at her and judging her, do you?"

Gradually, Wren's distress quieted enough for conversation to resume.

Deliberately changing the subject, Stahlia said, "Tell us. What about your babe? What about your sailor?"

"There was no babe. There was no sailor."

"I knew it!" cried Percia. "But then why did you leave us?"

Wren shook herself and stood up, twisting her hands together.

"I'm sorry. You must know that I didn't leave you out of choice, and I've thought of you every day, regretting the pain I caused you. But the night I left I learned I was in danger, danger that might spread to you." She held up her hands. "I can't tell you *anything* now; I will tell you *everything* as soon as I am able."

"*What?* Why the delay?" Stahlia asked. "You owe us—"

Tilim interrupted her harsh tone. "Because Percia will be safely married off, and Marcot's father won't call off the wedding because of our feckless sister!"

Wren managed to half smile at him. "Something along those lines. I know it's unfair. I know I owe you all an explanation. But I can't give it now." She stood even straighter now. "And I ask—this is serious now, Tilim—that you not talk about how closemouthed I have to be. I ask that you just tell everyone that I am your foster sister who lived with you in Wyndton and recently took a sea voyage to settle some personal affairs. By the Grace of the Waters, I managed to arrive in Cascada for the wedding." Her expression was steady and searching. "Can you do that? Will you promise to do that?"

Percia spoke up. "You are very mysterious, Birdie, but I'm so happy to have you back, you could ask for Nargis Ice and I'd climb up the Fountain to give it to you."

Stahlia gazed at Wren, so familiar and yet so changed, with narrowed eyes. "You'll tell me everything after the wedding?" she probed. "You'll hold nothing back? You won't disappear? Your word on the Waters?"

Wren held out both hands to Stahlia and looked her straight in the eyes. "I vow, Teta."

A soft knock on the outside door interrupted their treasured retreat.

Stahlia swiftly glanced around to ensure that all of her charges had arranged their faces for public scrutiny. "Enter," she called out.

Brother Whitsury opened the door with an apologetic expression. "I am so sorry to intrude, madam. But the chamberlain worries about our keeping to the day's schedule. . . ."

Lordling Marcot joined Brother Whitsury in the open doorway. "The day's schedule be hanged! We'll change the damn schedule if need be. Mistress, take all the time your family needs. Is there anything I can get you—do you need anything?"

"No," said Stahlia firmly. "We are recovered now. It was quite a shock to have my other daughter appear like—like an apparition in the church. A wonderful shock . . . Thank you for granting us these precious moments to catch up. We are sorry to have kept everybody waiting. We are ready now to return to the rehearsal."

"But, Teta, I'm not fit for grand company," Wren said, with a significant glance at her own clothing. She looked very rustic indeed, and she had ink splashed down her trouser leg. "Might I, perhaps, be excused to join you later . . . ?"

"Chamberlain Vilkit would be pleased to see to your guest's

comfort," said the lordling. "Percia, would you be so kind as to introduce me to the apparition?"

Although her face was still blotchy, Percia glowed. "This is the best marriage gift ever! Lordling Marcot, may I present my *sister,* Wren of Wyndton. Wren, this is my *betrothed,* Lordling Marcot."

Marcot made a formal bow to Stahlia's second daughter.

"I am delighted to make your acquaintance," said her future son-in-marriage. "Percia has often spoken of you. I am so happy that you are able to join us for this occasion. The Waters have blessed us with their favor."

Wren curtsied in return, with downcast eyes. "You are too kind, milord."

Now that's the quiet, humble Wren I know, Stahlia thought. *But can this modesty be put on and off, like one of these oil cloaks hanging here?*

41

An under-footman stood before Vilkit's desk in his office, the "command post" of a massive campaign. The room, usually a paragon of order, showed the stress of combat, with heaps of bills of lading bedecking tables, masses of flowers that had yet to be arranged temporarily left in buckets on all his chairs, and a table linen with a burn mark wadded up and thrown in the corner.

Vilkit had been chamberlain of the palace for three years. This wedding presented the biggest challenge of his career. If all went off well, he might retain this position for life, and laurels would be heaped upon him. If a terrible slipup occurred, he would be held responsible, regardless of actual fault. Lord Matwyck probably wouldn't have him killed, but Vilkit had discovered that the Lord Regent was not above a small physical cruelty, such as a broken hand or a punctured eardrum. This hardly endeared the Lord Regent to his chamberlain, but Vilkit was prepared to tolerate a modicum of terror for this prized position. Besides, he didn't intend to fail.

The trouble with food was that ingredients had to be fresh; thus only so much could be delivered in advance. The head cook worried so over whether the provisionaries would deliver enough geese, his anxiety had become contagious.

On the day before the wedding, however, everything had elapsed according to Vilkit's schedule and plans. The two paltry mishaps—a visiting duke complaining his rooms were not grand enough and the wine steward noticing that the vintner had overcharged them—Vilkit had handled with his usual efficiency.

But this under-footman cringing before him presented the chamberlain with a novel and potentially bigger quandary.

"How was I to know who she was?" the man whined. "No one told us about a *sister,* and she's dressed like a carter."

"And you say you treated her roughly?"

"No! I didn't touch her. Well, aye, I did grab her arm. But that wasn't rough. I didn't cuss her, not really. We was just being careful, as we was ordered to be. You know our orders about strange visitors."

"Give me a straight answer: Will Lady Percia have cause to complain that you treated their nearest kin without due deference?"

The under-footman scrunched up his whole face. "Aye, chamberlain."

Vilkit rose. "I will have to see what I can do to remedy this situation. Leave me and try not to commit any more blunders."

Vilkit hurried to the Church of the Waters, where Duchette Lolethia breathlessly informed him of the melodramatic event—a lost sister's return! The Wyndton family were currently sorting out their messy personal affairs in the coachmen's vestibule (of all places); meanwhile, Lordling Marcot, Duke and Duchess Naven, a Brother of Sorrow, and two councilors were just waiting, kicking up their heels, on this, the busiest of all days.

Vilkit paused to run his hands down his uniform to smooth any creases and pat down his hair, lest his haste had caused any disarrangement. Then he approached the Brother of Sorrow.

"Brother Whitsury, you need to be done with your rehearsal by midday bells because of the midmeal. Lord Matwyck will be waiting. I am afraid we really must try to keep to the schedule."

Just at that moment Lordling Marcot managed to extricate the bridal party from the vestibule. Marcot introduced the late arrival to him.

"Wren of Wyndton, may I introduce Chamberlain Vilkit?"

Vilkit immediately decided not to be harsh on the under-footman; really who could imagine this slops boy to be someone of importance?

"Oh, milady"—a title she didn't deserve, but flattery usually oiled gummed works—"I regret that the staff has not shown you all due courtesy. If only we had known you were coming to join us on this special occasion! My heartfelt apologies! Please, milady, tell me how I may be of service to you?"

"I am pleased to make your acquaintance," said the young woman, offering her hand to shake, a strangely masculine gesture.

Vilkit took her hand, smoothly turned it over, bent and touched it with his lips as he made a deep bow.

"I take it your arrival in time for the wedding is just fortuitous?" he asked. "We must make you welcome! Where is your baggage? I shall have it fetched. Have you dined? Would you care to come this way?"

"No luggage," answered the sister. "No, I have not dined."

"Vilkit, please, will you see that my sister is made welcome and cared for?" said Marcot.

"Of course, Lordling. It will be my honor. Milady, if you will follow me?"

Where am I going to put this new guest? All the rooms in the palace are full of visiting gentry. I can't insult her by putting her in a servant's room. I dare not ship her out to an inn. Not after the way she's been treated.

And now she needs clothing too! What a nuisance—these country-folk! Showing up for a palace wedding without proper garments! This woman's needs are going to occupy a servant's whole afternoon. Who can I assign to her who isn't essential elsewhere?

While pondering how to handle this increasingly messy

complication, Vilkit also led the guest into the palace through the ornate "Church Entrance."

"Your first time in Cascada? Your first time in the Nargis Palace, I presume?" he said to the young woman. He would flatter her with some of his time and a look at the palace's grandeur. "Let me show you a sampling of our treasures." He escorted her through a hallway and past a few lesser rooms.

"Here we are: this is the famous Gallery of the Queens and Consorts. This long hallway connects two wings of the palace. On the right you will see portraits of all the queens of Weirandale. Well, not all, because several queens ruled before Chista the Builder had the palace constructed." He pointed to the first portrait. "You see, we start here with Chista herself."

The country girl came to a dead stop in front of Chista, examining the painting closely.

"Ahem. Let me show you just the highlights. Now, if you will please come this way, milady, here is Cenika the Protector."

"Her Nargis Ice is a shield pendant!"

"Yes, isn't that stirring? And, here, everyone loves to look at Chyneza the Wise."

"Because of her lovely crown?"

"How very perceptive you are, milady; yes, the Nargis Ice tiara is stunning, is it not?"

"Where is Carmena?" the guest asked, gazing down the expanse of portraits.

"How odd that you ask for her; despite the famous lay we don't often show her off."

"Why not?"

"Well, her Royal Stone is very plain, you see; just this odd, mis-shapen rock around her neck." In unconscious mimicry, Vilkit made a fist in front of his own throat as he led her several paces forward. "I wonder what Nargis was thinking of. And the queen, while estimable of course, is not, well, the most striking-looking of the queens."

"Hmm." The guest made a noise so neutral he didn't know whether it signaled assent or disagreement. "Is that a dagger she wears around her waist?"

Vilkit looked closely. The portrait was dark; he wondered if one could clean oil paintings and if he should have done so before this fête. He could hardly see the detail that interested the country sister. "Many of the queens wear much nicer swords. Chaynilla the Warrior has a sword studded with diamonds. She's down here a ways. Let me show you."

"Just a moment."

The girl seemed lost in reveries in front of Carmena, despite her strong jaw and wide forehead. But she barely flicked her eyes over Chaynilla's beautiful sword or Clesindra the Kind's perfect teardrop of Nargis Ice, which affixed to her cheekbone so magically and which never failed to impress other visitors. A couple of aristocratic visitors to the palace strolled through the gallery, and Vilkit bowed respectfully.

She asked to see Ciella the Patient, probably because of the sentimental song about a love affair that lasted after death, and then she thoughtfully walked across the gallery to look at her prince.

Vilkit worried about geese, wine casks, and whether the scullery maids were breaking dishes. He really had to get back to his office. Servants might be looking for him; all hell might be breaking loose in the stables between temperamental coachmen.

"Ahem," he coughed discreetly. "We need to move on, milady; 'tis such a busy day in the palace."

"Just two more, Chamberlain Vilkit," she replied unhurriedly and without apology. "I'd like to see Queen Catreena the Strategist and Queen Cressa the Enchanter."

Vilkit led her down to the far end of the row of portraits. He tried to point out the significant details in the paintings of the last two queens, such as the map in the background of Catreena's picture, and the way the folds of Cressa's gown hid her pregnancy. But this rustic lass shushed him, staring at the queens with deep concentration, as if she would drink them in. Then she walked across the gallery to gaze at King Nithanil of Lortherrod, consort to Queen Catreena. When she turned to Lord Ambrice's portrait she gasped. It was a very nice portrait; Vilkit had heard that it caught the very essence of the man, standing with feet firmly planted and nautical instruments on the table beside him. The country lass reached out as if to touch the Lord of the Ships.

"Oh, I'm afraid no one is allowed to touch, milady! The oil paints are precious, as you can imagine, and we wouldn't want the artists' work besmirched by dirty hands."

The visitor turned to look at Vilkit then, and her eyes had a spark in them. Vilkit had the uneasy feeling that she had registered his remark about "dirty hands."

"Tell me, Chamberlain," she said, "were you employed in the palace during the reign of Cressa and Ambrice?"

"Alas, no. I have been here only three years."

"Then you never knew them?"

"Alas, no. Only by reputation, in the way that everyone knows the rulers of Weirandale."

"So you serve Lord Matwyck?" she asked, returning back to gaze at Lord Ambrice.

"I do serve Lord Matwyck," he replied. But then, perhaps because they had spent all this time in this gallery, he added with more forthrightness than was his wont, "Because he is the present regent. But my title is 'Chamberlain.' I actually serve the palace. The palace includes"—he swept his arm in a grand gesture—"all these queens, all this history, going back forever and ever."

Finally, the guest allowed him to escort her to the room where he had decided to lodge her.

"I will send a maid to wait on you momentarily," he informed the last-minute arrival. "Normally, we do not allow visitors to stay in these chambers. But since you are kinswoman to the bride, I am happy to make this exception."

He threw open the door, adding a touch of drama. "I am lodging you in the Princella's Bedchamber!"

42

Nana was bone-tired. Vilkit had been working them all at a furious pace for the last moon, ever since the public announcement of the wedding. These final days he had placed her as supervisor of the china closet, instructing the footmen and maids as to which plate and glassware to lay for which meal, and checking that each dish came back from the scullery spotless and unmarred. She'd been at it for the last two days since dawn. With luck she could snatch a few hours of break now to put her feet up, because the pre-wedding sup-per table had been set, though later tonight she would have to see the dishes returned in proper order and every piece of silver counted twice.

All in all, she thought that Vilkit had managed everything quite well. The staff worked with a will, though whether out of fear of the Lord Regent, or affection for Lordling Marcot, she couldn't tell. It could be that the palace workers shared the anticipation of the city folk; all Cascada flapped about in an excited hubbub about the gen-try's luxurious gowns and the rare feasts and the fireworks. Nana reflected that someday the inhabitants would rue the taxes levied to pay for these festivities.

But just now a sheepish under-footman came to tell her some

long-winded tale about how he'd been rude to a late-arriving guest and Vilkit had put her in the Princella's Bedchamber, and he hoped Nana would not be wroth but would help placate this country lass by attending to her as only Nana could.

Nana was not happy to hear her domain had been invaded in this manner. The Princella's Bedchamber should never be used for guests; it should be kept inviolate. Furthermore, by lodging someone there Vilkit had also ensured that Nana would have to wait upon this guest day and night and she'd get no free time. And Nana's feet hurt and her eyes felt gritty.

She knocked sharply on the door of the Princella's Bedchamber.

"Enter!" called a female voice.

Nana opened the door, walked in, and closed it quietly. Standing in the middle of the room, gazing out the window toward Nargis Mountain, stood Queen Cressa. Nana automatically made her curtsey, asking, "How may I serve Yer Majesty?"

The queen started and turned in her direction. Only—it wasn't—it couldn't—be the queen. Her darling, her Cressa, had been dead these ten years, leaving Nana with a hole in her heart.

This was the country girl Vilkit wanted her to care for. Her brown hair was fixed in a foreign-looking plait, and she was wearing rough breeches splashed with ink.

"Oh, beg pardon! My eyes are playing tricks on me and I'm an addled old fool," Nana said.

The girl stood frozen, perhaps in awe of her surroundings or in shock at Nana's odd slipup.

Why did I think this stranger was the queen? There's something about the way she stands, the shape of her face—everything is the same, but different too.

Oh Nargis!

"Chickadee!" Nana whispered, sinking to her knees. "At last! I've been waiting so long! Where have you been?"

"Nana! Could it be?" The young woman stood transfixed for

another moment; then she rushed over to her and got down on her own knees to embrace her. "I'd hardly dared hope that you would still be in the palace! And in my chamber!"

"And where else, pray tell, would I be?" Nana replied with asperity. "I told you that I'd be waiting right here. Well, here I be, practically in the exact same spot, on my knees in yer room."

"Oh, Nana! I've missed you so! I've felt so forsaken, down to my toes."

"Tush! You've never been forsaken, not for one instant." Nana patted her cheeks. "Nargis has always been watching over you. Didn't you know that, girl? And I've been waiting for you. Took yer time, didn't you, getting back here!

"Come now; let's get up. Hurts my knees, and it won't do for a Nargis Queen to crawl about on the floor!"

The young woman helped Nana to her feet. Nana took her by the arm and tugged her into the light from the window. With her soft, wrinkled fingers she traced her former charge's features: her velvet eyebrows (so well remembered), her cheekbones and jawline (which exactly repeated her mother's), her chin (which used to jut so stubbornly), and her lips (which used to be so saucy). Her eyes were brown whereas Cressa's had been stormy gray, and her lashes showed recent weeping. Her hair was a surprise, but it took more than hair color to fool her nursemaid.

Then the princella smiled her very own dazzling, joyous smile—the smile that used to cajole Nana out of being cross at her, the smile that was broader than her mother's and had a touch of her father's sunny confidence. She patted Nana's shoulders, and Nana felt years of fearful waiting lift, like a mist rising off a wet flagstone, warmed dry by a daybreak long awaited.

"Are you well, Nana? No one has hurt you?"

"I've grown ancient, girl, and I'm tired. It's been hard to bide my time, and I've had so many duties. I've been trying to get ready for yer return."

Nana's searching fingers found the burn scars on her neck. She stroked them tenderly. "My little one. What kind of trials have *you* gone through? And to return and be treated rudely by a footman! I'll have his scalp. That man is gonna be gutted and boiled alive!"

"You leave him alone now, Nana, so he's not suspicious."

The princella captured Nana's hands and squeezed both of them within her own. The roughness of the girl's skin and the ridges of scars and calluses—speaking of a life of toil and want—scandalized her former nursemaid. But rather than scold any more, she bit her tongue.

Cerúlia kissed Nana on the brow, making tears spring into her eyes.

"Where have you been?" Nana asked.

"I grew up in Androvale, but for three years I've been traveling. Oh, it's a long, long story—much too long to recount today."

"Well then, girl, as to the present—how do we get you safely Dedicated and sitting on top of that throne?" Nana asked. "Matwyck would clap you in a dungeon if he knew you was here."

"Aye, I've got to find a way into the Throne Room."

"The usurper keeps it locked up tight and patrolled day and night," Nana warned. "And once you're inside, even if you claim yer name and yer own Nargis Ice from the Fountain, what's to keep him from arresting you or something worse?"

The young woman waved away these warnings as if they were a minor inconvenience.

"Nana, revealing my identity and claiming the throne is only the beginning. All these years, I've had a lot of time to think. To think about how Matwyck got so strong in the first place and why the people didn't rise up to defend my mother. Why our gentry live so rich and the rural folk so poor. Why Oromondo hates us so. How am I going to bring Matwyck and his confederates to justice without a civil war? My task is much larger than just getting my backside on the throne."

The princella collapsed down on the divan, as if the mere thought of the challenges ahead exhausted her.

"Nana, I've not been trained to be a queen, and all these years I've longed to know loads of things—oh, like how laws get enacted. But lately I've wondered: What if our veneration for the queens has hidden their faults? I was just looking at their portraits. What if Clesindra 'the Kind' was also Clesindra 'the Stupid'? What if Cenika 'the Protector' was also Cenika 'the Vain'? I know Catorie swam the Bay of Cinda, but was she good at managing the treasury?"

"Queens are women, girl. Though Nargis blesses them with Talents for their times, they have their faults and they make all kinds of errors. Queen Catreena, yer grandmother, wise as she was, had a cold heart—that I remember well."

"I need to talk to Tutor Ryton and Chronicler Sewel. But right now, Nana, you must tell me." She looked in Nana's eyes as if this was the most pressing issue at this perilous moment. "Was my mother a good ruler?"

The nursemaid took the liberty of sitting down on the divan next to her former charge and patting her hand. "I might be the wrong one to ask, being as I raised her. I know she tried every day to do right. And she loved you with all her heart." She paused a moment, considering. "But the whole country and the palace factions . . . Mayhap it was all *too big* for her, if you catch my drift."

The princella sighed. "Yes, I understand. And what I wonder is . . . if I'm up to these challenges, not just getting Dedicated, but ruling."

Nana didn't know what to say that would give the princella confidence. In all her planning for the return of the Nargis heir, she had just assumed that once Cerúlia took the throne, all the realm's problems would melt away.

"Well, yer certainly not up to the task looking like that!" Nana said, rousing herself. "Is that ink?"

"I think so," said the princella, tugging at her spattered trousers.

"Don't scold. Ruining these clothes is the least of it. Nana, I've not eaten today; I crave a bath; and I must have a dress to wear tonight to the dinner and to the wedding."

Nana noted with mingled approval and disappointment that despite her trials the girl sounded exactly as if she had been giving orders all her life. "I will start the tap for the bath, then send for a tray."

When she came out of the bathing room after turning on the faucet she saw that Cerúlia had taken off her boots and begun to unlace her bodice. "Nana, did you know that Percia of Wyndton is my sister, my foster sister? Do you remember the day I met her, in West Park?"

"*You* know Lordling Marcot's intended? Oh, aye, that muckwit of a footman said that yer her sister."

"How did it happen that I arrived the day before her wedding?"

Nana lifted her hands in a helpless gesture at the coincidence, though privately she suspected Nargis's intervention. "Spirits save us, Chickadee, even if we don't know why.

"As for garments, yer dear mother's wardrobe lies through the passageway. I've been watching over it for years—turning the gowns so they don't set wrinkles, airing them out, keeping the moths away. I imagine I can find something to suit."

She took a measuring look at Cerúlia. "Though girl! Yer father gave you a bit of his height! Yer taller than Queen Cressa was. If I hadn't shrunk over the years you'd be as tall as me. I'll have to find one of her longest skirts."

"Who is this?" said the princella, bending to stroke the orange cat that had just slipped in through the Passageway of Lost Babes. He arched his back and held his tail straight as he vigorously rubbed against her leg.

"Don't you recognize Plump-pot? He was one of yer kittens when you left. He's an old man, now, but he seems to know *you*. The last thing you asked me was to watch out for yer pets, and I did."

"Ahhh. I knew you would. I've worried about many things over the years, but I never worried about that."

"Humph," Nana grunted, feeling both taken for granted and gratified, as she strode to the doorway to send under-maids a-scurrying.

43

Matwyck didn't like surprises. Part of his sense of control came from always being well-informed. A new guest at his table? A traveling sister who fortuitously appeared right before the wedding?

Thus, Matwyck was relieved to see that Naven and his wife recognized the woman.

So she really is a Wyndton lass. Very well. I will question her later.

He might have thought more about this provincial visitor, but several knotty situations swirled about him in the Salon of Queen Cinda, one of the rooms that ringed the upper stories of the Throne Room with a balcony. Moonlight shining through the panes of stained glass of the Throne Room leaked in through large, window-like openings onto this balcony. The light added a prismatic halo to the lantern glow that shone on the guests' jewels and gowns, on the sparkling table settings, and on the centerpiece ice statues. All in all, the room presented a magical sight, but Matwyck was beset from all sides.

His intended, Lolethia, was jealous about the amount of money and elaborate pomp going into Marcot's wedding. She complained that it would drain the treasury and upstage her own nuptials.

Of course Matwyck couldn't tell her that after the assassination attempt had failed he'd had to pretend that he was wholeheartedly behind this match in order to assuage suspicion. Marcot was no fool, and even that buffoon Naven could be wily. Besides, with the marriage going forward, Matwyck decided he could turn it to his advantage after all: it might be good for his image to embrace this commoner—show his sympathy with the little folk and such. So he had ordered a large wedding. Surely Councilor Prigent could squeeze the money out of one cache of the treasury or another. That weasel had his tricks. He smiled benignly in Prigent's direction.

At every course, every new bottle of wine, and every new china setting, his sweet little crumpet sent daggers at him.

"Darling, wait until you see what I have planned for us!" he whispered in her ear.

"Will we use the plates with golden patterns?"

"Everything will be the best in the realm."

Tirinella would never have shown such petty jealousy. It would have been beneath her to dwell on such trifles.

The room did look quite grand. The forty-odd dukes and duchesses, his own factotums and key allies, and the family of the bride sat dispersed amongst two long tables. Matwyck was seated, of course, in the middle of the High Table raised up on a dais, with Lolethia at his side, and Marcot, seated in between his betrothed and her mother, across from him.

The bride's family caused no trouble. They had agreed to all the arrangements, respectful and uncomplaining. No, the second problem lay in the fact that most of his invitees behaved arrogantly toward his new relations. Matwyck didn't appreciate it when they raised their eyes at the little brother's country manners or tittered at the mother's unfashionable dress. He tallied up the cutting remarks; someday those snobs would pay. They had forgotten that he, Matwyck, was lowborn as well, and he took their insults as personal slights.

But while Matwyck could watch the nobles and keep count for a later reckoning, Marcot was having a very difficult time stomaching their condescension toward his betrothed and her party. Matwyck had to keep one eye on his son, ready to intercede to keep him from speaking his mind, causing a scene, or worse.

Duchess Latlie was sniggering about something with Lady Dinista. Matwyck couldn't catch their words, but their glances revealed that the object of their scorn was the weaver. Marcot glared at the women and opened his mouth.

"My son, you are failing at your host duties," Matwyck smiled as he intervened just in time. "Pray, refill Mistress Stahlia's glass. And let's get your lovely bride another serving. . . ." He summoned the servant and managed to distract Marcot from responding in anger.

By dint of adroit machinations, Matwyck succeeded in steering everyone safely through the main courses. Before sweets were served, preparations commenced for the evening's entertainment, a presentation of the Wedding Pageant.

Showing this one flash of stubbornness, Percia had insisted that the Wedding Pageant be part of the ceremonies, but she had acquiesced, with maidenly grace, to Matwyck's suggestion that it be performed at this smaller, prenuptial banquet rather than tomorrow. Marcot (so besotted) insisted on dancing with her, and had arranged for Cascada's troupe of Royal Dancers to fill out the corps.

The meek sister helped Percia by tying her hair up in a ribbon that matched her peach-colored gown, detaching her outer skirt, and sliding on a pair of golden wrist cuffs. Marcot took off his constricting jacket and handed it to a servant. The musicians took up their instruments to play a prelude. Many of the guests stood up or turned their chairs so as to have a better view of the entertainment. The dancers took their places in the portion of the large room purposely left uncluttered by tables.

The Wedding Pageant, Matwyck discovered, is a narrative dance. Percia and Marcot walked to meet one another in the middle; they danced with their raised hands just barely touching one another's.

Then the troupe separated them—Percia to the left and Marcot to the right of the room. The dancers surrounded the lovers with obstacles by enclosing them in rings of crossed arms, or by having new people try to entice them away from their betrothed. As the music rose to a crescendo, the lovers evaded the obstacles and came together again in the final figures, to dance arm in arm under a canopy of sprays of willow branches held by the troupe.

Marcot's joyous face when the dance brought him back to Percia tugged (a bit) at his father's heart.

I wonder if they will be happy together after the initial infatuation has worn off. But why not let the boy follow his groin for his first wife? I will have many opportunities to get rid of her if a better match comes along.

Matwyck thought the folk dance rather pretty, but he saw his guests smiling to one another condescendingly.

As the Royal Dancers departed and the wedding guests regained their seats, his own betrothed wrinkled her darling nose at the elegant pastries sculpted in the shape of swans, which arrived on silver trays decked out with blue silk. When her pastry was set down in her plate, Lolethia leaned forward and caught the eye of General Yurgn's younger son, Burgn. Yurgn had snubbed the wedding, sending this substitute in his place, claiming—or feigning—illness. Lolethia gave him a smoldering glance while licking custard off her spoon with long strokes of her little red tongue.

You can misbehave in private, my little kitten, but never in public.

Matwyck snuck his left hand under the table, grabbed a pinch of her soft flesh from her inner thigh through her silk gown, and twisted it, *hard*. She put the spoon down with a slight clatter.

"Forgive me." Matwyck turned to Duchess Pattengale on his right-hand side. "I didn't hear your last comment."

"Oh, I was just saying how delightful the young couple looked dancing together," repeated Pattengale, whom Matwyck had chosen as an inoffensive table companion, and one whose loyalty he rarely got the chance to put to the test.

"Indeed!" agreed Matwyck, bringing his left hand back on top of the table and raising his glass in a half toast to his son and the flushed bride-to-be across the table.

Pattengale moved on to discussing the financial stability of her duchy, a topic that interested Matwyck more than topics she had previously offered. He was occupied with trying to calculate in his head whether the taxes she remitted to the royal treasury were on the square; otherwise he might have noticed the stir at the Lower Table earlier.

Duke Naven, whose face showed the effects of quite a bit of wine, presided there as host of the lesser nobles and lesser guests, such as Favian and Gahoa of Maritima, who had tottered out of their reclusive snootiness to attend this event. Percia's sister had been hastily seated at Naven's right hand. (Matwyck had moved Prigent to sit on her other side to try to draw her out, but she appeared too meek to converse with him.) Naven's lady-wife sat at the foot of the table, with the gauche brother at her side.

Someone had said something, and Naven had retorted and banged his hand down on the table in anger, which was what caught Matwyck's attention. Silence fell at the Lower Table. Marcot had overheard the jibe; he turned around in his chair and sprung up—the chair falling down behind him—a look of righteous indignation on his face.

"How dare you, Duke Inrick!" cried Marcot in a fury. "Your thoughts would shame a tavern rat! I will not have my bride insulted by a lickspittle like you—a *corrupt* lickspittle!"

Inrick rose too, swaying slightly, his hand reaching toward his sword's hilt. "Lordling Marcot, you may have a taste for country flesh—I've sampled those wares often enough in my youth—but, my fine fellow, surely you can't object when people of quality find humor in your buttermilk craving!"

Marcot launched himself down the dais straight onto the table-top of the Lower Table, landing with a crash. He then leapt off the table to stand facing Inrick. Dishes and glasses flew everywhere, breaking and splashing the guests' finery. Marcot grabbed a nearby water flagon and threw the contents into Inrick's face.

Meanwhile, the young brother jumped from his seat, pulling his sword from its scabbard. It was only half size, but its glint showed its quality as fine steel.

"My sister is worth twelve of you!" cried Tilim. "Take it back— whatever it was you said."

Inrick lazily wiped the water from his face and laughed at the lad, pointedly ignoring Marcot. "Oh, bravo, the milkmaid is defended by the pig's boy!" He clapped his hands slowly and dramatically, looking around the tables for appreciation of his jibe.

Duke Favian stood up on his tottering legs. "Gentlemen, gentlemen—" he began with his hands outstretched, taking a placating tone.

Marcot had pulled his sword and started to advance on Inrick. "You will answer—"

Matwyck had to take charge before events got further out of hand; certainly he was not going to let *Maritima* interfere. "Duke Inrick," he interrupted, speaking calmly, even lazily, "I know you have a pressing engagement elsewhere. It was so kind of you to join us this long." He paused and sipped his wine. "We won't keep you from it."

Inrick looked thunderous; he pushed Marcot out of his way and strode out of the room, his whole body stiff with fury. Burgn threw his napkin into the closest pastry swan, breaking its delicate neck, and followed with deliberate swagger.

Matwyck motioned to the guards in the room with his eyes so that they followed Inrick. Then, before the guests could stir or discuss the scandal, the Lord Regent stood up, holding his wineglass.

"My friends," he said, "I can't tell you how touched and honored I am to have you at my table to celebrate the upcoming nuptials of my only son, Marcot, to the lovely Percia of Androvale." He turned to the Lower Table. "Naven, your duchy grows fine hardwoods and fine apples, but nothing nearly so fine as its womenfolk.

"Although personally, another duchy's bountiful beauty has caught my eye." (A ripple of polite laughter made Lolethia smile with her little white teeth.)

"Before us tonight we are graced with several exquisite examples: your lovely lady-wife, the duchess (polite applause); my newest and dearest friend, the tapestry artist Mistress Stahlia, who is as talented as she is gracious (polite applause); and my lovely daughter-to-be, Percia of Wyndton (polite applause). Oh, and her sister, her sister . . ." Prigent mouthed the name to him. "Her sister, Wren, another forest marvel."

"You will join me in a toast to the loveliness of the ladies of Androvale!" Matwyck raised his glass. His guests dutifully moved to raise theirs, but Matwyck was not satisfied. "Gentlemen, please!" He looked around the room. "Is *this* the gallantry of Weirandale? When we toast beautiful ladies, we rise to our feet!"

Marcot and Tilim still stood in anger. His nobles, stuffed with his fine food, sleepy with his fine wine, knew who held the strings of power in Weirandale. They all obeyed his tug—the puppets rose off their comfortable seats at his command and raised their glasses.

Matwyck's eyes flicked over the assembly. Percia and her mother looked embarrassed. Marcot's knuckles were bloodless around his wineglass stem. Naven, mollified, quaffed down his glass. Duchess Naven, who had a quicker mind, was more aware that she had just been used as a distraction; she averted her face. The duchess of Maritima had placed a calming hand on Tilim's wrist, which was trembling.

The plain sister in an ill-fitting green gown looked down at her plate and then looked up. For half a second her glance met Matwyck's; then she looked down again. He'd had a fair bit of wine himself; for a moment he couldn't think of the word to describe the expression on her face.

Weighing?

A common wench from Wyndton judging me?

44

A remembrance of bedtimes past—of her mother's affectionate visits—pervaded Cerúlia's old bedchamber, so despite the tension of the banquet, her heartbreak over Wilim, and her dread over trials to come, she slept soundly in the bed she had used as a child.

Nana woke her up with a tray in the midmorning sun, and when she opened her eyes, the first thing she realized was that today was Percia's wedding day.

In yesterday's flurry, Nana had not had the opportunity to fit the green gown to Cerúlia's form. However, Nana had insisted on pinning the dress she'd selected for the wedding—a beige-colored brocade gown with a brown lace overlay—and during last night's supper she had cajoled her friends amongst the seamstresses to use the lace from the back panel to add an extra flounce at the bottom and wide circle lace cuffs. These three extra thumb-widths were all the dress needed to fit.

Cerúlia complimented Nana on her choice and her hard work (though what mattered most to her was if a gown allowed her to secrete her dagger on her person under the lace panel). She had felt naked without it last night and would feel doubly naked without it today. Especially after attracting Lord Matwyck's attention. She feared he would grow suspicious of her and that he would try to question her today.

And he had—or Lady Tenny had had—a magic stone.

"Nana, you recognized me immediately. So too, once long ago, did a noblewoman, Lady Tenny, who spoke with me in Gulltown. Will she be at the wedding today?"

"Lady Tenny! Haven't heard that name in years. No, Tenny has joined the Eternal Waters."

"What? Her too? How did she die?"

"The rumor is that she jumped off of SeaWidow Cliff. But there's them that wonders if she crossed Matwyck and was pushed. Tenny was smarter than most. And she knew your sweet mother well; I can see how she'd be able to recognize you."

Nana lay the dress down carefully and picked up both a hair ribbon she had chosen to accompany it and an argument she kept harping on.

"Girl, I don't understand. *Why* won't you use the distraction of the wedding to breach the Throne Room?"

Cerúlia strode over to the window, looking out at Nargis Mountain for strength.

"All my life I have *used* people, Nana," she said. "Put them in danger to hide me. Lied to them. Deserted them. My foster father *died* to protect me; he was as dear a man as drew breath, and his suicide has devastated my Wyndton family. Perchance even this Lady Tenny died because she protected me.

"I always believed that I had the right to do whatever I had to do because of the higher calling of reclaiming the Nargis Throne. This has to stop sometime. It has to stop today. It's dishonorable.

"I will not assume the throne by disrupting my sister's wedding. I can't believe that Nargis would want me to."

Nana made disapproving tongue clicks. "Sometimes duty comes

before druthers. And it's hard to know what a Spirit wants." She gave a huge sigh. "Sometimes I'm not sure the Spirits know what they want."

Cerúlia felt her nursemaid's pressure, but she kept quiet. She had decided, and she did not intend to yield.

"Well, since yer so intent on going to this fest, let's make sure you blend in. Yer braids are coming undone, and they're such a foreign style anyway. Let me wash yer hair and pin it up in a Weir fashion."

"Very well." Cerúlia walked into the bathing chamber and leaned over the basin as Nana undid her plaits, wet her hair, and started to wash it with the elderflower soap that was kept on hand in the Royal Chambers.

"Oh, Waters!" Nana shrieked.

"What's wrong?" cried Cerúlia, opening her eyes. But she saw the problem herself: the brown dye that had colored her hair for so many years was dripping off Nana's hands and running in rivulets down the side of the white basin.

"Is it the soap?"

"Could be," said Nana. "Or could be the Water itself. The Spirit's wishes. The Water we get here comes from the spillover of the Dedication Fountain." The nursemaid poured more Water on the young woman's hair. "Why and how is your hair *brown* anyway?"

Cerúlia had neither the time nor patience to explain her disguises and her hair's permutations over the years. "Well. Obviously Nargis has decided I should return to my natural color. Keep going, Nana. Let's see what it looks like."

Nana washed and scrubbed until all the dye came out. Cerúlia's hair, which had grown to reach the middle of her back, was completely transformed. Instead of the dull brown she had worn since she was eight, or the patchy yellow she'd assumed for half a year in Alpetar and Oromondo, it was blue. A shimmering light blue with a hint of green—some strands darker, some lighter—the shades of the feathers of the blue tanager.

Cerúlia was entranced. She gazed at her hair in the looking glass; she ran her fingers through the curling lower locks like a sieve through a stream. The change in hair color turned her into someone completely different; it made her resemble one of the queens in the portraits.

Nana seemed less impressed, but then she had attended blue-haired queens all her life.

"But what are we going to do with it?" Nana fretted. "Since you refuse to attempt the Throne Room today, yer gonna have to be sick and hide in here. No one can see *this*."

"You're right about that. But I don't want to miss the wedding. Amongst my mother's things, couldn't you find a kerchief, a wimple, something that we can hide my hair inside?"

Leaving the bath chamber door open, Nana went to search while Cerúlia, sitting on a stool, continued to rub her new blue hair dry.

A knock on the hallway door startled her from her reverie.

"Who is it?" she called.

"Duchette Lolethia," said a female voice, and the handle turned as the Lord Regent's intended walked in without waiting for an invitation.

Cerúlia, sitting in the bath chamber in a damp, borrowed night shift, had just time to curse herself for not locking the door and to wrap her head in the towel before the woman sauntered into her room.

She jumped up. "To what do I owe this honor, Duchette?" she said, casting down her eyes, bobbing a curtsey, and generally assuming Wren's shy persona.

"Lord Matwyck sent me to see if I could help you in any way. I heard that your wardrobe . . . has been misplaced. I am sure that you're anxious to put in a good appearance on your sister's special day! Mayhap I could loan you a gown?" Lolethia sized Cerúlia up. "We are close to the same size, I think?"

"That is so kind of you, milady," said Cerúlia as Wren. "But—"

Lolethia's eyes had been raking the room, intently looking for information about this last-minute guest. She saw the gown laid out.

"I see, entirely unnecessary! Where did *you* get this lovely gown, my dear? The lace is so delicate! An antique pattern, I'd wager."

Cerúlia wished that Nana had chosen something plainer; Lolethia feeling jealous of her clothing was a complication she didn't need.

"A servant found it for me, milady. I am afeard to wear it. 'Tis much too grand for a Wyndton girl."

Out of the corner of her eye she saw that Nana had returned to the inner door of the passageway, closed it a bit, and was hiding out of sight.

"Nonsense," said Lolethia, holding the dress up to her own body and registering that it was clearly too small to fit a woman as tall and buxom as herself. "You must wear it. I insist."

Cerúlia had come out of the bath chamber. It was vitally important that Lolethia didn't see the catamount dagger, which lay in plain sight on the bed.

"Milady," started Cerúlia, saying the first thing that came to mind, "how do ladies wear their hair at fine weddings? I had mine in plaits, because while voyaging it has gotten all dried out by the sea air." She continued in a confiding tone, "And 'tis so hard for me to be surrounded by such beautiful amber hair. Like yours."

Lolethia patted her own wavy amber ringlets with obvious satisfaction. "Nonsense, my girl. Country people don't have amber hair—everyone accepts that. Brown hair can be quite nice."

"My hair will never look right for the wedding. . . . Mayhap, milady, you might own a gable hat or a coif that I could borrow to cover it up?" Cerúlia managed to reach the bed and sat down, her body now in front of the dagger.

"I'll have my maids rummage about when I'm back at my rooms. I'm delighted to help your sweet little family in any way. We are all so fond of our Percia. So humble and polite."

Lolethia sidled over to the chest and began fingering the objects on top of it. She picked up a perfectly ordinary Weir boxwood comb.

"Is this a souvenir? Where is it from? I hear you have been traveling, my dear. Tell me, where have you been? I do so love to travel myself."

"Nowhere special."

Lolethia pressed, "Oh, but you are just being modest, I suspect. You must have had exciting experiences. Or maybe a beau in every port?"

"Nothing like that," said Cerúlia. "Wyndton girls tend not to have too many suitors."

"Oh, I don't know about that!" said Lolethia. "A young woman has got to use her charms while she's got them. Goodness knows, your *sister* has."

"My sister—" Cerúlia wanted to protest at the inference, but Lolethia didn't give her a chance.

"Time flies, and our youth goes with it. Pretty soon we'll all be wrinkled and droopy." The duchess sat down, spreading out her gown with care, and patted the couch next to her. "Now, let's have a good gossip, shall we?"

"Milady, you honor me, but I'm late already. I should go and help Percia get ready. In Wyndton, a bride would want her mother and her sisters to dress her."

"How quaint. In the palace, we have maids to assist her, I'm sure."

"Really? But I bet Percia would be shy to use a maid. The maids here have attended such fine ladies. Goodness, they know so much more about dress and clothing than we do. I'm afeared to ring for one to help *me*. You're so kind and friendly; mayhap you would help me lace the back of this fancy gown so I don't have to call for help?"

This finally succeeded in dislodging the duchette, who rose with a bounce of vexation at the thought of serving as a ladies' maid to a country lass.

"Aren't you quaint, little Wren, keeping up country customs! I'll leave you to it. See you anon, my dear. And then you'll have to tell me about all your travels." She moved toward the door. Cerúlia stood up in relief, making certain to position herself between the duchette and the dagger, to escort her out.

"And, oh yes," said Lolethia, "I promised to look for a wimple. Let me see how much hair we need to cover." She turned about and reached for the towel.

Although Cerúlia belatedly attempted to swat her arm away, Lolethia yanked it off—and the shimmering blue hair fell down in a tumble.

"Oh! Oh!" Lolethia sputtered, confused. Then with terror, "What is this? *You?* No! Guards! GUARDS!"

Nana rushed into the room at the moment of revelation, clasping her hands over Lolethia's mouth from behind to muffle her scream. The duchette bucked and twisted vigorously; she was a big woman, and terror made her strong. She tried to twist away from Nana, and she fought to wrench herself away from Cerúlia's instinctive grasp on her arms. Cerúlia let go and dove for the catamount dagger.

In one continuous movement she grabbed it by the hilt, pulled it free of its scabbard, and rose on her toes to drive it straight into Lolethia's jugular. The startled woman coughed out a bubble of red spittle; then blood began pouring down her chest and her knees started to buckle. Eyes wild, her hands reached out toward Cerúlia, who held them, hoping to provide a modicum of human connection at this last moment of Lolethia's life. The hands went nerveless and slipped from her own as the noblewoman's weight sagged to the floor.

She was dead.

Cerúlia and Nana looked toward the corridor. No pounding footsteps. No clatter of weapons. No one appeared. Nana crossed the last steps and latched the door.

Panting, they regarded the body. For all the moons Cerúlia had spent with the Raiders, this was the first time that she had ever killed someone outright with her own hand. She was shocked to discover that she experienced regret, because Lolethia was a young woman who should have had years ahead of her, but no horror or guilt. Not all enemies of the Nargis Throne wore Oro uniforms. This woman had posed an immediate danger.

"Are you hurt?" Nana asked her. Cerúlia shook her head. "Sweet Nargis!" Nana sighed. She touched Lolethia's body gently with her shoe. "There's a shit no one will mourn, certainly not the maids she abuses."

"That's hardly the point," Cerúlia rebuked her.

The stress of the moment led Nana to hector her. "You did right. See, girl, sometimes, to protect the throne, one has to do unpleasant things."

"I am—as you witnessed—quite prepared to do unpleasant things. Nana, you forget I am no longer an eight-summers child. 'Girl' is no longer appropriate." Nana scowled defiantly for an instant, then closed her mouth. "And I have been away a long time and gone through trials you know nothing about; you do not understand me as well as you may think."

Her former nursemaid glanced at her for a moment, undoubtedly taking in the bloody dagger and the flowing blue hair. She closed her mouth and bobbed a small curtsey.

Already Cerúlia's mind had moved past the ethics of the killing or Nana's temper to practical matters. "Who knows the duchette was coming to see me? We must both say that she came, stayed a few moments, and left."

She gazed down at the gruesome sight. "Where can we hide the body? What about the blood?"

"We could drag it into the passage between the bedchambers," Nana offered. "I don't want to put it in your mother's room."

"No, I'd rather not have it near me either."

Cerúlia walked a few steps away. "Wait. I have a thought. Last night I saw her flirting with a big young man. The duke said his name is Burgn. Is he staying in the palace?"

"He's staying with the other gentry in the Guest Wing."

"Is there a way to carry her to his chambers?"

"Oh, it's much too far for us to lug her." Nana twisted her hands. "But I have a page I can trust to send for someone strong enough . . . wrap her in a horse blanket . . . When everyone is at the ceremony . . . we could make some good use of the distraction of the wedding after all. . . . The blood's no problem—I'll scrub it up myself."

"Will people be looking for her?" Cerúlia asked.

"They might," Nana considered, "but this day's going to be busy and confused."

"Let's hope so. What a calamity if she'd managed to sound the alarm!" Cerúlia shook her head, now second-guessing her instinctive response. "I wonder if I could have taken her captive instead of killing her? But she was much too strong, and we didn't have the help of Damyroth or Whaki."

Nana looked puzzled by the unfamiliar names but her mind was on practical matters. "Leave the mess to me, Your Majesty," said she, calmly stepping over the corpse as if it were no longer a matter of concern.

"Now, let's go into the Queen's Chamber to get you robed and fix your hair." She stooped to pick up some items she had dropped in her dash out of the passageway. "This hat would work with a bit of veil, but this kerchief would be easier to tie so as to cover every bit quite securely."

"One moment, Nana. First, I need to wash off this blood."

From the washing room she called back, "Could you sew on a loop or give me a belt so I could carry my dagger on my person today?"

"No one will be going armed to a palace wedding, Your Majesty. It would give you away."

"I guess you're right," Cerúlia conceded, though she stared at the golden catamounts with regret.

The cat, Plump-pot, rubbed against her leg, his whiskers twitching. *Your Majesty, thou smellest.*

Do I smell of blood? Cerúlia asked, with a little shudder.

No, thou smellest of thee.

I don't understand—don't I always have my own scent? Didn't I smell like myself yesterday?

Before, thou hadst thine own scent, but masked by other strong smells.

Really? I wonder . . . My hair dye had an odor of coal tar and bergamot oil.

Those smells are gone now. Now thy scent wafts without such mask. He rubbed against her again, turned around, and brushed against the back of her calves. *Every animal—far and wide—with a nose will recognize thee.*

Ah! I understand. I thank you, Plump-pot, for the warning.

"Nana," she called, "is there some perfume in my mother's chambers?"

45

The frustrations of the last weeks had stretched Marcot to the breaking point.

Percia had asked him to find her childhood friend, Lemle, whom she'd expected to see when the family arrived in Cascada. Marcot had sent his personal manservant, who reported that the Type and Ink was boarded up, and no one knew what had happened to the owner or the workers; in fact, the neighbors acted skittish to even discuss the subject. Marcot had broached the topic with his father, who had shown concern and vowed that he would look into it. But Marcot had learned to doubt such reassurances, and indeed, no tidings about the printer's apprentice were forthcoming.

Then he had been shocked by the way his father's associates had treated his new relations. He shouldn't have been—he'd known these gentry all his life—but the wedding had brought to the surface their snobbiest behavior. Marcot missed his mother, with her unfailing grace. She would have known how to protect Percia from the likes of Inrick or Lolethia. She would have pressed his father to take a stronger stand. She would have understood.

In the Church of the Waters this morning, however, all his worry of the last weeks melted away. All he saw was Percia's smile; all he felt was her hand in his; her waist against his arm. Lit by the sun-beams shining through the church's windows, she looked so radiant; and Brother Whitsury smiled at them so benignly that Marcot's heart lifted. The cup of Nargis Water they shared quenched a thirst that Marcot hadn't even known he suffered. Marcot wished he could stand forever in the center of the church with just Percia and the cup.

He only became aware of the audience in the pews when Brother Whitsury led everyone in the traditional hymns "Happy Be the Life Entwined" and "May You Fill One Another's Cups." Then he caught sight of Stahlia, Wren, and Tilim sitting together in one section of the church, singing lustily; and the duke and duchess of Maritima, who looked so frail, holding each other's hands tightly, their eyes closed, with Duke Favian leaning his head on his wife's shoulder.

Marcot searched for his father and found him sitting alone in a front pew, his eyes hooded.

When the wedding party moved into the Great Ballroom, Marcot walked in a daze. People asked the cost of Percia's lovely pink gown, which he didn't know and wouldn't discuss if he had. So he merely smiled. Stahlia said something about wishing her husband could have been present. Naven kept bragging about being the one who had brought them together. His father hissed furious comments about Lolethia missing the ceremony.

But Marcot floated above it all, his ears attuned only to the sound of Percia's laughter. He looked to see what pleased her at this moment and discovered that she and Tilim were giggling at the way the champagne tickled their noses.

Their long and painful separation was over; now she would be close by. *During the days I will hear her laughing, and at night I will hear her breathing.*

After the opening toasts and courses, Marcot roused himself from his reveries. He moved to another seat to concentrate on having a substantive conversation with his new sister, noticing that today she wore a tight cream-colored kerchief, twisted in the front of her forehead. This was the way peasants wore their hair while working in the fields and it clashed with her dressy gown, but Marcot was prepared to use his dinner knife to gut anyone who so much as looked at her askance. Or anyone who pointed out that she seemed to have put on essence of roses with too liberal a hand.

"Are you enjoying the goose?" he asked.

"It is tender," she replied, "but this is too emotional a day for eating."

"I know. I hardly taste a thing." Marcot beamed at her. "You know, Percia is so overjoyed to have you here." They both glanced across the table at the bride, who caught their eyes, lifted her cup in their direction, and then turned to answer something Stahlia said to her.

"Wren," Marcot confided, "I was an only child. One of the many wonderful things Percia has brought me is a little brother; I am delighted to now have a sister too!"

"And I am delighted to have an older brother, Lordling Marcot. But if you are not kind to Percia *every single day* you will face my wrath."

They both laughed, but Marcot heard her deep loyalty to Percia and liked her the better for it.

Marcot was well content to sit next to someone who shared his appreciation for his bride. He waxed on about Percia's delightful qualities for several minutes, letting the food grow cold on his plate.

"Tell me stories about her childhood," Marcot begged, and Wren related the whole tale of how Percia's dancing talent had become apparent when she was very young. Marcot noticed that as she talked she tore the bread into smaller and smaller pieces that she rolled about and toyed with; he chalked this up to nervousness about being suddenly thrown into a palace and amongst gentry.

His intuition turned to certainty a few moments later when Wren broke the flow of their conversation. "One boon, I beg of you. I am frightened of the Lord Regent. If your father engages me in conversation, could you find a way to interrupt?"

Perchance over his shoulder she had seen his father working his way through the room, because only a few moments later he and Prigent swooped down upon them. Both Wren and Marcot rose to their feet at their greetings.

"Ah, lad," said Councilor Prigent, with a hearty friendliness that Marcot did not share. "What are your plans for your nuptial retreat? Somewhere *conducive,* I trust."

Marcot wondered if Prigent had drunk too much, because he was certain he had told the whole Circle Council that Percia and he would leave this evening by coach for a seaside estate the duke of Maritima had offered them. But politeness demanded that he repeat the information to the councilor, who kept peppering him with more queries.

When he glanced over Prigent's shoulder, he saw his father engaging Wren in conversation. She offered one-word answers and darted a glance in his direction. Marcot had an image of a raptor attacking a small bird.

Without explanation he stepped away from Prigent.

"Excuse me, Father," Marcot said. "Percia made me promise to bring Wren to her now." And with no further ado, he tucked her arm over his and walked across the mirrored ballroom. Noticing that Wren's hand trembled and her face looked strained, a surge of protectiveness rose in his chest.

Percia found gentry eccentric—too stiff to dance, but unabashed about getting drunk, falling asleep in their chairs, saying rude things, and spilling gravy on their expensive gowns. And they stuffed their faces with more food than would feed a Wyndton family for a week.

Marcot's father had made all the arrangements for the wedding banquet, and Percia knew that precious few of the guests attended out of genuine warmth for the couple. She didn't like feeling ungrateful, but she would have had a more joyous time at the Wyndton Arms with ale, boiled eggs, and her friends.

Could they make a life separate from these people? Marcot had promised her that if his father made conditions too unpleasant, they would relocate to Maritima. Duchess Gahoa, who had made Percia a present of the antique pearl earbobs Percia wore with her wedding dress, had charmed her. It was too bad that the Maritima couple hadn't felt up to this showy party after the ceremony, for Percia thought she would have enjoyed conversing with *them*—but then Percia barely felt up to this raucous party.

Marcot and Wren pulled her aside from the esteemed and (to her eyes) soulless duke and duchess of Lakevale, with whom the officious chamberlain had seated her.

"Do you wish to stay for the rest of the banquet?" Marcot inquired in her ear.

"Oh, no! That is, not unless you do."

"I can't take another moment. No more speeches, no more courses, no more toasts. No prolonged farewells from people who don't truly give a fig about us and really just want to butter up my father."

"Thank the Waters," breathed Percia in relief. "Wren, could you find Mother—I think she's seated over in that direction—and bring her to our chambers?"

Percia excused herself to the Lakevale gentry, saying that she needed to leave the table. The duke made some rude jibe about her bladder not being used to all this wine and pointed toward the relieving room. Percia feinted in that direction but slipped away to her chambers as fast as she could.

Wren and her mother joined her there in a few minutes. While they helped her take off her gown, the Wyndton women discussed the highlights of the wedding.

"The light shining into the church!" Mother enthused. "It made such a warm, soft glow! And the way your gown pooled on the floor! Marcot's deep blue, Brother Whitsury's black, and your pink! A picture I will treasure as long as I live."

"You looked so happy, Percie! Were you nervous?" asked Wren.

"Not nervous, but it all went by so fast. I wish I could have seen the picture you saw."

"You saw the most important thing—the expression on Marcot's face as you shared the nuptial cup. He looked so transfixed. And even into the banquet, he was having a hard time focusing his eyes." Wren clapped her hands. "Percie, I am so happy for you! Marcot thinks you make the rain fall."

Percie kissed her sister's forehead. "Someday you will find someone too."

After unfastening a ridiculous number of hooks, laces, and petticoats, the women laid the wedding gown reverently aside on Percie's bed. Percia sighed with relief as her mother gently rubbed the red marks the corset had left around her torso.

Wren held out the waiting yellow-and-black traveling frock. Mother pinned a jaunty little hat with yellow feathers onto Percie's hair.

"Shall we take these off?" Wren asked, lightly touching the pearl earrings.

"No, leave them."

"You look adorable," Wren whispered in her ear.

They heard footsteps outside, and Marcot knocked at the door. "Lady-wife, your carriage awaits below. Do you intend to always keep me pacing at your door? I have waited for you for a long, long year."

Percia threw open the door with a mocking smile, but sparkling eyes. "And pray, whose fault was that? Not mine, I'm sure. I'm ready—my husband, I have been waiting for *you*. Let me just say farewell.

"Wren, you must promise not to disappear again!" Percia enfolded her sister.

"Percia, I assure you: the only way I would not be here to meet you is if I have joined the Eternal Waters."

Percia laughed off the dark comment. "Where's Tilim?"

"He's with Duchess Naven," Mother answered, "probably giving himself a bellyache. She's been very motherly to him; she may enjoy a boy after all those girls. I'll tell him that you asked for him.

"Come here, lamb." Mother kissed Percia on both cheeks. "How I wish your father were here to see you!"

Marcot entered the room and bowed over her mother's and sister's hands with the gallant grace and manners that always smote Percia's heart.

"Thank you, Mother Stahlia, for everything. Sister-mine, I look forward to getting to know you better."

"Enough charm!" Percia smiled a teasing smile at Marcot. "Race you to the carriage?"

Feeling as if they were runaways, escaping not only from their own wedding banquet but also from looming clouds, they raced through the palace corridors, laughingly tumbled into the waiting vehicle, and made their getaway.

46

Sitting in the window seat of the luxurious second-floor suite that had been allotted to the Wyndton family, Cerúlia and Stahlia watched the wedding carriage as it rolled away down the avenue and out the palace gates. Then, sniffling a few times, Stahlia rose and went to hang up Percia's wedding finery in a nearby wardrobe.

Cerúlia sat watching her foster mother, the woman who had adopted her out of compassion and had cared for her the very best she could, even when her foster daughter had been secretive or cool. Stahlia may not have been as pretty and refined as the beautiful mother in the portrait gallery, and her manner decidedly less indulgent, but she had nurtured and protected her second daughter with a fierceness that had had as much of an influence on Cerúlia as heredity.

Stahlia had designed and sewn the gown she wore herself; one could tell from its stark simplicity. The gray velvet dress had a narrow skirt and severe lines, softened only by blue cuffs and a blue collar. Stahlia had included none of the lace, embroidery, or jewels that other women in the ballroom had worn; her only concession to vanity was the inset of an intricately woven wide waistband in which blue alternated with gray, yellow, green, lilac, magenta, and gold.

Cerúlia interrupted their quiet moment by stating, "I don't want to return to that banquet. Must we?"

"Definitely not. But I don't want to stay here, in this empty set of rooms. Do you think, perchance, we could take a turn in the Palace Gardens? I haven't had time before, and tomorrow Tilim and I will move into our new house in West Park." She amended her statement. "That is, me, Tilim, and *you*."

"I will be quite thankful to leave the palace, but I'd like to see the fabled gardens."

"Going outside sounds lovely." Cerúlia checked that the knot on her head scarf was still tight, then pushed herself to her feet and led the way to the door.

Declaring that she had seen an exit down a corridor, she led them instead into a dead end. Laughing at their confusion, the two women blundered around until at last they came to a grand first-floor entryway attended by a footman.

"Where are we?" Stahlia asked the man.

"We call this 'West Door,' madam," he replied.

"And the Palace Gardens?"

"They are that way, madam, to the east of the palace." He walked a few paces outside, pointing. "From here you have to walk past the Church Entrance, the rear of the Throne Room, Kitchen Door, and Servants' Door."

"Thank you," said Stahlia, following him and looking where he pointed. "Is it far?"

"Well, yes, madam, it *is* a bit of a distance."

"I don't care," Stahlia said to Cerúlia. "I'm so happy to be outside and away from that party."

They walked east around the massive building, recounting again to each other the details about the wedding that needed to be savored.

"Marriage is a big step," Stahlia said, with a meditative look in her eye. "When I meet a couple, I always try to figure out if they're happy—or at least content—with one another. How much trust, how much comradeship, after the courtship days? I can usually read at a glance how tight a marriage is. The duke and duchess of Lakevale would actually like to kill each other. That elderly couple from Maritima, now *they* have a rare bond."

"Hmm-mm," Cerúlia commented, not really listening, because she was scanning their surroundings.

"My feet hurt in these fancy slippers; a maid dug them out for me, but they don't fit well," she said. "Can we stop a minute?"

"Mine too," agreed Stahlia. "Let's kick them off!"

"*I* was just going to adjust the strap. How would that look—the lordling's mother-in-marriage walking barefoot in the grass like a village girl!"

"Do you think I care what *these people* think of us?" Stahlia said. "What you've seen is only a portion of the indignities these 'high-class' people have heaped upon us. I fear for the country, Birdie, in the hands of this lot. Duchess Latlie wore baubles that would feed all the orphans in Northvale for decades. Not that she ever sees those orphans; I learned she lives full time in the capital rather than take care of her people. Naven often grates on me, but at least he truly cares for the folk of Androvale!"

Cerúlia, bent over her shoe, didn't respond.

Her mother continued, "I think the world of Marcot, and Percie's happiness lies with him, but all week I've been dying to sail back to Wyndton. Wouldn't that have caused a scandal!"

Stahlia kicked off her shoes vehemently.

Cerúlia laughed at the force of the kick. "Are you thinking of kicking that cad of a duke who insulted Percie at the dinner last night?"

"Oh, if only I could!"

"Just a moment—my buckle is caught," Cerúlia said. While she pretended to work on the shoe, she also sniffed her wrist to see if the rose water still lingered. She didn't want all the animals at the palace racing to her side. She had closed her mind to them but she feared their recognizing her scent. The perfume was still noticeable, though much fainter.

"I'm not sure, though, whether it would even be safe to return to Wyndton," Stahlia mused. "Did Duke Naven tell you about what happened last fall?"

"No," said Cerúlia, a touch absently, still bent down.

There! Is that bit of rumpled earth, hidden under that bush, the exit of the catamounts' tunnel?

"Do you need help with that?" offered her mother.

"Oh, no, I've got it. See?" said Cerúlia as she pulled off her second shoe and stood up. "What happened last fall?"

As they continued strolling Stahlia told the story of the attack on the cottage.

"Did Hecht ever find out more about the ruffians or their goal?"

"No. I've a suspicion, but I'd rather not speak such dark thoughts aloud."

"Was Tilim all right afterward?"

"Aye. He's a wonder, that boy. What pained him most about everything was leaving Baki behind. The dog was too old for a voyage and a new life. Lemle took him in for his last moons."

Stahlia stopped walking a minute. "Lemle, now, there's another worry!" And she filled Cerúlia in on Lemle's baffling disappearance.

When the apple fritter woman had spoken of an acquaintance going missing, Cerúlia had sympathized, but she had not completely understood what this felt like: now this same anxiety and dread had fallen on her. She wanted to reassure Stahlia that she would find him and free him, but could she promise such a thing?

Aloud, she said, "Oh, for Water's sake! This is horrid news!"

"Aye," said Stahlia, with a grimace. "But I'm getting used to people disappearing on me."

Cerúlia flinched at the blow—accidental or intentional—but she couldn't blame her foster mother for being angry at her. She could imagine how much that anger and heartbreak had smoldered over three years.

"Look, Birdie"—Stahlia put such love into the old dear name that her foster daughter heard an apology—"this must be the original garden laid out by Queen Calendula. Oh, it has not been well tended for some years! So overgrown and weedy. How could they let it go like this? I'm sure I read that famous statues stand in the center. . . ."

They wandered through the gardens alone together. Enough of the original lines were visible to show how magnificent they must have once been. Cerúlia thought she must have run through these paths as a child, perchance with her parents or Nana chasing after her. Now she looked about with Gardener's eyes, seeing that the shrubs needed pruning and the flagstones wanted mortaring, but that hardy bulbs still persisted in pushing through the leaf clutter to reach the sun.

The two women found the marble statues of select Nargis Queens arrayed around a "river" designed out of blue flowers, early spring snow glories that poked up amongst weeds and debris.

"I'll bet in its day, the landscapers designed this bed so that blue and white flowers changed with the seasons." With lips compressed, Stahlia dropped to her knees and began pulling up the biggest and ugliest weeds around the blooms, heedless of how the activity stained her hands and her dress. Cerúlia took half a step forward to help but then stopped; she couldn't bring herself to dirty Queen Cressa's beautiful lace.

"Tell me about the statues," Cerúlia tried to distract her foster mother.

Stahlia left the river of flowers, straightened, and studied the weathered marble. "Well, this must be Carra the Royal. This has got to be Cinda the Conqueror. And here we have Cashala the Enchanter. How dare they let creepers grow around her robe!"

As they walked by each statue, Stahlia told Cerúlia the story of each queen's reign. All the while, her angry hands yanked away the worst of the vines.

The last of the marble queens was Carmena the Perseverant.

"I'm surprised to see Carmena honored," said Cerúlia. "Chamberlain Vilkit implied she's out of favor."

Her mother scraped some moss off the statue's bare marble toes with her fingernails. "I don't know who chose the queens. But she's a good choice, right? All any of us can do is persevere."

"Teta . . . it must have been so hard for you and Percie and Tilim," Cerúlia said. She was thinking about the pain of Wilim's death, but reluctant to say his name.

"Well, it hasn't been easy," Stahlia admitted. She managed a small smile. "But there's others that have had it worse. And we had friends in Wyndton, good friends, loyal friends."

Stahlia patted Carmena's feet and then turned to her daughter. "You write a fair hand, as I recall; mayhap you'd help me write to Sister Nellsapeta and all the Wyndton folk, telling them the good parts about the wedding and about your return. They'll sleep easier for the news."

Her mother gathered up the vines she had torn away. "We won't tell them about Lemle. Some of them aren't fond of him—and anyway, we still have hopes of finding him safe and sound."

Placing the weeds in a neat pile under a shrub, Stahlia continued, "Percia's settled now, though I foresee a whole new set of problems for her, living amongst those people. And I fret at night about Tilim, growing up without a father, in a new, unfriendly city."

Stahlia met Cerúlia's eyes. "And I've anguished over *you* these past years, and even without your telling me *anything* yet, I know that you're in some kind of trouble."

This was an invitation to confide in her strong teta. Cerúlia had to beat back her longing to throw her arms around Stahlia's neck and lay all her burdens on those sturdy shoulders. But she had to keep to her vow of honor.

"Let's not disrupt our memory of Percia's wedding day with me and my troubles," she answered with a self-mocking smile. "Tomorrow is soon enough." Stahlia bit her lips at the rejection.

Cerúlia swung her dressy shoes in her hand. "Teta, tell me the story of how Percia and Marcot met. Duke Naven jabbered at me last night, but I was distracted. I'd love to hear the full story."

They wandered through the rambling garden paths as they talked, occasionally pausing to pick up a fallen branch or marvel over an overgrown arbor. The spring light started to fade, and the air crisped. Their bare feet began to grow chilly. Reluctantly, the women turned around to head back to the interior of the palace.

Throughout this excursion, shades of the dead stood between them. Ambrice and Cressa had always lingered in Cerúlia's heart, keeping her from committing fully to the foster family that offered her love, and yesterday she had learned that Wilim had joined her birth parents. Desperate for reconciliation before tomorrow's peril, Cerúlia intertwined her arm around her foster mother's waist. Stahlia kissed her on the top of the head and intertwined her own arm, each dangling their worthless slippers in her outside hand.

Cerúlia relished her touch, but fear still coursed through her.

She will never forgive me when she learns that Wilim died on account of me. Will she blame me for killing the duchette? Will she love a murderer?

Cerúlia felt overwhelmed and dizzy from the rush of events. But in this instant one need pushed to the fore. *Stahlia is my true mother now. This may be the last moment she loves me. I want to hold on to it.*

As an invitation, she sang the opening notes of "The Lay of Queen Carmena," an overture to a duet. Stahlia, smiling, let her carry the melody while she joined in down a third with the harmony. They leaned close to one another, blending their voices.

Gaining confidence, they sang louder, and the breeze swept up their ballad.

Scullery maids paused before the tower of wedding china. Footmen counting their tips, stable boys carting clean straw, and guards on patrol heard the music carrying through the twilight. Even those gentry smoking at their windows caught the whisper of the tune. All who heard it were seized with nostalgia and yearning—yearning for the heroic era of the Nargis Queens, when Weirandale lay secure, or at least *felt* secure, in Nargis's Blessing.

Evening birds broke out in background accompaniment, and after a moment one particularly enthusiastic participant caught Cerúlia's eye.

Tanager! There you are. Thank goodness you haven't retired yet. I would talk to you. Meet me at the window of my chamber. We must make plans for tomorrow.

47

When he returned to his quarters at the end of the exhausting day, Matwyck's thoughts churned with fury.

After all he'd done for this wedding! All the treasure he'd lavished! The address to the townspeople tonight in the Courtyard of the Star was to have been a crucial capstone.

My son will pay for this insolence when he returns.

Matwyck poured himself another glass of claret.

As for Lolethia . . . he initially chalked up her absence to childishness, and he had spent the day fuming that she should embarrass him in public this way. Matwyck had decided he would have his guards whip her; then he amended this plan by resolving he would flog her himself.

The image of a horsewhip biting into her soft back or bare backside while she wept and pleaded provided him a pleasant distraction.

But to enact this scenario, he needed the woman in his possession. He summoned his valet.

"I want you to go to the duchette's suite. Take two guards with you. Bring her—drag her, if necessary—to these rooms immediately."

In a few minutes, his valet returned with the report that her maids had not seen her since early morning, which was puzzling, but he wouldn't put it past the sulky minx to hide from him.

He ordered his most trusted personal servants to begin searching the palace discreetly.

While he waited in his chambers, he shrugged off his expensive coat and loosened his cravat. He removed the heavy rings he had recently taken to wearing. He sent a page for a riding whip and paced the room flicking it, enjoying each time it made an audible pop. He opened a window, hoping that the cool evening air would settle his frayed nerves.

Briefly, he wished that Tirinella were still alive to massage his neck with her long fingers, as she sometimes had in the early days of their marriage.

Pouring another glass of claret, a new thought assailed him.

That sister. I don't trust her at all.

Well, with Marcot gone from the palace, there was no reason why the Lord Regent could not question her firmly. If he detected any prevarication, the Truth Stone would pry out the secrets of her mysterious comings and goings.

Matwyck pulled the bell. At least he could make one of these aggravating women bend to his will.

"Guards, I want you to find Wren of Wyndton, the sister of Marcot's bride. Once you've got her in your possession, take her to my business office, keep her there, and send me word."

The guards bowed and departed on this errand.

He was pouring more claret when his valet appeared in his doorway. The man was shaking.

"Lord Regent," he said, neglecting to make obeisance, "the Duchette Lolethia . . . has been located."

"Aha! Well, what are you waiting for? Bring her here at once."

"Lord Regent, I regret—this—this is impossible. She's been found in Captain Burgn's chambers."

In Burgn's chambers! Matwyck saw spots in front of his eyes. *She*

has gone too far. To cuckold me with Burgn on my son's wedding day!
The whole court will know!

They will be executed. Publicly.

I will have him castrated first.

But his valet's lips were still moving. "What did you say?" Matwyck asked over the roar in his ears.

"We are unable to bring her here, my lord, because—because she is no longer among the living." The man blurted out, "Someone has cut her throat!" and then fell to his knee.

Matwyck sucked in a gulp of air and steadied himself with a hand against a table. "Tell me you have apprehended Captain Burgn!"

"Alas, my lord. He is missing from the palace. His carriage left this morning."

Matwyck realized that he had not seen Burgn at the wedding or the midmeal feast. "Take me to his chambers."

A small crowd of servants and guards—gossipmongers and telltales—already hovered in the doorway. A murder in the palace would stir people's base curiosity.

"Disperse!" Matwyck barked.

Maids had not attended the room today. The bed was rumpled, but only on one side. Lolethia lay fully dressed on a couch, gently arranged, with her eyes closed but a bloody gash at her throat and blood pooled on the carpet beside her. Matwyck found the blood distasteful, and he saw nothing appealing in her inanimate body. He wondered why he had ever thought he wanted her.

He knelt by the body and forced himself to grab her dangling hand. It was cold. "He killed her. She came to him this morning with some innocent request, and the brute tried to force himself upon her. When she defended herself, he drew his knife and cut her sweet flesh. Oh, my darling girl—too innocent for this world. So cruel of the Waters to take you from me so soon."

Matwyck rose to his feet, addressing a nearby soldier. "Go fetch your officer. I want fifty of my men to leave in pursuit of that brute immediately."

He looked around at the people in the room. "I am cursed. Born to suffer the worst of losses, the worst of solitude. First my beloved Lady Tirinella was taken from me, now my sweet Lolethia."

As he left the room, he noted several heads hanging in sympathy, and it occurred to him that the situation might well work to his advantage. Indeed, he may have just been spared from another mistake.

Lolethia was a passing fancy, nothing more. I will find a more suitable and less capricious partner. The public will see me as a suffering lover and a bringer of justice.

When he returned to his room he saw the palace guards whom he had sent after the Androvale sister lounging in the corridor.

Seeing him approach, they snapped to attention and then bowed. "The woman is not in her chamber, milord. A footman told us she is touring the gardens with her mother. Do you wish us to apprehend her there?" said a soldier.

"No, not in front of Stahlia! That would be ham-witted. Tarry until you can get her alone."

The men set off down the hall.

"Guards!" Matwyck called after them. "Wait. I have other things on my mind. Leave it for now. We'll attend to that tomorrow."

EPILOGUE

The four catamounts stalk the Weirandale Throne Room. Sometimes they switch their tails in anger. Sometimes they rub their bodies against the throne's leg or scratch their faces on its arm. On occasion they roar in vexation.

The dusty throne sits empty. The room shouts its stillness and quiet, locked tight. With long tongues lapping, the catamounts drink from the pool under the Dedication Basin.

These last days the air currents that filter into the room have offered many new scents, but the mountain lions ignored them.

Finally, a waft from the gardens brings them a hint not only of new-grown greenery, but of something long awaited. The catamounts twitch their whiskers and taste the breeze. Their ears twist backward and forward, scanning for a particular quality of voice. All of their ears point east.

They stretch their claws out and knead the hard marble floor.

They purr.

APPENDIX ONE

CHARACTERS AND PLACES IN ENNEA MÓN

The Spirits

'Chamen, Spirit of Stone

    Agent "Mason," chosen realm, Rortherrod

Ghibli, Spirit of the Wind

    Agent "Hunter," chooses no country

Lautan, Spirit of the Sea, "the Munificent"

    Agent "Sailor" (first unnamed, then Mikil), chosen realm, Lortherrod

Mìngyùn, Spirit of Fate

    Agent "Spinner" (Destra)

Nargis, Spirit of Fresh Water

    Agent "Water Bearer" (first Tiklok, then Nana), chosen realm, Weirandale

Pozhar, Spirit of Fire

    Agent "Smithy," chosen realm, Oromondo

Restaurà, Spirit of Sleep and Health

    Agent "Healer" (Myrnah), chosen realm, Wyeland

Saulė, Spirit of the Sun

Agent "Peddler," (Gunnit is agent-in-waiting), chosen realm,
Alpetar

Vertia, Spirit of Growth

Agent "Gardener," chosen realm, the Green Isles

Weirandale

THE EIGHT WESTERN DUCHIES (WEST TO EAST)

Northvale

Prairyvale

Woodsdale

Lakevale

Maritima—includes city of Queen's Harbor

Riverine—includes Cascada

Crenovale

Vittorine

THE THREE EASTERN DUCHIES ACROSS THE BAY OF CINDA (WEST TO EAST)

Androvale—contains Gulltown (port city) and Wyndton (country village)

Patenroux

Bailiwick—Barston (major city)

THE FORMER GENERATION ON THE THRONE

Queen Catreena the Strategist (deceased)

Consort: King Nithanil of Lortherrod (abdicated)

THE ROYALS

Queen Cressa the Enchanter (deceased)

Consort: Ambrice, Lord of the Ships (deceased)

Cerúlia, the princella

People in Cascada

Lord Regent Matwyck

    Lady Tirinella, his wife (deceased)

    Lordling Marcot, his son

    Eyevie, his (lost) favorite sister

    Duchette Lolethia, later Matwyck's betrothed

    Heathclaw, his secretary

Gourdo, seamaster currently in port

Gunnit, a goatherd, sent to Cascada

Hiccuth, a stableman

Lemle, Wren's friend from Wyndton, now in Cascada

Murgn, nephew of Yurgn; leader of Matwyck's Marauders

Nana, a nursemaid, now Water Bearer

Ryton, Cerúlia's former tutor

Vilkit, chamberlain, appointed by Matwyck

Whitsury, a Brother of Sorrow

Lord Matwywck's Councilors:

    Duke Burgn, second son of General Yurgn

    Lady Fanyah, formerly Cressa's lady-in-waiting

    Duchess Latlie

    Lordling Marcot, the regent's son

    Prigent, also treasurer of the realm

    General Yurgn, also general of the Armed Forces

Visiting Weirandale Aristocracy:

    Lady Dinista, former lady-in-waiting to Queen Cressa, now married to younger Lord Retzel

    Duke Favian of Maritima

        Duchess Gahoa

Duke Inrick of Crenovale
Duchess Pattengale

THE QUEEN'S SHIELD: QUEEN CRESSA
Sergeant Yanath

Branwise

Pontole

WEIR SEAMASTERS
Gourdo

Wilamara

IN OR NEAR WYNDTON
Duke Naven

   Duchess Naven

   Five unnamed daughters

   Captain Walmunt, head of the duchy guard

Stahlia, a weaver

   Percia, her daughter

   Nettie, friend of Percia

   Dewva, friend of Percia

   Tilim, her son

Ackerty, a landowner

Carneigh, a blacksmith

Goody Gintie, the midwife

Goddard, a healer

Hecht, peacekeeper who replaced Wilim

Rooks, retired/injured sergeant

   Lemle, Rooks's nephew, Wren's friend

Nellsapeta, a Sister of Sorrow

Alliance of Free States:

Fígat—contains Latham and the Scoláiríum

Jígat—contains Jutterdam

Vígat—contains Sutterdam

Wígat—contains Yosta

IN SUTTERDAM

Hartling, a potter and owner of a once-thriving pottery business

    Jerinda, his wife and business manger (deceased)

    Hake, their eldest son

    Thalen, their middle son

    Harthen, their youngest son (deceased)

    Norling, Hartling's older sister

Ikas, a wheelwright, squad leader of the Defiance

    Sansam, a member of Ikas's squad

Pallia, a candlemaker

IN JUTTERDAM

Bellishia, a leader of the Defiance from Yosta

Dwinny, a healer

Hulia, a fisherwoman

Nothafel, a boatman

Rellia, the overall leader of the Defiance

THE SCOLÁIRÍUM OF THE FREE STATES, LOCATED IN THE TOWN OF LATHAM, REACHED BY FERRY FROM TROUT'S LANDING

Rector Meakey

Andreata, tutor of Ancient Languages

Granilton, tutor of History (deceased)

    Graville, his son (deceased)

RAIDERS (SURVIVORS)

Commander Thalen

Cerf, a healer

Dalogun, seventeen-summers-old archer

Eli-anna, an archer from Melladrin

Eldie, her sister who stayed in Melladrin

Fedak, cavalry

Hake, quartermaster, Thalen's older brother

Jothile, cavalry

Kambey, weapons master

Kran, swordsman

Quinith, quartermaster, originally a reader at the Scoláiríum

Tristo, Thalen's adjutant, formerly a street orphan from Yosta

Wareth, cavalry scout

ORO OCCUPIERS

Lumrith, fifth-flamer

Murnaut, head of the Occupying Force

Lortherrod

King Nithanil, abdicated
   Ilkula, his mistress
King Rikil, the current king
   Unnamed wife and two sons
Prince Mikil, the king's younger brother
   Arlettie, Mikil's wife
   Gilboy, Mikil's adopted son

In the Green Isles

SLAGOS (SECOND-LARGEST ISLAND)

Gardener, Agent to Vertia

Shetdrake, an officer of the Green Isles Bank who travels to Pilagos

Zillie, innkeeper of the Blue Parrot

PILAGOS (LARGEST ISLAND AND CAPITAL)

Magistrar Destra, head of the government, originally from the Free
    States

Bajets, seamaster of *Island Dreamer*

Hake, Thalen's brother, quartermaster to the Raiders

Mikil, prince of Lortherrod

   Arlettie, Queen Cressa's former maid, now Mikil's wife

   Gilboy, adopted son of Mikil and Arlettie

Olet, owner of Olet's Olive Oil and Spicery

Quinith, former student at the Scoláiríum, quartermaster to the
    Raiders

Oromondo

Smithy, Agent to Pozhar

Sumroth, rises from commander to general

   Zea, his wife, works for the Library of Reverence

Alpetar

Peddler, Agent of Saulė

Culpepper, a hostler in Tar's Basin

The Sweetmeadow Refugees

Gunnit, a ten-summers-old shepherd
  Linnsie, his mother
Saggeta, Gunnit's neighbor and friend
Orphans
  Aleen, eight summers old
  Addigale, a toddler
  Alloon, four summers old
  Limpett, four summers old

Wyeland

SALUBRITON

Betlyna, an assistant healer
Ciellō, a mercenary from Zellia
Myrnah, a healer, Agent to Restaurà
Hunter, Agent of Ghibli
Tockymora, landlady of the Bread and Balm Recovery House
  Damyroth, one-legged amputee
  Hope, a melancholic
  Jitneye, heart patient
  Lymbock, hepatitis sufferer
  Phénix
  Sezirō, wounded patient from Zellia

APPENDIX TWO

NOTABLE HISTORIC QUEENS OF WEIRANDALE
IN CHRONOLOGICAL ORDER

Cayla the Foremother

Carra the Royal

Chista the Builder

Cayleethia the Artist

Carlina the Gryphling

Charmana the Fighter

Cinda the Conqueror

Chyneza the Wise

Crylinda the Fertile

Cashala the Enchanter

Catorie the Swimmer

Ciella the Patient

Cenika the Protector

Chanta the Musical

Carmena the Perseverant

Callindra the Faithful

Cymena the Proud

Clesindra the Kind

Crilisa the Just

ACKNOWLEDGMENTS

In the years that I worked on this series I incurred debts, large and small, to those who guided, helped, and encouraged me.

I am grateful to Vassar College, which has always valued creative pursuits on an equal plane with traditional scholarship, for travel funds and the William R. Kenan Jr. Endowed Chair.

Throughout the drafting, Lt. Colonel Sean Sculley, Academy Professor and Chief of the American History Division at West Point, generously shared his military, historical, strategic, and sailing expertise. (I drew specialized information from Angus Konstam's *Renaissance War Galley, 1470–1590* and Sean McGrail's *Ancient Boats in North-West Europe*.)

Professors Kirsten Menking and Jeff Walker of Vassar's Earth Science Department led me away from grievous errors concerning world-building.

Stefan Ekman, Professor of English at the University of Gothenburg, took the time to share his unique knowledge regarding fantasy maps.

Professor Leslie Dunn of Vassar's English Department, a Shakespeare scholar, studied my poetry with the seriousness and skill she applies to more exalted works.

Professor Darrell James, who teaches stage combat in Drama, showed me his swords and taught me about their use.

I was fortunate indeed to find Penelope Duus, Vassar '17, who was trained in cartography. She started the map of Ennea Món when she was a senior and has patiently, loyally tweaked it for years. For the final corrections I am grateful to Amy Laughlin of Vassar's Academic Computing office.

A professional editor, Linda Branham, critiqued the first fifty pages. Friends who read drafts—in whole or in part—provided comments and encouragement that kept my roots watered. Thank you for your time, Fred Chromey, Joanne Davies, Madelynn Meigs '18, and Molly Shanley. Feedback from Madeline Kozloff, Daniel Kozloff, Bobbie Lucas '16, and Dawn Freer came at particularly timely moments or was particularly influential.

I tapped Theodore Lechterman for his knowledge of the Levelers (the historical analogue of the Parity Party) and his linguistic skills. Tom Racek '18, captain of the fencing team, helped me choreograph some of the fight scenes. Dr. Sam Kozloff diagnosed a fictional patient.

Rather late in my writing process I was lucky to find a writing partner with whom I exchanged manuscripts. The fantasy author James E. Graham provided irreplaceable assistance by reading nearly all of the series and filling the margins with passionate comments.

Others were kind and patient in giving a novice advice about how to publish in a new field, including Susan Chang (Tor), Alicia Condon (Kensington), Diana Frost (Macmillan), and Eddie Gamarra (The Gotham Group). Without their guidance these manuscripts might never have been published.

My husband, Robert Lechterman, supported me in this endeavor as selflessly as he has throughout our life together. Without him, the appliances would have just stayed broken and I would have subsisted on frozen fish sticks.

Martha Millard—my original agent at Sterling Lord Literistic—

knew and delighted in the fact that she was changing my life when she pursued me as a client and sold the series. She has retired and I shall miss her, but Nell Pierce of SLL has now ably filled her shoes.

At Tor my manuscripts fell into the hands of Rafal Gibek (production editor) and Deanna Hoak (copyeditor), who saved me from myself.

My editor, Jennifer Gunnels of Tor, took a leap of faith on a nontraditional debut author, a four-volume series, and a rapid publication schedule. She also found the balance between corralling me when I wandered astray and giving me freedom. "You really need to research X," she would advise, and I would obediently get busy. Other times, when I fretted over whether I should change something, she'd remind me, "It's *your* book, Sarah."

It is *my book, Jen, but in a larger sense it belongs to everyone mentioned here, to a dozen others who offered a hand, not to mention the books, films, and teachers who formed me. Except the mistakes and infelicities, which pool around my feet, mewling like attention-mongering kittens—those poor things are mine own.*

THE
CERULEAN
QUEEN

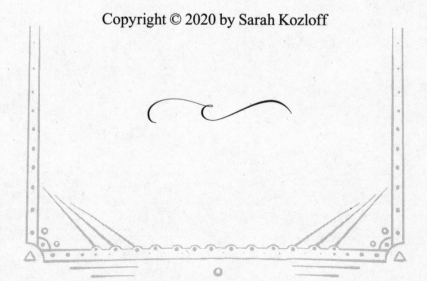

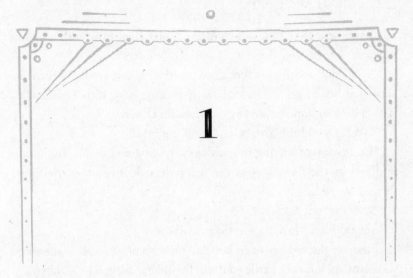

1

Alpetar

Smithy woke early with a feeling of deep unease. While General Sumroth had gone on with thousands of his troops to the shipbuilding center Pexted, pursuing his plan of vengeance against Weirandale, Smithy had stayed in Alpetar with the refugees in Camp Ruby, situated where the Alpetar Mountains slid down into fertile plains.

Camp Ruby, the first of four camps established along the Trade Corridor, lay closest to the Land.

He strode out of his tent into the dawn air, gazing northward in the direction of his homeland, as he always did. He saw fingers of smoke far away and read these as a sign that FireThorn yawned and stretched.

Around him the camp stirred as the other exiles from Oromondo woke and began their days.

Pozhar's Agent stoked his nearby fire, adding coal and blowing up the flames with a hand bellows. He had no real forge here, and he missed the high, cleansing heat. But he had his hand tools, and he used this outdoor fire to soften metal and shape it as best he could whenever one of the Spirit's children approached him with a commission.

As if conjured by his thoughts, a girl of about twelve summers appeared before him, a little slyly, thrusting out at him a tin kettle with a broken handle. Smithy examined it closely.

"Aye," he told the girl. "Come back tonight."

But instead of leaving immediately she lingered by his fire, mesmerized by the flames. And the fire reflected in her eyes, making them glow red.

"You like my fire?"

She nodded. "It makes me warm all over."

He read the answer from her lips' movement. "Good. Make sure you come back for the kettle yourself. I will have a small treat for you."

Smithy had found another; this girl made three Oromondo children who harbored a spark of Pozhar in their souls. He would tend these flames cautiously, to see if any of the children would develop into new Magi. The death of those Eight more than a year ago counted only as a setback, not as the end of the reign of the Magi.

Smithy walked to the camp's communal kitchen area and pointed at a bowl of bread dough, which the baker gave him without question. When he returned to his tent, he reached under his flimsy bed for the canister he kept hidden. He used his thick fingers to add large pinches of volcanic ash to the glutinous material. After mixing in the additive, he set the bowl to rise in the warmth of the stones ringing his fire. Later in the day he would bake biscuits (it didn't matter if they looked misshapen or got singed), which he would offer to the three prospects. The ash did not contain as much Magic as cooled lava, but it would serve. These children would gain the Power, abilities that demonstrated their devotion to Pozhar and illustrated the Spirit's might and majesty.

That fool Sumroth believes that because the Eight past Magi perished, he will rule Oromondo. But he would rule as all dictators rule: for himself. Only Magi will keep the Land of Fire Mountains for Pozhar. I

will aid General Sumroth in enacting retribution against Weirandale,
and then the Spirit will deal with his pride and blasphemy.

The fire he sat by rose higher than the fuel he had given it should burn. In the crackle of the flames, Smithy heard the voice of his master.

The witch's spawn has returned to Weirandale.

Smithy pounded one fist into the opposite palm.

What can I do, Mighty Pozhar, to stop this?

Thou canst do nothing, Smithy. But I have other servants. Tend thy flames and keep watch over my children.

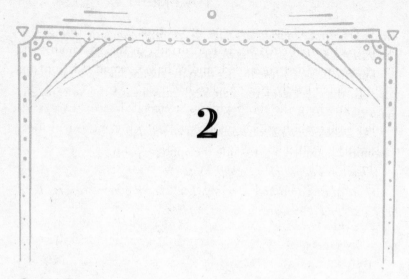

2

Cascada

Ciellō and the dog, Whaki, set out from the Sea Hawk inn in the pearly dawn light. Both felt too restless to stay inside the lodging house environs a single moment longer. Despite his remonstrance, the dog had been whining and scratching at the fence gate throughout Ciellō's morning exercise routine. He could hardly get Whaki to wait while he scrubbed and dressed.

Together, man and dog surveyed the empty streets of the capital city. Last night these same streets had been crammed with townsfolk celebrating some wedding amongst the gentry by feasting at squares where soldiers roasted pig—carving off generous slices— and poured hard cider into whatever vessels the citizens proffered. Street musicians played while people danced and cavorted, happy with the free victuals. When night fell, fireworks set off over the harbor burst out in patterns of blue and white.

Ciellō had partaken of the pork, and Whaki had scarfed down dropped tidbits until the fireworks started; these sent the dog into paroxysms of terror. So the Zellish bodyguard had taken him back to the Sea Hawk and coaxed him into a nearly closed wardrobe to muffle the noise of the explosions. By the time the men with whom he shared the room returned, dead drunk, in the wee hours, the fireworks show had concluded, and Whaki—exhausted from his fright—snored loudly under Ciellō's bed.

This morning the thoroughfares stretched deserted except for the loads of rubbish strewn about and a few unconscious drunks curled up on their sides.

In Zellia, after a fête, the mayor would hire the poorest of the poor to sweep up the refuse. Ciellō wondered if that was the custom here. Certainly street sweepers needed to clean these streets; their disarray offended his sense of order. The whole city had an air of mismanagement.

Ciellō allowed the dog to lead the way. This morning Whaki didn't detour to sniff or eat the meat scattered on the ground. His nose stuck high in the air, and he loped onward without wavering. Whatever was bothering Whaki this morn, Ciellō knew it had to do with damselle. Whaki rushed up the streets so urgently that Ciellō, supremely fit as he was, had to struggle to keep up.

The white towers of the Nargis Palace, perched on the top of the hill, flashed in the morning sun, and grew larger as they approached.

Regent Matwyck had tossed and turned the whole night through, disturbed by the rich fare of his son's wedding feast, and, more than he would care to admit, by the image of his intended, Duchette Lolethia, lying murdered in Burgn's chambers.

The hole in her throat had gaped with an almost lewd intimacy, and her blood had soaked the floor black. A small quantity of this blood had stained his shoes and the side of his doublet, both of which he tore off with disgust and ordered his valet to burn, even though they were new and quite costly. Even after washing his hands three times, he still felt the touch of her clammy palm in his own.

Although the Lord Regent knew he had no cause to feel guilty—*he* had not killed the girl, nor ordered it done—an unease lingered, perchance because of how angry he had been when she failed to appear for the wedding and the banquet. While it explained her absence Lolethia's murder did not really douse his fury. Even if she had not, after all, purposely missed the grand wedding, he could conjure no innocent explanation as to why she had gone to Burgn's chamber.

Giving up on sleep, Matwyck pushed aside his bed-curtains and rang for his valet. His head pounded fiercely so that he poured himself a glass of wine while he waited for the man to appear.

"No word yet from the Marauders who went after Burgn?" he barked when the valet entered, carrying his fastbreak tray.

The man shook his head.

Matwyck was not surprised. It really was too soon for them to have caught up with the shitwit and returned. He would have to think of the proper way to punish the man once he had him in his possession.

"Fetch Heathclaw and Councilor Prigent," Matwyck ordered as he sat down to his food. Undoubtedly, he was the most put-upon of men: after all the time and treasure he had lavished on the wedding his son had run off early, skipping the capstone events, and then that damn minx Lolethia had gotten herself killed. And when Prigent arrived, he would bring the latest expense receipts and wave them under his nose.

His valet dispatched a guard with his requests, received a pitcher of wash water from a chambermaid, and started to lay out an outfit for the day.

"Not brown today, you shitwit," Matwyck corrected. "Black. And I'll need a circlet of mourning."

The valet nodded, replacing the offensive clothing with black silk, and pulled a box of accessories out of the wardrobe. Matwyck gave up on moving the food around on his plate and crossed to his washbasin, waiting for the valet to pour the water and hold a towel. When the man started to sharpen his razor, however, Matwyck shook his head—his unshaven appearance would show the court just how little he cared about appearances in the midst of his grief.

Matwyck had dressed in fresh smallclothes, trousers, hose, and boots, but he still had his sleeping shift keeping his upper body warm when Heathclaw and Prigent bustled in together. Both of them looked hastily prepared, as if they had been roused earlier than they had expected. But why should they loll in bed when there were so many things to attend to?

"Lord Regent," they murmured as they bowed.

"Prigent, I want a report by midday of every remark the visiting gentry make," Matwyck ordered. "Get our people amongst the servants to write everything down. Everything about the wedding and the unfortunate events concerning the duchette. They will chatter like magpies during fastbreak, and I want to know who says what.

"And Heathclaw, I want you to take three guards and summon Captain Murgn."

"Where should I bring him, Lord Regent? Is he under arrest?" Heathclaw raised his brows.

"Not yet. We don't know if he was in league with his cousin in this crime, and he's been extremely useful to us over the years. Take him to my office. We will let him dangle for a while before I question him.

"Now, what do you have for me?" he asked, because both men had lists and leather portfolios tucked under their arms.

Prigent, distressed over how much it would cost to feed the visiting noble folk, wanted to talk about how long they would be staying in residence.

"No, you idiot," Matwyck cut him off. "We *want* them to linger where we can keep an eye on them. We need, however, to provide entertainment tonight, something fabulous that will wash away any negative impressions. Perchance the Aqueduct or Peacock players could be induced to give a private performance? Bring me a list of possibilities in an hour.

"And what is already on my schedule for today?" Matwyck turned to Heathclaw.

His secretary consulted his list. "Mostly formal farewells and a few 'private meetings' that dukes have requested—these are probably appeals for loans."

"The farewells are so tiresome," Matwyck said, steepling his fingers. "The carriages are never ready on time, and the guests themselves are worse; thus I'm forced to stand in the entry hall making empty conversation while the spouses or insipid offspring make excuses."

"Perhaps you'll be able to directly glean information about the gentries' reactions to—recent events?" Prigent offered.

"Hmm," Matwyck assented with a grudging nod. "Who's specified a leave-taking time?"

Heathclaw consulted his list, "First up, at ten o'clock, is Mistress Stahlia and her dependents, though I hardly think *they* are worth your time, Lord Regent. I could represent you, if you so desire."

Matwyck slapped the table with his hand, because so far this morning he had forgotten about the Wyndton sister. His suspicions about her mysterious appearance and his memory of her judgmental eyes came rushing back.

"Fetch a brace of guards," he ordered. "I want to examine that sister right away."

Gunnit had been in Cascada several moons, often stealing away from his page duties to serve as liaison between Water Bearer and her allies outside the palace. Yesterday, he saw Finch—no, now he had to think of her as "Cerúlia"—from a distance: she was strolling in the gardens as he hustled out the Kitchen Gate with a note. He had longed to run to her, but Water Bearer had told him that his errand was urgent.

His job today had been to unlock and unbolt West Gate two hours before dawn. He took down the crossbeams that held it shut. As soon as he poked his head through, he saw more than thirty people waiting in the shadow of the stone wall in dark garb.

After they slipped into the grounds, however, they paused. Each tied on a sash and reversed their capes. As the sky lent more light he saw they wore black trousers, black shirts, dazzling white sashes (elaborately knotted), and blue capes sparkling with silver thread. Three of them, including Captain Yanath, also wore breastplates and helms so polished they caught the fading starlight and rising sun. Gunnit's mouth fell open at their splendor.

"I take it you like the cloaks?" Yanath asked him. "My wife— she's such a clever seamstress—she's been working on them in secret forever. Uniforms matter, especially when you need to impress. We are the New Queen's Shield, or whatever we're going to be called, and anyone who crosses us better drought damn know it."

Yanath turned to a woman with a peeling red nose to whom he seemed to defer. "Ready, seamaster?"

She, in turn, surveyed the men behind them. "Don't let your mace clatter," she said to one with very bowed legs. Then she nodded at Gunnit. "Lead on, lad."

Moving at a gentle lope, Gunnit shepherded the troop across the grounds. The soldiers clutched their weapons so they didn't jingle as the boy wove them through the deeper obscurity of shrubs and trees for over an hour. By the time the white stone of the palace loomed before them, the sun had risen.

Palace guards positioned in a loose formation—much looser than the nightly cordon created by Matwyck's Marauders—were keeping watch in a desultory fashion. Yanath gestured to his followers and singing arrows struck two guards who stood in their immediate way, while slicing daggers made sure they didn't cry out. The New Shield pulled the bodies from where they tumbled, hiding them under nearby shrubs. Then the captain had everybody double over into a crouch while moving to reach the shelter of some hedges, then crawl on their bellies to a small, unremarkable door through which footmen usually brought firewood into the Great Ballroom. They paused, taking deep breaths and passing around water bags.

Gunnit whispered to the captain, "Wait. There will be a signal."

"What kind of signal?" Yanath asked.

The boy had no idea, but he placed his confidence in the Spirits. "We'll know it," he answered with conviction.

They waited. Everyone had already readied his or her weapon.